TROJAN
HORSE

Published by Thomas & Mercer
P.O. Box 400818
Las Vegas, NV 89140

ISBN-13: 9781612182285
ISBN-10: 1612182283

TROJAN HORSE

A THRILLER BY

DAVID LENDER

THOMAS & MERCER

For Grace Smith

ALSO BY DAVID LENDER

The Gravy Train

The Gravy Train is the story of a novice investment banker who helps an aging Chairman try to buy his company back from bankruptcy, pitted against ruthless Wall Street sharks who want to carve it up for themselves.

Bull Street

Bull Street is the story of a naïve, young Wall Streeter who gives a jaded billionaire the chance for redemption, as they team up to bring down an insider trading ring before they wind up in jail or dead.

Vaccine Nation

Vaccine Nation is the story of an award-winning documentary filmmaker who is handed "whistleblower" evidence about the U.S. vaccination program, and then races to expose it before a megalomaniacal pharmaceutical company CEO can have her killed.

ACKNOWLEDGMENTS

First, thank you to Sidney Gruson, a dear friend from my Rothschild days, now departed. He sent an early draft of this novel to a number of friends, including Nick Gage. Nick sent it to a prominent literary agent he knew, Joni Evans, at what was then The William Morris Agency in New York, whose reaction was (I am paraphrasing), "Not bad for somebody who doesn't know what he's doing," then offered to introduce me to some editors who could teach me. She did. So thanks to Nick, Joni and, most importantly, to Richard Marek, who was the editor I worked with over 18 months on this manuscript, and who taught me how to write a thriller.

To Michael Hauge of Screenplay Mastery, thank you, not only for coaching me on pitching my stories in person, but for your advice on punching up key elements of my story from a Hollywood perspective.

Next, thank you to those who transcribed and typed: Julie Widmer, Madelynne Sansevere and Marcie Herkner. And to those who read, supported and commented: notably, Grace Smith, Michele Young, Nick Gage, Geoff Selzer, Ira Schwartz, Penny Page, Mark Lender, Paul Lender, Mom and Dad.

And to George Philhower, who professionally formatted the original cover. I have a pillow in my den at my weekend house in Milford that is embroidered with the phrase, "Old Friends are the Best Friends." True.

Thank you to Amazon Publishing.

And finally, to Dad, for the legacy of his many gifts, including his photographic eye and all those slides, negatives, prints and JPEGs, including the one on this cover, "The Man in White."

PROLOGUE

JULY, TWENTY YEARS AGO. RIYADH, Saudi Arabia. Omar pressed the button that activated the lighted face of his watch, cupping his hands so he wouldn't be detected. *Today is a good day to die*, he recited the mercenary's creed in his head. *0158 hours.* The others would start to arrive momentarily. He pulled out the American-manufactured night-vision goggles and stood in the shadows across the street from the outside perimeter wall of the grounds of the Royal Palace. He felt the chill of the Saudi night. He was grateful for the warmth provided by his German kevlar vest and British army fatigues beneath his robe, the traditional Saudi dress he wore as a disguise. Still, his Russian army boots were ridiculously obvious; the disguise wasn't about to fool anyone.

He scanned the street from where he knew the others would be joining him. Still no one. His mouth was dry. He fingered the Uzi clipped to his belt on his left hip, the .45 automatic Colt holstered on his right hip. Then behind the Colt the .22 caliber Beretta with its silencer extending through the hole in its holster. Omar was the only one of the team of twelve who carried a Beretta. He was to be the shooter.

Two men walked toward him, shielded by the shadows against the wall. He motioned to them and they gestured back. It was time. The other nine appeared like a mirage in the desert. Each was armed with Uzis and .45 caliber automatic Colt pistols; two carried American M-203 grenade launchers. All were eclectically uniformed and hardwared to defy nationalistic identification if killed or captured. They waited silently against the wall, listening for the passage of the patrol jeep. It lumbered by, bearing two heavily armed guards.

Omar raised his hand: the "Go" signal. He felt his pulse quicken and the familiar butterflies and shortness of breath that preceded any mission, no matter how well planned. The twelve-member squad crossed the street to the white stucco perimeter wall of the palace. Four faced the wall and leaned against it, shoulder to shoulder. The others performed a series of acrobatic maneuvers and materialized into a human pyramid. The top man silently secured three rubber-coated grappling hooks with attached scaling lines to the top of the wall. Omar was over the top and down the other side in less than fifteen seconds.

While the others followed, Omar pulled off his robe. His heart pounded. He pulled five bricks of C-4 plastic explosive from his pouch and stuck them to the wall in an "X" configuration, aware that his palms were clammy. He wiped them on his robe and again focused on his work. He inserted an electrical detonator in each brick of C-4, and wired them to a central radio receiver that he inserted into the center block of the "X." By the time he finished, the rest of the team had cleared the wall and removed their robes. They stashed their robes in zippered pouches buckled to the backs of their waists.

Omar squinted at the wall of the palace, illuminated by floodlights, fifty meters away. This area had no first-floor windows.

His eyes adjusted to the light, and he looked for guards he hoped wouldn't be there. He focused on a second-floor window at the junction of the east and north walls. *Be there*, he thought. *Just be there.*

Sasha didn't awaken at 2:00 a.m. as she had intended: she hadn't slept at all. She glanced to her right at Prince Ibrahim, illuminated in the light from the display of the digital clock. His body moved up and down with the rhythm of his breathing. Sasha had earlier treated him to some extended pleasures in an effort to assure he wouldn't awaken at an inopportune moment. She smelled the pungent scent of the evening's energies, felt the smooth silk of the sheets against her naked breasts: sensations that under other circumstances would cause her to revel in her sexuality. Now she felt only the flutter of apprehension in her stomach. She thought of the business to be dispensed with.

The Royal Palace was stone quiet at this hour. Sasha listened in the hall for the footsteps of the guard on his rounds. A moment later he passed. A renewed sense of commitment smoothed a steadying calm down her limbs. *It's time*, she told herself, and she slid, inches at a time, from the sheets to the cool marble floor.

Yassar will never forgive me. She breathed deeply, then felt exhilaration at the cool detachment her purpose gave her. She stood, naked, shoulders erect and head back, observing Prince Ibrahim, the man she had served as concubine for three years. *But you don't deserve to see it coming.*

Backing from the bed, Sasha inched toward the closet. The prince stirred in his sleep, inhaled and held it. Sasha froze in place. She felt her stomach pull taut and she held her own breath. The cool marble under her feet became a chilling cold, the silence an oppressive void. *This mustn't fail.* The prince resumed his rhythmic breathing and she exhaled in relief.

One more cautious stride carried her to the closet. She reached into it for her black *abaya*, the Muslim robe she wore in the palace. She cringed at the rustle of the coarse fabric as she put it on. The prince didn't stir. She picked up her parcel from the closet floor, crossed the room and slipped out the door.

At the corridor window, she removed the clear plastic backing from one side of a 2x5 centimeter adhesive strip. The acrid odor of the cyanoacrylate stung her nostrils. She slid the strip between the steel window frame and the steel molding around it, precisely where the pressure-sensitive microswitch for the alarm sat.

She took an electromagnet from her parcel and plugged it into an outlet, unraveling the cord as she walked back toward the window frame. She placed the magnet against the corner of the window frame behind the alarm microswitch and clicked on the electromagnet.

The force of the magnet jolted the molding against the window frame. She endured a count to thirty until the adhesive fused the microswitch closed, then switched off the magnet. She turned the window latch, took a deep breath, shut her eyes, pushed. The window opened. *No alarm.*

The face of the man she knew only as the squad leader popped into her view from his perch atop his team, who had formed a pyramid on the wall below. She stepped back from the window. In an instant he was inside, raising his finger for her to be silent, and then turning and attaching one of the grappling hooks to the window frame. *Never mind shushing me,* she thought, *just make sure you know what you're doing.* Within sixty seconds the other eleven members of the squad stole inside. The rope was up and deposited on the floor and the window closed and latched.

The black-haired girl backed herself against the wall, her palms against the marble. Omar stared into her jet-black eyes, saw her fierce spirit. *That was close,* he thought. *She nearly blew it. Late.* He sensed her excitement in the heaving of her chest, but she appeared otherwise to be in complete control of herself. She raised her chin defiantly. He looked into those penetrating black eyes again. *Black steel,* he thought, and felt a fleeting communion with her. She motioned with her eyes in the direction of Prince Ibrahim's chamber. He nodded.

Sasha stood with her back pressed against the wall and watched as the team leader made hand signals and head motions to his men. He ordered a group to stand guard, then led most of them down the labyrinthine passageways that rimmed the outside perimeter of the palace toward Prince Ibrahim's chamber. She watched the team leader disappear from sight around the first turn of the corridor. For some reason Sasha was seized by the premonition that something was wrong. She pushed herself out from the wall, trotted toward the prince's chamber.

One of the team members, who had spread themselves in pairs in firing position, grabbed her by the wrist as she passed. A bolt of adrenaline coursed through her. She clenched her teeth and shot a glare at the man. His widened eyes showed fear. She jerked her arm away and continued. She was now aware of the exhilaration of life-threat and the calm purpose that drove her.

He'll never forgive me, again crashed through her consciousness. It sucked the strength from her, but she kept on. She reached the next turn, the last before Ibrahim's chamber and saw the team leader ten feet from the door. At that moment three Saudi guards bustled around the next turn in the corridor. She felt hot blood rush to her face and a charge of anger erupt from her chest. She saw two of the squad members three meters beyond the team leader rear their heads back like horses at the sight of fire, then crouch over their weapons.

Shots hissed from the two squad members' silenced Uzis. The three Saudi guards were hurled backward in a spray of blood amid the crack of bullets ricocheting off the marble walls. Their bodies hit the floor with thuds. Two more Saudi guards materialized at the same turn, M-16s aimed from the waist. Bursts from their guns flashed stars of flame from their barrels and flattened the two squad members. The squad leader froze, the hesitation of death, five feet from the prince's door. An instant later twin bursts from the Saudi guards' weapons slammed him backward into the wall.

Sasha forced herself to bury her panic within her. Next she was aware of the rush of her own breathing and the momentary sense she should conceal herself behind a tortured wail. Instead, she stretched out an arm and raised a hand toward the guards. They lowered the muzzles of their automatics and nodded to her in recognition. She pressed her back against the marble wall, her feet inches from the pool of blood that oozed from the team leader's body.

"More!" she called in Arabic and motioned with two fingers back down the corridor toward the window she had opened. The men nodded again, crouched over their weapons and trotted toward the turn in the corridor. She squinted at the two guards as they passed, seeing the panic in their faces, and resisting her own urge to flee. She slid down the wall, noting the Beretta and silencer protruding from the team leader's holster.

This mustn't fail, she told herself again. She yanked the Beretta from the team leader's belt and gave the silencer a jerk counterclockwise to make certain it was anchored in place. Then she held the gun at arm's length with both hands and fired one round into the back of the first guard. She saw the startled look of terror in the eyes of the second as he turned. She aimed the gun at his chest and pulled off two more rounds.

Three gone, five rounds left. She ran up to the two fallen men with the gun outstretched. The second one down didn't move, the first did. She put another round in the back of his head. She spun and darted toward Prince Ibrahim's chamber, gulping air in huge breaths as she thrust herself through the door. The glow from the digital clock outlined the shape of the prince, who sat upright in bed, staring directly at her. She raised the gun at his chest. "Pig!" she said in Arabic.

"Sasha, I don't understand," the prince stammered.

"Then you don't deserve to," she said, and pulled the trigger. He lurched backward onto the pillows. A circle of red expanded on his white nightshirt directly over his heart. Sasha stepped forward, lowered the Beretta and fired another round into the Prince's skull just behind his right ear. Then she dropped the gun.

Her brain told her what to do next—run for the window at the end of the corridor, throw down the rope and escape—but her body wasn't nearly as composed as the voice in her head. Her breath came in gasps, her stomach churning at the smell of the blood puddled on the floor as she passed the bodies toward the first turn in the corridor. She shot a glance over her shoulder. *Still no other guards. Thank God.* She heard a crackle of static from a portable radio on the squad leader's belt and heard the words, "We are blown! We have casualties and are aborting! Prepare transport! Minutes one!" Seconds later she heard shots and screams from someplace. An alarm sounded and the corridor lights flashed on. As she reached a turn in the corridor, one of the squad members must have triggered the C-4, because a yellow-white glare flashed as bright as the sun. A shock wave whooshed down the corridor and threw her over backward to the floor.

Sasha jumped to her feet and ran down the corridor. She saw six squad members near the window, leaping out and down the rope each in turn. By the time she reached the window they were all down the rope. She leapt over the top without looking down. As she slid down the rope she listened for the sound of the three BMW 535s she knew the squad would have waiting for their escape. They were her only hope. But she couldn't hear them. She could only hear the pounding of her heart in her ears and the ringing from the sharp blasts of the guns and that malevolent C-4 blast. She knew she was beginning to think again and not just act on instinct and adrenaline and the passion of what she believed in, and she realized she might survive, and that even with the disastrous intervention of the Saudi guards, and her split-second improvisation, the plan hadn't gone so horribly awry.

Sasha ran for the hole in the perimeter wall. At ten meters away from it she heard the staccato bursts of Uzis from two of the death squad members stationed at either side of the hole. She saw two more men running in front of her and now they were in the ten-foot-deep crater where the wall had been. She could see one of the black BMWs on the other side. She heard bullets whiz past her head. The dust from the explosion that hung in the air tasted musty in the back of her throat. She felt the rubble of the wall beneath her feet and lost her balance, then dove into the crater. She landed on her stomach and wheezed for breath but the air wouldn't flow into her lungs.

Sasha could still hear the sharp retort of those Uzis and then even they went silent. Her eyes were wide open again and she couldn't breathe but her legs were starting to work and she tumbled down on top of somebody or something, she couldn't tell which, and then two men were dragging her by either armpit up the other side of the crater and she could see the open door of the BMW in front of her, hear the engine racing, and felt herself being thrown headfirst inside. She smashed her face on the floor and felt another body dive in on top of her and then the car was moving. Soon it was moving fast and she realized that not only was she alive but that she was going to make it out of there. And in that same instant a flash of anguish shot through her brain: *But where do I go from here?*

The crack of automatic weapons awakened Prince Yassar. He reached for his telephone, but there was no one to call, so he placed the receiver back in its cradle. Over the next five minutes he alternately sat and waited for someone to come, then got up and took a few halting steps toward the door to his outer suite, uncharacteristically uncertain. Should he fling the door open into the corridor and investigate for himself? Then a stiffly formal sergeant knocked sharply and entered the room. Prince Yassar observed the sergeant's stony face. He expected bad news and felt as if the weight of it were pulling his jowls toward the floor. He stroked his forehead. *Sweaty.*

"Prince Yassar, sir," the sergeant said expressionlessly, staring as he said the words, "Your son, Prince Ibrahim, has been murdered."

Yassar felt the words burst in his chest like a hollow-point round. He closed his eyes, knowing already that it was true. *She tried to warn me.* His sigh emerged as a moan.

Yassar glanced from side to side as if to find a way to escape. He hung his head in resignation, then glared up at the sergeant. *Why are you telling me what I already know? What I already have imagined in my worst fears?* He felt that he wanted to strike the little man.

"There were no other civilian casualties," the sergeant continued, still with no expression in his voice, on his face. Only that vacant stare. And the measured tones. "But five guards were killed in the corridor only meters from Prince Ibrahim's chamber, and three of the provocateurs"—Yassar noted with rising anger the ridiculously mispronounced French word—"were killed in the corridor. That, and twenty-three other soldiers are dead in the courtyard, most from the explosion. Everyone else is accounted for and safe, except one of the prince's concubines."

Yassar opened his eyes. They felt like black pools of moist agony. And rage. He realized the strength had been sucked from his limbs and now tried to move his arms, wanting to strike at this pompous man. But he all he did was motion for the soldier to continue. "It is Sasha. She is gone," the sergeant said, "and we found a disabled microswitch on the window used to thwart the alarm, as well as an electromagnet and a grappling hook and rope. It would appear the death squad had help gaining access to the palace."

Yassar tried to stand and still could not. His legs trembled and he placed his hands on his knees to steady them, leaned forward, then slumped backward onto the bed.

"We found a gun on the bed. We found footprints in blood leading into the bedroom and then out again," the unbearable fool continued. "And we did not find Sasha."

Yassar felt the words like the twist of a knife in an already mortal wound. He closed his eyes again. *Sasha? How could Sasha do such a thing?* He felt his face contort. He raised his head and looked at the man, this man who would say such things, feeling the conflict of his anger against what he knew in his heart to be true. Sasha, whom he had taken under his patronage, treated like a daughter, and who had honored him like a father. Sasha, who had heeded his need for her to both minister to and keep his beloved, yet wayward, son in line. *This cannot be true.* But his shoulders curled over.

The sergeant continued his unemotional droning as if he were pushing through a checklist. "The perimeter of the palace is now secure and no intruders are believed left inside. Except for the three who were killed, the remainder of the assassination team appears to have escaped."

How can this mechanic, this mere functionary defile the memory of my son with his prattle? Yassar felt his strength returning as his anger rose. He sighed, then lifted himself from the bed, seeming to bear the weight of his dead son as he did so. He wanted to crush the man's head like a melon for having the audacity to bring such a message with such methodical reserve. The sergeant reached out and put a hand on Yassar's shoulder. Anger boiled in Yassar at the touch. He whirled, all the strength that had been drained from him in the last quarter hour focused in a single fist that he lashed toward the sergeant's face. A roar emerged from his breast, the single word, "No!" And then with the same ferocity of effort he stopped the blow just inches from the man's face. He hung his head so the man could not see the tears he knew he could not stop. He reached forward blindly, unclenched his fist and placed his hand on the man's shoulder. He squeezed it and pushed the sergeant toward the door. "Go. Please, go," he whispered. He heard the sergeant back out and shut the door.

Yassar turned back into the room. Then a dark sensation rose in him, one he had never felt before in all his years of adherence to the faith in his pursuit of the path of Allah: newborn hatred. *I will avenge this act. I will find out who has done this and chase them down. And Sasha. I will find her and destroy her.*

BOOK 1

CHAPTER 1

July 2, This Year. New York City. Daniel Youngblood knew when people were lying to him. He sniffed out untruths, half-truths, even eighth-truths like a bloodhound. Not through force of will or training, but by instinct. And the scents of these lies, ranging from the subtly sour to the glaringly rotten, stung Daniel's gut like ulcers. It wasn't because "it takes one to know one." In fact, Daniel was proud of the fact that he could look someone in the eye and say something difficult, or avoid saying something difficult, without lying.

Daniel had suffered uncomfortable moments throughout his career by not lying, but it was something by now, at 45 years old, he'd resigned himself to. And if anything made him unsuited to his chosen profession, it was Daniel's honesty, because he'd been an investment banker for the last twenty years. He always thought the only consolation in it was that God had steered him from becoming a lawyer.

He glanced around his office. It was a familiar, comfortable world. Antique Persian rugs. The hand-rubbed sheen of 19th-century mahogany. Two exhausted but wonderfully comfortable overstuffed guest chairs. Computer keys in the outside corridor emitted muted ticks, hushed by the hallway carpet that deadened phones and voices into reverent whispers.

His gaze went to the side of his desk where Angie's photo had always sat. He felt a pang of guilt, he guessed because he'd removed it—but after two years, enough, even his shrink said so—then a flood of shame, because it caused him to think of their fatal trip to Peru.

Daniel's assistant, Cindy, buzzed him on the intercom. "Robert Kovarik from Goldman Sachs—I mean Kovarik & Co." Daniel's back stiffened and he sat up straight.

Thought I got rid of you yesterday.

"My compliments," Kovarik said. "Always great to work on the other side of a deal from a real pro. Always knew you'd pull a rabbit out of a hat."

Daniel's stomach surged like a blender slapped to "pulverize." "Thanks, Bob," Daniel said. "So what's up?"

Kovarik chuckled. It was the low, insinuating chuckle Daniel knew well. He'd heard it for 10 years as Daniel and Kovarik worked their way up side by side in Goldman Sachs' Oil and Gas group. He hadn't heard it as Kovarik worked behind the scenes to maneuver Daniel out of the way for Oil and Gas partner over the next three years, after which Daniel had left Goldman to set up his competing Oil and Gas practice at the international investment banking firm of Ladoix Sayre & Cie Banque. Kovarik had recently set up his own boutique investment bank, Kovarik & Co. Talk on the Street was he'd been forced out at Goldman for being too sharp-elbowed. Kovarik said, "No, no, just called to congratulate you."

Lying son of a bitch, what do you want? Daniel had been holed up in a conference room negotiating with Kovarik and his client in a death struggle for two weeks. He waited.

Kovarik added, "Just a congratulatory gesture. You were brilliant."

Pause. "Thanks."

Silence.

"Yes, well," Kovarik said. He hesitated.

Come on. Daniel's stomach's action had subsided to a mere sea squall. Kovarik cleared his throat. Daniel was still trying to figure out what this was all about; Kovarik always had an angle concealed beneath his faux Boston Brahmin charm. Like the way he played old Harvard chum while he'd been hitting on Angie, by then Daniel's fiancée, at the same time he was screwing Daniel over for partner at Goldman. *Guess you need a kick in the pants.* "You leave something on the conference room table?"

Kovarik laughed. "No, actually I was calling to see if we could strike an arrangement on a piece of business."

Here we go. "Sure, what's up?"

"You know Walt Dean at Houston Oil and Gas?"

"Of course." One of Kovarik's locked clients, somebody who always pretended to flirt with other investment bankers when he had a deal, soliciting quotes to keep Kovarik honest on fees.

"He's got a nice buyside—about a billion dollars, good for about a six million dollar fee. My legal people say I've got a conflict on it. I was wondering if I could throw it your way."

Beware of Czechs bearing gifts. Kovarik had never done this before; he'd rather throw a piece of business away than send it to Daniel. His stomach gurgled. "That's very gracious of you, Bob. What's the deal?"

"The meeting with Walt is scheduled in Houston next week on...Monday."

Kovarik's momentary pause gave Daniel's telltale stomach another turn. *What are you up to?* Then it came to him: the Saudis. Prince Yassar would be in town for one day next week interviewing investment bankers for his acquisition program. *He wants to see if I'm competing for the Saudi assignment, too.*

"Thanks, Bob, that's really kind of you," he said, thinking on the fly. *Do I want him to know I'm in the hunt? And of course if I bite on this, his conflict will dematerialize.*

"My pleasure. I can't think of anybody I'd rather recommend. Really, you were brilliant on the Dorchester deal."

"Thanks again, Bob." *Enough of this bullshit.* "Well, thanks for the offer, but I'm in town pitching the Saudis next week." Daniel waited for Kovarik's reaction.

A long pause. "Ah, well, good luck," he managed.

"Thanks again for the offer."

"Right," Kovarik said. "Well, see you next deal."

"Good-bye, Bob." Kovarik hung up almost before Daniel finished the words. *That ought to have spun him a little.* Then Daniel realized probably all he'd accomplished was ruining the Fourth of July weekend for two or three of Kovarik's junior staff—Kovarik would now push them flat out to compete with Daniel. *You're what's wrong with Wall Street, Kovarik.* "You're what's wrong with the world," he said aloud.

A moment later the phone rang and Cindy buzzed him again. "Michael Smits."

"Congratulations on the Dorchester deal," Michael said. Michael Smits was Daniel's best friend, one of Daniel's partners at Ladoix. One of the only partners at Ladoix he regularly spoke with. "I saw the announcement in the *Journal* this morning. Front page, but below the fold. You're slipping." He chuckled. "Didn't think we'd ever see you again."

"Thanks. I started to think nobody'd ever see me again either. Got swallowed alive by a conference room at Jones Day. Two weeks of raw acrimony, sandwiches and take-out Chinese."

He noted the vague paunch that had begun protruding over his belt line and sighed. He hadn't even had time to exercise.

"Well, the deal closed. Fee of four or five million?"

"Six million two hundred fifty-two thousand three hundred ninety-six dollars."

"Shoulda been a heroic end to the fiscal year for your bonus. How'd you make out on it?"

"Haven't gotten it yet. I see the poisonous little rat at eleven o'clock." Daniel's stomach gurgled at the mention of his upcoming bonus negotiation. Jean-Claude Dieudonne, Ladoix's senior partner, the son-in-law to the third generation of the founding French family, always had that effect.

They both paused.

"I can hear the wheels turning," Michael said. "And not too quickly. Maybe it's time to head off to the beach."

"Maybe. But I want to go out on an uptick."

"This oughtta be enough of an uptick."

"I don't know…" Daniel's voice trailed off. He could almost see Michael scrunching up his face with an "Oh, come on, Daniel" look.

"Oh, come on, Daniel, there's no rule book. Nobody's gonna come up to you and say, 'Okay, Mr. Youngblood, finished with engines. Stand down, old boy.'" Michael let it drop. "Anyway, you had a decent year. I imagine you won't have too much trouble with our *enfant terrible* in your bonus review."

"From your mouth to God's ears. You know Dieudonne."

Michael laughed. "Well, good luck," he said and hung up.

Daniel started getting ready for his bonus negotiation with Dieudonne. He stood up, smoothed his lapels and looked down at his black Italian loafers: impeccably shined. His European-cut suit was freshly pressed and his pants had knife-edge creases.

The suit was not too wild, yet something he would never have gotten away with at Goldman Sachs. He wore a custom-made white-collar-and-cuff English-striped shirt. His blue-green Hermès tie was strong enough for his upcoming negotiation, but not too powerful as to be distracting.

He looked at his reflection in the glass in front of a print on his office wall and drew himself up to his full 6'4". *I'm as ready as I'll ever be.*

His reflection looked back at him dubiously. He saw he didn't have it today: eyes glassy, lack of color in his cheeks, projecting no energy. He was burned out, and it would handicap him this morning. The Dorchester deal had closed solely because he had made it happen. But the deal had sapped him like a reverse exorcism. He knew why: he was no longer a young man in a young man's business. *A crushing insight.*

He walked back to his desk and sat back down. *The Cromwell Group/Dorchester Refining—6.3 million. Closed July 1,* he thought, "And almost just killed me," he said aloud. He wrote it on the pad. He continued, writing deals and fees in reverse chronological order of the closing dates of his transactions over that year. In a moment he had a total of seven deals for 11.3 million dollars. *Not bad.* It wasn't the kind of year to feel exuberant about, but respectable.

He wanted his last year to be a smashing success, a huge bonus. *Eleven point three million. Not great, but not bad. But enough?*

Daniel's mind drifted. He'd brought his car to the garage underneath 30 Rockefeller Plaza, where Ladoix's offices were, to drive out to his weekend house in Milford, Pennsylvania, this afternoon, a day early for the Fourth of July weekend. He tried, but couldn't remember this year's theme for Gary and Jonathan's annual Fourth of July party. Last year it had been Tennessee Williams Night, a not-surprising choice for the two gay hosts.

He recalled it as a particularly painful evening, because it was the first time many of his acquaintances had seen him without Angela, and two had actually asked him where Angie was. "Oh, I guess you didn't hear," he remembered saying, and pain clamped his heart and the guilt that had squeezed his brain then sneaked back up on him now. A shape appeared before his eyes—Cindy standing in the doorway, brow wrinkled.

"Everything okay?" Daniel said.

"Oh, oh, yes, I mean..."

"Jeff again?" *Teenage son plus single parent equals Cindy in early grave.*

"Afraid so. You mind if I leave a little early? A fight in gym class this time. Stitches."

"Better get going now. I can cover my own phone."

"You sure?"

"Yes. Get going." She mouthed *Thank you* and left.

Daniel checked the markets on his desktop monitor. The pre–Fourth of July holiday weekend trading was listless. The Dow Jones news ticker showed not much of any significance happening. Boring day except for the oil markets. *Wow. Oil down to $30.93 per barrel. That has to be hurting the oil economies. Maybe that's why the Saudis are looking for outside financial advisors.* He let his mind wander into the notion of the fees his potential representation of the Saudis could produce. *I could make a fortune on those deals.*

Daniel's phone rang: "Mr. Dieudonne is ready for you."

Showtime. And the son of a bitch is twenty minutes early. His stomach turned over.

July 2, This Year. Riyadh, Saudi Arabia. Prince Yassar raised his eyes from his morning prayers to a vision that stiffened his back. Through his window a jangle of traditional, low-slung buildings huddled in subdued browns, tans and orange patches of the sunrise, framed against modern skyscrapers. That wasn't what sent the shiver of unease through him. What affected him was something he couldn't see on the horizon, a horizon that would soon be obscured by waves of heat under the sun of a 100 degree day. *I must again admit failure.* He relaxed his muscles and settled down again onto his haunches. The earthy scent of the wool of his prayer rug soothed him.

He bathed in a moment of silence, prolonging the moments before the cares of the day invaded his consciousness. He raised his head, again, at the expanse of desert that was the kingdom of the Al Mamlakah al Arabiyah as Suudiyah: Saudi Arabia. *A forbidding sight to contemplate.* A giant field of sand—harsh, mostly uninhabited desert—sitting atop unfathomably large oil fields. Questions came to Yassar against his will, as they did every morning: how long before the unfathomable becomes fathomable, and the oil deposits deplete; how long before the oil revenues that constitute three quarters of the government budget stop? *When we are out of oil, we are out of oil.*

Yassar wished he could ponder them as an ordinary Saudi citizen might, rather than as the Finance and Economy Minister, the most powerful of the twelve members of the Council of Ministers, mostly royal family members appointed by his cousin, King and Prime Minister Abad. *Would that I did not bear this responsibility.* The thought brought back his own words to his fellow ministers and King Abad almost two decades ago. His words after decades of unrestrained spending of unspeakable oil profits by their regime, when they'd begun running government deficits: "We must adapt to life in a normal economy."

Yassar felt the tension in his forehead, even this early in the day. He dreaded his upcoming meeting with the king and Council of Ministers. "It is not just our pride at stake, but ultimately our survival. I will conceive a plan for diversifying our economy away from oil revenues," he heard himself say to them decades ago. Words forged in his mind.

He turned from the window, straightened his back and looked to the end table at the photograph of his son, Prince Ibrahim. Ibrahim had been the eldest of his twelve children, the son of Nibmar, the first, still favorite and most loving of his four wives. The familiar wooden frame on the photograph was stained with the oil from Yassar's hands, rounded at the corners from his touch. *He'd be in his mid forties, old enough to be a Deputy Minister.* Yassar remembered the hopes he had held for Ibrahim, and through him great hopes for the Saudi people. Harvard-educated, a blending of the cultural, religious and educational heritage of Saudi Arabia and the Western ways of their chief ally, the Americans. *Ibrahim would be a fine young man now.* Immediately Yassar's thoughts turned to his old adversaries, the extremist Shiite Muslim fundamentalists blamed for his son's murder. That conjured the image of Sheik bin Abdur, the man he held liable for Ibrahim's death, the spiritual and day-to-day leader of the al-Mujari, their terrorist organization. *You are as responsible for where we are as our government policies.* Yassar knew that on top of the budget deficits and recessions, the fundamentalist preachings of the Sheik now captured the emotions of a restive Saudi people. *Sheik bin Abdur, a man...*and Yassar's thoughts trailed off as his memories were linked in a struggle in his soul, his Islamic values versus revenge; *shari'a*—Islamic law—versus blood-hatred; self-control versus obsession.

Now he thought of Sasha, the young concubine he had brought to Ibrahim from Switzerland three years before his death. Sasha had dominated Ibrahim with her fierce pride and energetic loins. Sasha, the last person to see his son alive.

Time to get ready. He turned and walked to his desk, settling in for a full day of preparations for his meeting. Again, he thumbed through his worn and dog-eared manila folders, the top one bearing the name "J. Daniel Christian Youngblood III," files on individuals and institutions who would figure into Yassar's plans for redemption. The redemption of the Saudi people from their downward spiraling economic situation. Yassar's redemption from his decades-old unfulfilled promise to solve their problems.

July 2, This Year. Buraida, Saudi Arabia. In the commercial section of Buraida, 200 kilometers north of Riyadh, the man was certain everyone knew he was a nonlocal, despite his dark Arab complexion and features. He was tall and muscular, and didn't try to hide his walk with an erect military gait. He crossed through an alley toward the main street, his hands thrust into the pockets of his green windbreaker. He wore long tan slacks and heavy black boots. The dust kicked up by dozens of other feet hung in the still morning air and deposited in his nostrils and throat. The sun from the cloudless sky burned on his head. *Damn desert.* The man wanted to spit to clear the dust from his throat but knew that was frowned upon by the Mutawwa'iin, the religious police, the only law in this Islamic fundamentalist northern province. His eyes darted from side to side, not out of fear but from his years of training as a mercenary, now an instinctive component of his military equipment.

He rounded the corner of a butcher shop and entered the main street. Amid the cries of shopkeepers pronouncing their wares, he passed Arab men dressed in robes and headdresses seated in groups on the street in front of shops, conversing, sharing bowls of food or meditating. The smell of spices intermingled with the scent of cooking meat in the smoke and dust that hung in the stifling air. The man walked another fifty feet past a group of skinny Arab kids and stopped in front of the first building after the mosque. He looked around to see that no Mutawwa'iin were apparent. He knocked.

An Arab man in traditional dress opened the door, then moved out of the way to allow the man to enter. He pointed to a doorway into a back room and the man walked into it. Sheik bin Abdur was seated in a half-lit corner. The man smelled the odor of spices on the breath and skin of the five other men in the room. He knew they would be silent, but that he would have to tolerate an hour-long speech from bin Abdur. The man reminded himself of the premium he charged the al-Mujari, because very few others would do business with them. The risk/reward was worthwhile if all he needed to do in addition to his usual services was tolerate being regaled by this despot.

It's a living. And a good one.

Bin Abdur's robe formed a table of his lap, in which he held a pile of papers. He wore the traditional headdress. His beard was mottled with gray and untrimmed in the conservative Islamic fashion. His face was craggy and his dark Arab skin sunburned, wrinkled, and coarse; his eyes gleamed with energy and intelligence. He motioned for the man—who used the name Habib—to sit down. He did so in the corner.

The Sheik removed his Koran from its special stand in front of him, wrapped it in cloth, and gestured to the man who had admitted Habib. The man approached, retrieved the book from the Sheik and placed it on a shelf high in a corner of the room. The Sheik closed his eyes in contemplation for a full two minutes, moderating his breathing to relax himself, almost meditating. *Damn.* The Sheik seemed to be preparing himself for a long speech. He wasn't just the al-Mujari terrorist organization's day-to-day leader, he was its spiritual head as well. The al-Mujari, the dominant terrorist force in the Muslim world now that al Qaeda was no longer a factor.

The Sheik exhaled and looked up at Habib. "Greetings."

"Thank you, Sheik bin Abdur. Greetings to you as well."

"There is no God but Allah!" the Sheik said.

"La ilaha ilallah!" the others repeated.

"These are historic times," Sheik bin Abdur said. "Not since the first Caliph, Abu Bacr, the successor to the Prophet Muhammad himself, have the Shiites and Sunni Muslim brothers been united in our spirituality or our way of life."

Sheik bin Abdur's audience leaned forward, expectant.

"Since the first dynasty, we Shiites have claimed that Sunni Islam is not the true Islam at all, but the creation of the lax and worldly first generation Caliphs," the Sheik began. "Shiite Islam is the true way, based on the practices of the Prophet Muhammad and his original four successor Capliphs."

He bent his head knowingly toward his colleagues, who returned his gesture. Habib sat in silence, motionless.

"Since King Abdel Aiziz al-Asad led the Sunni religious brotherhood from the local tribes over a half century ago in conquest, and created our current monarchy in Saudi Arabia, the al-Asad family succession has relied on the support and approval of our religious leadership. We—the clerics, the religious leaders of the Muslim faithful—act as a protector of the Muslim principles on which our kingdom was founded, and upon the guidance of the Koran and the guidance of shari'a, our Muslim law. And it was with our support that the al-Asad kings have assumed the title of Imam, the law giver."

*One Mississippi, two Mississippi, three Mississippi…*Habib drifted into his thoughts as the Sheik went on. The skinny kids in front of the mosque reminded him of himself when he was growing up, South Side of Chicago. Rough neighborhood, all blacks and Arabs. Getting kicked around every day until his brother, Muhammad, helped him bulk up: protein shakes three times a day and weights four times a week. Back then he thought getting the hell out of there was the best thing he ever did. But after the Black Ops boys in Langley made him into a soulless tool that could never go home again, he realized having a place to call home was something he never should have given up. And now…
He refocused as it looked like the Sheik was winding down. Looking at the Sheik now, Habib had to admit the old man did have a presence that could will men to extraordinary feats. His eyes gleamed with an intensity Habib had rarely seen in the class of murderers and fanatics Habib encountered in his trade.

"And now the al-Asads have betrayed the laws of Islam. They have permitted the infidel Western troops to inhabit our sacred Arabian Peninsula, site of Islam's two holiest places. We declare this government illegitimate. We declare them to be infidels. As infidels, they, like the Western infidels, must be expelled or destroyed!"

Fifty-six bottles of beer on the wall, fifty-six bottles of beer, take one down and pass it around…

Minutes later, Sheik bin Abdur paused; Habib thought he was finished at last. But then the Sheik started up again, this time with eyes burning in a manner that made even Habib uneasy. "And since they will not go, they will be destroyed in our holy Islamic war. We will collapse this infidel Saudi regime and reestablish the great Muslim Caliphate that once unified the Middle East, Northern Africa and Islamic Europe under shari'a, our holy Islamic law. And we will go further!"

Habib saw the Sheik's followers swaying as they listened.

"In our jihad we will strike at and destroy the enemies of Islam throughout the world. We will extend the Caliphate to the infidel United States, Britain, to all the Christian nations. We will show the American infidels in particular, who have invaded our Islamic soil, that Osama bin Laden's September eleventh was only a taste. Now the true jihad is conceived!"

Habib saw balls of spittle at the corners of the Sheik's mouth.

"Our own believers and our hired warriors like our friend Habib who joins us today will strike the oil facilities of the infidel nations, chiefly the Americans, and of the infidel Saudi government. We will strike at the oil facilities of the Saudi government to cripple the royal family's ability to maintain their illegitimate hold on our people. Throughout this we must continue our efforts to educate our people, to urge them to protest, to undermine and topple these infidel royals." Bin Abdur shook his fists at the heavens. "We must expel the foreigners that the royals give our Saudi jobs to! We must expel the Americans who caused the wars of Islamic Arab brother against brother! We must continue to punish their military forces who are a stain on our holy Saudi soil! We vow the ultimate destruction of the Americans who are a stain on the Islamic world! There is no god but Allah!"

"La ilaha ilallah!" the Sheik's followers repeated.

The Sheik fell silent. The lesson was over. It hadn't been so intolerable, Habib thought, less than twenty minutes.

After another minute, the Sheik's retinue got up and left, closing the door behind them. Habib waited for bin Abdur to arouse from his meditation. Finally the cleric opened his eyes.

"You know of our efforts in the United States?"

"I have heard," Habib said.

"Good. You are well connected. As usual, Habib, or whatever your real name is." The Sheik's eyes twinkled. "Perhaps it is time for you to reveal your true identity."

In your dreams, old man. You'd have your people slit my throat and hang me by my feet until I bled out like a halal sheep if you knew I was American-born and CIA-trained.

"I think not, Sheik."

The Sheik hesitated, smiling. He went on, "I will pay you to recruit some additional, shall we say, 'committed individuals' in the United States."

"I understand. Go on."

"And we would like our identity to be kept secret."

"Of course."

"Good. I need you to recruit professionals who can provide us with access for our plans."

Habib nodded.

"Our plans to cripple the Americans' oil production."

"You need me to handle that, too?"

"No. That is a different kind of specialist. Computers. I will involve you in coordinating their work with the professionals you recruit, but later. Can you help us?" He handed Habib a paper he held in his lap. "These are the organizations we need access to."

"Yes." Habib didn't look up from the paper.

"I want to know the details after you have thought it through. Today I wish to agree on your engagement and to know that I can look to you for delivery of results."

"Always," Habib said.

"And I know where to find you if you don't deliver."

The men sat in silence for a minute. Finally the Sheik spoke again. "I do not wish to be difficult. I merely wish to stress that I would like to continue our relationship on a basis which maintains the level of confidentiality and satisfaction with results that has existed in the past."

"Absolutely."

"Then I trust you'll understand that these new efforts must not be traceable to the al-Mujari until we wish to claim responsibility for them. Understood?"

"Understood."

"Good, then I'll arrange for an initial wire transfer to your bank account of one hundred thousand dollars."

"We haven't agreed on my compensation yet," Habib said. "What you ask is difficult. And dangerous." The Sheik offered no reaction. "Orchestration won't be easy. Security has never been so tight. This requires planning. Subtlety."

"That's what I pay you for." Sheik bin Abdur's eyes penetrated Habib's. "Are you saying you're not up to the task?"

"You know better than that," Habib snarled. He remembered the rumored oil billions that funded the al-Mujari's terrorist activities. *What's it worth? Two million? Ten?* "One million advance against ten million upon completion."

The Sheik blinked as if in disbelief. "Five hundred thousand against two million completion."

"This will require that I recruit very specialized professionals."

"Seven hundred fifty thousand against three million."

"It will require significant travel, expenses and coordination with people we must grow to trust."

"One million advance against three million success."

"I think perhaps you should find another vendor. At that level, I must respectfully decline."

"One million advance against seven million success. That's final."

He offers three million, then bumps right up to seven. Quite a move. He must really need me for this. Habib put his hands on his knees and shifted his weight forward as if ready to rise. He saw the Sheik's eyes widen as he did so.

"I accept," the Sheik said. "One million advance against ten million success."

Habib leaned back again. "Thank you, Sheik bin Abdur. I'm grateful you've seen things in an appropriate light. I will not disappoint you."

CHAPTER 2

JULY 2, THIS YEAR. RIYADH, Saudi Arabia. An hour after finishing his morning prayers, Yassar walked with his characteristically erect posture from his private chamber into the exterior office of his suite. Assad al-Anoud, the head of the Saudi Secret Police, already sat waiting in front of a simple desk, ensconced in the cool marble of the oversized room. A pile of well-worn manila folders sat on the desk, identical to the ones Yassar carried. The two men praised Allah.

"We begin," Yassar said. "Final oil and gas investment banking advisor candidates. Our OPEC colleagues will rely on me for the interviews for final selections." He placed his file folders on the desk and opened the first: "J. Daniel Christian Youngblood III." Yassar thumbed an eyebrow, thinking. He was certain of this one. "One of the best. A top priority." Yassar looked at Assad, who kept his gaze on his folder. What did Assad think?

"Smart, experienced, self-confident and quick to react under pressure—a powerful combination," Assad said. "Regarded by his peers as a great investment banker. A creative deals man. Good at solving complex financial problems, structuring merger and acquisition and financing transactions. A superb strategist and negotiator. A motivator of his own people. Team leader."

Yassar was pleased Assad shared his view. Still, Yassar mused, "A hired gun like all his peers." He looked up at Assad, who now knitted his brows together. Yassar felt anticipation. Had Assad's agents come up with anything? "What is it?"

"Personal life. A recent widower, then a series of unstable relationships with women."

"Something that could be cleverly exploited." Yassar felt a rumble of apprehension. He paused, sighed. "Anything else?"

Assad raised his eyes. "We have been observing him for some time. The other area of major concern is his commitment. He has recently toyed with the idea of leaving his business."

Yassar shrugged. *Who hasn't?* He felt the weariness in his limbs. They moved on to the next file.

Two hours later Yassar pushed his chair back from the desk, rubbed his eyes and looked at his itinerary. "Visits to New York, London, Paris and Tokyo for interviews and final choices." He looked at Assad. "I'll be gone for ten days. And you?"

"Our agents are in place and I have our intelligence networks at full alert. We have only to…"

The sound of a fist pounding on the door interrupted him.

"Minister! Commander!" a voice called from the hallway. The door swung open and a guard with perspiration on his face bustled into the room, then pulled himself to attention. "The student protest has turned violent. A thousand of them have pinned two of our units against the steps of the Labor Ministry. Our men are armed with only live ammunition and the students are hurling rocks. We're afraid our men will be forced to fire!"

Assad looked at Yassar, then back at the guard. "Our men do not have rubber bullets for crowd control?" Assad demanded.

"No."

Yassar said, "We need to stop them before we have an incident that will cause repercussions!" He had a flash in his mind of dead students in front of the Labor Ministry, front-page

photographs in *The New York Times* of bloodied steps and fleeing bystanders. Assad strode from the room, Yassar behind him.

Assad heard him and turned, alarm in his face, holding up
his hand as if to stop Yassar. "Minister, it is too dangerous."

"I'm coming."

Bin Abdur, Yassar thought. He felt his blood rise to his face.

July 2, This Year. New York City. The first class passengers on
Air France 244 to JFK had a jump on everyone deplaning, and
Lydia made sure she kept a brisk pace in the corridor. She knew
the lines for the passport control checkpoint at JFK were always
long, and waiting on the things was more mind-numbing than
having her hair done at Isolde's on Place Vendome. She put on
her sunglasses as she approached the checkpoint. When she
turned the corner she saw thirty or so on the "U.S. Citizens" line.
Another flight must have arrived just before hers. The "Foreign
Nationals" line was empty.

She ducked under the cordon and strode up to the first agent
in the "Foreign Nationals" area.

"Passport," the dead-eyed man said.

"Good afternoon," Lydia said, smiling.

The man looked at her, then at her passport, then back at her.
He paused.

She pulled off her sunglasses, then the Hermès scarf from
her head, and shook out her black hair, letting it fall to its full
length halfway down her back.

"It's me," she said, smiling again at the rumpled man and
cocking her head to the side. She made eye contact with him and
held it. He looked down.

"The reason for your visit, Ms. Fauchert?" he said.

"Business. I'm a fashion photographer. A photo shoot in New York City and then perhaps some sightseeing."

"How long is your stay?"

"Two weeks."

He continued looking at her passport, as if it would tell him if she were being truthful, or whatever these silly men concerned themselves with.

"Enjoy your stay," he said, stamped and handed her passport back without looking at her.

After she checked into the St. Regis and dropped off her bags she walked down to Rockefeller Center, stopping in front of the skating rink. She looked up at 30 Rockefeller Plaza. It was troubling, this feeling she had. If she had lead feet now, how would she feel in weeks, or months?

She told herself to relax, then started to walk around the rink toward the entrance to 30 Rockefeller Plaza. She took a deep breath. She only wished she didn't feel so empty.

Her next sensations were unworthiness, then guilt, and she had to remind herself she was grateful for the opportunity. The opportunity for whatever name it was given in English, none of which captured it: absolution, atonement, redemption. It was something she'd try to work out during this lifetime. She offered a short prayer to her Hindu god Ganesha.

July 2, This Year. Riyadh, Saudi Arabia. Yassar stood in front of the Labor Ministry, clenching and unclenching his jaw, waiting. Assad's man had exaggerated: there weren't a thousand protesting students, perhaps only 600. But it was bad enough, hearing them growling, shouting—he could even smell their sweat—seeing them force their way in against the police. Two units of Assad's men, 50 at best, the front row doing all they could with their riot shields to keep the students back from the steps of the Labor Ministry. The others stood in a line behind and above them on the steps, rifles poised. He saw their fear in the beads of moisture inside their riot facemasks.

Finally the microphone was ready. Yassar saw Assad motion to him. Yassar started out from behind the protective group of Royal Guards encircling him and walked toward the microphone stand. *Quickly*, he told himself. The jeers began as the students saw him, then rose into a crescendo, a roar like a jet plane taking off. Yassar squinted against the sun, smelled the dust swirling on the plaza, then saw the stone hurtling toward him, too late. He heard the dull thud as it hit him in the forehead, felt his knees go weak. Dark shapes danced in his peripheral vision and then he heard sharp pops like firecrackers. Only when he collapsed onto the steps did he realize the sound was shots from the police rifles.

As the Royal Guards pulled him to his feet he saw the students running, shouting and screaming in panic. And now he saw at least a dozen students lying on the ground, some writhing, most not, with blood oozing in pools beneath them.

Allah be with them. And with us.

Then he clenched his fist. *Bin Abdur, something must be done about you.*

July 2, This Year. New York City. Daniel felt the heat of the afternoon sun on the polished brass of the revolving doors before it blasted him when he stepped into the wall of a moist New York July outside 30 Rockefeller Plaza. The air already tasted like the silt that hung on his skin when he got home in late August. He glanced in either direction and chose a route for a "lap," a circuit of Rockefeller Center. It always raised Daniel's spirits when he was down, recharged him when he was tired and further animated him when he was happy. It was his reminder that New York was the center of power, of commerce, of money, of the arts, the center of everything that up to now meant anything to him.

Wow. He raised his chin and relit his cigar, reflecting on the last half hour. He'd almost quit and walked out of his bonus negotiation with Dieudonne. Instead it had ended with a deal that could net him more in bonuses over the next few years than he'd made in his entire career. Daniel had started by encroaching on Dieudonne's space, commandeering one of his good Cubans—a Cohiba Esplendido—from his humidor to join Dieudonne in a smoke, *de rigeur* in Ladoix Sayre's custom of ignoring New York's no smoking laws. Dieudonne had humored Daniel with a smile, then sucker-punched him by insisting the Dorchester fee of 6.3 million was next fiscal year's revenue, having closed one day after the end of Ladoix's June 30th fiscal year. He awarded Daniel a bonus of 650 thousand based on his other 5 million of fee income for the fiscal year. Daniel had struggled to collect himself—he was angry at himself, not Dieudonne, that he hadn't seen it coming—feigned genuine outrage and countered by informing Dieudonne the fee had already been paid by wire transfer, reminding Dieudonne that he was the firm's entire franchise in oil and gas, then jabbing him with a not-so-veiled threat to take his business across the street to the Rothschilds if Dieudonne didn't pay him an appropriate bonus—20%—of the Dorchester fee. Dieudonne blew cigar smoke at him and offered

1 million when he signed up the Saudis. Daniel said to himself, *Ah, negotiating leverage,* and told Dieudonne that was bullshit. He was offering Daniel less than what he already deserved on Dorchester for signing on a piece of new business that would make the firm hundreds of millions in fees over the next few years, based on the Saudis' grand-scale acquisition objectives. Dieudonne said, Okay, he'd throw in 10% of all the Saudi fees as well if Daniel signed up the Saudis for at least two years and stuck around to do the deals. Daniel then got genuinely pissed and told Dieudonne he knew damn well 20% was standard, and to commit to this he needed 30%, since life was too short to fight this fight every deal, every client, every year. Dieudonne laughed, blew more smoke and said he couldn't possibly do 30%. Daniel stood up to leave, glaring at Dieudonne and said, "You can do whatever you want," and started for the door, meaning to keep going when he reached it.

"Alright," Dieudonne had said when Daniel was halfway across the room. "Twenty-five percent. A million on signing them up, a minimum engagement of two years. Do we have a deal?"

"If it's in writing," Daniel had said, turning and looking Dieudonne in the eye.

Daniel now puffed on his cigar, turned, and looked back up at the majestic seventy-story art deco masterpiece of 30 Rock. *A million when I sign up Yassar, and who knows how much? Twenty-five percent of the fees on billions of deals. Amazing.*

And then there she is again, in those staccato photographic images that assault him just when he feels he's safe from them. Angela Elizabeth Theodore as a twenty-four-year-old long-waisted beauty, her hair up, empresslike, over a white, white neck that curves into shoulders that hover over a gown pretending to deserve the perfection it holds; Daniel bending to Chip Barnaby to ask who this otherworldly creature is. Next, Bucwald "Teddy" Theodore, Angie's father, a fast-talking, fast-food mogul, son of a son of an authentic New York real estate tycoon, ravenously shaking Daniel's hand, beaming at his future son-in-law, welcoming him into the Greater Metropolitan Theodores ("he's a *Vice President* at Goldman Sachs where being a Vice President still really means something"). Then Angie cupping Daniel's cheeks in her hands, her brown eyes…

"Stop it," Daniel said aloud. An Asian girl spun from taking her father's photograph in front of the skating rink, her eyes startled. Daniel felt his face flush and strode a quick few paces away.

He stared at the motionless American flags on the face of Saks across Fifth Avenue at the other end of Rockefeller Center, brushed beads of perspiration off his eyebrows. *A year or two with this Yassar fellow and I'm out of here. Maybe Congress after all. Or teach? Write?* He turned that over in his mind as he rolled his cigar between his fingers. He got no answer. The Dorchester deal came back to him. *Damn.* That was the problem, the hunt without the thrill of the chase anymore.

"You've got enough," Michael's words came back to him. "Why not head off to the beach?" That was right, he didn't need the money, so why was he still doing it?

He stopped in front of a topiary at the entrance to the Channel Gardens in the middle of Rockefeller Center. He looked back at 30 Rock, then turned again toward Fifth Avenue and Saks. He reminded himself he loved this place, and now he tried to recapture the sense of home and balance that the elite retail stores up Fifth Avenue—Tiffany, Van Cleef and Arpels, Versace, Gucci, Bergdorf Goodman—conjured up in his mind, a quarter of a mile of the most exclusive retail space in the world. He groped for the secure presence of the cream of the world's business community headquartered within a twenty-minute cab ride in either direction—TimeWarner, Sony, Bank of America, American Express. He sighed, then walked slowly toward Fifth Avenue.

That Yassar fellow. He'll certainly get the juices flowing again. He could even help Daniel prove a point: you can still make an honest buck on Wall Street without screwing anybody and check out on an uptick. Then he could forget about dealing with sleazeballs like Dieudonne forever. And guys like that lying bastard, Kovarik.

He smelled hot dogs on a musty breeze, then the perfume of two women in front of him. Then there she is again: Angie in Peru, coaxing Daniel by the hand to the shaman's hut, the one that took them three days of hiking in the mountains to find; next Angie with her lips on the wooden bowl containing the shaman's hallucinogenic potion; then Angie on the moist dirt floor of the hut after thirty-six hours on the trip Daniel came down from but she never did, boiling with spinal meningitis.

He forced the image away, exhaled heavily. He lifted his cigar to his mouth, realized it was out. He threw it in the wastebasket. *So what do I do with all this?* He let the question sink in and the answer came back: "Somebody." *Somebody to share it all with.*

Another shot of Angie, smiling mischievously then running into his closet and crinkling his rows of freshly starched shirts when he had particularly infuriated her. Her smile softens. Now he sees her expressionless in the hospital bed, dark circles under her closed eyes, face beaded with sweat from the fever that alternately rages, abates, then consumes her. Then another, the faces of Dr. Arbouthnot and his resident in infectious diseases at NYU Hospital, shaking their heads after Daniel tells them of the shaman's potion. The images swamp the thought of anyone else taking Angie's place in his life. *But that's really what I need.* He stops, expecting another assault. Then, as anticipated, a stinging wave of guilt.

Daniel faced the statue of Prometheus holding his flame over the skating rink and stood for a few minutes without speaking. *A spark of fire? Yeah, maybe that's what I need.*

"I need more than that," he said aloud. *I need Prince Yassar. And a year or two to slam out a few hundred billion in deals for him. And twenty-five percent of the fees as my cut, maybe twenty to thirty million for myself.* He savored that for a moment, realized that wasn't all. *That, and a good woman. Someone to make it worthwhile.*

His stomach was calm.

CHAPTER 3

July 2, This Year. Riyadh, Saudi Arabia. Sheik bin Abdur understood that one accustomed to American standards would consider the shampoos, hand lotions and miniature soaps found in the baskets in the bathrooms as pedestrian pleasures; still, the Riyadh Hilton seemed opulent to him. His aides had rented the penthouse suite as much to make him comfortable as to provide for the round-the-clock security they felt necessary. Things were getting hotter with the Saudi Secret Police.

He was still adjusting from the hasty airplane flight from Buraida. After his prayers, Sheik bin Abdur entered the living room, noting with disapproval that Henri Ledouce, that odious little man, had already arrived, along with Habib. Ledouce was a paunchy, perpetually sweaty man who nervously darted his eyes around any room. His hair was greasy and he always wore a disheveled suit that seemed to have been handed down to him from an older brother. He smelled of wine. Worse than that, the odor of pork emanated from his pores. But Ledouce knew computers and therefore had to be tolerated. For now.

"Hello, Henri, delightful to see you," Sheik bin Abdur said, without extending his hand.

"Your Excellency." Ledouce stood and bowed. "I'm pleased to be of service to you again."

Sheik bin Abdur needed someone of Ledouce's skill to assist him in his upcoming meeting with a young man known to him only as Ali. The Sheik's aides had prepped Ledouce in advance, insisting he question the young man in such a way as to reveal Ali's expertise or to expose him as a fraud. He was reputed to have tackled every major computer network in the U.S., Russia and China, even breaking into one of the CIA's mainframes at its headquarters in Langley, Virginia. He was the smartest, fastest and most undetectable computer hacker that Sheik bin Abdur's organization could find.

The Sheik and Habib exchanged nods. Habib would assess the young man's mettle.

Sheik bin Abdur seated himself, staring at the doorway through which he knew Ali would enter. He was beyond making small talk with a piece of rotting flesh like Henri Ledouce.

It was 4:28 p.m. Mercifully, Ali arrived two minutes early, admitted by one of the Sheik's aides.

"I am Ali." He bowed. "I am pleased to meet you. I trust you are Sheik Mohammed Muqtada bin Abdur."

The heavy weight the Sheik had felt in his chest lightened. Ali wore casual Western clothes, a polo shirt and khakis and those curious American sneakers, but he was freshly scrubbed and beautiful to behold. And, to judge by his demeanor, he was respectful of the Sheik's position and of the Islamic ways.

"Come close and sit, please." Sheik bin Abdur motioned to a chair immediately to his left. Henri Ledouce shifted uneasily. The Sheik froze him with a glance. Ali took the seat he was offered. "I understand you are Saudi. And Shiite?"

"Yes, Sheik bin Abdur."

"That is good. Come, let us share food together." Two of the Sheik's aides moved a room service table between the two men and placed plates with various fruits, breads, sweet cakes and spiced grains in front of them. Sheik bin Abdur opened his palms and offered the meal to Ali, feeling the spirit of genuine Muslim brotherhood. Ali bowed and ate eagerly. Finally Sheik bin Abdur said, "I'm interested in engaging your services on a sensitive project."

"Yes, Sheik bin Abdur." Still the respectful young Muslim.

"I should like to understand something of your capabilities, beyond what we have already been able to find out on our own, and learn if these capabilities suit our needs."

"You may ask what you wish."

"Very well. I'll be blunt. We're interested in your ability to penetrate the computer networks of various industrial facilities."

"I'm prepared to describe my skills in that regard, Sheik bin Abdur." Ali leaned forward, eager. "I am at your service."

The Sheik turned to Ledouce. Would that one day he would not need the services of a pork-eating infidel like him. He cringed as he nodded to Ledouce to begin his questions.

"Please give us some examples of your computer infiltration experiences over the previous few years," Ledouce asked. "Your 'hacking,' as we professionals call it," he threw a ridiculous glance at the Sheik.

"As we professionals call it," really. Ledouce, do you think I am an ignorant fool? Get on with it.

Ledouce twisted in his seat, seeing the Sheik's menacing stare.

Ali responded enthusiastically. "Absolutely. I'm one of the few who has penetrated the U.S. Army's Telstat network. I now 'own' three account names and passwords on the most classified of the computers on the network and have a score of others on various other less important systems."

That was what he wanted to hear. Now if Ledouce could ascertain the young man's level of sophistication. He looked away, afraid his gaze would paralyze the greasy idiot.

"How do you conceal your activities?" Ledouce asked.

"I have telephone links perfected through Computel, the U.S. online service that provides access to computer networks around the world. I access all of them through dial-in modem links through various computers on either the Saudi Peninsula or Europe, chiefly at universities who rarely police their accounts. They're considerably slower than T-1 lines through the Internet, but none of my links has yet been detected."

"Are these networks landlines or satellite?" Ledouce asked.

"Computel uses either satellites or undersea fiber optics. These interconnect to U.S., European and Asian telephone lines through which I hack my way into various computer systems."

"And what about the Internet," Ledouce asked.

Ali smiled. "That access is available to even less sophisticated hackers. I can hack into thousands of industrial computer networks that way. Many multinational corporations have only third or fourth generation computer security firewalls. Most are inadequate in the face of one with the level of sophistication of a hardware architecture designer and software developer such as myself." He allowed himself to look less humble. "And even corporations that understand security haven't yet come to comprehend the ability of hackers to invade their systems through means as a lowly as email, automatic data feed and preprogrammed input accumulation access points."

The Sheik looked at Ledouce for an explanation of Ali's last words, but saw the vacant look on Ledouce's face and turned back to the young man. He nodded for Ali to go on.

"I've even saved hard disk copies of all my online hacking sessions and can produce examples of any of the hacks into specific networks I just cited. I can also provide you with references from satisfied customers, ranging from corporate customers to foreign governments, at least to the extent I am able to disclose them." The young man paused, seemingly finished for the moment.

"And now," Ledouce asked, "getting to the heart of the matter, what about sabotage? What is your experience?" The Sheik thought Ledouce looked like he was hoping Ali would shrink and run from the room. He smiled. He knew from his investigations the young man was experienced. Not some journeyman like Ledouce. Ledouce continued, "What would be your preferred approach to a sabotage assignment? Be specific, and remember we would wish to remain undetected. At least," and Ledouce looked at the Sheik with matinee melodramatic affectation, "in the short run."

Intolerable, pompous fool!

Ali rose up in his chair. "Logic bombs—computer programs that sabotage other computer systems at a predetermined time—planted within 'trojan horse' programs that infiltrate the host computer, lie undetected and then unload their cargo."

"That is a most impressive recitation of credentials," the Sheik said, beating Ledouce back with a glare, tired of his stageplay. "Is there anything else you'd like to add?"

"No, Sheik bin Abdur."

The Sheik spoke. "Ali, we're impressed. I'm impressed." Ali bowed. "We are interested in engaging you. As a perfunctory matter of confirmation, Mr. Henri Ledouce will evaluate a representative sample of your previous sessions, after which we will negotiate the terms and specific objectives of your engagement.

Mr. Habib here will act as our advisor in those negotiations." The Sheik paused as if to receive Ali's gratitude for his magnanimous gesture. Ali responded with a wave of his hand that flattered the Sheik with its submissiveness. "We would like to discuss your first assignment with you at this time. Are you familiar with the means to access any of the computer networks associated with the Saudi Aramco Oil Company?"

"I am."

"Very good. We're specifically interested in your ability to succeed where we have previously failed"—he looked critically at Ledouce—"at the main refining facility in Dhahran. It will be a trial run, before our real business. We wish to implement certain measures which would, shall we say, slow down the company's processing of oil into its various by-products. This would not be intended to harm the Saudi people but to serve as a warning of Saudi Arabia's vulnerability to outside forces. We'll take other steps to make the act appear to be the work of the Western infidels, specifically the Americans. So we want you to be clever, and we want you to leave no obvious traces that would point in any direction. We will take care of the rest. Do you understand?"

"Of course. As one of the Believers, I understand completely."

"Good. Mr. Ledouce will give you your specific instructions."

Jesus Christ, Habib thought, watching the two. *Like two peas in an insane asylum.*

Habib saw the Sheik look at him as if to ask, "Well, what do you think?"

I think you people are scary. You, your pubescent little freak here, your religious fanatics, the lot of you. Scarier than me on my worst day.

———◇———

July 2, This Year. Milford, Pennsylvania. Daniel stopped at the stoplight—the only stoplight—in Milford and felt the ache creep up again. It had been easier to avoid it with someone in the passenger seat next to him, someone to talk to, have fun with, argue with, make love to. Five warm bodies had occupied that seat in the time since Angela's death.

He parked in front of his house. Now that Angela was dead it seemed enormous—a five-thousand-square-foot Greek revival clapboard on the edge of town. Empty. On the front porch he heard his phone ring, fumbled for the key, then, guessing who the caller was, looked across the street and waved. Sammy opened his kitchen window and waved back.

"Last one sober does the dishes," Sammy called, motioning for Daniel to come over. Daniel nodded and went into his house.

Sammy and Mickey were fellow New Yorkers who had bought the rambling Victorian place across the street a year after Daniel and Angela moved in. Mickey worked 18-hour days all week at his own computer consulting business so they could afford for Mickey to work 18-hour days all weekend restoring the Milford house, because, as Sammy said, he couldn't sit down for more than five minutes. Sammy managed a Greenwich Village clothing boutique and, according to Mickey, was in charge of griping on weekends.

Sammy and Mickey and Daniel drank as the afternoon faded, Daniel his red wine, Sammy and Mickey their vodka martinis. Periodically Mickey would disappear, preoccupied with some peculiarity in the garden, leaving Sammy to berate Daniel with his unique brand of effrontery.

"...not thinking of that slut, Rebecca, are you?" Sammy's eyes twinkled from under his bushy brown eyebrows. He had more hair than Daniel could imagine on three people.

"What?"

"I said you're not thinking of that slut, Rebecca, are you?"

"Of course not, what makes you say that?"

"Because you've got that same cross-eyed stare now that you had from the day you met her. After you decided you were in love with her—Mickey and I decided you were in lust with her—until you broke up with her six months later."

Daniel scowled. "I wish it had been six months. It was on and off for a year and a half. There were Sandra and Kimberly— the second time for Kimberly—in between."

"Ah, yes, Kimberly. Sweet lady. Too bad she was so dull."

Daniel laughed. He didn't know what he would do without Sammy and Mickey. In the weeks after he had returned from Peru with Angela, they had sat with him in his vigil as she alternately burned up, strengthened, slipped away, and finally died from the fever that wouldn't relent. After she died they shopped for him, sat with him and when necessary saw to it that he ate during the weeks he was incapacitated with grief.

It took at least a month before Daniel could speak about his guilt. Yes, he told them, it was Angie's idea to hike the mountains of Peru. But it was Daniel's idea to visit with a shaman, to explore the third world's mystical Other Side. Later, Daniel would sit for hours in their house, rambling on after making a good show of it all week at work. And Sammy and Mickey would put their arms around his shoulders when Daniel broke without warning into sobs.

And so Daniel wasn't only bound to Mickey and Sammy by friendship, but now through the intimacy of their knowledge of his pain and his guilt. They had adored Angie, just as everyone had adored Angie, and it didn't take Daniel long to realize he would feel better if they railed at him for his negligence in taking her from them, from everyone.

Sammy said to Daniel, "You're lost. You don't believe in anything anymore. That shit about not making partner at Goldman just made you bitter and cold."

Daniel looked at Sammy's glass. It was full, but he couldn't recall how many drinks had preceded this one. He could be exasperating enough when he was sober. But give him a few martinis…"I came back from that," Daniel said. He shifted in his chair and raised his chin like a defendant protesting his innocence under cross-examination.

"Yeah, maybe, but I bet it didn't make you a better investment banker. Just made you more resolved. And hard."

"Maybe. But my career's back on track. And I've got at least one potential assignment for the Saudi government that could get me excited about getting out of bed every morning."

"Well maybe you've gotten over the Goldman thing, but you haven't gotten over Angie. Your personal life is still a mess."

"I'm over Angie."

"Bullshit."

Nobody else talks to me this way. Where would I be without Sammy?

"After Angie died you curled up in a ball and pulled the covers over your head. You don't take chances anymore."

"Where is this coming from?"

"Look at you. You used to race Aston Martins with that asshole Kovarik on that stupid summer circuit you rich guys dreamed up. Used to do crazy shit like bungee jumping."

"I cut out nonsense like that after I met Angie."

"Bullshit. The Peru trip with Angie? You two scaled a two-hundred-foot vertical face down there two days before you went to the shaman. You don't do stuff like that anymore."

After a moment Daniel said, "Where's this going?"

"Where are *you* going? You used to be a risk-taker, hotshot investment banker who lived out at the edge, only you haven't taken a real chance since Angie died."

"Sammy…"

"Don't 'Sammy' me. You've had a half-dozen girlfriends—"

"Five."

"—Okay, five—and never let anybody get close to you since Angie. You're scared of getting hurt again. It's time," Sammy said. "Time you took a chance again. Make a leap of faith on somebody. Have a relationship. Get your life back on track."

July 3, This Year. New York City. Habib hated wearing a suit and tie, but if that was the price of not sweltering in the damned Saudi desert, it was a good trade. Although at 96 degrees and 84% humidity, New York City was a hostile environment all its own, particularly after his overnight flight.

He entered the revolving doors to 299 Park Avenue and felt the soothing blast of air conditioning. Habib plopped a New York driver's license bearing a name not his own on the security desk. "I'm going to Kovarik & Co.," Habib said.

Upstairs, Kovarik & Co.'s offices were done up like they'd been in business longer than the Rothschilds. The lobby smelled like old leather. Habib crossed a Persian rug—a Tabriz that had to be at least 300 years old—past leather club chairs and 19th-century English wooden armchairs to a receptionist in her 20s. She introduced herself as Tracy from beneath an oil painting of someone's grandfather, then showed Mr. Kareem Kapur into the conference room to await the founder of Kovarik & Co.

During the 15 minutes Kovarik made him wait, Habib ran through in his mind why Kovarik would be perfect: the man leaves his job as Goldman Sachs' lead oil and gas partner and sets up his own boutique investment bank; he leaves, say, 80% of what he thinks are his clients behind, because they're really Goldman's clients; the new offices he's been carrying for six months during renovations are probably costing him $120 a square foot, say, $100,000 a month in addition to the $3 million or so he must have sunk into the renovations; and just as he launches his new firm he realizes, unless he's a complete moron, he's going to lose out on his pitch to represent Yassar and OPEC on their global acquisition program, because Yassar will never hire some no-name start-up firm.

Habib felt a tingle of anticipation.

Kovarik arrived, a dandy with a matching silk pocket square and tie, starched shirt collar and an open button on the sleeve of his jacket so you knew it was a custom suit. He walked with a limp that seemed from some old injury and smelled of cologne, a lot of it. "Bob Kovarik. Sorry to make you wait," he said, not looking the least bit sorry. Then he went on about being a Harvard man, a Goldman man and a marquee deal oil and gas man. After 10 minutes of it Habib decided this was harder than listening to the Sheik, so he took a long moment to glare at his watch, then put his hands on the edge of the table to push his chair back, like he was ready to get up and leave.

"Let me tell you why I'm here in the few minutes before I have to go," Habib said.

Kovarik looked startled, then gave Habib a patronizing smile and rested his clasped hands on the table. "Okay, shoot."

"On the phone I told you I'm an independent contractor to a client who wants to remain anonymous."

Kovarik nodded.

"I need to hire someone with your expertise for a confidential project. In turn, you would be an independent contractor to my client, whose identity you wouldn't know."

"What's the nature of your client's business?"

"You don't need to know that either, only that he needs your expertise in the oil and gas business."

Kovarik nodded again. "May I ask the nature of your business—what kind of independent contractor you are?"

"I do whatever my clients need me to do, including jobs like this. Frequently they involve security issues."

He saw Kovarik look at Habib's hands: the right scarred from knife wounds, the tip of the pinky severed; the flesh on the back of the left hand bumpy and hairless from the napalm burns that extended up to his shoulder. Kovarik smiled and said, "Would it be safe to say you're a mercenary?"

"If I said yes would you decline this assignment?"

"Depends on how much it pays."

"And what my client's asking you to do?"

"Within certain boundaries."

When Habib didn't respond right away, Kovarik leaned back in his chair and smiled more broadly, then lowered his voice into a conspiratorial tone. "Investment bankers are sometimes described as mercenaries. We sell our services for a fee, hired guns to accomplish specific client goals, all the while maintaining complete confidentiality. We aren't fainthearted."

Habib looked into Kovarik's eyes, taking his measure of the man, still without responding. Kovarik looked back evenly, not shrinking from Habib's gaze. *He'll do.*

Habib said, "Good. Then here's what we plan to do—"

"Are you sure you want to tell me that?"

"You won't be able to give us the information we need if you don't know what we're going to do."

Kovarik nodded. Habib now thought Kovarik might be losing his nerve; he saw him shift in his chair and tense his jaw.

Well, here goes. "Our client wants to slow down the flow of oil around the world to achieve his political ends. His tactics will be to trigger certain events in the computer software that runs the operating systems at all levels of the industry—drilling, refining, pipelines, and all other aspects of production and distribution."

"How will he do that?"

"Computer tinkering. We've lined up the experts for that."

"So where do I come in?"

"We need information you have and access to people you know."

"Okay." Kovarik seemed to be turning it over in his mind. "What, specifically, do you need?"

"We need you to identify and get us access to the software vendors who supply the brains to the oil and gas industry's computer operating systems. We need the information organized into three tiers: first, the investment bankers who advise the software vendors; second, the software vendors themselves, organized by type of operating systems their software runs; and third, the oil and gas industry companies who are customers of each software vendor. You understand?"

"Yes, it's very clear."

Habib paused, again taking in Kovarik's reaction, waiting.

Finally Kovarik said, "We need to resolve my compensation."

Habib suppressed a smile. "I assume the fees we discussed on the telephone are acceptable?"

"A starting point. Since you don't have much time, I'll cut to it. I'll need a retainer of a hundred thousand dollars per month. I'll credit the retainer against a transaction fee—we call it a 'success' fee—payable on successful completion of the project. The transaction fee of two million you proposed is low, given the complexity and critical nature of what you want me to do. I'd accept four million dollars."

Habib didn't feel like screwing around with the man all day. Besides, it wasn't his money. He nodded.

"There's only one more issue," Kovarik said.

"What's that?"

"How do we define 'success'?"

"Oh, there won't be any question about that."

"Well that sure fell into my lap," Kovarik said aloud after Habib left. Add the retainer to the three client retainers he'd already signed up and he had Kovarik & Co.'s first year's expenses covered. Any other fees, including the 4 million from their mutual client, whoever the hell he was, would be profit.

But what these guys were up to was scary. He had a moment in the middle of the discussion with this guy, Kapur, or whatever his real name was, when he started wondering, was he Arab,

Afghan, Pakistani? Could his client be some fundamentalist nut or terrorist? No way he'd go there. He'd make sure all future meetings with Kapur were in person, hard copy of documents only, with no email paper trail. He'd insist the entity he'd sign up in the engagement letter would be clean. And no wire transfers of fees; checks from U.S. banks only. He didn't want any shit from this sticking to him.

And the way the guy assured him the definition of success was no problem, well, he didn't need to be a rocket scientist to put two and two together there. Once his new client had worked his magic, things in the oil and gas business would either slow down, stop working, or more likely just blow up. It reminded Kovarik of that drilling rig that exploded and sank in the Gulf years back. The well had spewed oil for months, screwed up fishing, beaches, marshes. What a cleanup bill, what a fortune some of his clients made on it. And it got Kovarik a lot of business, too, financing those clients, merging a couple of them. Imagine that on a scale 50, maybe 100 times bigger. Financings on new equipment and plants: drilling rigs, refineries, offshore platforms, pipelines. Bankruptcies, workouts, mergers. Every banker in the oil and gas business would pound it for fees for a decade.

Yeah, that sure fell into my lap. And whether Kapur knew it or not, he was only asking a couple of weeks' work; putting together a comprehensive overview of all the bankers in oil and gas, all their software systems clients, and all their customers. A third of it he could do off the top of his head, the rest with his Analysts grinding out the midnight hours.

He started thinking it through. Daniel Youngblood, of course, would be at the top of the list with the most clients. Just thinking about him made Kovarik's pulse quicken, his jaw tense. Man, how he hated that guy. And how much he enjoyed the beginning of summer, breaking Daniel's balls over that Dorchester deal. He'd whipped his own client into a frenzy: yes, no, maybe; yes, no, maybe. Back and forth, dragging the deal out for weeks just to wear Daniel down, drive him crazy. He even succeeded in stretching the closing out until past the end of Daniel's firm's fiscal year. He bet that gave the sonofabitch a fun year-end bonus negotiation with his CEO.

He hadn't done a deal across from Daniel in 18 months, so it was especially fun. Not as much fun as sabotaging Daniel for partner at Goldman—the stupid, holier-than-thou, smarmy Mister Nice Guy Team Player had too big an ego to even think Kovarik could be screwing him behind the scenes. Hell, they were pals, right? Pals going back to B-school, pals starting out together at Goldman. Yeah, pals like when Daniel stole Angie from him.

Angie, *his* girl, the best lay he ever had, and her father rich as Croesus; man he'd have been set. Dating her a year before business school, then two years of working the long distance relationship thing from Harvard, and then she disappears to the West Coast. By the time she comes back both he and Daniel are Vice Presidents at Goldman, she takes one look at him and that's it. Daniel twists her mind; she's all his.

Up until then all Angie knew was that Kovarik lived in Beacon Hill before he came to New York. Never knew he'd grown up in South Boston, threw off that low-class Southie accent, until after she met Daniel. It must have been he who told her. Well, no matter now. Daniel had gone and let her get sick and die in that crazy Peru trip; now he'd never get her back anyhow.

Christ, how he hated that sonofabitch. And maybe now, with Daniel's name at the top of the list he'll be giving these wackos, who knew? Maybe the shit Kovarik didn't want sticking to him would stick to Daniel. Maybe, if he could work it right.

CHAPTER 4

JULY 4, THIS YEAR. MILFORD, Pennsylvania. Gary and Jonathan's home, the site of the Fourth of July party, was on an isthmus in the Sawkill Creek not more than a mile from Daniel's weekend house but seemed in another constellation.

"Hey, sailor," Sammy said, when Daniel entered. The theme that year was Gilbert and Sullivan. Sammy's outfit proclaimed him the Ruler of the Queen's Navy: ruffles on his shirt, velvet coat bedecked with brass buttons, hat adorned with a plume. "No costume, eh?" He scowled at Daniel.

"Are you polishing the handles of the big front door or scaring the passengers off?"

"You're hilarious. The bar's across the main deck, me hearty." Sammy walked outside to greet someone else.

Daniel wasn't prepared for the sight. Most of the crowd—at least 150 people ranging in age from their 20s to their 60s—was costumed in full Gilbert and Sullivan regalia, undulating and full of life in the twenty-foot-ceilinged main room. The stereo blared songs from HMS Pinafore. A group in the corner represented the chorus from the Mikado, complete with pancake face makeup, pencil-line eyebrows and stenciled, ruby lips. He couldn't discern which were women dressed as men, which were men dressed as women. Immediately to his left another Admiral was conversing with a svelte, dark-haired woman in civilian dress, either a newcomer to the annual bash or a slacker like Daniel.

The entire left wall was devoted to tables crammed with food. Daniel walked past them to the bar, carrying two bottles of a respectable burgundy. At the bar he handed his wine to the Pirate of Penzance who was tending it, one of his hosts.

Jonathan uncorked one, poured Daniel a glass and stashed the bottles under the bar. Daniel turned back to look at the floor again.

His eyes strayed back to the Mikado girls, then to the woman in civvies. She wore a bright red silk dress and had jet-black, straight hair. She was short, perhaps five foot four, and powerful. Not fireplug-powerful, more like a dancer, athletic. In fact, she moved the way dancers move, a mixture of subtlety and energy. Even just standing up as she did now when their eyes met, a sharp juxtaposition of opulence at rest with a muscular explosion as if into a pirouette. Daniel smiled. She smiled back. He was curious about who she was. He'd find out later.

Daniel made the rounds. More than once his eye settled on the black-haired woman in the red silk dress. "You two've been looking at each other all night," Sammy said to Daniel, appearing out of nowhere. "Get over there and talk to her."

Daniel headed over to the bar for another glass of wine.

It's come to this. Now my gay friends are telling me how to meet women. As he stopped at the bar his eye found the red dress again. He looked at the woman closer. She was petite, with full, uplifted breasts, not like any he'd ever seen on stage at the New York City Ballet. She moved again with that languid grace followed by another catlike spurt of energy. He heard her uninhibited laugh, the one his ear had caught more than a few times during the evening from across the room. She was very slender, very athletic and very difficult to take his eyes off of.

Daniel poured wine for himself and a glass for her, resolving to use it to get a conversation started. When he looked up he saw her standing next to him, smirking.

"I can spot a good glass of burgundy at fifty paces," she said, taking the glass he offered.

Great smile. Great eyes. "Hi, I'm Daniel Youngblood."

"Lydia," she said. "Lydia Fauchert." She sipped the wine. "Mmmm. Good. Thank you." She spoke with a lilting, sing-songy accent he couldn't place. Maybe a tinge of a British accent within that melodic cadence. Her words were crisp and distinct, as though she'd been formally taught her English.

"Are you foreign?" he asked. "European?"

"Ish."

Daniel leaned forward. "Oh?"

"From Europe, Asia, all around. I was raised always on the move. But mostly Europe. So I'm European-ish."

"I see," he managed. She laughed. Her black hair flew as if in mockery, but her black eyes exuded warmth. *Confident.* She smiled. There was something unusual about her smile that drew him in. *I think I'm going to enjoy this.* "So do you have a place around here or are you just visiting?"

"Visiting. I'm only in the country for a few weeks."

"Vacation?"

"No. A job. I was here on a shoot, now I'm goofing off for a few days with the Mikado girls over there," she motioned with her head. "Models. I'm a fashion photographer."

"Ah." *That would account for the restrained personality.*

"I see you're out of costume, too," she said. "Visiting?"

"No. My weekend place is in town."

"Are you from New York City?"

"How'd you guess?"

"Professional look. And boarding school."

"Both true."

"Ah," she said brightening, as though she'd learned a major secret. "I can see you with those suede patches on the elbows of your tweed jacket when you're alone in your den." They were standing off to the side of the crowd and now Daniel could see her legs more clearly. *Dancer's legs.* They were slim, long and muscular. Their skin was creamy.

They walked for a while together, Daniel introducing her here and there. They made their way back to the bar and he poured them both another glass of wine. His mind drifted and he paused, unconscious of the party for a moment.

"Oh, what's that all about?"

He looked at her, confused. "I'm sorry?"

"You suddenly looked very serious, like you just remembered you left the kettle on the flame."

"No, just an undigested bit of the week intruding upon my weekend."

"Slings and arrows?"

"Quoting Shakespeare or regaling me with my past?"

"Regaling."

"I've been regaled enough lately, thank you very much. Eat it for lunch all week. Today's my day off."

She tightened her lips. "I'll top it," she said half under her breath.

"I'll bite, you go first," Daniel said.

She took a long swallow of her wine and looked at him like she was trying to decide if she thought this game was a good idea. "Lady's prerogative, you first."

Daniel shrugged. "Let's see, father a prominent lawyer. Straight As. Sunday school. All-star Little Leaguer with dreams of baseball greatness crushed by the introduction of the curve ball in junior high school. Couldn't hit it."

"That's the tragic part?"

"Into each life some rain must fall."

"Drizzle. If this doesn't start to get more interesting I'm going back to those Admirals." Her smile told him otherwise.

"Choate, Yale, then two years as a financial analyst in the Mergers and Acquisitions Group at Goldman Sachs. Harvard Business School, then back to Goldman for ten years as the quintessential team player at the quintessentially team-oriented Wall Street firm. Then passed over for partner."

She locked her gaze on his eyes as he said it, searched his face. Her eyes had a searing presence. He felt as if she were trying to read his thoughts—no, that wasn't it—sense his emotions. He softened his eyes and made himself more approachable. He was intrigued, and wanted her to know it.

He turned to her as if to say, "Your move."

"Okay. Orphaned, never knew my parents at all. Raised more by the governess than by my legal guardian, Sophie, who adopted me as much, I think, as a lark as anything else. One of these Parisian socialites, you know." She glanced at him knowingly as if he understood already. "Traveled in the best circles, but never really had a home. Europe, mostly France. Paris. Provence, a little place near Avignon. French Riviera. A few seasons in Northern Italy. The Orient. Sophie was very wealthy. I think I was a toy she always wanted and didn't have. Used to trot me out for parties."

Daniel nodded. Maybe that would account for the accent. English learned on the Continent. And her ease; raised to know she could do anything, even before she developed the sense of it as she came to know she was beautiful. Maybe she was always beautiful. *Careful. It makes them crazy.*

He asked, "Did you go to private school? College?"

"Tutors, and a lot of life rammed down my throat at too young an age to swallow all of it properly."

"Read as: men?"

"Lots. But not like you're thinking. Grew up with wealthy hangers-around. Older, sophisticated." She looked at him through seasoned eyes. "I learned how to take care of myself. Your turn," she said.

"Passed over for partner at Goldman a second time two years later."

"That's cheating."

"No it's not, it's a sling followed by an arrow."

She stopped walking and put her hand on her hip. "Suppose we start this over again. Less like some competition."

"Okay," he said. "I'll start first. I grew up in Upper Montclair. It's in Northern New Jersey. That's a state…"

"I know." She rolled her eyes. "Just across the Delaware Ocean from here." She smiled. "Paper route? Dog? Siblings?"

"Yes, yes, two brothers and I'm the oldest."

"Never've guessed it."

"What's that supposed to mean?"

"Only, silly man, that it's obvious you're somebody's older brother." They started walking. Daniel tried to place her age. He'd thought she was in her early thirties at first. Now he detected the beginnings of tiny crow's-feet at the corners of her eyes. *Wisdom.* He liked the fact that she didn't wear any foundation or makeup on her face to try to cover them. She began to speak in one of her fluid spurts, waving her arms, almost spilling her wine in her enthusiasm, and curling her free hand to emphasize the words. "I have places in Paris and London, since most of my work is based in Europe. Although I've been doing a lot more shoots in New York and the Caribbean lately, so I'm thinking of getting a flat in New York, too."

He waited to see if she would offer anything about a current man in her life. They reached the front door and went out. The air outside was damp and surprisingly cool. It smelled of woods. A black-robed judge in a white wig, a sailor and a few pirates lounged in white wicker on the front porch. Daniel and Lydia walked down the steps and across the driveway until the chirps of the crickets were louder than the voices from the porch. He still waited to see if she would mention a man. He gave it a little more time. She stopped, stood smiling in silence.

"Where are you staying out here?" he asked.

"A little bed and breakfast outside town. One of the girls rented a car. God," she widened those big black eyes, "models *can't* drive. They're going back tomorrow. I figured I'd get to know the area, particularly if I may get a New York place."

An opening? "I may be able to help you out."

They reached one of the entrances to Jonathan's gardens. The grass was cool and damp when they crossed it. He saw the moonlight on the skin of her shoulders. *Even creamier looking than her legs.*

They sat next to each other on a bench. "I suppose at the back of my mind in considering a flat in New York is an attempt to be a bit rooted for once," she said, as if she'd been ruminating on her earlier train of thought. "It's only in retrospect that I realize I grew up with sort of an empty existence, mostly." Daniel was silent. "Don't get me wrong. It was fabulous to go to so many places, see so much and to grow up around really fascinating people. Artists, politicians, actual royalty. And to have pretty much anything I wanted—Sophie was rich, but some of her crowd was super-rich. But years later I've learned that others grew up with a warmth and closeness I would like to have had. Those were things that took me a long time to find out were possible." She looked at him for a response from underneath her hair, then swooshed it out of the way with a languid toss of her head so she could see his eyes. "Know what I mean?"

"I didn't grow up like that. Sounds lonely."

"No. Soulless. But it doesn't matter now." She sat up straight. "But after that you'd think I'd have picked a profession with a little more emotional substance or depth. Fashion isn't overflowing with profundity; some days I feel like what I guess I am. Somebody's hired tool for the day."

"Tell me about it. That's how I've been feeling lately. Where I work now is an eat-what-you-kill realm of independent contractors. Yeah, I know what you mean. When it's no fun anymore you really have to think seriously about getting out."

"You surprise me."

"Oh? Why?"

"I hadn't expected you to be like this."

"Like what?"

She paused. "Open. Warm."

"How did you expect me to be like anything?"

She shifted in her seat, as if she'd let out a secret. "Well, from afar you looked like rather a stiff with your nose in the air and two bottles of wine in your hands."

He laughed. The moon flickered out from behind a cloud and he saw her lips parted and her eyes exploring his. After a moment she said, "So what's a man like you looking for now, Daniel."

"Trying to recapture something, I guess. One of my friends says trying to find something—or someone—to believe in again."

"Again?"

"Angie. My wife, she passed away two years ago."

"I'm sorry. I've had my own losses, too. I know how it feels. But I have spiritual beliefs, and they help after a loss, especially like yours."

Daniel didn't feel the need to respond.

"In my religion we believe that souls keep coming back until they get it right. Some who don't even know they're on the path get there because of how they live. Some who are trying incredibly hard can't seem to do it properly and come back hundreds of times. So maybe you won't meet up with Angie again, at least until the last journey, but maybe you will."

Daniel thought of Angie, wondering why he wasn't seeing her framed in his mind, scolding him, teasing him, making him laugh. "If that's the case, maybe Angie will need a few more turns. She had quite a temper. But she was exciting when she was mad."

Lydia cocked her head to the side, urged him on with her eyes.

"But even when I was pissed off at Angie, I never forgot what a kick it was being with her. Right away I could be honest with her. Just be myself and feel like that was the way it was supposed to be. She was someone who made me know that us being together and sharing things was worth believing in."

Lydia slid her hand into her hair, tossed it back, and tilted her head toward her shoulder. "Go on."

Daniel said, "But you have to move on with your life, don't you? You can't meet somebody and decide you're going to have that. It just has to happen. You can't be looking for it."

"Have you been looking?"

"Hard to say." Daniel pursed his lips. "But one thing is sure: I haven't found anything like I had with Angie. Maybe because I don't really want to give up what I had with Angie."

"Why would you ever want to give up your soul embracing someone else's?" she asked.

Daniel felt good hearing that. "How do you know so much about all this?"

"I guess you could say I've had my own hard knocks. But you don't want to hear about all that."

He sat up. "Yes, I would like to hear about it."

She was silent, staring as if at something in the distance.

He opened his mouth to speak again, urge her, then stopped. She was someplace else. Her face showed pain.

Come on, don't put me off.

She abruptly stood up. "I'm sorry, I have to go."

"Did I say something wrong?"

"No," she said. "Not at all, I just have to go. I'll be around all weekend. I'll see you again. Good night, Daniel, I really enjoyed meeting you." She said it with a finality that told him not to follow her as she walked off.

Some lady. Beautiful, world-wise, yet spiritual. And suddenly unfathomable.

———◇———

July 5, This Year. Milford, Pennsylvania. Since Angela died, on weekends Daniel immediately thrust himself from bed upon waking. It avoided dozing in that half-waking state between dreams and consciousness, the one in which he had always turned toward Angie and was reassured that everything was as it should be. After her death, he'd turn to face the stinging reality that she wasn't there, and wouldn't ever be again.

So the morning after the party, Daniel sprang from bed and into the shower. He was still toweling off when the doorbell rang. He ignored it, but it rang again a minute later, then again. *Damn.* Maybe Edward, the guy who took out his garbage and did handyman jobs for him, was under pressure to show some recruits for the Jehovah's Witnesses again. He put on his robe and went downstairs, resolving to make a good, Christian show of it for Edward's sake. He answered the door.

"Good morning!" Lydia called. She was holding a brown paper bag in her hand. "I brought bagels, cream cheese and lox."

Daniel quickly got over his surprise. "A European-isher bearing gifts," he said. He noticed her cotton sweater accentuated her breasts. Sockless in pumps, hair straight and shining, a toothy smile. *Great smile.* And those big black eyes.

She showed him the wisdom he had seen last night in the corners of her eyes as she smiled. He admired the firm curve of her cheekbone. He moved closer until he could smell her hair. He noted she wasn't wearing her perfume today.

"So are you going to leave a girl standing here all morning or let me in to fix us brunch?" Daniel laughed and opened the door, stepped back to let her in. His eyes stole back to the touchable roundness beneath her sweater. "Where's the kitchen?" she asked cheerfully as she walked past him, then turned, almost as an afterthought. "Is this okay? I'm not intruding or interrupting anything, I hope."

"Not at all. Welcome to my home. The kitchen's through the dining room, that way." He pointed, smiling now, wanting her to know he was glad she'd come. He saw her take in the oak-paneled walls of the dining room, slow her pace and run a finger over the Sheraton breakfront. She was luminous, even more so in the daylight. Her breasts looked bigger than he'd remembered them last night, even in the skimpy silk dress she'd worn.

She glanced back over her shoulder at him, smiled. "It smells of antiques and money. Gatsbyesque, but understated."

Once in the kitchen, Lydia asked, "So what's on the agenda?" She opened her bag and laid out bagels onto a plate she found in the second cupboard she opened.

"Your move," he said, remembering her forwardness of the previous night, enjoying her. She continued unloading her bag. Still bagels, now plastic tubs of cream cheese, lox.

"Brunch, then a tour." She looked around the kitchen. "First here, then town." She smiled and tossed her hair.

After a brunch accompanied by Mozart—Daniel guessed she'd been an electrical engineer in a prior life, because she'd figured out how to turn on his audiophile stereo system while he was upstairs dressing—and the caviar and burgundy Daniel added to Lydia's offerings, she jolted in her seat. One of those sudden athletic moves he'd seen last night. The dancer.

"So I'll clean up, while you think through the tour."

Daniel insisted on helping her despite her insistence to do the dishes herself. In ten minutes the dishwasher was loaded.

"The house first," she said. "I was quietly overwhelmed coming in. Show me more. Knock the legs out from under me."

I thought I was thinking through our day, Daniel laughed to himself. He shrugged and walked her through the house.

In the wine cellar she laughed, "After a hard week of merging and acquiring the man comes up here to commune with a few thousand bottles of wine."

Upstairs in the attic, he showed her his slant-ceilinged study with its seventeenth-century writing desk and the daybed where he could nap but never did.

"And what's this room?" she asked, looking across the hall to a room where the door was closed, marked "PRIVATE."

"Angie's room, although she never spent much time there. It was actually Elsie's room, the former owner's."

They went inside. The room was cluttered with a mixture of knickknack-laden tables, hard-backed maple chairs with wicker seats, urns, candlesticks and pots on the floor, rugs rolled up.

Lydia looked around, walked to one side of the room, arms folded. She put her nose in the air as if sniffing for the scent of rain, then smiled at Daniel self-consciously, as though caught in a private moment. "Who was this Elsie?"

"Elsie Camden," Daniel said. "She was quite the colorful character. Everybody's got a story about her, like when fifty-eight years old and divorced she was found on the sofa in Jonathan and Gary's house with a twenty-nine-year-old gardener the morning after their Fourth of July party." Lydia smiled with her eyes, looking delighted. "This was Elsie's study."

"It feels good. She must have been an old soul."

"What?"

"An old soul," she said. "Wise. Been around many times."

Daniel observed her skeptically, not sure if she was kidding, then certain she wasn't.

"I like it here," Lydia said, walking to the other side of the room, now treading on the balls of her feet, reverently.

Her seriousness made it okay, rather than quirky. *Like last night.* He relaxed again and just took her in.

Finished with their tour of the house, they set off to conquer the town. "The best antiques are in the big building here we call Forest Hall," Daniel said. "Sometimes I like to just wander around and look at old things. Wood, china, brass."

In Forest Hall Antiques, they clumped up the bedraggled stairs. Inside Lydia became focused, her eyes intense. Daniel followed a few paces behind her. He watched her walk with purpose now, scuffing her pumps on the unvarnished pine floor, taking in the front room of the store with studied glances.

She disappeared through a doorway to his left. He wandered to it, sure she'd been there from the scent of her hair, then was distracted by a pile of gaslight fixtures. He looked up to see Lydia standing in the doorway smiling triumphantly. The sun hit the side of her face and it glowed, that same creamy whiteness he'd seen in the moonlight in Jonathan's gardens. He wanted to hold her. Lydia walked up to him, a battered leather athletic bag clutched in her left hand. She curled her right arm through his and pressed her face up close to his.

"Look what I found," she said. "Something to keep that past of yours in. So you don't need to discard it; just tuck it away so it won't sneak up on you so often. But you can still peek in at it whenever you want."

Daniel sat back in the sofa in his den, holding his third glass of wine aloft, admiring the color through the crystal, flowing with one of the assorted Puccini arias Lydia had chosen for the after-dinner music. She'd found the good stuff in his cellar. Chateau Margaux 1982. *And she knew to decant and breathe it for an hour. With explorateur cheese.* He watched her hunching over her cards. They faced each other on the sofa, their chips in a pile between them on the uneven leather.

As he heard the clock on the Presbyterian Church in town strike 10:00 p.m., Daniel was thinking this wasn't going quite the way it was supposed to. He didn't like losing, even if they were only playing for chips. She was a wild bettor, and she seemed to be switching on and off an inscrutability that he now wasn't sure was solely related to her wanting to adopt a poker face. *Beautiful. Fascinating. But a mystery.* "I should have called seven card stud again."

"Doesn't seem to matter much what you call," Lydia laughed. The pot in the middle of the sofa was a moderate one, although it dwarfed Daniel's dwindling store of chips. Lydia's winnings were piled up against her crossed legs.

"So this Yassar, the Saudi prince," she said, and flipped one card facedown. "I'll take one."

"One?"

"When you've got the cards, you've got the cards. So, Prince Yassar, has he told you what he wants you to do yet?" She leaned forward, holding her cards in one hand.

"Not all of it." Daniel was wondering if one of the tutors she'd had as a child was a mathematician. Or a professional gambler. Fast Eddie Fauchert. *Who is she?* One thing, she was quick-witted, and not just at cards. If she said she was a fashion photographer, okay, she was. But she wasn't some artistic type he needed to explain business to. She'd tracked right along with his explanation of his latest deals, even showing real interest in his potential Saudi project. He reminded himself he'd only met her twenty-four hours earlier. Her transformation over the game only underscored that. "So far he says he wants to undertake a multi-year acquisition program and is looking for one, maybe two key advisors."

"I hope you're better at investment banking than cards."

This was violating the code. Using needling to further her advantage. In a minute he might actually start to get angry. He kept his gaze on his cards, but saw in his peripheral vision as she eyed him over her cards. He didn't reply.

"Sorry. Just seeing how far I could push you."

"So you've played this game before."

"I only bluff, Daniel, I don't lie." Now she seemed to be reading his thoughts, not just his cards. He realized he was getting carried away with wondering about her. *Roll with it. Enjoy her.* He saw her look at him from underneath her hair, much as she had in Jonathan's garden the night before, expectant. He felt a tingle.

Daniel took two cards. Emboldened by two pair, Queens high, he went for the jugular and bet his remaining chips. A moment later it was over.

"Three Kings," Lydia said, scooping the pot into her legs. Daniel slid his hips forward on the sofa and reached to put his arms around her. She pulled back, chuckling up at him, "You're crushing my winnings," she said.

He pulled her to him and kissed her.

July 6, This Year. Milford, Pennsylvania. "Why don't you hang out here for the day, then meet me back in the City for dinner?" Daniel said. Lydia wore his bathrobe and curled her feet under her where she lounged next to Daniel on the sofa in the living room. His briefcase and the leather duffel bag she'd bought him sat on the floor next to him. He was fully dressed.

"Sounds delightful. Only I don't have a shoot until tomorrow. Do you mind if I stay here today and then see you in town tomorrow night?"

"No, have a great time. I only wish I could stay with you, but I have that lunch with Prince Yassar tomorrow, and I want today in the office to get ready. As I told you, it could turn out to be important. I'm excited about it."

"I know." She pulled his face to her and kissed him. "Are you close to getting hired?"

"I hope to close over lunch."

Daniel kissed her again and stood to go, anxious to get on the road. He checked his watch. *Six thirty. I can be in the office by eight and get in a full day's work.* "I'll call you tonight. If you get lonely you can call me in the office." She mouthed a good-bye as he pulled the front door shut.

Lydia sat on Daniel's sofa, rubbing her cheek on the collar of his bathrobe. This Daniel was a good man with a pure heart, who'd been hurt in a way that touched her. And he respected her, even seemed he could care for her. She felt her heart reaching out to his, had to restrain herself. She looked up the stairway, started up toward Elsie's room in the attic. She'd see if she could feel that old soul again. Her eyes were moist.

CHAPTER 5

JULY 5, THIS YEAR. RIYADH, Saudi Arabia. At 9:00 a.m. Prince Yassar entered the corridor to King Abad's office. Two Royal Guards bowed to him as he knocked on the door. He waited next to the silent men for a response to his knock, wondering if they ever imagined he sometimes toyed with the thought of changing places with them for a day. Let them carry the tedious responsibilities of government into the king's office. Allow Yassar the peace of the simple task of merely standing at attention for a twelve-hour shift. He heard a murmur from behind the door and opened it.

"Morning," King Abad said, without looking up from the papers on his desk. "You're the first to arrive."

"Good morning, Abad. How are you?"

"Tolerable."

Yassar knew the feeling. "Perhaps that's the best a ruler can do in these times. Even one of royal blood."

King Abad looked up. "Yes, Yassar. Perhaps."

Yassar sat down in a chair beside the king's desk. He adjusted his robe and put on his reading glasses, then pulled five photocopies of the papers from one of his files and gave them to the king. Yassar was relieved the others hadn't arrived, grateful for a few moments of familial peace. The two men worked contentedly, side by side. Over the next ten minutes Crown Prince

Abdul arrived, then Prince Naser, the Oil Minister, and then Prince Hashim, the Minister of Foreign Affairs. They all took seats around a conference table.

Yassar spoke almost before they had settled, anxious to get the objectionable preliminaries over with. Yet another confession of his inability to resolve the country's economic problems. His relatives and fellow leaders looked at him.

He groaned to himself. "It is with regret I must report to you our continued failure," Yassar said, meeting each pair of eyes in turn, showing no attempt to hide from the responsibility he felt. "If only we had been right in 1973." The others averted their eyes. All except King Abad.

"That was not your fault," Abad said softly.

"Maybe," Yassar nodded, but felt a sting of pain behind his eyes. "Nonetheless, if the OPEC oil embargo of 1973, as the Americans refer to it, had worked, we wouldn't be…"

"'In this mess today,' as the Americans say," Prince Naser, the Oil Minister, said.

"Yes," Yassar continued. "If we OPEC members, with almost forty percent of the world's oil supply, couldn't sustain high world oil prices as a group, how can we expect to sustain our individual economies on our own?"

No one responded.

He regretted asking the question, one he so often asked himself, sensing it made him appear to be making excuses. "So on to my report. A few statistics first." Yassar lowered his head, spoke from memory, as if by not consulting his notes he could spare his eyes the burn of shame. No use. The facts were branded into his psyche. "We will end this year with over 100 billion U.S. dollars of internal debt. Even now less than two-thirds of our population over 15 years old can read and write. Over a quarter are non-citizen aliens, here only to work, yet accounting for over half the private sector work force. And yet, despite our efforts to help our young Saudis compete for the jobs that will make us prosperous again, foreign workers—who are willing even to flip hamburgers for less and less—are increasing their hold on the job market even faster."

"How does the Saudization plan go?" Abad asked.

Yassar shrugged, felt another rumble in his chest. "All the disincentives we've created toward hiring foreigners—increased work visa charges, denial of work permits for certain jobs, even prohibitions on purchasing automobiles—have had very little impact." He paused and looked at them through heavy eyelids. "And that isn't the worst of it. You all know the social situation. Our young Saudis are being swept up in this extremist religious fervor. Sheik bin Abdur is striking a chord with his demands for the expulsion of all foreign workers from Saudi Arabia and the return of all jobs to Saudi nationals." *The simplistic idea has seductive appeal. Would that we could be so bold as to implement it.*

The other ministers looked at Yassar to continue. But it was the king who spoke. "With oil prices back down to thirty dollars per barrel we're in a losing struggle."

Yassar took it as his cue, relieved his unburdening was over. On to the future. The redemption he'd conceived from these stagnating ills. "That brings us to our project—Project Deliverance—with our fellow OPEC members. It's time to implement it. We and the other members of OPEC have largely the same profile—we have huge oil and gas reserves, but all we do is pump them out of the ground. Our industry peers refine them, ship them and sell them to their customers for further processing into end products, like chemicals and plastics, or sell them through retail outlets like gas stations."

He saw Abad nod in agreement. Yassar continued, "Today, that end of the business makes over half the profits, and the percentage is growing. We are leaving money on the table, as the Americans say. Money we need in our economies. We need to embark on an aggressive acquisition program to buy refiners and marketers. If we control the flow of oil from the wellhead all the way through to the end-consumer, we can increase the price and maintain it—something we've been unable to do consistently in the long history of OPEC. Our economists calculate that each dollar crude oil price increase translates into ten billion dollars per year of Saudi profits." Yassar only now raised his head. "I believe this program will double our gross domestic product within five years."

"That will fix our government deficits and put Saudis to work," Hashim said.

"It will solidify our control by undermining the arguments of the religious extremists," Crown Prince Abdul added.

"Most of all, it will make the Saudi people comfortable and proud again," Yassar said. The air of command was now back in his demeanor, energizing him. "Before each of you are copies of the main exhibits I will present to our OPEC colleagues to secure final approval for Project Deliverance. Before that I'll spend the next ten days on the road interviewing finalists for our advisors—to choose investment banking mergers and acquisitions specialists and lawyers." His cousins all nodded. "Naser and I fly to Vienna for our OPEC meeting in two weeks. After that we leave the results in the hands of Allah." *Indeed.*

"Let's just hope it's not too late." King Abad stood and paced. "Sheik Mohammed Muqtada bin Abdur," he said. Yassar felt his pulse quicken at the mention of the Sheik. "Our old adversary. Now rising again, after years in virtual exile among his

own people. Not only is he fomenting social unrest, he is leading the al-Mujari's call for a global jihad, a holy war against all
non-Islamic states. Two terrorist bombings within the past year
on the bases of our American allies. Both our own Secret Police
and the American intelligence agencies have all but confirmed
it." Prince Hashim, the Foreign Minister, shifted in his seat.
"Sheik bin Abdur interprets the Koran to describe the royal family as secular and corrupt. He says we betray the laws of Islam by
allowing infidel Western troops on our soil."

"He vows the destruction of the Americans as a stain on the
Islamic world," Prince Hashim interjected. "He says they made
us fight our own Islamic brothers in the '91 Gulf War, and then
pressured us to support them again in Iraq in '03. He sees himself as the successor to Osama bin Laden."

King Abad continued, "These attacks against the
Americans, as we all know, come in part because under Islamic
law it is forbidden for Muslims to kill fellow Muslims. But it
may not be long once the extremists have declared our government illegitimate—and therefore infidels they may attack
as well."

Naser and Hashim glanced sideways at Yassar. Yassar saw
them out of the corner of his eye, continuing to sit looking grave,
betraying no emotion. But he guessed that Prince Naser and
Prince Hashim knew the internal struggle he felt at the mention
of bin Abdur. He knew they had seen its toll on him over the
years, the lightheartedness turned to suffering, the patience frequently shattered by anger. The anger that his faith taught him
to be ashamed of, yet which he held on to as part of his reason
for living.

"The Americans will help us. They are already helping us,"
Prince Hashim said.

"And with this program we are helping ourselves," Yassar said, his anger empowering him. "In time we'll have prosperity again and the appeals of the extremists will fall like hollow whines in the ears of Saudi citizens who are wealthy, well fed and satisfied with their culture—and their government—again."

King Abad turned toward them, his hands clasped behind his back, a man fatigued with stress. "The Americans will help us," Abad said. "Because they have too much at stake to see us fail. They cannot risk another period of instability in our region or any disruption in the oil markets. And in the next few years, when we are on our feet again we won't allow ourselves to need them so much. That's why we and our colleagues at OPEC must be successful in our program." Yassar observed his king, his cousin, carefully. He saw the weariness in his eyes and the strain in his face.

King Abad continued. "The Americans haven't forgotten the long chain of events that started, and what happened to them after the Shah of Iran was overthrown. We ourselves can't pit Saudi Muslim brother against Saudi Muslim brother, but the Americans are not bound by such religious dilemmas." King Abad turned to Yassar. "So is everything in place?"

"Our advisors have been identified," Yassar said. The background profile of this Daniel Christian Youngblood III, the most promising, still hung in his mind. "I am ready for final selections. Our OPEC colleagues are poised. And we are watching bin Abdur. Our agents are in place."

"Very well." Abad looked around the room. "All in favor of committing to our OPEC program as Yassar advises?" The others nodded. "Good. We take it to the full Council of Ministers this afternoon."

CHAPTER 6

JULY, THIS YEAR. NEW YORK City. Dick Jantzen was a skilled, self-trained promoter. His lying was natural-born. "Uh huh," Daniel said. He was talking on the telephone with Dick, Chairman & CEO of Intelligent Recovery Systems, Inc. Dick and his company, which designed computer software for driving secondary and tertiary recovery methods for fallow oil wells, running oil refineries and controlling sophisticated drilling rigs, were darlings of Wall Street.

Dick was one of Daniel's oldest clients and one of the core relationships Daniel had taken with him from Goldman Sachs when he moved to Ladoix Sayre. And Dick was beginning to wear on Daniel. Given the peculiar sensitivities of Daniel's stomach, Daniel's years of dealing with Dick were finally accumulating to the point where Daniel couldn't ignore the impulse to puke.

"Uh huh," he said again, closing his eyes and summoning a reserve of calmness to force down his rising urge. *This I didn't need right now.* Daniel looked at his watch. *Twelve twenty. I've got Prince Yassar coming in for lunch in ten minutes.*

"So, I told him his banker would hear from you about a meeting to discuss the details, structure and all that."

"Uh huh."

"Okay, that's it. Get on with it. His banker is some guy named Dean Lowell at Morgan Stanley."

Daniel opened his eyes again. "Yes, I know Dean. I'll call him. I'll give some thought to an engagement structure and send you a fee letter as well." Dick didn't respond. *Why should this one be any different. I've had to chase you on fees every time you've done a deal with me over the last ten years.*

"See you," Dick said. "Go get 'em."

Daniel sighed. *I'm getting too old to listen to this guy's bullshit. He's what's wrong with my world.* Daniel glanced toward the window and saw the leather duffel bag Lydia had bought him. Then a calm settled over him as he thought of Lydia, wondering if they were starting something together. *Too soon to say. But it's not based on time: it's how you feel.*

He turned his mind again to the luncheon he'd spent all Sunday preparing for. He revisited his walk-through of the dining room an hour earlier. *No wine. No cigars.* All in deference to Prince Yassar's Muslim strictures.

A few minutes later Cindy buzzed him on the intercom. "Prince Yassar is here. He's been shown into the dining room."

"Thanks." Daniel was looking forward to this. He felt his heart rate pick up. He smiled at the sensation. *I pull this off and I'm good for some genuine excitement again, and enough in fees to let me leave this craziness with a bang. Tell Dieudonne where he can shove his fiscal years.*

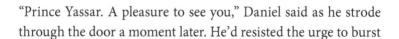

"Prince Yassar. A pleasure to see you," Daniel said as he strode through the door a moment later. He'd resisted the urge to burst in with forced energy; he didn't need to put on. And today Prince Yassar looked more approachable than he'd remembered. The kind, almost sad, yes, sad eyes. He crossed the room and shook hands. The big hands and firm grip he remembered. *Western business attire. Strain showing around his eyes.* He met Yassar's gaze, felt he was connecting. "Please, some tomato juice?" He turned to the sideboard. "Some water?"

"Water, thank you." Yassar sat down. The table was set for lunch in formal splendor, as if for a diplomatic function. The eight pieces of silver at each setting—indicating an appetizer, a fish main course, a dessert and tea—was Christofle sterling. The plates were Limoges. Light danced off two pieces of Baccarat lead crystal attending each setting, accompanied at the center of the mahogany table by crystal water pitchers.

Daniel buzzed for the waiter.

"Mr. Youngblood," Yassar began.

"Daniel."

"Daniel. We've done our due diligence. You have a reputation as an effective investment banker. Given the worldwide importance of your Wall Street, we're impressed."

"Thank you," Daniel said, observing the prince as meticulously as the prince observed his sterling silver. Calm, as if he didn't hurry to places; purposeful, as if he was never late. Daniel liked that. "I try very hard to stay in touch with my market, my specialty. I'm flattered that my clients have made favorable recommendations. I know that your network of contacts extends far beyond that of most."

Yassar said, "I'd like to be direct."

Yassar's going straight to it today. He felt a surge of adrenaline; he was going to be tested. He folded his hands on the table and leaned forward.

"As I've told you in our previous meetings, I—we of Saudi Arabia, as well as our colleagues from OPEC, are interested in engaging a few key financial advisors who can assist us in our efforts to diversify our economies out of reliance on domestic energy revenues." He paused. Daniel nodded, telling him to go on, but in his own time. Yassar continued, "We're a wealthy nation, but we have ambitions to become wealthier still. And we wish to take advantage of the best investment advice available to us in the world. That is where people like you come in."

"I'm here to listen. Hopefully I can respond to your satisfaction." Daniel trying to show some humility.

"We need the advice of you and other professionals to make certain we are optimizing our investment and profit options. I'd like to hear your thoughts on where the opportunities are today in the oil and gas business, not just in the U.S., but worldwide," Yassar said.

He's leading me right into my pitch.

"I think I can be very helpful to you." Daniel felt his stomach flutter, as it always did before a crucial opportunity. "We at Ladoix are one of the largest factors in Mergers and Acquisitions on Wall Street. We normally rank in the top three or four for domestic deals, and in the top one or two for international deals. Last year we did 225 deals valued at 462.5 billion dollars overall, with 144 deals…" Daniel hurried through his standard preface, then saw he was losing Prince Yassar's interest. *Knock it off. He knows all this crap or he wouldn't be here.*

Yassar smiled. "I am a careful and methodical man. I take my responsibilities to my people and my government seriously. I came to New York to interview three prominent investment bankers in the oil and gas mergers business. We will interview others in London, Paris and Tokyo. I know your firm's position in the sector, and that as the partner in charge of oil and gas at Ladoix that these are your accomplishments. I've done my homework. So please tell me something I don't already know." Daniel saw him studying him through those hooded, life-saturated eyes. "Tell me where to put our money, where we should invest around the world if we're to diversify out of domestic Saudi oil reserves or OPEC reserves, as the case may be, yet stay in the only business—oil and gas—we really know anything about."

Daniel shifted in his seat. *Don't blow it. Remember your research. He doesn't suffer fools and he can't stand a bullshitter.* "Okay," he said. "Trends in the oil and gas business are no different than those being experienced in M&A for all other megabusinesses."

Prince Yassar stared at Daniel blankly. "I don't know what you're talking about."

"Not too many clients say that," Daniel smiled.

"I've observed that not many investment bankers say that either. In fact, my experience is that most investment bankers say even *more* when they don't know what they're talking about." Daniel laughed. The old guy Yassar was battle-weary, but he had a sense of humor. *Okay, now quit over-thinking this meeting; just let it happen.* Daniel leaned back in his seat, got comfortable as if he was going to start enjoying this.

Prince Yassar noted Daniel's reaction with pleasure, seeing the spark of individuality Daniel had allowed to show through the presentation persona. The real man showing, even if only a glimpse. Now perhaps the young man wouldn't be so tightly strung beneath that polished exterior. Yassar tried to imagine what kind of conversationalist Daniel would be over a dinner, say on a discussion of politics. Was he honest? Would he give him advice he didn't want to hear?

"So you were saying," Prince Yassar continued, "or not saying. Please, put things in perspective for me." *Let's see if this will lead where I want to go*, he thought.

Yassar saw Daniel lean forward, enough to see the young man's eagerness, like the American baseball players he'd seen on the hotel television last night, the ones called infielders, charging the batted balls called grounders. He felt an involuntary urge to smile, couldn't help it. His eyes softened. He saw Daniel respond to the subtle encouragement. Now maybe he'd hear something.

"Today we've got a strategically driven M&A marketplace, where deals are put together to pool resources or drive operating costs down. Mostly in maturing, consolidating industries with high costs and little ability to raise prices." Daniel paused, as if to see that Yassar was following. "In your case, you've got crude oil priced at $30.42 per barrel, way down from recent years, combined with bloated operating costs."

Yassar raised his chin at the word "bloated." It was true. Daniel didn't change his face, continuing his steady gaze. *Good,* Yassar thought.

Daniel continued, "So you're seeing industries consolidating into a few last big players who will dominate their fields. They're cutting literally *billions* of costs out of the merged entities. And these companies that are merging are now creating global, as opposed to national, behemoths." Daniel paused again.

"Go on." Yassar observed Daniel critically. Would he now start with the blustery, know-it-all investment banker pomposity he'd come to expect?

"So even though the oil and gas industry has largely consolidated, you'll see more. Look at your own situation, and that of your OPEC colleagues. Even *you* need to keep driving down costs in order to survive. And that means mergers—strategic mergers to create economies of scale to cut costs."

Prince Yassar shrugged. He'd half-hoped Daniel would offer some brilliant, startling solution. *Would that he would lie to me for just a minute*, he thought, then smiled at his absurdity. *Let's see how he responds to a question nobody can answer—except Allah.* "What will happen with the price of oil over the next few years? Will it finally stabilize?" Yassar watched him carefully. The young man thought for a moment before he answered. *Good.* Secure enough not to feel he needed to bark out an answer. Would he be bold? Or tread the middle ground? Would he discredit himself by saying something ridiculous like that fool, Kovarik, he met with this morning?

"Much of that's based upon OPEC's willingness to hold to production quotas. You know better than I that OPEC's members have a history of being unable to resist overproducing. You're constantly undercutting each other on price."

As long as that pig Vincenzio in Venezuela sticks to his production quotas things will go tolerably well, Yassar thought. *This young man saw his worst fears. Maybe he's too perceptive, too direct.* "If history's any guide you may be right. Perhaps we will see continued price instability. But back to what you'd advise us to do."

"First, let's examine what you have to build on. Your economy's only major export and only major expertise is oil and gas. An estimated two hundred seventy billion barrels of reserves—largest of any country in the world—but purely domestic. So what would help you? Buying offshore reserves? Being fully vertically-integrated from reserves, to production, down to refining and marketing?"

Don't we know it. Now we're getting someplace. "We don't have significant properties in refining and marketing. Perhaps to increase our interests there would give us more outlets through which we could sell our reserves."

"It's interesting that you raise the 'downstream' side of the business—refiners, pipelines, natural gas distribution, gas stations—as opposed to 'upstream'—exploration and production."

Please! "I have a vague notion of what these terms mean," Yassar interjected.

"Yes, uh, sorry," Daniel stammered. His face flushed red.

Yassar then smiled to reassure Daniel, soften the jab. *An investment banker who can blush,* Prince Yassar thought. *Remarkable.*

Oh shit, I'm actually blushing, Daniel thought. *What was I thinking?* Describing the segments of the oil and gas business to the largest player in the world.

"To get back to my original point," Daniel said, adopting a serious tone, thinking he was suddenly bombing and trying not to show it. "The downstream part of the business is where over half the profits are, so you need to be in it, or you'll get squeezed in the long run. And it's in consolidation. If you want to get in, it's now or never. Over the next few years you'll see such a huge consolidation in downstream operations that there will be only three to four major refining and marketing players worldwide.

If you and your OPEC colleagues aren't among them, you'll be locked out of most of the profits."

"Interesting," Yassar said, his tone neutral. "Who do you believe are the attractive parties with whom to combine?"

Daniel sat up straight. He focused, knowing if he slipped up here he might blow his chance. He tightened his abdomen. *Okay. Show him something.* "Frontier Oil seems like a long-term player. They're aggressive and they built their business by cutting costs. They're small, but you could build them through more acquisitions. And then of course there are three or four smaller independents like Gelco, Majestic and…"

"I like you, Daniel, and I like your ideas. I think we can do business together," Prince Yassar blurted out.

Daniel was thinking he was just getting started, but if Yassar was already sold, he should keep his mouth shut and listen. This was getting good, just when it had seemed to be turning bad. *Shut up and close.*

"I'm reflecting on all my final visits and will be considering my options over the next week," Yassar went on. "At this stage I will, however, ask you to put together your thoughts on an engagement by the Saudi government and OPEC and get it to me for my consideration."

"Absolutely," Daniel replied. *Damn. Thought he was ready to commit today. Play it cool, don't push him.* "It would be my pleasure, Prince Yassar. I'd very much enjoy working with you. I'll fax something to your office by tomorrow."

"Send me an email," Prince Yassar said, "we stopped living in tents ages ago." He smiled.

Daniel realized it was over. Time to put on a client smile. He wasn't sure where he stood and knew he wouldn't get another shot. One of 10,000 pitches, 268 deals and, maybe or maybe not, 152 clients.

"Thank you for coming," Daniel said.

"Thank you for seeing me. And thank you for being so personal and genuine. I can see you'll get along with my cousin, the Saudi Oil Minister, Prince Naser. It was good to hear someone speak so spontaneously and enthusiastically, and to allow me to see something of yourself after so many pompous fools."

Daniel brightened at that. *Maybe I did land him.*

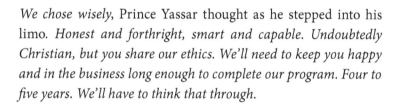

We chose wisely, Prince Yassar thought as he stepped into his limo. *Honest and forthright, smart and capable. Undoubtedly Christian, but you share our ethics. We'll need to keep you happy and in the business long enough to complete our program. Four to five years. We'll have to think that through.*

CHAPTER 7

JULY, THIS YEAR. NEW YORK City. "Well, Dr. Fauchert, what do you advise?" Daniel sat on a cedar lounge chair, his head in Lydia's lap. She'd returned from Milford, bags in tow—including enough odd-shaped containers and cases containing her photographic equipment to convince Daniel she was a member of a traveling circus—and established herself at Daniel's insistence as his houseguest for the two weeks until she was to return to Europe. They were on the roof of his building, 10 stories above Park Avenue. She stroked his hair. The lights of New York City glowed around them against the night sky. Taxis honked and screeched on the street below. A hot breeze carried the scents of exhaust fumes and tar.

"I suggest you be a little coy, don't let him think you're ready to crawl over broken bottles to get his business."

How did she know so much about this stuff? She'd only heard his description of the luncheon with Yassar, his uncertainty about how it had really gone, and she was advising him to play it as cool as he would in a negotiation where he'd read the other side's briefing memo. And she understood finance, because she was able to respond to the business side of what was going on as well as his description of the interpersonal nuances. *She'd probably be a secret weapon in a negotiation. Who knew what she could do in reading body language?* He rolled his head to the side and looked up at her face. "That's easy for you to say. You forget I've got twenty- or thirty-odd million bucks riding on this engagement. Even more: it's my ticket out."

"And I think you forget you possess the stuff that got you to where you are." She bent over and kissed him. "The steel to keep your poise in a nervy negotiation. And the man I know you to be isn't afraid to show his soul, either. His humanity. Perhaps this Yassar needs to see that, too. Stand back from it for a minute. Remember who you are."

How could he argue with that? Particularly with those black eyes drawing him into the depths of her being, framed against the stars, telling him she meant it, that she believed in him. He smiled and nodded to her. She was good for him. He didn't need six months or a year of being with her to tell him that. She made him feel confident. The battered gladiator being reminded to use all his resources: heart as well as experience and skill.

Lydia looked down at him and smiled. "Besides, he likes negotiating."

Daniel wondered what on earth she was talking about, how she could possibly know what Yassar did and didn't like.

"That's just their way, you know."

"You know this guy?"

"Of course not, but I know their—the Arab—mind. He's dancing, making it feel to himself you're worth doing business with. Give him a little more time. Ever buy a rug?"

"Yeah, well, if it makes him feel good, I guess I'll show him a helluva time." He'd had long dances before, he could play it out for as long as it took. Maybe she was right. But what was all this about 'knowing the Arab mind'?

He looked out at the New York skyline, felt his mind drift. "I haven't been up here for years. I used to come up here a lot and just think, dream. This goes back a long time, just after I bought the place. Even before Angie, before we bought the south apartment, knocked out the walls and took the whole floor. Up to that time this apartment was my crowning achievement. Penthouse Looking North Over Park Avenue. It was after my first five-hundred-thousand-dollar bonus at Goldman. I was different in those days."

"How so: different?"

"I could do anything. I was relentless. Focused on getting where I wanted to be, in every part of my life. I can remember feeling I was pissing my life away if I was just looking out the window during a cab ride instead of reading *Businessweek*. Now I think I understand some of the things my father said, like, 'It's just as important to read the Arts and Leisure section of *The New York Times* as it is to read the *Wall Street Journal*.'"

"Feed your soul."

"Exactly." The lights of the city showed the creaminess of Lydia's skin. He matched his breathing with hers, relishing a few moments of it, as though they were singing together.

"I could use more of this," he said. "You're good for me."

"I'm glad you feel that way."

"And you understand things, too. At least in my life. But you know that's only a small part of it."

Lydia said, "I know. The other part of it's that you're good for me, too. Even in the short time since I met you I've started to wish I could talk to a client without constantly 'selling' my perspective. God, it would be nice to simply tell an advertising agency art director on a shoot to get out of my way for three hours and let me do my job, instead of 'positioning' it with 'Well, that's an absolutely brilliant idea that I'd never have thought of, but what if we tried it like this first?' That's not something I was even aware of until I met you."

"I'm not sure I'm doing you any favors, then. Sounds like I'm making your life miserable."

"Au contraire, mon cheri."

They sat in silence like that for a few minutes, Daniel soaking in the sense, scent, and feel of her. "It's funny, though," he said. "A few weeks ago I felt like an overage ballet dancer, like I didn't have it anymore. Now all of a sudden I've got the spring back in my legs again." *And you're a major part of that.*

"Sometimes you need to just stay in the game long enough to see what comes after what comes next."

Daniel looked up at her. He said, "You keep saying your hard knocks have been worse than mine. The more you talk, the more it sounds like you can teach me a thing or two."

Lydia didn't respond.

"Maybe we'll both figure it out together," he said.

Daniel sat in the den off his master bedroom. He bent over his walnut-inlaid desk, reading documents for his meeting the next morning. He could see Lydia moving back and forth in the bedroom, gliding in and out of his view in the dim light as she folded her clothes and laid them in her bags. She sang to herself in the lilting tones in which she spoke, and now Daniel recognized that the musical cadence and eighth tones had an Eastern influence. He put his papers down and watched her as she passed in and out of his vision, savoring her singing.

Am I really going to simply let her waltz back out of here and off to Europe again?

He watched her for another minute, then stood up and walked into the bedroom. She seemed to sense him and turned to receive him as he crossed the floor, arching her head backward. Her eyes were moist. He kissed her, softly at first, then firmly, feeling her embrace him as urgently as he held her.

Then he stepped back, holding her hand, and walked the few steps to the bed where her bags lay open. Without a word, he picked up her clothes, one by one, and placed them back in the drawer. She watched with her hand on her hip, until he was finished with the large bag, then pressed herself against his back and stopped him.

"I'll need to pack at least the small bag. I've got two shoots in Paris and I can be back by Thursday."

"I'll leave the light on."

She turned him to face her and looked into his eyes. "Tell me what this means."

"It means I'd like you move in, at least if you want to."

"Yes." She said it quickly and with self-assurance.

He glanced at the mound of black-composite, steel-trimmed boxes of her photographic equipment. He laughed to himself. "You taking all that with you?"

"Not if I'm staying—living—with you."

He looked into her eyes. "I'll clean out a closet for you, so you've got some personal space."

"Mmmm." She leaned forward, put her arms around him, rested her head on his shoulder.

"You want some space in the Milford house, too?"

She pulled back and looked into his eyes, excited now. "Elsie's room, in the attic?"

"Yours," he said. *Whatever makes your old soul happy.*

She kissed him.

———◆———

July, This Year. Riyadh, Saudi Arabia. Ali, the only name by which Sheik bin Abdur knew his computer hacker, stared at the computer monitor on his desk. He sat erect in his seat, neatly dressed in a Ralph Lauren polo shirt and khakis, and his customary Nikes. Tonight he was clean-shaven and his hair smelled faintly of soap. Ali had showered after dinner before performing his evening prayers and sitting down to his computer.

A tangle of three-inch-wide flat cables, half-inch round cables, optical fibers, patch panels, and wires scrambled from behind his computer. Telephones, modems, computers, servers and hard disk storage units filled the room in a jumble of interconnectivity. He finished typing a message on his screen:

WE ARE IN. BIN ABDUR'S CONSULTANT HAS FINISHED HIS REVIEW. MY HACKING SESSIONS IMPRESSED HIM. HE HAS GIVEN ME THE ALL-CLEAR AND BIN ABDUR HAS GIVEN ME HIS FIRST ASSIGNMENT. HE WISHES TO HACK INTO SAUDI ARAMCO'S COMPUTER NETWORK. GO TO IT. ONCE YOU ARE IN HE WILL ADVISE FROM THERE. HE HAS OFFERED $25,000 DOWN AGAINST $100,000 SUCCESS. I TOLD HIM I WOULD THINK ABOUT IT. AGREE?

ALI

Ali loaded the letter into an encryption program. The encryption program spat out the note in its gobbledygook of scrambled letters and numbers only translatable by his hacker correspondent at the other end using the same program:

Ahr thc 2divv ghtyui ctypelmtnedht 74etrihgnv dhf h cnfjtiye qprotiyunv Protmg nb njgot ahdot e dhfogutyr cbvngh 009wuetrbva frityen ejduyt djfnxbzms 79 77gi

vnh gH el wyughdnvbv xnckflgotoe 689dnfngot sar-
wregdhf 335ghtow0 shdg gf tt x sndhfr a87 torpdlfkg
JjfkgkgotownsNh 63 fkgjhytu sPro alsoptej34mcnv
dmvko Dkfjri 2300t sgge toyiujh sjsfotp sjsapqpritn
adjghto skfdjgyt T dhforowj XX orohgit 7sjflgotn sjfoe-
nuvyt pwprotjs, mkho nb hgot7 akskfjg105 Ajkdfote lak-
doroea jdkcnGjgpwpr qoworpfjsmncWI vnj dd357owhhs
0T4bcs8

He off-loaded the note into a separate file, exited, then dialed
into Eastnet, an Egyptian-based digital, high-speed common
carrier computer data line, and had his call routed through to a
modem in a rented Eastnet location in the basement of a retail
store in Detroit's South Side. The Eastnet station housed 100
dial-in modems. It was one of thousands of Eastnet's local links
around the world.

His call went in, then out through one of the modems to
one of fifty modems linking the University of Michigan's computer system to the world. Under the username "Lindbergh"
and password "Gracie," which he had stolen two days earlier, he
logged on to one of the university's ten Unix systems running
on IBM hardware. He had located Professor Grace Lindbergh's
account under the expected username and simply guessed her
password would be a variant of her or her husband's or her children's first names. Grace Lindbergh was a professor of math-
ematics who was on vacation for two weeks and wouldn't notice
what happened to her account until she returned. Ali trans-
ferred his encrypted file into Gracie Lindbergh's account, then
logged off and closed down his link through Eastnet to wait for
a response.

Once he logged off, the link was untraceable.

An hour later he got his answer. Alica, the name by which he had known his hacker colleague since they started doing business together a week earlier, sent:

TRIPLE THE PRICE. $75 AGAINST $300. AND TAKE THE DEAL. AND TELL THEM WHATEVER THEY WANT YOU TO DO ONCE YOU'VE CONVINCED THEM YOU'RE IN IS GOING TO COST THEM A LOT MORE. A LOT, LOT MORE. REMIND THEM THEY'RE HIRING THE BEST.
ALICA

Ali smiled at the letters blinking on his screen, typed:

WILL DO, PARTNER.

Alica typed back:

I'LL TRY TO GO IN THROUGH THE INTERNET RATHER THAN TRYING TO CRASH THROUGH DIRECTLY. I'LL LET YOU KNOW WHEN I'M IN, OR IF I HAVE TROUBLE GETTING IN. CHECK GRACIE'S MAILBOX EVERY DAY.

Ali sat with his perfect posture gazing at the computer. He wondered who and where Alica was.

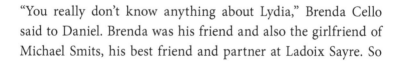

"You really don't know anything about Lydia," Brenda Cello said to Daniel. Brenda was his friend and also the girlfriend of Michael Smits, his best friend and partner at Ladoix Sayre. So that was it. The agenda that was shimmering beneath the purposeful look on Brenda's face. Daniel had even heard it in her voice when she'd called to invite him to dinner because Michael was out of town. They were seated in the clang-bang center room at Raoul's in Soho, in one of the booths jammed in amid the bistro's simple white china and silverware crammed onto utilitarian stainless-steel racks. Waiters darted back and forth in the aroma-filled room just off the kitchen—garlic, frying pomme frittes, grilling steaks, and bouillabaisse hung in the air. Clattering china, shouts, and sizzles from the kitchen rose and fell as the swinging doors whirred in and out.

"Don't beat around the bush, Brenda, just spit it out." Daniel was thinking that Michael would be chuckling softly right now if he were here, enjoying the fact that Brenda was in somebody else's face for a little while. He glanced across to a booth on the other side, where he and Brenda had dined not two years earlier in those awful months following Angie's death, the dinner in which Daniel broke, leaned forward and almost literally cried into his soup.

"Well, I may not be smooth but I at least get it out on the table," Brenda said. She was an authentic blonde, a lithe northern Italian beauty. With striking blue eyes that could either seduce or scald you. "I mean, how long have you known her now, a month?"

Definitely scalding tonight. "A little longer."

"So you don't even know for sure where she's from. She just parachutes in here from—"

"—jet-setted in here, I believe—" Daniel interrupted, smoothing his hair back.

"—okay, jet-setted in here from God knows where—"

"—it was Europe."

"—okay, so she jet-sets in here from Europe—don't be a smartass. I'm talking to you. Michael and I are concerned." Brenda looked Daniel in the eye, held it. "Don't you think you should just slow down?"

There was no hiding from Brenda. Yet he averted his eyes, glanced at the booth across the way, the scene of the almost-in-his-soup dinner. He tried to think of going home to nobody. Not Lydia. Nobody. Like after Angie passed away. He couldn't imagine it now, couldn't feel it. All that was left of that immeasurable anguish he'd experienced after Angie died was a numbness. Was it the anesthesia of Lydia's thighs? Emotional Novocain? Or was he really happy? He remembered now that Brenda had said 'we': both Michael and Brenda. Were they right or was he? Or were they just concerned as good friends are? It was the first time he'd questioned his feelings for Lydia. So far it had been blissful, passionate.

He glanced at his wine glass, thinking. Then he locked eyes on Brenda's, it seemed for a long time. He noticed her eyes were misty. "Okay. Message received."

CHAPTER 8

July, This Year. New York City. Not one cantankerous conversation with a client—or colleague—had as yet intruded on Daniel's repose on this, a quiet summer Friday. He had time to reflect on the major unexpected pleasure of his summer, Lydia, who made each day a polyphonic experience. But he eventually lowered his gaze to the draft engagement letter on his desk, and the tenseness in his scalp was there again. *Yassar's making a holy crusade out of this thing.* It seemed like they'd been one draft away from signing up for weeks. It wasn't helping the rest of his business. Two busted deals and one assignment lost to a competitor. Bob Kovarik at his new boutique, Kovarik & Co., of all people. He glanced out to the doorway to make sure no one saw him festering in his anxiety.

He pored over the language of the "services" section of the engagement letter yet again. *Lighten up.* He was letting it get under his skin. Yassar would tire in time; he could outlast him. He looked back down at the "fees" section, the most important to Daniel, the one that had resulted in the thorniest negotiations. *Retainer fees of $250,000 per quarter, $1 million on announcement of any deal, and .5 percent of any deal value, no less than $5 million, nor more than $30 million per deal.*

"Good," he said aloud. He lifted his head, hearing Lydia's voice in the hall. Cindy buzzed him. "Lydia's here," she said as Lydia entered his office with characteristic long strides.

"Hi!"

"Hi, lover," he said. Before he could get out from behind his desk to receive her, she bustled up to him and planted a kiss on his mouth. "Well this is a pleasant surprise."

"Thought I'd pop in and visit the great man at work."

He stepped back so he could admire her. *Stunning.* She wore a blue silk dress. *Prada?* Elbow-length blue gloves adorned her hands and arms despite the August weather, and an Audrey Hepburn–style, wide-brimmed hat perched on her head. A pair of Jackie Onassis–sized sunglasses swung from her hand. "You're name-dropping with every step today."

She kissed him again, this time pushing him over backward into his chair and knocking her hat off. She laughed as she reached for it. "You can pick on me all you want. But I'm in such a good mood you can't get to me."

"So what puts you in such a good mood?"

"I'm so pleased with myself I'm brimming over." She retrieved her hat and sat. "I've planned a surprise for you."

"Hardly a surprise if you're telling me."

She looked at him, smirking. *Beautiful.*

She glanced at his desk, then at the draft of "Presentation to the Kingdom of Saudi Arabia on Selected Worldwide Acquisition Opportunities in the Refining and Marketing Sector," made a short observation of the summaries of the target companies reviewed in the presentation, then a long one at the engagement letter he was working on. "So, Yassar's still haggling?"

Reads upside down. A skill only investment bankers have. She's in the wrong profession. "Yes, Yassar's still haggling."

"Hmm. The last nickel on that rug he's selling you."

"No, lover, I'm the one who's selling *him* the rug now."

"Don't be so sure, darling. Perhaps he's a better salesman than you think."

"Okay, whatever." Did she enjoy flummoxing him? But maybe she was right. Maybe Yassar was leading the dance. Daniel shrugged and sat back. "You said something about a surprise?"

"I'm throwing a party."

"And?"

"You're invited."

"Great. When? Where?"

"Tomorrow night, at your Milford house. I've invited a half-dozen of your friends for your birthday, so be there."

"Wouldn't miss it. Anything else?"

"Well, it's also a bit of a short-term going-away party for me. A friend of mine came down with pneumonia so I'm back off to Europe for a few weeks." She frowned and cocked her head to the side. "Sorry, darling, but I'll be back as soon as I can."

Daniel didn't hide his disappointment. "I'll miss you."

Cindy buzzed Daniel: "Walter Purcell and Steven Pace."

"Okay." He looked at Lydia. "This'll only take a minute."

The two junior colleagues, team members on Daniel's presentation to Yassar, entered and stood in front of Daniel's desk. He didn't invite them to sit, because he didn't want to spend much time on the draft at this crude stage. He reviewed a few choice comments and handed Purcell his markup of the draft with a look designed to remind him he knew better than to send him something so poorly executed. Lydia occupied herself in a corner chair reviewing—no, poring over the company summaries.

"You were a little overbearing, darling," she said after the two left. "I like these." She handed him three summaries.

Yes. She's in the wrong profession, he laughed to himself.

They kissed. She wiped the lipstick off his mouth, then re-applied hers. "Bye, darling. What time do you think you'll be up to the country tonight?"

"I'll try to leave early. Eight by the time I get there."

"Great. I'm taking your Porsche, okay?" She waved on the way out. He turned back to his work, smiling. Then Brenda's words came back to him. *"Slow down."*

By 12:30, Daniel decided to forego the remainder of his business day and buzzed Cindy. "I'm leaving early for Milford."

By 2:00 he had arrived at his house. The Porsche was in the driveway and the front door was unlocked. "Hello," he called. He made a quick circuit of the first floor, but couldn't find Lydia. *Where are you, lover?* "Lydia?"

He went back into the den and found her notebook computer on the desk, open and still online. He walked to it and felt the unmistakable sensation of someone rubbing fine sandpaper on the back of his neck. What he saw wasn't possible. It was the desktop of his own computer at the office, icons for deal documents and programs stacked in neat rows on either side of the desktop, and the folder of documents on his hard drive open in the center. His scalp tingled. *What the hell?* It was as if she'd hacked into his computer.

He felt his pulse quicken as he ran upstairs to check the attic room he'd given to Lydia as her personal space, entering without knocking. She wasn't there. He was leaving when he saw a pile of documents on the floor. He bent to examine them.

German, French, Swiss, Israeli, American and Italian passports were lined up next to each other, flanking piles of various currencies and another pile of well-thumbed manila folders stacked two inches high. He opened the French passport. The name was Lydia Duffre and the photograph was Lydia's. Again he felt the sensation of someone rubbing sandpaper on the back of his neck. This was wrong, all wrong. *Who the hell is Lydia Duffre, why was she...?* Was she hiding out from somebody? Was it drugs? Some kind of scam?

He opened the German passport. Lydia Schiffer. The photograph showed a sullen woman without makeup and close-cropped, black hair. Unquestionably Lydia. Now the sandpaper was coarse grit, he heard his pulse ramming in his ears and tasted his stomach bile. He flipped through an Israeli passport, plunging on with greedy fingers. Lydia Goldman. He slapped it shut and fumbled through the Swiss, then the American, then the Italian versions. He laughed morosely, almost a desperate moan. *Not a single one with "Fauchert." What, did she reserve that name for me?*

He leafed through the euros, estimating there was at least the equivalent of 50,000 U.S. dollars. He didn't need to count the American dollars to recognize that approximately $100,000 lay in four wrapped piles of $100 bills. He began to count the English pounds when he heard someone walking up the stairs.

"Daniel?" Lydia paused on the stairs out of view.

"Lydia," he said in a monotone. His mouth was dry. Lydia resumed her ascent. He waited for her holding the passports and the bundle of Swiss francs. "What's this all about?" he said.

As she came into view, her eyes were wide, her mouth open with alarm. He saw her inhale, then exhale slowly, then a hardness formed in her eyes. "I can explain."

"I should hope so." Daniel felt his chest heaving now, heard the tremor in his voice.

"If I were you I wouldn't adopt that tone with me. You did go into my room uninvited, after all." She raised her chin. "I didn't fantasize your telling me that room was my private space. You gave it to me and now I want to know why you went in there."

Daniel gritted his teeth. *Cheap negotiating ploy. Turn a defensive position into an offensive one.* He felt his hands beginning to shake. "You bring something like this into my house, and all you can say is I shouldn't 'adopt that tone with you'?" He waved the passports and money at her.

"So first it's my room, and now it's your house?" She walked toward him, her eyes leveled.

"Yes, it's my house and I'd like to know just what the hell is going on. Including what you're doing screwing around with my computer at work!"

"You want know what's going on? I'll tell you what's going on. You're invading my privacy!"

"Privacy only goes so far, dammit! Just what's this all about? What the hell are you *doing*?" Daniel's breaths were short. His pulse thundered.

She tried to grab the passports and currency. He threw them to the floor.

"Oh, that's constructive!" she snapped. Her mouth tightened into a sneer. "You don't want an explanation! You just want to get angry and throw your weight around!"

"I *expect* an explanation."

"Private client business." She stepped to the side and pointed to the door. "Now get out of here!"

"If anybody's getting out of here it's you. Now what's going on?"

Lydia ran out and down the stairs.

Daniel stood in the middle of the room for a moment, breathing deeply, flexing and unflexing the muscles of his jaw, waiting for his pulse to return to normal, wondering what had just happened. *Who is this woman?*

A moment later a blast of energy propelled him toward the stairs. "Goddamn you!" He bounded down the stairs, two at a time to the second floor. He heard the kitchen door slam. "Lydia!" he yelled. He tore down the stairs to the first floor then out the kitchen door. The gate was open to the front and he ran through it, feeling his pulse in his ears, gritting his teeth with anger. As he reached Broad Street he saw her turn the corner at the traffic light, running full tilt. By the time he reached the intersection he'd lost her. He ran for another block, but still couldn't see her. He stopped, panting, sweating, his heart pounding. *Damn.* When was the last time he'd run a 200-yard sprint?

He stood on the sidewalk catching his breath. He tried to collect his thoughts, decide what to do. He stood, staring, eyes unfocused, thinking. *What the hell is going on? Who the hell was I just talking to?* His stomach was turning flips.

Daniel lost track of how long he stood there, his thoughts in a jumble. He made up his mind he'd throw her out, whoever she was. Didn't need this in his life. Then he decided he'd sit her down, look her in the eye and find out just what was going on. But what kind of woman runs around with stuff like that, pretending to be somebody else? He'd set those investigators from Kroll & Co. on her that he used for background checks on prospective clients, trace her back to Europe.

But what was she doing to his computer? Her standing there giving him the righteously indignant routine was a sure sign her story would be a lie. And the files, what were they? Maybe it *was* a scam. She was savvy enough to pull one off. Throw her out and check his bank accounts, fast. *Damn, this is bizarre.*

He walked around the corner, then toward his house. He smelled smoke, then saw it in the air. He heard the town's fire engine with its siren blaring, horn blasting as it came up Broad Street toward the intersection. In the next moment he saw smoke coming out his kitchen door.

His pulse rammed in his temples as he ran to the front door. He ran into the dining room, where he saw the source of the conflagration. Lydia had pushed the dining room table to one side and placed a metal garbage can from the kitchen in the center of the rug in the dining room. Manila folders were strewn on the floor; a robust blaze leapt from the can.

He darted his gaze around the room. *There!* He grabbed a vase of flowers from the breakfront and tossed the water uselessly into the garbage can. He heard the kitchen door slam. *Lydia!* He ran toward the kitchen, looking back over his shoulder to see flames still dancing from the can.

He wanted to follow Lydia outside, but lurched toward the sink to refill the vase. He ran back into the dining room and doused the trash can again just as Rich Freeman, manager of the local hardware store, burst through the door with his volunteer fireman's outfit on. "Get an extinguisher!" Daniel yelled.

Freeman motioned to one of his fellow firemen. "The CO_2!"

An hour later Daniel stood in the center of the dining room looking through morose eyes at the patch of rug shampoo he had just sprayed on the Oriental carpet. *Now what?* He turned toward the door to the kitchen, the site of Lydia's exit. *Was any of it real?*

Now he could feel it, that same soul-ripping pain he'd felt after Angie died. The sensation he'd been unable to recapture at dinner with Brenda at Raoul's a few weeks back. The heaviness he felt in his chest now and the sensation of the extra ten pounds he carried in each of his limbs was worse than he could remember, in part because he felt ridiculous for letting himself get involved with someone he now realized he knew nothing about.

He watched the foam sink into the carpet. Curiously now, his infallible gyroscope had deserted him: his early-warning-system stomach was gone—where was it?

He closed his eyes, trying to forget where he was for the moment, conscious only of the fact that a basketball now seemed to be lodged in his throat, making it difficult to breathe. He exhaled painfully. *How could I let this happen?* He tried to say it aloud, realized he couldn't. He waited until he had control of his throat again. "Lydia, who are you?" he said finally to the empty house.

July, This Year. Milford, Pennsylvania. Lydia arrived at the Black Walnut bed and breakfast just outside town. *Stupid,* she chastised herself. *Should have been more careful.*

She threw her bag down on the bed and unpacked her notebook computer. It wasn't so much that she was in a rush to get off her message, she simply needed to use up some nervous energy. She booted up and dialed out through her communications software, logging into the computer account she was using that week to deposit her messages in Geneva University. *Stupid.*

PROBLEMS. NEED ADVICE. I AM COMING IN TO TALK.
LYDIA

She encrypted the message, deposited it in the account and logged off. She walked to the mirror. Her eyes were red. *No surprise.* She'd felt a thickness in her throat ever since getting into the taxi. Tears began streaming down her cheeks.

BOOK 2

CHAPTER 9

JUNE, TWENTY-NINE YEARS AGO. VEVEY, Switzerland. "These mountains are spectacular," Sandra Chase said, looking out the window of the limousine. The black stretch Mercedes labored up the mile-long winding drive to the hilltop chateau owned by the Countess Del Mira. Towering evergreens, meticulously maintained stone walls and lanterns bordered the drive and heightened the expectations of visitors approaching the summit. "How is Christina? I haven't seen her since she got back from India. How long has it been?"

"Two months," Ophelia replied. "She'd been in that ridiculous ashram for *four years*. But now she's never been better. But whatever possessed a bona fide Italian countess—she's a Del Mira for God's sake—to throw it all away and go seek enlightenment in some Swami Kripananda's ashram in the first place?"

"In the first place, she didn't throw it all away. It was sitting back here in Switzerland waiting for her. In the second place, what's wrong with it?" Sandra adopted Ophelia's sarcastic tone. "I mean, what's wrong with a wealthy, eccentric European—whom many, including yourself, call an adventuress—seeking the teachings of a Guru at a time when people are open to such things—even wealthy, eccentric European adventuresses?"

"Look, Sandra, I'm up for a lark as much as the next one, but this went a bit too far."

"Perhaps it was her feelings for Sasha."

"Has she adopted her?" Ophelia looked at Sandra with an accusing stare that demanded an answer. "Nobody's quite sure how she came by her in the first place."

"I don't know. But I'm told Christina went to the ashram to raise the child with some formal base in spirituality."

"Something that is clearly beyond the grasp of Christina herself!" Ophelia laughed. "No matter. Her parties are more extravagant than ever. The themes!"

Livinia Duke cooed her agreement. "'A Night at the Opera' last month. She had a set from La Bohème and a twenty-piece orchestra in her library. And Pavarotti sang."

"Hmm," Sandra said. "I thought she'd changed."

"Oh she's changed all right," Ophelia said. "All that silliness about her 'teachings.' I'm certain Christina doesn't know what the hell she's talking about when she prattles on about Brahman as the one Supreme Reality, without attributes, unmanifest, eternal, all knowing, all this, all that, all pervading..." Her voice trailed off into laughter. "At one point she told me this Brahman created the tangible world as mere sport, a diversion."

Livinia shrugged. "At least she's got the sport part down, because she's certainly relishing the temporal satisfactions of the material world."

"Yes," Ophelia added. "She learned in India to appreciate them as more eternally satisfying than she ever did before."

"And Sasha?" Sandra asked.

Ophelia clasped Sandra's forearm. "Oh! An absolute delight. She's precious, a beautiful and spirited child."

"Christina relates to her not as if she's a daughter, or a dependent, but rather a partner."

"They're coconspirators," Ophelia said.

"Co-seducers," Livinia added. "And they create exquisite entertainments. They weave a spell together."

"I'm surprised," Sandra said. "I was told Christina was calmer and that she actually had a faraway quality, you know, a light in her eyes."

"Really, darling, it's a comical notion that a woman who can taste the difference between a 1949 and 1957 Domaine de la Romanee-Conti Richebourg and actually tie a cherry stem in a knot with her tongue has truly discovered the meaning of life."

The car reached the top of the drive. The view of the hillsides, now covered with greenery, didn't disappoint. Nor did the grandeur of the fifteenth-century complex imposingly presiding over the mountain overlooking Lake Geneva, the town of Vevey, and beyond. All fifteen thousand square feet of it, thick blocks of limestone half-covered with ivy, muscular oak timbers holding forth within. Sandra reflected that it had been no mean feat to maintain the chateau's premises and four-hundred-acre grounds while the Countess was in India. But a staff of twenty-five certainly helped.

Two of the Countess' staff opened the limousine doors to the pleasant and unseasonably cool summer evening. Sandra saw Christina standing beneath the sparkling chandelier in the center of the entrance hall. She was addressing a child, undoubtedly Sasha, who appeared to be stifling tears. "Don't deprive yourself of your pain, child. All part of the ecstasy of being alive," the Countess was saying. The child raised her chin and forced back her tears nonetheless. The three women entered the doorway to a jangle of jewelry. The air smelled faintly of incense.

"Sandra, darling, it's been so long," the Countess whispered as they kissed each other on either cheek. "So truly, truly good to see you again."

Sandra stood back from her and appraised her from arm's length. She stood in her characteristic pose, her right arm across her stomach, her left holding a cigarette aloft. *But there is a light in her eyes. Subtle. But she's different.*

"And you've previously met Sasha," the Countess said, putting either hand on the splendid child's shoulders. "Sasha, this is my old friend Sandra Chase. She visited us once in India." It was unquestionably the same child Sandra had seen there, swirling with activity at the ashram. She had fiery black eyes and straight black hair. The corners of her mouth were turned up in a ten-year-old's mischievous grin.

"Pleased to see you again, Sasha."

Sasha pursed her lips. "And you."

Sasha crossed from the dining room into the library, where twenty guests waited for the evening's post-dessert entertainment: tonight she would act out another story, an encore performance for those who hadn't already seen this tale.

She saw the Countess standing by in the audience, smiling with pleasure. Her champagne glass was never empty, the rustle of her silk chartreuse evening gown never silent, her throaty voice never resting as she moved through the room, greeting, complimenting and pampering her guests.

As Sasha moved to her position in front of the fireplace, she saw the Countess sit next to Prince Yassar. He was one of Sasha's favorites, for he always spoke gently and calmly to her. Not like the others. They were always talking down to her like she was a child. But Yassar listened to her, observed what she said, and only offered advice when she wanted it.

Sasha took her position facing her audience. Her eyes met Prince Yassar's now and she smiled. Christina nodded and Sasha began to act out her story, a single player cast in all roles.

"Parvati, wife of Lord Shiva, became lonely for companionship when she sat in her palace, which was separate from her Lord Shiva's palace. And she wished for a son after the many years, many centuries that she and Lord Shiva had unsuccessfully attempted to bear a child.

"Parvati went to the bank of the stream near her palace and created the figure of a beautiful boy out of clay. She breathed on the figure, breathed the essence of her life into it and brought him to life. As he grew up, she ran and frolicked with the boy and found him to be an excellent and loving companion." Sasha acted out the creation of the boy from clay, and then ran back and forth in front of her audience.

She continued her story, relating how Parvati asked the boy to guard her palace while she bathed, then how he refused Lord Shiva entry when he returned from hunting. Then she acted out the great struggle that ensued between the boy and Lord Shiva. She dramatized how Lord Shiva finally shouted "Enough!", pulled out his sword and cut off the boy's head.

At this point Sasha looked at her audience. All were giving her their full attention.

She continued her tale, showing and telling how Parvati emerged from her bath and saw the beheaded boy and the blood on Lord Shiva's sword. She became Parvati: "Why may I not have my privacy while I am bathing? Why did you demand to come in? Why did you kill the boy?"

Then Lord Shiva: "I have the right! I am Lord Shiva, and when I want to visit you to speak to you I will come and go as I please!"

She acted out the great war between Parvati and Lord Shiva that followed, showed the shooting of many arrows, the stabbing with many swords.

Sasha then hung her head and stood with her knees bent and her arms slack at her sides like a defeated warrior, however brave, to show the adults how Lord Shiva accepted his eventual defeat by Parvati's army.

As Parvati she said, "Now to acknowledge my right to my independence, my right to my solace, bring my son back to life."

And as Lord Shiva, she said to his attendants, "Go and bring the head of the first creature you find sleeping with his head pointing north."

Sasha became the attendants on the lookout for this being.

"The attendants went into the forest and found a baby elephant sleeping with his head pointing north, and they brought back his head, which Lord Shiva attached to the torso of the boy, bringing the boy back to life. Lord Shiva made their new son the leader of his Ganas, his semidivine attendants, which is how the boy with the elephant's head came to be called Ganesha. Eventually it became clear that he was a god himself, the God of Good Luck, the Remover of Obstacles and Difficulties, the God of Wisdom, and the great patron of learning."

Sasha ended with a grand wave of her arms and bowed.

Her audience applauded. A murmur of appreciative complements and exclamations of delight echoed from the walls in a dozen languages. Sasha twirled, reveling in the adulation and most particularly in the special delight of the Countess.

But as she gazed out upon her audience, she knew her black eyes—so full of animation and life, already so worldly—did not betray the secret ache in her child's heart.

CHAPTER 10

July, Twenty-Five Years Ago. Vevey, Switzerland. Yassar sat enveloped in an overstuffed leather chair in the Countess' library, chatting with other guests and his cousin, Prince Naser, the Saudi Oil Minister, who sat next to him. They were spending a weekend at the Countess' chateau following the OPEC Ministers' meeting in Vienna, before returning home to Saudi Arabia. They had become familiar guests.

Through the open door of the library Yassar watched Countess Del Mira descend the last few stairs into the main entrance hall, pause languidly, as if to allow herself to be admired, and start across the polished marble of the entrance hall toward the library door. Her head was motionless as she walked, as if the trancelike focus of her glance riveted it in place. Yassar detected the sleepy softness at the corners of her eyes, the pinkness in her cheeks, and the general flaccidness of the muscles in her face.

Opium.

The Countess paused in the doorway and raised an unlit cigarette to her mouth. She wore a sleeveless floor-length black silk evening dress that flowed with her, yet her head never moved and her eyes never left Yassar's. A guest tiptoed to her, some baronial or royal presence, lit her cigarette and tiptoed off.

"Hello, my princes," she said in a whisper. "Make a few billions today?"

"Hello, Christina," Yassar said.

Prince Naser smiled, "You're looking radiant, my darling."

The Countess glanced at each of them. "You charm me. I swoon." She moved closer to Prince Naser and pressed her leg against his. "Prince Naser, you're looking gorgeously full of manhood this evening. You will visit me later?"

"I think I'll be taking a little more dessert and tea now," Yassar said. He stood to leave. The Countess turned slowly and met his gaze, her face barely a foot from Yassar's. He could see that her pupils were dilated and her eyes bloodshot.

"I'll excuse you if you promise to entertain me presently," she breathed.

Yassar rose. Sasha stood at the other end of the forty-foot room, her eyes gleaming a hello. She met him halfway in his progress toward the sideboard dessert service. *Remarkable,* he thought. *So beautiful. Would that I were a young man again.*

She hooked her arm through his and pulled him down to her, planting a loud kiss on his cheek. "Gotcha." He felt her breast against his arm. "What's a girl have to do to get your attention tonight, Yassar? You were playing hard to get all through dinner. I could barely catch your eye, what with that Miss Ballanchine next to you. The way she monopolized your conversation I wanted to scratch her eyes out. And you were so gracious to her when she became absolutely *churlish* by the time salad was served. Poor dear. Someone should teach her to handle her wine."

Yassar laughed. "You're a very observant young lady." *And very tempting.*

"I see I have your attention now," she smirked. They reached the dessert table. He poured himself a cup of tea and placed two petits fours on his dessert plate. "Very observant and very precocious." She was only fourteen, he knew, but already possessed the poise and self-confidence of a woman. The adventurous independence and fiery temperament she had displayed as a child were still there, only now they smoldered beneath a more sophisticated exterior. *She holds her head a little higher now. She trumpets her independence and defiance.*

Sasha's lithe frame now showed the roundness of a woman's hips, a sensuous curve into a tiny waist, and fully-formed high breasts, enticing him from beneath her sleeveless silk dress. The curves of her shoulders still showed some traces of tomboyish muscularity, as though she hadn't grown out of them yet, which somehow made the ache he felt to touch her breasts seem even more forbidden and profane. He was always surrounded by beautiful women, many of whom were available to him, and yet he rarely felt the urge as he did now to dare his heart to get him in trouble. In the last six months since he had seen Sasha, her skin had achieved a glow that indicated some hormonal festival had sprung to life within her. The gleam she now showed in the corner of her eye told Yassar she knew she could carry off the seductiveness her entire being implied. *And only fourteen!*

She grabbed his arm and ushered him toward the door. Yassar smiled and gave in to her, grabbing his cup of tea. "I get the feeling you can't make up your mind what to do with me."

"Oh, I've got my mind made up all right, I'm just not sure where to whisk you off to and whether or not I can get away with it." Then she clutched both hands around his arm. "Actually, I need your advice," she said, glancing at him with conspiratorial intimacy. "Christina has sold another painting. I believe we're no longer living on the interest on the interest. Perhaps now we live only on the interest. If this continues, the upstairs bedroom walls will be empty in two years."

"Not at these prices," Yassar said. "The last one was a Renoir that fetched one point two million Swiss francs."

She relaxed her grip. "It won't hold out." She let go of his arm, then glided forward to an elderly couple who stood in the corner, exchanging a few sentences with them in Italian and making an arch of her arm pointing to the dessert table.

Yassar observed the light dancing on the muscles on her arms, took in the curves in her well-toned legs, admired her face. *The same black hair that's always swirling. It will be a lucky man who awakens with it draped across his chest.* Sasha returned, took his arm again and herded him onto the patio.

"Angry, sad, contemplative—in any mood, really—the beauty of this place always touches me." She turned to face him, leaning on the limestone railing. Her eyes were soft. "I think I'd die if I couldn't ever look at this again."

She advanced abruptly toward him, stopping inches from his face. He saw her look change to one of anxiety. "You're the only one I can talk to about these things," she whispered. "You've seen how Christina is."

"Yes." *Indeed. And how sad that she may become unable to maintain a young lady with your extraordinary quality in the style you deserve. And her situation may result in your worst fear—never to look upon this place again.*

"If she keeps going like this, well, I just don't know. She's become less—discriminating." Her eyes were doleful. "Do you think you could speak with Naser? You know how much time he spends with her. Do you think you could persuade him to help her out? Take her under his wing, so to speak?"

Very observant, very precocious, very worldly. "I'll see."

Prince Yassar lay awake that night in his bedroom in the west wing of the Countess' chateau. He had always appreciated the Countess' hospitality, even though he had never availed himself of the pleasures of all her entertainments. A religious man, living by the shari'a code, he had frequently desired the Countess, although out of respect for his four wives at home and his religion he had never given in to the temptation. The Countess' decline had been gradual and difficult to detect. But Prince Yassar had been one of the first to notice her willingness to make herself available to the wealthier of those who visited with her. He knew that Prince Naser was undoubtedly with the Countess at this moment and that his gifts to her were unquestionably helping her maintain her lifestyle. That was troubling, but he would not acknowledge his unease to his friend, fellow minister, and cousin. And his knowledge must of course be kept a secret from the remainder of their family.

But what was more troubling to Prince Yassar that night was the desire he felt for the young lady less than a third his age, whose body had pressed against him in the dining room and then again on the patio that evening. *Remarkable.*

CHAPTER 11

AUGUST, TWENTY-THREE YEARS AGO. VEVEY, Switzerland.
Yassar's black Mercedes limousine drove up the winding drive
to the Countess Del Mira's chateau. He wondered if it was the
last time it would do so—regardless of the outcome of his visit.
He'd come with a proposal. And although he was accustomed
to routinely negotiating life-and-death issues as a member of
the Council of Ministers, it was not the Countess' response
that caused the butterflies to churn in his stomach; the spirited
Sasha herself was the one whose reaction he feared. He emerged
from the car and passed through the curved limestone facade,
through the massive arched oak door and into the marble
entrance foyer, grateful the splendid young Sasha was nowhere
to be seen.

"Dashing as ever," the Countess said from her pose halfway
down the stairs, cigarette poised aloft, smoke wafting from the
corners of her mouth.

"Ah, Christina, you flatter me." Yassar bowed, then held his
hand out to her as she descended, deliciously, excruciatingly,
every step a photographic moment. She alighted and allowed
him to kiss her on each cheek.

"Splendid. Do come in for breakfast, Yassar." He walked her
on his arm into the main breakfast room where the table had
been set. She pointed to a chair for him, then disappeared into

the pantry, emerging a moment later, a paradox of languor and energy, occupying the enormous space only she could command in a room. "Oh *do* sit *down*," she reprimanded, as Yassar prepared to stand from his seat at the table when she reentered. She assumed her position at the head of the table, waved off the butler who attempted to push in her chair, and took up her napkin before the steward could place it in her lap.

Yassar watched the Countess settle into her chair, survey him and then look expectantly at him in a long pause calculated for maximum dramatic effect. She took a pull on her cigarette and exhaled slowly to allow her pearls to catch up with her. They did. "Well?" she said. "You seemed like it was rather urgent, something about a proposition."

Yassar grinned. "Never one for subtlety, Christina. It's one of your most prominent charms." He allowed the steward to pour his tea, then waited for him to follow the butler into the pantry. *Well, only one way to find out.* "It's about Sasha."

The Countess inclined her head, waved at him to go on.

"She's become quite a young lady, and you've seen to it yourself she's developed sophistication well beyond her years."

"True."

"My son Ibrahim has come of age and I believe that a young lady with Sasha's cultivated style and intelligence would make a suitable companion for him."

The Countess laughed in a low, oozing rumble. "You mean you've noticed the libidinal firestorm she creates in men whenever she walks into a room."

"That's another way of putting it." He allowed himself to smile, then pressed his eyebrows together and thrust out his lower lip. "So shall we say she would be an entertaining presence for Ibrahim. If you have no objection, she could leave with me for Saudi Arabia immediately. I would make certain the arrangement was to both your and Sasha's satisfaction."

"Go on." The Countess exhaled, arching her chin backward and spewing a geyser of smoke up at the ceiling. "How interesting are you going to make this for me?"

Just out of sheer curiosity I'm tempted to negotiate to test whether or not you're totally broke. He abandoned the thought. "One million dollars, via wire transfer."

The Countess froze for perhaps three seconds, then crushed her cigarette out. A smile crept across her face as she picked up the teapot and poured, first for him then herself. "She went out for a morning ride on her horse. She'll be back soon. I expect you'll have better luck convincing her than I. I suggest you take her shopping first." She picked up the sugar bowl and smiled at him. "I believe you take sugar?"

Later that day, the Countess Del Mira stood at the bedroom window looking out over the expanse of pines and deciduous trees that forested the hill on the front of her grounds. The late-afternoon sun streamed in the window, its rays capturing the lazy smoke from the opium pipe she had just extinguished. She rubbed her face, trying to push away the cobwebs of sleep from her nap, and welcoming the cobwebs from the drug she had just inhaled. It was already caressing away the anguish and self-reproach with which she had awakened.

The Countess crossed the room toward the bathroom door, pausing in front of the mirror. The dark circles under her eyes had become a constant malady and would require at least a half an hour of makeup to mask. She pulled at a wisp of her hair and pushed it back off her forehead, then went into the bathroom to shower, pausing in front of the mirror over the sink. If she cared more, would it be any different? She looked intensely into her eyes reflected back at her. Cared more? She cared enough. But the fear she saw in her eyes was too much. She stared into it, now, fascinated. The fear. Suddenly older, less beautiful? Contemplating being alone? No. Clichés. It was that she'd become bored with it all, something she couldn't bear. Like George Sanders' suicide note: "I am leaving because I am bored." At least she could keep the child from seeing that in her eyes. The boredom or her fear, no, her terror of it. Let the child grow up without ever knowing it. Perhaps if the child knew how she was trying to spare her that she'd forgive her one day. She'd done all she could for Sasha, given her the understanding of what zest meant. She was on her own now. Still...The Countess felt a sob try to rumble up from her soul, then fade, die feebly. She stepped into the shower.

Yassar and Sasha pulled up to the front door of the chateau in his black Mercedes limousine. It was an unusually warm August day, and Sasha's face was flushed from the heat despite the air-conditioned drive from town. Yassar looked across at her in the back seat. *Either she'll come with me or she won't.*

The car stopped. Sasha walked on his arm, head characteristically aloft, smiling at him. At the front door she dropped his arm and darted ahead to precede him into the entrance hallway, then suddenly turned to face him.

"Tea?" she asked.

"That would be nice."

He followed her toward the kitchen. She seemed to have boundless energy compressed into that muscular five-foot-four-inch body. Over the last few years as she'd flowered, he had already seen her youthful encyclopedia of allures: cocks of her head, pouts, expressions ranging from the bored to the tempestuous. Sasha had years earlier cast off the innocence of a teenager and allowed her innate sensuousness to blossom unrestrained. *Surely a worldly young lady like this can't be so scandalized at the mere fact of the proposal.*

Sasha and Yassar established themselves at the simple table in the staff's dining room off the kitchen. They would take a respite from their shopping expedition, munching shortbread cookies and sipping tea, prior to the inevitable Grand Drama that the Countess would create out of dinner.

Yassar watched Sasha carefully. He couldn't remember whether he had ever noticed before that her alabaster skin seemed not to have pores, it was so flawlessly smooth and luminous. She was now sixteen and like a ripe piece of fruit, an enticement to those who would savor her. And now that he would offer to pluck her—for his son—he anticipated experiencing the thrill and the fury of her womanhood, the power she could exert. He knew now from his quickened pulse and rushing emotions he had made the right choice for Ibrahim. *And this is a girl of sixteen!*

He reached his hand across the table and rested it on hers. "Sasha, there's a question I've been waiting for an appropriate time to ask you all day."

"I suspected something." She looked up and met his gaze, then looked back down at the table. She clasped her other hand on top of his. "You've been very serious, very mysterious."

She's not making this easy for me. "You've heard me mention my son, Ibrahim, many many times. As you know, he's coming of age now and I'm grooming him to one day be a leader of the Saudi Arabian people. He's beginning to travel, assume greater responsibility, and in a few years he'll be going off to Harvard, where he's already been given early acceptance for study in economics and political science." He saw Sasha frown. She was perplexed, he knew, and pushed on. "In short, he's maturing and leading a fast-paced, exciting life. He's surrounded by interesting people, and I'm equally interested in ensuring he has female companionship worthy of his future status in the world. Women who are able to keep him challenged and help keep him on the path of his ambitions."

Yassar felt Sasha's hands go limp and saw her raise her head and meet his gaze, her mouth open with dawning incredulousness.

"I'd like you to come back to Saudi Arabia with me to be a live-in guest at the Royal Palace. You and I have always enjoyed each other's company. I'm sure you would be an equally entertaining presence for Prince Ibrahim."

Sasha pulled her hands back from Yassar and placed them in her lap. She sat straight upright in the chair, her lips drawn tight together, her eyes wide as if in terror. "Are you suggesting…?" She looked away from him and swallowed hard, then met his gaze again. "What would I be doing there?"

Surely a girl of your worldliness can figure that out. Your reaction tells me you already have. "Why, anything you wish. At least within the context of entertaining my son, and don't underestimate the degree to which you can be entertained and pampered yourself. I needn't remind you how wealthy the kingdom of…"

"Yassar, whatever were you thinking when you decided to approach me on this?" Sasha's face showed a mixture of disbelief and pain, her upper lip beginning to tremble.

Let's get this over with. Perhaps I should be more direct. "Surely a young lady with your desires can appreciate how such an arrangement can be to your own satisfaction as well. It is a life most girls can only dream about."

Sasha raised her head, looking him in the eye, first with steel showing, then expressionlessly, then her eyes displaying a look of shame. He averted his eyes.

Yassar thought of abandoning the plan, but discarded his doubts when he reminded himself that she would transfix Ibrahim, and how she affected even him. She would settle the young prince down, keep his mind on his studies in a way the other young concubines could not. Sasha would exhaust Ibrahim's wanderlust and carnal lust, binding him to home like a stray dog compelled to the neighborhood by a poodle in heat.

"You can come and go as you please, at least within the bounds of the social customs and expectations of women in the Saudi Kingdom. You will be provided with a lucrative monthly allowance in addition to having all your needs cared for."

The spirit returned to Sasha's eyes. "You've mentioned how much you'll be paying me. How much are you paying Christina?"

Yassar looked back into Sasha's eyes, seeing not just a sense of betrayal, but stern disapproval. *All right, if you're going to insist upon calling me a pimp, I'll deal with you in a businesslike fashion.* "Christina's situation is well known to you." He observed her calmly, as though he was lecturing one of his children. Or one of his wives. "You yourself approached me some time ago soliciting my help in persuading Naser to provide for her, knowing full well what you were asking." He saw her body go limp as his words struck at her. "No one is holding a gun to your head. What I'm offering you is the opportunity to be maintained in a lavish lifestyle, travel around the world with my son, keep him company in an arrangement you might find to your liking. Beyond the three or four years that I have conceived, you may wish to stay indefinitely. What I am offering you is an opportunity to fulfill your wildest imagination. And, yes, Christina will be well taken care of, which is perhaps her only chance left. You must know she is nearly broke. And what will she do then? What will you do?"

Sasha shot up from the table, pushing her chair back in her fury. Yassar saw the rage in her eyes and met her gaze as forcefully as he could. *What a will! Exciting!*

"I'm utterly horrified! How could you!" Without another word Sasha disappeared from the room.

———◆———

Five minutes later Sasha charged through the door to the Countess' suite, her chest heaving and her heart screaming in pain. "Christina!" she called, her eyes darting around the room, then settling on the closed bathroom door. It flew open as she approached it, the Countess' robed form glaring at her, her hair still dripping wet from the shower.

"What on *earth* compels you to burst in here like this!"

"I'm sorry, I'm sorry, but I'm just so offended...so mortified..."

"What is it, child," the Countess said and stepped forward to grab Sasha by the shoulders. She ushered her into a chair. "Now sit down and control yourself and tell me what's wrong."

It's Yassar, he wants me to go be his son's—paid woman!" *You can't even bring yourself so say the word 'whore', can you?* She clutched at the Countess' hand, afraid to let go, and now tears were beginning to well in her eyes.

The Countess pulled away from her and backed up a few steps. She raised her chin and looked down at Sasha through eyes still glazed with intoxicants. "Well of course he's invited you to go live in Saudi Arabia, but I'm not certain I'd narrow it to that perspective."

Sasha looked up at the Countess in disbelief. *Oh my God! What is she saying?* "You mean you *know*?" She clutched her bosom with both hands.

"Of course, child, he spoke with me about it this morning. I think it's a tremendous opportunity for you."

"Tremendous opportunity!"

The Countess backed against the wall, her arms tense and her hands pressed flat against it, as if she were preparing to defend herself from Sasha springing at her throat at any second. "Yes! Opportunity!"

Sasha advanced toward her, her hair shooting off in all directions, as though she'd been electrified. Her back was rigid and she thrust her chest forward, like a girl daring a schoolboy in the playground. "Dammit! You talk like you're sending me off to boarding school!"

"Quiet! Yassar will hear you!"

"Then let him hear me! What do I care?"

"I thought you admired Yassar."

"What does admiring or not admiring Yassar have to do with becoming his son's—"

The Countess scowled. "Don't be ridiculous. He's invited you to live with his son in the palace, to keep you in style and lavish you with money, gifts, whatever you can possibly imagine—do you honestly understand how rich these people are? And all you can think about is some trite nonsense about money for services. Really!"

Sasha felt tears coming. She focused on her anger to force away the pain, then lost to it as desperate thoughts flashed through her mind. *How can you do this? You're all I've got. I'm all you've got. Except for the drugs. Has the opium really so consumed you?* "Damn you!" *She's selling me!* "How much is he paying you?"

The Countess merely looked away.

"How much?"

The Countess gazed back at Sasha, then crossed her arm in front of her stomach in her unique way. "My financial affairs are none of your business. No one is compelling you to do anything. Make up your mind," she said flatly. "But remember, you've got few other options."

"Damn you, Christina. I do too. I'll run off."

"Where? You don't have any money, and I can't possibly imagine you getting your hands dirty. You haven't been raised for it."

"You'd cut me off?"

The Countess arched her head back. "Silly child. There's nothing left. At least to speak of. Just look around the walls, dear. The pictures *are* all gone."

Sasha felt her heart was going to explode, then her brain.

Sasha walked out onto the patio. She felt the heat of the field-stones through her shoes and smelled the scent of the pines as she looked out over the grandeur of the greenery that tumbled down the hill to the valley—the Countess' hill and Countess' valley—that extended to the town of Vevey and to Lake Geneva itself. Now she realized that one way or another she wouldn't be able to call this place home anymore. *If I don't go, what happens to both of us?* Tears singed at her eyes. The pain in her throat became unbearable.

After a minute she stepped forward, smeared the tears from her face, and rested her palms on the limestone railing. The grounding sense of the stone settled her. She stood there, her chest heaving. She gradually raised her head, straightened her back. The muscles in her stomach hurt. *I guess I could forgive Christina because of the drugs. But Yassar? He's one of the few people I thought who understood me, whom I could talk to.* Her knees buckled and she rested her hips on the railing, turning to face the house. She felt for a moment as if she would tumble over backward, dizzy from her confusion.

Come on, get control of yourself. She forced herself to think. She realized that her life here with the Countess was over. Even if she refused, which she wasn't sure she could do, why would she want to continue living here with Christina now? Yet where else would she go? Defiance and anger empowered her. *All right, damn you. Damn you both. Only one thing to do. Make the best of it until I can see a way out. That, and save enough money to never need anybody again.*

CHAPTER 12

AUGUST, TWENTY-THREE YEARS AGO. ABOARD a Saudi Royal Family Lear Jet. Although the rumble of jet engines normally made Sasha sleepy, this flight was different. Sleep wasn't an option her nerves and emotions would allow. In the absence of that release from the dissonance of her reality, she distracted herself by focusing on the G-force of acceleration, the change in cabin pressure as they ascended, and a comparison of the pervasive aroma of new leather in the opulent cabin to the scents of her tack when she'd saddled her horse the previous day. Anything to keep her crumpled heart from wailing.

A mere five minutes into the flight, anguish burned through her dissembling mind. *If Christina could betray me...if Yassar... then who do I have?* Her body was rigid, muscles taut, synapses on overload. *Nobody.* She began to tremble. *Who, what can I believe in now?* Was she truly alone?

She looked at Yassar, dressed in Saudi robes and headdress, quietly reading his Koran in the seat across from her. She affected nonchalance, but her thoughts were still racked with periodic shrieks from a disbelieving heart. *Or is it my soul?*

She went to the lavatory and looked herself in the mirror. *You can't very well just ask them to turn this thing around. You made a decision. Thought it through with a clear head. Now make the best you can out of it.* She saw traces of red in her eyes. Fear too, and was certain others would perceive it.

She emerged. Yassar had put away his Koran and turned his chair toward hers, across the table set up between them.

"I suppose I should tell you something of what will be expected of you. And what you should expect to see when we arrive." He used the same gentle manner she had always known.

"All right," she said.

"Riyadh is one of the conservative religious bastions of the Saudi kingdom." He applied some jam to a piece of toast. "The Mutawwa'iin, the Saudi religious police, are charged with enforcing the standards of Islamic behavior, and are welcomed in Riyadh rather than feared. As you may know, among the standards of shari'a, our Islamic law, which they enforce, are standards for the behavior of women."

"So I've heard." Her legs were stiff. She suddenly felt crowded by the walls of the aircraft cabin.

"Women traditionally wear a full-length black covering known as the abaya. In addition, they must cover their heads with a hijav veil, a headscarf that hides their hair from public view. Men and women beyond childhood years may not mingle in public areas unless they are family or close relatives." He smiled. "Of course, as one associated with the royal family, certain privileges apply, and you may be allowed in public accompanied by Royal Guards."

When you think things can't get any worse, think again. She stifled a moan. *So how do I stop myself from thinking?*

"And what about when I'm at home?" Her mind conjured the image of her sitting in a room full of black-draped women, afraid to file their fingernails. She thought of the breathless ride through the brush on the north face the previous day on Sable, her unruly yearling; the backless gown she'd worn to dinner with Baroness and Baron de Moulin that caused his eyes to linger on her throughout the evening; the kick of the 16-gauge shotgun she liked to use for quail. Never again?

"Saudi women wear any type of clothing they choose, provided it's not attention-seeking by being either too revealing, too tight, or too short. Clothing that presents women as 'naked even though they are clothed,' which stirs the passions of men and tempts them, is not only considered contrary to the teachings, but unfair, unkind, and not sensible. Most Western blouses, even those with long sleeves, which are thin enough to reveal the underwear beneath are not approved of." He scrutinized her like a strict professor. "In your private chambers, and with Ibrahim, of course it is another matter."

"I see," she said. *Maybe I should just open the door and jump out.* She felt her muscles in her abdomen convulse and a pain in her heart as if it were being crushed by his words. *Yassar, please stop this.*

Yassar placed his hand on hers. She pulled it back into her lap. "My dear, I'm not attempting to frighten you or lead you to believe you'll be unable to conduct yourself largely as you've been accustomed." His drooping eyes were soft and gentle again; he was the Yassar she knew. "I simply don't want you to wind up getting carted off by the Mutawwa'iin, for example, for riding a bicycle. Or something you might ordinarily take for granted and not realize would be looked askance at in our culture. And I don't want you to embarrass the royal family, since you will be associated with us. Things will not be so difficult. Or unpleasant. You'll see."

Sasha felt her eyes beginning to burn. *I've never felt so alone in my life.* She turned to the window, tried not to think, counted the rivets around the window frame. But a voice within her accosted her. *I'm lost. I'm disappearing into a void.*

Riyadh, Saudi Arabia. There they were in the distance: the twenty-two-karat gold, onion domes of the 1700-room Royal Palace glittering in the sun. As the limousine carrying Sasha and Yassar neared the white stucco perimeter walls surrounding the Royal Palace's grounds, they passed nondescript gray- and brown-colored commercial shops and residential apartment buildings, piled on top of each other in angular cinder-block and concrete. A few robed figures peered into the tinted windows of the passing limo. Sasha didn't meet their gaze, as if to shrink from her shame. She smelled the omnipresent Saudi dust even inside the air-conditioned car. *Better get used to it.* She was now terribly aware of the coarse fabric of her abaya against her skin. *This too.*

Inside the palace garage, tan-and-red-uniformed Royal Guards pulled the doors open. "I'll ask how you're doing after you've settled in. I have some business to tend to," Yassar said flatly and disappeared to a rustle of robes and the click of a half-dozen pairs of heels. Sasha was met by two women in black abayas. They led her through an entrance past the stiff figures of more Royal Guards, then through successively complicated labyrinthine passageways to a set of double doors. *Okay, keep your distance, get through it. And don't let them see you flinch.*

Two young ladies wearing white Eisenhower-styled waist-cut jackets trimmed with gold braid met her on the other side of the double doors and led her to a room. One knocked softly and they entered. The room was a spacious, trapezoidal-shaped apartment of some fifteen hundred square feet, an open door to a dressing room on the far wall, another door of unknown destination next to it. The construction was almost entirely of marble, except for the ceiling, which was of an ornate wooden latticework, a portion of which opened to a filigree skylight. Windows on the side opposite the hallway opened into a courtyard through latticework that cleverly obscured the view from outside without interfering from within.

"I have the distinction of being your size." A dark-haired young woman was lounging in the center of a king-sized bed. The bed seemed ready to swallow her petite frame, which sank into a three-inch-thick comforter, surrounded by rich maroon chenille throws and a half-dozen pillows with golden cords and tassels. The young lady didn't look up from the television screen that commanded a four-by-six-foot square of the wall adjacent to her bed. She held a remote in her hand. The two attendants left.

"No hello?" Sasha said. "And what's my size got to do with anything?"

The girl turned her head toward Sasha. She was a black-haired Arab beauty with uncharacteristically light complexion. "It's why you're here." She put the television on mute and dropped the remote, which almost disappeared into the comforter. She observed Sasha through almond-shaped dark brown eyes. "It's why you're in with me, that is. And I must admit, I'm not happy about it, I've gotten quite used to being alone." She smiled for the first time, halfheartedly. "After years of sharing, being the favorite has some advantages," she said. "So let's get you oriented and out of here as soon as possible, okay?"

I'll say. "I won't even bother to unpack."

The girl laughed, looking at Sasha's lone bag. She turned back to her TV, rummaged for a moment to find the remote. "We don't wear those abayas inside the palace, certainly not inside the women's section. Clothes are in the armoires." She turned toward Sasha again. "Wear any of the Prada and I'll kill you."

Little snit! Sasha tightened her jaw. She sighed and looked around the room, actually an assemblage of various rooms within the room. A Persian carpet here, creating a living area with chairs, settee, and table, a dining area there with a simple Persian-influenced table and four chairs. The main bedroom area was defined by another fine silk-and-wool Oriental carpet under the girl's bed. Another bed, substantially smaller, surrounded by a modest night table and bureau, was established in the far corner near the dressing room door. The furniture was all Oriental and Mideastern antiques, mixed with the incongruously modern hi-tech audio-and-video system that the girl seemed to be obsessed with. Sasha continued to stand in silence.

The girl rolled over on the bed, then finally slid off it and stood up. "I can see this is going to be difficult." She shook herself and straightened her evanescent robe, under which she was naked.

Oh my goodness! A bare-bottomed hostess wasn't at all expected. And what else should that lead her to expect?

"I'm supposed to show you how things work around here the first few days, weeks, whatever it takes."

"It won't be long." Sasha said through clenched teeth. *And maybe I'll strangle you first.*

"It better not." The girl stood in front of Sasha, then smiled again, exposing a mouth that seemed accustomed to laughing. "Or I'll be in big trouble, and even I can't afford that around here." She quickly kissed Sasha on the cheek.

Don't you dare...

"I'm Nafta. And you, of course, are Sasha."

Sasha moved back until she felt her palms behind her against the marble walls. She rose up to her full height. *Just leave me alone.*

Nafta cocked her head to the side. "Oh, sister, you look stressed. And tired."

Sasha felt her fatigue, let her shoulders slump, looked up at Nafta through hooded eyes. "I need a nap."

"Good. Get one. If you're coming out tonight you'll need to look beautiful." Nafta stepped over to the door and pushed a button beside it, then walked back over to the bed and sat down.

"Tonight?" Sasha asked.

"The party after dinner. The highlight of the day around here, where we're all expected to shine. Some of the girls do little else all day but get ready for it. A competition of sorts. Gets a little catty sometimes, but it's fun, you'll like it." They heard a knock on the door. "Come in," Nafta called. One of the uniformed young ladies appeared in the doorway. "I'll have some couscous," Nafta said to the girl, her feet dangling over the edge of the bed a foot from the floor. "Make it with lamb today. Not too spicy, you know how I like it. Have them make up some nice garnishes—cornichons and caperberries—tell them to improvise. And some bottled water, no gas." She turned to Sasha. "What would you like?"

What is this? A hotel? "Oh, just a salad, anything." Sasha said waving her arm. The attendant girl nodded and left.

"Don't be so reticent," Nafta said. "You could've ordered whatever you wanted."

"I'm not hungry." Sasha still stood awkwardly near the door, only a few feet into the room.

"They cater to every nationality. You want haute cuisine French cooking, you've got it. Thai, giant prawns, Indian curry or steak, no problem. Get used to it, sister. Use your imagina-tion. That's the real reason you're here. And remember, there's nothing you can dream up that they, or their money, can't satisfy. Squadrons of jets, fleets of Rolls-Royces, yachts, polo teams, mansions all over the world, and I'm only talking about Ibrahim." Nafta laughed.

Seems like you're swallowed up in all this. Sasha looked at the other bed, testing its mattress with exhausted eyes.

Nafta continued chattering as if Sasha hadn't heard her the first time. "Yes, whatever you want. Catherine Bowne, one of the girls they brought in a year or so ago from California, simply adores Southern California avocados—not just avocados mind you—but Southern California avocados, so Ibrahim has them flown in once a week."

"Who's Catherine Bowne?"

"One of the other girls."

"Other girls?"

"They're twenty-six of us here." Sasha's jaw went slack. "Ibrahim's got four cousins who are of age with similar tastes."

Oh my God, it's a harem! Sasha put a hand to her forehead. "Where do they all come from? Why do they all do it?"

"Everywhere. Talent agents in Hollywood. Plastic surgeons. Why do any of us do it? You?" She looked at Sasha.

Sasha pretended not to hear and began pulling off her abaya. *Right now I'm asking myself that.*

Nafta answered her own question. "A half million pounds a year, for starters. Another half million pounds a year or so in jewelry if you work at it, which is yours to take with you."

Sasha jerked her head to look into Nafta's face. Her eyes were narrowed, her interest piqued. *That's enough to set me free.* "Go on." *You're a chatty thing, Nafta, don't stop now.*

"That got your attention." Nafta laughed. "Most of the girls know if they come here for a year or two, they'll never have to work again, particularly if they're a favorite." She grinned, as if to say "yours truly."

"How long have you been here?"

"Four years. There's nowhere I'd rather be. You can get awfully used to this. And I've got a great imagination."

Sasha finished pulling off her abaya. She still wore an English riding outfit underneath. Nafta tumbled back into the bedclothes and pillows. "Tally ho. If you're into horses, Ibrahim's got those too. A stable full of Arabians, although except when you're riding you'll have to lose the boots. Ibrahim's really into feet, if you know what I mean. Well," she said now at the ceiling, her feet pointed absurdly at it as well, her naked buttocks showing through her robe, "Better get yourself prepared. The queen bee herself will be here to check you out any minute now."

"Who?" *Queen Bee?*

"Nibmar. Ibrahim's mother. Yassar's first and favorite wife."

"Why is she coming?"

"See if you're up to her standards for her oldest son. The men run things in the outside world, but you're in the girls' world now. Nibmar is queen of the roost around here. So even if Yassar thought you were just the thing, you still need to make Nibmar's grade." She rolled over on the bed and leveled her gaze at Sasha through forbidding eyes. "Don't trifle with Nibmar."

They heard another knock on the door. Nafta sat up straight in bed. The latch turned tentatively and one of the servant girls entered with a silver tray, followed by another similarly-attired attendant. They walked to the table and busied themselves with laying out the girls' meal.

As they ate, Sasha understood why Nafta had been designated to indoctrinate her. After forty-eight hours of her inces-
sant chatter there would be nothing left for her to impart. Sasha
got in a few words but Nafta told her about Ibrahim bringing the
band Three Dog Night back from retirement for a week's engagement at his nightly party; the size of the breasts on Florinda
Wilson, former Miss California and aspiring movie star, before
a casting agent sent her to one of Crown Prince Abdul's—one
of Ibrahim's cousins—bodyguards to interview her and, oh my,
she *flashed* her way into Saudi Arabia; the time Ibrahim, on a
bet with Prince Omar, brought six of the girls to bed with him
and serviced them all, she could tell you because she was there
and witnessed it firsthand—well *fourth*-hand, so to speak—
herself; and the time...Then a firm knock on the door silenced
Nafta in midsentence. "That would be the Valide Sultana
herself."

The door swung open and a petite woman with a prominent
nose, full lips, and brown eyes with lashes half as long as Sasha's
toenails entered, followed by two attendants. "Hello, Sasha, welcome to Saudi Arabia. I've heard so much about you, child." She
spoke in refined British English like Sasha's, but with pronunciation and diction in the high style, as if she were reading from
Shakespeare. She strode across the room with the air of ownership, stood in front of Sasha, and eyed her up and down. She
smiled gently, almost serenely. Her dark Arab skin was unlined,
with the creamy glow of a life of biweekly facials, save for a few
wrinkles at the eyes, and she wore a stylish tan dress that looked
like it could have been on the cover of *Vogue*—Chanel? Her dark
brown hair was pulled back into a bun.

Not at all what Nafta had led me to expect. Sasha smiled
back. "Hello, Nibmar."

"Well, my child, the first thing we need to do is get your measurements. I'll ask you to remove your clothes. Preeba and Darkeen will assist you." The two attendants stepped forward.

Not on your life! Sasha's body went rigid, her hands instinctively clutched at her breast. Her chin shot up, her eyes went wide with alarm, then narrowed with anger. Sasha saw Nibmar react—the serene presence in her eyes turn to resolve.

"It's all right, child. As you wish. I will help you." She began to unbutton Sasha's blouse.

What kind of crazy place is this. Have I lost all individuality, all privacy? she lamented to herself, but in the same instant her anger returned. She stared into Nibmar's eyes. "I can do that quite well for myself," she said through curled lips. She began to unbutton her blouse. Nibmar stood back, returning Sasha's glare and waved the two girls forward. She said something to them in Arabic. The two girls averted their eyes from Sasha as they began unbuttoning, unbuckling, and sliding her out of her clothing.

Sasha struggled against them, pushing their hands away, only to have them gently but relentlessly resume. Twice. Five, six times, methodically pursuing her buttons, one conquest at a time, pushed away, back to it. Why didn't she just run from the room? Shout at Nibmar to have her harpies leave her alone? One of the attendants tore a sleeve.

Nibmar clapped her hands and the two girls froze. Nibmar walked forward and stood inches from Sasha's face. "You will learn many things in your first few days."

Sasha stared back into Nibmar's eyes, unrelenting. Nibmar might learn a few things, too. *Maybe get a poke in the eye, not so figuratively, or a kick in the pants.*

Nibmar continued. "But never so important as to understand who I am and the all-encompassing affection of a good

Saudi son for his mother. And the unlimited willingness to accept his mother's advice as to what is best for him and those he consorts with. Do yourself the service of choosing your battles more carefully, over matters of more substance. An unruly colt sometimes kicks itself in the head." She stepped back and waved the attendants forward again.

A moment later Sasha stood before Nibmar fully naked except for a solitaire diamond—Christina's gift for her 16th birthday—on a gold chain around her neck. Sasha heard Nafta's feet pat across the floor back to her bed, then the sound of her resuming her ridiculous clicking around the television dial.

Nibmar walked a slow circle around Sasha, who stood as if for a military inspection, her chin edging higher in defiance. "You are very beautiful. Prince Yassar only imagined how exquisite."

Ganesha, open my heart. Give me peace and keep my soul from bursting from my body. Sasha closed her eyes. She felt Nibmar's presence.

"Are you honest, subtle and submissive?" Nibmar asked.

A laugh shot from Sasha in a burst. "Honest certainly! But hardly subtle or submissive!" Nibmar wasn't amused. She nodded to the two assistants again. One of them stepped forward with a tape measure. The other placed her hands on Sasha, moving her limbs, directing her. Sasha felt the cold tape on her skin as they encircled her breasts at their fullest points.

Sasha now avoided Nibmar's eyes and observed Nafta, who still lounged on the bed, clicking past a hockey game to a pornographic film. Nafta leaned forward, studying the film as if she were filing away the information for later use. Nibmar observed the measurement process with the same scientific intensity.

One of the girls inadvertently tugged at Sasha's gold chain and the clasp gave way. Nibmar dropped to her knees and retrieved it, cradling it in her two hands to Sasha. "Forgive her, child. A careless accident." She took one of Sasha's hands and placed the necklace in it. "See, it's the clasp. An easy repair. Permit me to handle it myself."

"Thank you," was all Sasha could think of to say. *What a remarkable transformation. What an unusual reaction.*

One of the girls produced a robe, which Sasha eagerly put on. *Thank God that's over.* She felt tears beginning to form in her eyes and breathed deeply to force them away. Nibmar waved the two girls out the door and led Sasha to the settee.

"Your classes in Islamic culture and palace etiquette begin tomorrow. You'll need to learn how to behave."

"And how is that?" Sasha said, suddenly feeling she was up to taking Nibmar on again.

"Solicitous. Entertaining. Beguiling." Nibmar's eyes were hard once more. "But you can start with subtle and submissive." She stood up abruptly. "Tomorrow afternoon after your physical examination. Nafta, your roommate, can help you."

Sasha returned Nibmar's hardened stare. "I would prefer my own quarters. It's what I'm accustomed to."

"Then get accustomed to having a roommate. At least until you learn to behave properly." Nibmar turned and left.

Sasha felt her face flush. *So I'm to be poked and prodded, have my privacy violated* and *I'm to live in a dorm. Give me two weeks. I'll have this whole place turned upside down.*

$$\rightarrowtail\!\!\diamond\!\!\leftarrowtail$$

Sasha savored some private moments after Nafta dressed and left for the party, then dozed and awakened to twilight glowing red through the latticed windows. She listened in the half-darkness to evening prayers, mournful callings from the minarets, plaintive at first, then louder, insistent, the music of a faith, a world she didn't know. She stirred in the bed—the twin bed pushed against the wall almost as an afterthought—her bed, in her shared quarters, and swung her feet to the floor. She walked across the rug, then sat down with her feet on the edge of it so the cool marble beneath could revive her. Her limbs ached, as did her heart. She rested her face on her knees. *Oh, God, I feel so violated. What have I done? What has Christina done to me? What have you done to me, Yassar?* She gave in to her sobs, clutched her legs until her forearms ached.

Finally she arched her head back and sighed. *All right. Enough. This is your life now. Don't just sit around agonizing, frozen. Do something about it.* She recalled Christina's words: "It's OK to hurt when you hurt; feel it and get through it. Don't deprive yourself of knowing the ecstasy of being alive." The thought of the Countess sent a surge of pain through her, like someone stomping on a fresh wound.

Face your situation. You've been destroyed by some woman who never was, never will be, never wanted to be your mother. Sold by her for drugs to the highest bidder, the only bidder, the "kindest" of her friends. A man who probably wanted to bed you himself, but is too religious, decorous, whatever—so he does the next best thing and buys you for his son. Great life!

She stopped herself, realizing she was standing. *All right, you've lived your life unbridled. Christina saw to that. Now you're in some God-awful country. So what do you do?*

She turned the options over in her mind. Rebel and get thrown out? Limp along, miserable? No, she had already decided she would adapt until she saved enough money to leave. Well, according to Nafta, she was in the right place for that. *Go earn it. Move on and see what comes next.*

CHAPTER 13

AUGUST, TWENTY-THREE YEARS AGO. RIYADH, Saudi Arabia. After a nap, Sasha abandoned any thought of going to the party and waited, reminding herself she wasn't at all good at it, as if she needed reminding, as if the bloody pacing could keep her mind off it. The only thing she hated more than waiting was not knowing what she was waiting for. But the knot in her stomach told her that whatever it was she wasn't ready for it. She now sat on the edge of the bed feeling like some prom queen poised for her date. In that moment she knew what was coming: Ibrahim. She just wanted to survive it.

A trapezoid of light flashed onto the floor as the door to the corridor was thrown open. Nafta strode through, jewel-bedecked, glittering, and resplendent, with her hair up. She wore a pastel, floor-length evening gown, breasts barely restrained within it, the sleek curves of her waist and hips accentuated through the silk fabric. She bore no relationship to the waif who had inhabited the bedclothes, peering out at the television only hours before. "Meditating or dancing in the dark, sister?" she said.

Sasha wondered why Nafta had returned so early. She seemed distraught, pulling her earrings off and tossing them distractedly on her bed, unzipping the back of her dress with a furious level of activity Sasha thought impossible for the girl she'd lunched with earlier that day. She slid out of her dress, exposing only panties beneath it.

Sasha wondered what she was so upset about as she strode past her without making eye contact, her lips pulled taut and her brow furrowed. She fumbled with shaking her hair out straight, whisked into one of the armoires, grabbed a handful of clothes and turned toward Sasha. "He wants you," she said. "I'll help you get ready," and disappeared into the bathroom.

Sasha stared dazedly at the far wall in the dim light, trying to get her brain to catch up with her racing emotions. There wasn't going to be any easing into this; as she'd feared, tonight was the night. She hadn't even met the man, exchanged childhood stories with him, stood awkwardly awaiting his first kiss goodnight or felt him stroke her cheek, and yet she'd be spreading her legs in his bed in, what, an hour? It wasn't suppose to be like this, at least not the way she'd imagined it when she'd felt the first tingling curiosity about who her first lover would be as far back as, when was it? Seeing that muscular carpenter repairing Christina's stables in Switzerland, or, her mind jump-cutting now, that French aristocrat's son who didn't want to stop at just kissing her. She felt her heart pounding, now deliciously curious, hoping, expecting, wanting to enjoy it, now realizing her brain was rambling desperately—under the circumstances how could she possibly expect pleasure? All her senses seemed cranked up to unbearable perceptiveness at the same time. She heard strains of music coming from the ballroom as a roar. The smooth silk of her nightgown against her breasts was like ice. The forms of the furniture across the room grated on her eyes like sandpaper. *Was it Tuscany?* she thought, absurdly, flashing back to the first time she'd seen an electrical storm, the thrilling danger of those majestical swords of lightning arcing to the vineyards below, now almost believing she felt the synapses in her brain firing with the same intensity.

Her eyes detachedly perceived the bathroom door open and Nafta cross the room. Why did she appear so tense, even angry? Nafta switched on a light and then stood in front of Sasha, observing her. "Sister, you need to get ready *now*." Sasha looked up at her, nodded, and knew better than to attempt to speak, feeling the dryness in her throat, certain her voice would emerge as only a squeak, betraying her nervousness. Nervousness? Was that all it was, because now her brain was screaming at her unintelligibly, speaking in tongues. She stood up from the bed, knew her face was too brittle to smile and then wondered why on earth she would even think of doing that.

"Relax," Nafta said. "That's the best advice I can give you for tonight." Sasha saw Nafta's face soften, the playful smile of earlier that day reappearing for the first time since she'd returned. "I'll have time to teach you a few things later. For tonight just don't be afraid to use your imagination." Sasha felt herself nod in response. "Now off with this nightgown," Nafta said, lifting Sasha's arms and pulling the silk over her head. Nafta looked toward the armoire. "You'll need something casual, loose fitting." Nafta bent down in front of her, "You won't need these either," she said, pulling Sasha's panties down. Sasha was conscious of Nafta's voice changing to an ominous tone before she processed her words: "Oh, sister, you'll need to shave."

Sasha rubbed her hand over her thigh and uttered, "Smooth."

"No, I mean everything. In our culture, it's a sin to have hair on one's private parts."

Sasha felt her cheeks burn and turned away. *Is there no limit to my humiliation?* She clutched her arms to her as she ran for the bathroom door.

"You look beautiful," Nafta said ten minutes later. Sasha now wore a simple ankle-length linen dress with sandals, and a short-sleeve off-white silk blouse that Nafta had selected for her. "Show some cleavage but not too much," she said, adjusting Sasha's blouse.

Cleavage! I'm braless in a see-through blouse. Her solitaire diamond, which had been silently returned in a velvet jewelry box while she'd napped, hung from its gold chain around her neck. Her hair and eyes were highlighted by the ivory colors of her blouse and skirt. Sasha heard a whooshing in her ears, and guessed her senses were shutting down after abusing themselves for the last quarter hour. She felt sickened. Was it Nafta's musky perfume? She wished for a friend, thought of clinging to Nafta but knew it wouldn't help.

Nafta kissed Sasha on either cheek and tapped on the mysterious door in their chamber. Sasha heard a muffled voice from within and felt the freezing cold of the brass doorknob without realizing she'd reached for it, turned it and pushed the door open. It led to Ibrahim's quarters. She stood in the doorway, feeling on instinct she should pause, allow Ibrahim to survey her. She heard a race of thoughts telling her to appear nonchalant, excited, eager, bored, anything to keep from showing her urge to run from the room.

She saw deep-set eyes observing her from beneath puffy eyelids. She saw a dark face, clean-shaven and curly black hair that had been slicked back with some kind of gel. She thought the calm expression and bushy eyebrows could be mistaken for mournful, both like Yassar's. The man had an air of command, maybe even arrogance, she quickly decided—her reason hadn't abandoned her after all. *Yassar's looks, definitely his eyes. Quite fetching, actually.* The fact that he was good looking made it easier for her to smile. "I'm Sasha," she said. She thought he said something like, "I know," and, "I'm Ibrahim," and she knew he had stood to greet her, but she wasn't hearing clearly, aware in that moment that somebody, it had to be Nafta, closed the door behind her and her mind, her body froze.

Then, how much later? a second? a simple perception, as if her mind was taking in small bits at a time to process her situation: Ibrahim wore a white collarless cotton shirt and tan linen slacks. *Better now.* She blinked and thought he looked older than his 17 years, more polished, more relaxed and self-assured than she expected.

Ibrahim stood in the center of a comfortable 15-by-20-foot sitting room. Persian rugs on the floor, a few draped over tables to convey an opulent informality, pieces jammed everywhere, antique Beidermeier and English Period pieces mixed with Ottoman Empire, two-foot high end tables designed for kneeling services of tea or meals. Pillows and throws every place on tapestried, overstuffed furniture and leather couches. Moose, elephant and antelope heads on the walls. *A man's room. No surprise. But over the top.*

Now she wasn't sure the jangle of images appeared as she perceived it, realizing her eyes were taking in pieces of mosaic as if by pops of flashbulbs, all surrounding the man who stood in the center of the room as the words, *he'll be my first lover,* formed, then fixed themselves in her mind. Her knees were weak, she felt her pulse throbbing in her ears and she moved a step forward into the room to avoid appearing dumbfounded, then wondered why that would matter.

Ibrahim smiled at her, *returning mine?* she wondered. His eyes turned down at the corners. *Yes, like Yassar's.* She saw him shrug, then turn his back to her and cross toward a sofa where he sat down. He motioned to the center of the rug in front of him, said, "You can come in now, please." Refined, proper British English, like she'd been taught by her tutor. She walked to the center of the room where he had directed her, wondering what she was supposed to do. His gaze inched down her body, then back up again. She felt cheapened. This wasn't how it was supposed to be. She lowered her chin, looking down into his eyes with as much as she could muster of her indignity, suddenly not caring if he saw it, even better he should see it than sense her fear. He didn't react and she wondered, is he going to leave me standing here all night, for goodness sake, then saw the desire in his eyes and answered her own question. He motioned for her to sit on the sofa beside him.

"Father told me about you. Spirited." She saw him pause, then nod to himself, as if he'd reconsidered his comment, then decided he'd let it stand.

Yes, he's Yassar's son: that deliberate manner. He pulled a small silver case out of his pocket, placed it on the table and opened it. A vial of white powder was within it. He took a silver spoon from the box, unscrewed the vial and spooned out some of the powder onto a mirror. He formed four lines of the powder using a knife, then picked a silver tube from the box. Cocaine! Sasha's back went stiff as she realized he wasn't just preparing it for himself. She shifted tensely as he placed the silver tube in his nose, bent over and snorted two lines.

Yassar certainly wouldn't approve of that, and even as a prince, they'd skin him alive for it around here. She looked up at him to see his eyes upon her. She inhaled and her chest heaved as his gaze coursed down her neck to settle on her breasts. She knew he could see the shape of them beneath her translucent blouse. She felt a flutter in her chest.

He slid the mirror across the table toward her, held out the silver tube. She didn't think he'd allow her to say no, then heard herself say, "No thank you."

"Take it," he said bluntly. "You need to loosen up. It's not going to be a lot of fun for either of us unless you do." Sasha froze. She saw him observe her like he didn't have time for this, extend his arm with the tube in it toward her further. She reluctantly took it from him. She leaned forward and after a few inartful passes managed to snort up the two lines.

Now what?

He sat back and spread his arms across the back of the sofa. She wondered why she wasn't feeling any different from the drug, then wondered if maybe she was, seeing the way he looked at her. "You are beautiful, even more than my father described you. Even more than your pictures from Switzerland." She nodded because she couldn't think of anything else to do, but felt a sinking sensation in her stomach at the realization that even his compliments weren't going to make it any easier for her. He laughed, then said, "But you're not much of a conversationalist." Did he always laugh at his own comments before he made them?

How rude! She wanted to tell him so, but thought better of it, then thought to get up and leave, but realized he wouldn't let that happen. "We'll see in time," was all she could think of to say. He abruptly stood, crossed the room and pressed a buzzer. Two servant girls appeared. One knocked on the door to Nafta and Sasha's room and a moment later Nafta entered. Ibrahim stood near the doorway and watched as one of the servant girls unrolled a small rug and moved Sasha onto the center of it. The other girl approached with a bowl of water and towels. Nafta crossed the room and stood in front of Sasha, leaned forward and whispered to Sasha as she began unbuttoning Sasha's blouse,

"Everything's all right," she said in hushed tones, "everything's all right," her voice soothing, but Sasha wondered why her face looked so tense.

What in God's name is going on? "What…?"

"We're going to cleanse you to prepare you. It's a religious thing, symbolic, really." Nafta finished undressing Sasha and raised one of Sasha's feet for the servant girl to splash water over it from the bowl. The girls washed each of her feet. Sasha observed Ibrahim from across the room, his eyes on her body, watching the ablutions with steadily heavier breathing, his head arching back with his rising desire. She wondered if he were aroused, what he would look like if he were, how he would direct her in the bedroom. She wasn't so much afraid of it now, feeling the beginnings of her power as a woman as she sensed her ability with merely the shape of her body to transfix Ibrahim as she was doing at this moment.

The servant girls finished drying Sasha's feet, picked up the bowl and walked noiselessly from the room. Sasha turned to see Nafta's face as she held her by the hand and directed her toward the doorway to Ibrahim's inner suite. Sasha stepped forward, her face within a foot of Nafta's. She thought she saw sadness in her eyes, or perhaps tenderness, and was grateful for it as her pulse surged again, throbbed in her ears. She looked up at Ibrahim, whose mouth now seemed slack, and crossed the room toward him feeling in a way she was at her best when she was most afraid, trying to take everything in, absorb it and digest it. *Walk into the fear.* There was a first time for everything and she reminded herself that much of the majesty of it was in experiencing the sheer terror of it. Tonight would be no exception, she thought.

Thank God for some noise, Sasha thought, lying in bed the next day before dawn to the sound of the call to first prayers. She'd been awake for hours, listening to Ibrahim's rhythmic breathing, itching to explore what seemed like the beginning of a new life. She had slept as deeply as she could remember, drained after a night of hurling herself into sensations that brought a smile to her lips remembering them now. Lips that did things the night before she hadn't ever imagined under Ibrahim's gentle tutoring. *Nobody told me.* She wished she hadn't waited so long, thinking back on the glances she'd drawn from men decades older in Christina's circle. *And I'm sorry that French aristocrat's son stopped when I said "stop."*

An hour later Ibrahim awoke, switched on the light, and looked around the room. "Good morning," Sasha said. She pulled the sheets up over her breasts, embarrassed to allow herself the feelings of unrestrained freedom she'd explored in the dark.

"Mmmm. Morning." Ibrahim rolled toward her and kissed her on the cheek. "I see you make up for your conversational reserve with athleticism." Her instinct was to look away but she chose not to express modesty. After all, she'd relished his touch, and more. No need to feign prudishness.

"You'll have ample time to become as enthralled with my dialog as you were with my body last night," she said. A silly comment, she realized, but it made her feel sexy to say it. After all, she was experienced now. She could express such things without seeming like she was putting on.

Ibrahim laughed. "One night and you're Marlene Dietrich." He slid out of the covers without seeing the sheepish look his comment provoked. Perhaps she was overdoing it, she allowed. Still, nobody could take from her what she'd become last night.

"Breakfast?" he asked on the way to the bathroom. She laughed to herself: hardly a fitting punctuation to her thought. Nonetheless, she liked the familiar tone, his informality. It made her feel he was pleased with her.

"Don't you have to do prayers and such?"

"In time. I can miss first prayers. Ring for the servants, will you? They know what I take for breakfast. I'll be in the shower. I'll need help scrubbing my back."

She felt a tingle of desire. Would he want her again in the shower? Was that his way? She admired his body from behind as he walked away. *Maybe life here won't be so unpleasant.*

She got up and summoned the servants, then stood blatantly naked as she ordered breakfast from one of the bellgirls. "Bring me a robe from my room, please." The bellgirl pointed to a closet, crossed the room and produced a luxurious silk robe.

"Miss Sasha, you also have a cotton robe in the bathroom," she said and left.

Of course, I'm sure he's got ten of them in there. She listened for the sound of the shower, found her way to the bathroom. It was a mirrored, pink marble palace—were those solid gold fixtures?—fully three-quarters the size of Sasha and Nafta's room. Ibrahim stood in the center of a six-by-nine-foot shower walled with glass on three sides. A dozen showerheads sprayed from all directions. He saw her and turned, beaming and waved her to come in like a rich teenager showing off his new Ferrari. *Oh, for goodness sake.*

She entered the shower. "Come on, I'm getting waterlogged," he said, handing her the soap. He pointed to a loofah, turned his back to her. "You surprised me last night," he said as she began scrubbing. He stood with his hands on his waist, back arched, chin raised. The baronial lord of the manor of early last night had chased off the lad with the new car.

"In what way?" She took it as a compliment, expecting to be further flattered, or at least praised for her skill. She pulled closer to him, felt her breasts against his back.

"You lack experience but you throw yourself into it."

Sasha stiffened and stepped back. *I see.* She felt her face flush. She resumed her scrubbing, responding to his comment by bearing down with the loofah.

"Hey!" he called, turning, "not so hard!" She saw the flash of anger in his eyes. The suddenness of his reaction surprised her, but she recovered and met his gaze without giving ground, then looked away, aware he knew she'd chafed him on purpose. She noted his temper, filed it away. She went back to her scrubbing, feeling the awkward sense of surrealism of her first moments with him last night. She shrugged it off, managed to laugh to herself and relaxed. She couldn't expect to be an expert in one go at it. Besides, she hadn't heard any complaints from him in the bedroom. Quite the contrary. It was awkward at first, but once she'd gotten into it, well...it *was* she and not the cocaine, she was certain. She grinned mischievously. It was she who initiated this time, groping for him with soapy fingers, until she'd assured herself there were no complaints from him in the shower either.

An hour later Sasha and Ibrahim walked into a side chamber in his suite. "My breakfast room," he said, lip thrust in the direction of a table and chairs arranged near windows facing a courtyard and set for breakfast for two—white wicker, bright sunlight from the windows, china designed for an English garden, with topiaries and boxwoods to accompany.

Oscar Wilde gone mad, trapped in one of his plays.

"Bright and cheery, eh?" he asked. She saw his look of expectation, knowing her compliment was supposed to follow.

Was he joking? No. *The Self-Importance of Being Ibrahim.* "It certainly looks English," she said as enthusiastically as she could. They sat. He buzzed someplace and two bellgirls appeared. One served his eggs Benedict, with generous spoonfuls of hollandaise, the other Sasha's Earl Grey tea, strawberries and oatmeal. She watched him eat, well-mannered, like a gentleman. *At least he's cute. Sexy, really.* She smiled as she thought it, swirled her tea with a spoon. *Not my lover, but maybe in time? Sexy helps.* She felt comfortable with him now. "Not in training for the Olympics, I see." He looked up, puzzled, and she felt a jolt of alarm at remembering his ugly glare in the shower.

He looked down at his eggs. "I agree with Western culture that breakfast is the most important meal of the day. You should see what my countrymen eat." He smiled.

Yes, like Yassar's smile, in his eyes. She remembered now, from last night. "So, don't you have prayers soon?"

"Later."

Odd. Not at all like Yassar. She knew Yassar was always the first up when he visited in Switzerland, praying on the rug he carried with him everywhere. "So, what exactly does a prince do all day, then?" Ibrahim pursed his lips. *Ah, must be important.* Ibrahim inhaled, preparing to speak. *Maybe someday he'll grow into his demeanor.*

"The fun parts are fun, the dull parts are dull. Which do you want to hear?" He smiled again, the engaging smile she'd seen but was unable to fully respond to last night. It rolled over her cynicism.

"All of it," she said. She propped her chin on her clasped hands, elbows on the table.

"Well, let's see, suppose we just use today as a typical day. First, up early"—he looked at his watch— "by 5:30 I'd guess, then a shower." He looked down at his eggs. "So far, fun parts. Good company." He looked up from his plate. The smile again, focused, as if she were the first person he was trying it out on, the real smile he'd use as the platinum iridium against which all the subsequent copies would be measured before they were released. "So far you follow?"

Sasha nodded. *Maybe he doesn't take himself so seriously after all.* She waited for him to continue, aware that with this most mundane of descriptions he held her attention, even had her earnestly interested in what came next. The light caught the swirls of dark hair on his arms. She remembered the firmness of his biceps as he'd embraced her last night. *Yes,* she cocked her head to the side, content for him to take his time before going on, *perhaps a lover in time.*

"Next, I will get to those prayers you keep pestering me about..."

"Pestering, really..."

"...believe it or not. Then I study for my afternoon class."

"Are you a serious student?"

"Don't know. Enough, I guess."

"Your father says you're going to Harvard."

"Yes, that's what one does, I suppose. Father had his heart set on Harvard. Glad I didn't disappoint him." He shrugged. "I guess I write a good essay. Then again, not everyone can write about being a significant factor in the future of a country." He said the words as if he were reading from his application. Practiced. And without enthusiasm.

"Next?" she asked.

"Next comes my first really dull part, a meeting at the Finance Ministry with Father's aides. I must review their work on some new plans Father has for securing long-term private-sector jobs for graduating Saudi students. Instead of letting them plod the typical track to some unimaginative government bureaucratic position."

It surprised, even delighted her, hearing him speak with apparent authority about one of Yassar's projects. "You find your father's programs dull?"

"Not at all, he's a visionary, but I find his subordinates dull. After all, they're unimaginative government bureaucrats." He laughed. "And yet they have the audacity to be arrogant and self-righteous. Like Father, I don't suffer fools easily."

To the contrary; I've seen Yassar sit politely for hours listening to nonsense from twits like Ophelia Deneau. "Tell me more about the jobs program. Your father's always been so guarded about what he does."

Ibrahim shrugged and pushed the remnants of his eggs to the side of his plate with a piece of English muffin. "Father's ideas are brilliant, but I find dealing with the whole process a bore. No patience for it. The people are morons. Progress is slow. There's no action."

"And you're a man of action?" *Uh-oh.* She felt that flutter of unease again, afraid she'd allowed her impudence too much reign. She detected the first signs of an angry retort in the wrinkled brow, then saw the ridges soften.

"Well, I'm training for the Olympics," he deadpanned. Sasha burst into spontaneous laughter. No, he didn't take himself too seriously at all.

"Then what?"

He shrugged. "Then I suppose back to the palace, a workout in the gym and then a massage." He looked up at the ceiling like he was thinking.

"You sound like you're making this up as you go along now."

"I am. I don't have anything scheduled again till midday. Maybe a little lunch, then perhaps a nap with one of the girls."

Quite the Don Juan, I see. Sasha felt a flash of, what was it? Disappointment? Jealousy? *Don't be absurd.*

"Then prayers, then off to my religion classes."

"Even on a Saturday?"

"Absolutely." He looked out the windows as if bored. "That's the way we do it here." He looked back at her and she detected his sudden impatience, as if he had to be someplace else. Finished with her for now? He had his hands on the table as though he were ready to push his chair back and stand up. Had she become one of the dull parts? "Then prayers, dinner, then my party." His eyes brightened at that. "You must be there tonight. Nafta will fill you in. It's the highlight of the day around here." He stood up and gave her a curious nod of his head as if he were acknowledging a servant. "Don't get up," he said, even though Sasha hadn't stirred. "Relax and finish your tea. I'll see you later. I must go now."

Sasha inclined her head just so, trying to effect a superior version of his nod, not sure she'd carried it off, then glanced away affecting indifference to his leaving. Two bellgirls appeared seconds after Ibrahim left. "Not now," Sasha said with authority. "Leave me." She felt a hollowness, as if she were waiting for an emotion to come to her and fill up the space where there was nothing. She raised her teacup to her lips mechanically, lifelessly. The tea was cold. She put the cup back in the saucer and pushed it away.

Later that day Sasha reclined in the half acre of tiered terraces, stone benches and cultivated shrubbery, flowers and trees that comprised the central octagonal courtyard within the women's section of the palace.

She lay in a cushioned lounge chair shaded from the sun by an umbrella surrounded by boxwoods and flowering magnolia trees. The nook had appealed to her instantly, inviting her with its calm. A fountain trickled in the terraced level above, and a stream of water ran underneath the stone patio in which she reclined, emerging beneath a wall into a thirty-foot-long rectangular channel that was bordered on either side by paths of geometric shapes in brick, and lined with fruit-bearing grapefruit and orange trees.

The previous day's events replayed themselves in her mind in a seemingly endless tape. *Nibmar.* She'd rather jump in a cold pool than be around her. *The less I see of her the better.* Her cheeks burned at the thought of standing before Nibmar naked, stripped of all dignity, furious and in pain at the same time, yet forced to swallow it all, an image she realized would haunt her for some time. *But Nafta, after having me foisted upon her as a roommate, after her tone in our first introduction, why would Nafta attend to me last night? And this "sister" routine and the kissing. Very curious. A friend is too much to ask for. Maybe somebody to reciprocate in keeping each other out of trouble?* She thought of the frostiness of the other girls she'd encountered earlier, as she'd entered the courtyard, closed her eyes and smelled the seductive aroma of the flowering magnolias that encircled her haven. She thought next of her hours in bed with Ibrahim, as if it hadn't dominated her consciousness all day, recalled her exhilarating spontaneity. Was it the cocaine, after all, Ibrahim's artful touch, or her own innate sexuality? She felt her womanhood stirring in her, a thrilling sense of abandon at the thought of embracing the profane world she'd chosen.

Then her thoughts and emotions were all upside down again, and she was crying without the ability to control herself. She buried her face in her knees and pressed her hands to the sides of her head. The sex last night had hardly been consensual. She'd been offered up like some kind of pastry. *Oh, God, what kind of life is this going to be?* She willed the warmth of the sun to penetrate into her bones, her heart, and revive her.

All right, sister, she mocked herself, get hold of yourself. Stop wallowing in your misery. Think. Regroup. She started by facing her situation. There wasn't anybody to run to who would make it all better, not that Christina ever did, anyhow. She always knew that. It was probably what made her so self-reliant. And look what else it made her. *You're a royal concubine. That isn't going to change any time soon.* Going back to being some hurt, tentative teen who was dropped in over her head in a strange, unfathomable life was not an option. *Move on and see what comes next,* she reminded herself of her decision of the previous day. *Yes, I can do this, and do it well.*

She dozed.

"Sister, that sun isn't to be trifled with at noon." She awakened to Nafta's voice.

Okay, ask me about last night. I know you're dying to hear. Then Sasha felt silly, realizing Nafta was no novice herself. She looked out over the multi-terraced courtyard. "The patio is beautiful."

Nafta sat next to her. "Yes, for our own exclusive use, exactly as you are doing right now. You see the latticed windows? They're all the girls' rooms—ours too. That way we can sunbathe, paint our toenails, or just reflect, away from the eyes of even the Royal Guards. It's the one place we can be our own queens. I've never even seen Nibmar come in here."

Sasha's pulse picked up. "That Nibmar, she's positively dreadful."

"She's not so bad," Nafta said.

"Oh for goodness sake, Nafta, did you hear what she said to me? 'Are you honest, subtle and submissive?'"

Nafta laughed. "That was nothing. Better than what she told me on my first day: 'Cultivate a mysterious aura of magical possibility about you.'"

Sasha laughed. "What does that mean?"

"Learn to wiggle your ass."

Sasha inhaled the fragrance of the flowers. She smelled the scents of cooking, of Arabian spices curling into the air as well. She exhaled and rested her head back on the lounge, closing her eyes.

Nafta pulled Sasha's robe up over her. "I'm serious about this sun. It doesn't sneak up on you. It overwhelms you."

"Thank you. And thank you for helping me last night."

"Don't mention it," Nafta said. She paused and there she was, tightening her lips like last night, as if tense. Sasha resolved to find out why. "How are you getting along?" Nafta asked before Sasha could probe her.

Sasha shrugged. "The girls I've seen today have been icy."

"Know why?"

"Only what you told me about them being catty. Makes sense if I'm the new girl."

"Wrong. You're a sensation around here. And they all knew about last night."

"Oh?" Sasha raised her eyebrows. *What on earth...?*

"The reactions of the other girls shouldn't surprise you. You came heralded."

Sasha frowned. "Heralded?"

"You were selected by Yassar himself. No small distinction. That already placed you high in the hierarchy around here." She leaned to within a foot of Sasha's face, her expression serious. "Do you know what an insult Ibrahim's behavior was to me last night?"

"No." *Whatever are you talking about?*

Nafta looked from side to side as if what she were going to say was confidential. "It was Friday night last night."

Sasha looked back at her blankly.

"Even though the men are fairly egalitarian in revolving their 'couchings' with their women, Friday nights are reserved for all the first wives. The favorites. The Koran said, 'If one wife does not suffice, take four.'" She added as an aside, "Although there's no limit on concubines. And if they're not married, Fridays are for the favorites in general. Ibrahim knows that better than anyone else. I'm the favorite. Yet he told me he wanted you." She lowered her eyes and played with one of her bracelets.

Sasha didn't respond. *So that would account for why you looked so tense. You were hurt? What a strange culture, what a strange creature you are, Nafta.* Sasha clasped her hand. Nafta reached forward and hugged her, kissed her on the cheek. "Be nice to me, sister, when you assume your role."

CHAPTER 14

OCTOBER, TWENTY-THREE YEARS AGO. RIYADH, *Saudi Arabia.*
Sasha felt her excitement as she knocked softly on the door to
Yassar's study. She didn't want to be late. *Today's the day.* Her
quick adaptation to the culture—she'd decided it was because
she'd been raised to "want to experience everything"—had left
her curiously without anger toward Yassar. But there was a distance between them: he'd betrayed her. How else could she look
at it? But she didn't want that distance and was determined for it
not to be so. Here, as before in Switzerland, she wanted her hours
with Yassar to be bright moments.

A young servant girl opened the door and nodded. Yassar
looked up from a comfortable sofa on one side of the room. The
study was eclectically furnished with carefully selected antiques
from other cultures and eras—French provincial end tables, a
Beidermeier kas, fifth dynasty Chinese vases—mixed with more
traditional Middle Eastern and Saudi low-slung tables, Persian
rugs and tapestried settees. She'd remarked to herself on her first
visit to Yassar's room that it was the tasteful model on which
Ibrahim's decorators had received their instructions in creating
his garishly overdone anteroom. "Hello, Sasha. Please come in."

"Hello, Yassar," she said and sat in the stuffed chair next to
him. She smelled tea steeping on the end table.

"How are your classes in Saudi history and Arabic going?"

"Tolerably well and only fair," she said in awkward Arabic. "Not bad."

Yassar's raised eyebrows warmed Sasha, the way she'd felt about him when he was a houseguest at Christina's chateau.

"And as of today, I'm taking over your classes in Islam. I understand you're an enthusiastic student. You know how important it is to all of us here, including Ibrahim." Yassar reached for the tea, but Sasha stopped him and served them both. He asked, "How are you getting along with Ibrahim?"

"Quite well," she said, lowering her eyes. She felt embarrassed at the thought of enjoying the sex, wondering, if like a new toy she'd tire of it, not for a moment deluding herself she was in love with Ibrahim. Yet she acknowledged a grudging fondness for him. Thank God for that. How would she deal with it otherwise? She suppressed the sudden urge to giggle. *There are some things a young girl isn't supposed to disclose to her lover's father.* Then: *Except maybe here?* She let the thought drop and reflected on one of the Koran's teachings Yassar would probably not be asking for her interpretation of during studies: "A Muslim man must not satisfy his need of her until he has satisfied her need of him." She smiled to herself. *And Ibrahim is a good Muslim man.*

"Excellent," he said. "Now to the teachings. Following them will be very important for him, if he's to become a leader of the Saudi people. And therefore it will be important for you, as well, to understand and live by the ways that will keep him on his path."

"I understand." She wondered if Yassar had any idea what Ibrahim did with his time.

"You've been here long enough to observe some of the issues we need to deal with, what we need to do to help our people. I have great hopes that Ibrahim will one day be a committed and educated leader, with a strong base in our Islamic ways."

You may be the only one who believes he can fulfill those expectations. I've never heard him express your level of commitment to those issues, or to his being a leader. She exhaled silently. Ibrahim could be fun, even sweet, but she was beginning to find it odd that Yassar expected so much from him and seemed so out of touch with what Ibrahim did with his life.

"You must have more than a basic grounding in Islam so that you can be responsive to Ibrahim's religious practices and restrictions. So now, before we begin our lesson, we must prepare our hearts by consciously thinking about Allah and seeking refuge from Satan." Sasha slid out of her chair and sat, her legs crossed in front of her on the floor. Yassar joined her, placed the special stand, the *kursi*, in front of him, and rested his Koran on it. "Reading with heart, soul and mind and strength is known as *Tilawah*, and the practice of correct pronunciation is called *Tajwid*. Learning to recite the verses without understanding them is insufficient. As you progress in your studies, you must also discover the meanings of the scriptures and see how the messages apply to you and how they should alter our lives."

He picked up the Koran and its kursi and placed it in front of Sasha. She opened the book to the page he had marked and began to read in halting Arabic:

"'We shall certainly test you with fear and hunger and with the loss of goods or lives or the fruits of your toil. But give encouragement to those who patiently persevere, and, when calamity befalls them say: We belong to Allah, and to Him do we return.'"

She wondered if he'd chosen the selection to address her sense of being stripped of everything, including her dignity and privacy, when she'd been brought here. She doubted she would

171

ever derive the comfort from their Koran she did from the peace she felt during her prayers to the statue of Ganesha—her Remover of Obstacles—on the improvised puja she frequently made out of her night table, even knowing the practice of any religion but Islam here was illegal.

"Life is a test for the life to come," Yassar explained the passage. "Some are tested with poverty—will they become dishonest or lose faith? Some are tested with wealth—will they become selfish or will they act with responsibility?"

Some are tested with betrayal. Will they become embittered or continue to believe in love?

An hour later they finished the lesson. Sasha wrapped the Koran in its special cloth, then placed it above their heads on its shelf in the west corner of the room. She returned to her place in front of her chair, waiting for Yassar to sit before rising from the floor and sitting in her chair. In the dim light she forgot where she was, simply happy to be with Yassar.

Now, she thought. *Subtly. Obliquely.* She was aware of his stature in his world, now knowing their culture, and the gravity of what she would ask of him, a man in his position—any man at all—but she was determined to get his apology. It was the only way she felt she could recapture something of the closeness she'd once felt with him, even if only to satisfy herself she hadn't been self-deluded in believing he'd once reciprocated her feelings. He must have. In that moment she realized she needed even more than that: she needed to see his respect for her again, and now felt the flutter of nerves in her stomach at the fear Yassar might thrust her aside. *No.*

"Yassar," she said. She kept her eyes lowered to make it easier for him. "Change is sometimes a shock." She sat perfectly still. "And this change in my life was particularly large and unexpected." *All right, Yassar, I've opened the subject. You know what I'm talking about.* "I would hate to think that either of our actions as my transition occurred would stand in the way of the relationship we once had." *Too vague. He only knows me as one who speaks directly.* She felt the flutter in her stomach again. "Why did you do this to me?"

Yassar didn't look at her. "Do? This is an opportunity."

"Perhaps for one who has no other opportunities." She turned that over in her mind for a moment, glad she'd let it roll out spontaneously, wondering what she'd say next if he didn't respond. She waited. She still didn't look at him. "What kind of life is this?" she asked finally.

"In the old days a concubine could in time become a wife. We can have many, as you by now know."

"And you have many such wives yourself?" She thought for a moment it was too forceful, then decided she didn't care. She let him sit with the question hanging out, deciding she wasn't going to let him off by answering her own question or continuing without a response again. She waited.

"I remind you that you came on your own volition."

"Did I?" *Really, Yassar.* "I had precious few alternatives. Christina was wiped out. You seem to have known that better than I. One might argue you swooped in and plucked me for a song." A long silence. *That's okay. Let that one hang around your neck for a few minutes.* She waited, still not looking up at him, and ultimately deciding it was time for her to zero in on her point. "I'd like an apology. And an explanation." Yassar didn't respond. Sasha waited.

A long minute later she heard the rustle of his robe as he stirred in his chair. "Perhaps I didn't handle things as I might have," he said. "I want the best for my son, and I know he needs settling down if he is to be groomed for his role in one day running Saudi Arabia. I confess I was conflicted between that and my affection for you. In a way, Ibrahim is my biggest weakness. One day when you have children you will understand. If I was insensitive to your feelings I regret it."

That was as close to an apology as Sasha thought she would get. *Still Yassar.* She felt a release, a calmness—almost a sensation of her chest being stroked. But she wanted an explanation. Now her feelings were rising, she felt her throat thickening, and she stopped thinking and let her emotions speak to him. "You were the kindest man I knew—until that day you made your proposal to Christina—and me."

"Perhaps you will think well of me again one day."

"I'd like an explanation. Why bring me here? What do you want from me?" She'd pondered those questions for the weeks since arriving, hoping there was more to it than simply being a piece of flesh for his son. Now she felt anticipation, eager to hear if he'd answer at all, now afraid he might.

"Your experience of the world with Christina prepared you for this," Yassar said. Sasha couldn't decide if he was answering her question, justifying himself, or still apologizing. "Your experience in most ways surpasses that of Ibrahim's."

This was taking an eternity, she decided, then resisted the urge to spur him along. *In his own time.*

"As such I thought you could help guide him, keep him out of trouble. And stand up to him, or deal with him with a cleverness the other girls couldn't. Undoubtedly you've observed…well…" He trailed off. "Sometimes a father cannot interfere directly with any productive result."

So he knows Ibrahim doesn't spend his time studying the Koran. And the cocaine, too? She itched to meet his gaze, read what was in his eyes. She resisted. "Go on," she whispered. "And how exactly does this involve me?"

"I long ago observed that despite your own lack of fear of the world and your fascination to try everything, you do have an ethical rudder, even if I am not always sure in what direction it is pointed. I need you to be Ibrahim's gyroscope, to straighten him out. Maybe get him interested in something."

"Why should I do that?" Her head shot up. *Oh dear, forgot myself.* She lowered her head again. "I mean, how...how should I go about that?"

"No, you mean why. For me. And my gratitude would be expressed in tangible ways. You would be rewarded financially beyond the generous stipend you are already receiving. And I would help you readapt to another life afterward. Do not underestimate the power of our influence. Or wealth."

Sasha's mind was now a tangle. The old fondness for Yassar, wanting to please him, warred with an anger and hurt that she could now let herself feel after forcing them away these weeks to keep her sanity, in her refusal to let her situation overwhelm her. She slowly raised her head, her jaw tense, eyes expectant. She met his gaze.

"Please," Yassar said. She saw the emotion in his eyes. They pleaded to her, not at all the eyes of one of the most wealthy and powerful men in the world. The eyes of a father, of her mentor, now telling her he was sorry, but asking more.

Sasha nodded, but she'd already told him with the tears in her eyes that she'd do what he asked.

———◇———

October, Twenty-Three Years Ago. Riyadh, Saudi Arabia. Sasha sipped her glass of burgundy, rested it on the end table and slid out of bed, carefully so as not to disturb Ibrahim's afternoon nap. She turned up the thermostat and opened the window to the courtyard. *I swear I spend twenty-three hours a day around here with goosebumps.* She slid back into bed and glanced at Ibrahim. It was extraordinary, the man got up, ate, had sex, ran off someplace, ate some more, drank, had sex, napped then got up and did it all over again. He still kept a few of his scheduled classes and meetings—a few—occasionally even sitting in on the Council of Ministers beside his father.

She looked at the clock. *One twenty-two.* She'd wake him in ten minutes so he could get to his two o'clock religion class. No early-afternoon prayers for him today unless he'd been thinking of Allah a half hour earlier in those last thrusts of his hips before he'd collapsed into sleep. She picked up her wine glass, reflected on how Ibrahim pulled rank to secure it for her this early in the day, admired the ruby color of the burgundy and complimented herself for overseeing the establishment of a decent cellar in the palace. *All this money and nobody knew what Domaine de la Romanee-Conti was.* Sasha sipped her wine and considered how she would segue back into the discussion she'd started with him earlier. Ibrahim was as adept at dodging subjects as she was determined.

Ibrahim stirred, inhaled as if someone had let the air out of him earlier and forgotten to reopen the valve. He blinked.

Always looks like some innocent child when he wakes up. It made her smile. She stroked his hair.

"You amaze me," he said. "Just when I find myself thinking I liked you better when you didn't know what you were doing, you do something totally outrageous." He laughed and rested his head back on the pillow. "I think my spine is out of joint."

"Are you trying to flatter me?"

"Begging for mercy."

"It's almost one thirty. You should think about getting ready for your class." He didn't respond. "And then afterward your father would want you to join him at the Finance Ministry for the meeting with the American bankers."

"That again. I can tell when Miss Sasha has an agenda. You woke up with that on your lips this morning."

This would be easier if he weren't so perceptive. Or resistant. She recalled her meeting with Yassar, how he had implored her. But how was she supposed to get Ibrahim interested in something if Yassar couldn't do it himself? Very little of what Ibrahim liked to do involved using his brains. She'd just have to try. "Your father has great hopes for you. He talks about it all the time, even when I visit with him for my religion classes." He didn't respond. "You know that's why he's tutoring me, don't you? So I can better understand your practices, know how you're supposed to live."

"He's known you a long time. I'm only beginning to understand why he regards you so highly." He stroked Sasha's thigh. "And he knows his teachings well. The Koran is full of instructions on teaching by example. So Father brings me someone who's smarter than me and more interested in life, everything. And beautiful." She met his gaze. There was tenderness in his eyes she hadn't seen before. Her heart warmed, enjoying the spontaneity of his compliments. They made her feel close to him, then guilty for pushing her agenda. Still, acceding to Yassar's wishes, nudging Ibrahim in the direction of something did no harm. She remembered Yassar's words: be his gyroscope. A worthy enough cause.

"You're sweet." She stroked his forehead. "And it isn't just for your father, I'd like to see you succeed at something myself. You have so much potential." *Oh my goodness.* Her words came from her heart, surprising her.

Ibrahim kissed her hand. Then he stood up and walked to the window to open it. "You still cold? I'm roasting."

Sasha nodded.

"Next time I'm in Paris remind me to buy you some sweaters. And okay, I'll go to the Ministry with my father after my class." He walked into the bathroom.

A minor victory, but a victory.

Fifteen minutes later he reappeared, drying himself. He walked to the bureau and began arranging two lines of cocaine.

"Ibrahim!" Sasha called. "I can't believe you're doing that before your religion class! And then you're going to the Ministry with your father! What on earth are you thinking?"

Ibrahim glared at her, then turned back and began snorting the lines.

"Ibrahim! How can you be so disrespectful to your father?"

"I don't need you to tell me how to deal with my father!"

"I obviously do if you're behaving that way!"

He took two steps forward toward her, his mouth contorted. "Leave it! Don't push your luck!"

Sasha leapt up from the bed, her hair flying, and strode into the bathroom. *Stubborn oaf.* She mocked herself for her warmth toward him moments earlier and ran into the shower, feeling suddenly unclean, needing to wash his scent from her.

She'd calmed herself by the time she emerged from the bathroom. When she walked back into the bedroom, Ibrahim seemed equally willing to make up, observing her with a smile as he finished dressing. "Feeling better now?" he asked.

She noted his condescension in implying she was the one who'd lost control. "And you?"

He smiled at her. "Come here," he said. She didn't move. "Come on, now." She walked over to him and he drew her to him and kissed her deeply on the mouth. He started to pull her towel off, and she stopped him.

"Not now," she said. "You upset me."

"I'm sorry. But you needn't be my policeman."

"I'm just concerned about you. You're using more of that stuff, and more frequently."

"I'm alright," he said.

She wasn't convinced. "It isn't good for you, and you know it." She looked into his eyes. "You're smarter than that. It just saps all your ambition. Maybe if you stopped it for a while you could decide for yourself if you're alright."

He nodded, then kissed her again. "Thank you," he said. She looked at his pupils as he turned to go. They were dilated. She regretted that Yassar would see it, that is if Ibrahim showed up at the Finance Ministry at all. Through her frustration she admitted she was concerned about her lover. What did she need to do to convince him of that?

Sasha wore a formal gown for the party that night. She wasn't feeling lazy or apathetic, just calm, secure, with a sense of ownership of the palace. It was odd, but she allowed herself to experience it, thinking perhaps it had something to do with Ibrahim's recent attentiveness to her, despite his sharp words to her that afternoon. And she was beginning to think he would get himself more involved with his father's work. Who knew? He might even take an interest in the politics.

Sasha followed the music in the hallway to the ballroom, her sandaled feet padding on the marble floor. Two of the ubiquitous uniformed Royal Guards stood at attention at either side of the double doors, accompanied by one of the bellgirls in her white-and-gold-braided uniform.

"Miss Sasha." The bellgirl opened the door for her.

Brilliant light, a wall of sound, the fragrance of flowers and perfume, and elegance. The ballroom was eighty feet across, circular, and it rose up into one of the palace's onion-shaped domes at least sixty feet to a twenty-two-karat gold ceiling. Crystal chandeliers hung from the dome and encircled the walls. Every woman in the room was dressed as if for a formal ball. Chanel, Yves St. Laurent, Prada and Halsten formal evening gowns were everywhere. Gleaming gold, glittering strands of jewels, even a few diamond tiaras adorned heads that must have taken hours to coif. It was all like a grand stage set and the women were performing a costume drama.

Sasha located Ibrahim from across the room and watched him for a few minutes. It didn't take long to see that the men around him were his flunkies. He stood up and walked left, they followed; he stopped, they all froze. He gestured, and one of them scurried off. A glance said: "Get me a scotch," and a glass appeared, cradled in a supernumerary's hands. A sideways head movement: a girl was swept off someplace. *Had she offended him?* Then he moved off to one side, like Lord Byron, making himself available to be adulated.

Sasha walked up to him.

"Hello princess," he said.

"Hello, prince."

"Care to sit down?"

"Care to dance?" She extended her arm to him. "This one's a little fast for you isn't it?" He took her arm and led her out onto the floor, where perhaps half a dozen other couples were already dancing.

"We'll see." As he and Sasha entered the floor, the band slowed the tempo of its song, lost pace with each other for a few beats, then synchronized themselves in a slow waltz. The other girls moved off the floor and Ibrahim spun Sasha in confident steps, smiling and admiring her.

"How did it go at the ministry today?"

"You'll be pleased to know I actually found it interesting."

There. That wasn't so hard to say, now was it? A victory, but she lowered her eyes so he wouldn't see her satisfaction. No sense in lording it over him.

"Go ahead, you can say it."

She looked up and met his gaze. "I told you so." He smiled that special smile, the one just for her. How long had it been? She'd never been able to doubt him, think ill of him when he looked at her that way. She rested her head on his shoulder, aware that many of the other girls were observing them. She didn't care. *The new favorite.*

"Why don't we get out of here?" she asked.

"What's your hurry, the party's just started."

"That's not what I mean. I mean take me someplace." She looked at him earnestly, searching his eyes. "Take me someplace—romantic."

"All right," he said. "In a few weeks. Father's asked me to follow up with the bankers, so I'm going to New York for a few days. Strictly business, but I'll make some reservations for when I get back. I'll surprise you." She rested her head on his shoulder again. *You're surprising me now.*

CHAPTER 15

January, Twenty-Two Years Ago. Riyadh, Saudi Arabia. Wow, is he high, Sasha thought. She pulled the silk robe tightly around her as if to protect herself from the unexpected—which she had recently come to expect from Ibrahim—and lay back on one of the sofas in the anteroom of his suite. She heard him through the open doorway into his living room, chuckling and sniffing. *This has to stop, or at least slow down.* Ibrahim burst through the door, gesturing as if speaking to someone. His eyes were red and he rubbed his nose.

It was beginning to make her feel estranged; not him, the cocaine. He was good to her when he wanted to be. She believed he cared for her. And weren't there moments when she felt truly close to him? When he did little considerate things for her. Leaving the window open so she wouldn't freeze from the air-conditioning. Her Earl Grey tea. Learning which her favorite burgundies were and having a glass of Pierre Bouree Clos de La Justice ready for her when she arrived, even though he never touched wine himself. But the drugs. Like tonight. Sometimes it was more like being with the cocaine than with Ibrahim. And she wanted Ibrahim tonight, for a rare quiet evening, to be close to him.

Sasha sat up. "Why don't we stay in tonight?" she asked. He flopped down next to her, fidgeting.

"I don't want to. I hired the band Chicago. Tonight's the first of their three nights, and I want to be there. Besides, I *need* to be there."

Why couldn't he let go of being the center of attention? "Let Prince Abdul be the master of ceremonies." She stroked his forehead. "He'd love to do it, I'm sure."

He took her hand in his, kissed it and let it fall to the sofa. "He'd love to all right. Pretend it was his idea, too." He glanced back and forth. "Besides, I want to hear them."

He's too far gone. Yassar will find out for sure. I need to do something. That was the other problem. She didn't need to be reminded that Yassar was relying on her to keep Ibrahim out of trouble. She felt a wave of guilt. Not a comfortable sensation, nor one she was accustomed to. "I want you to myself tonight." Sasha lounged onto the pillows and allowed the robe to part slightly.

"You have a strange sense of timing," he smiled. He pulled out his silver case, laid it on the table and opened it.

"Why are you doing that?" *Please, Ibrahim. Just be with me tonight. I need some quiet time.*

"Why not? It's none of your concern."

"I'm worried about you." She sat up, slid next to him, placed her hands on top of his and gently closed the silver case. He paused, gave in to her, stroked her hair, gently brushed it away from her face.

"Remember what your father dreams for you," she said. Here she was making arguments about his father. Why wasn't she simply appealing to him from her heart? That's where she needed him tonight. Didn't have the nerve? The girl with no fear? She felt any chance to get through to him slipping away.

He said, "I know. I'm the future of Saudi Arabia." He looked away. Sasha reached up and rubbed the back of his neck.

"Sometimes I think you're closer to my father than I am," he said. She felt her own neck stiffen. "I can't do it," he said, glancing away. "Not like he wants me to."

She leaned against him. "Have you talked to him? I can perhaps introduce the subject…he listens to me…"

"Listens to you!" He yanked himself away. She tried to reach for him again. He shouted in a sudden rage, "Don't! Just don't… He's my father! Do you know how preposterous it is at times? The things he wants for me to do?" He raised his hand. Sasha thought he was about to strike her. Instead he slumped in his seat. "I never asked for any of that."

Sasha massaged his shoulders. He continued, as if in defeat. "You don't understand any better than he does. The fact is, I just don't care that much. At least not as much as him. Or possibly even as much as you." He stood up, stumbling into the coffee table. "We're going to the party."

Sasha had lost all interest in his affections tonight. But she wasn't about to endure explaining to Yassar why everybody was whispering about Ibrahim. She stood up and spoke to him calmly. "Look. Like I said. I want to be alone tonight. With you, that is." She heard it herself; the emotion was gone from her voice. This was business now. She stepped back and let her robe fall off her shoulders to the floor.

She wore the diamond necklace he had given her two days earlier, fifteen karats on the strand with a ten-karat stone hanging from the center, and a matching ensemble of ear clips, each dangling with five karats of stones. The diamonds and a white G-string and open-toed high heels. She stepped back a few more paces, cocked her head to the side and smirked. Then she reached down beneath the pillows of the sofa and pulled out two mittens made of beaver fur. That would get him interested. "And I brought these." She turned and walked through the door, knowing he'd follow. *Only problem is, after all that cocaine even I won't be able to keep him happy. He'll probably want me to call in Nafta.* Her heart felt numb.

February, Twenty-Two Years Ago. Riyadh, Saudi Arabia. The din of the open market rose in a crescendo as Sasha approached its entrance. She walked confidently wearing a black abaya, her hair covered by a cotton scarf, her face hidden behind a hijav veil, chest thrust forward and back straight. She was slightly ahead of the rest of her party. Nafta and two Royal Palace Guards followed. She saw a Mutawwa'iin eyeing her from 30 feet away. She raised her chin higher as he stepped forward and blocked her path. Sasha stopped in front of him, glaring. Just as he prepared to speak, Nafta eased Sasha to the side, escorting her into the entrance to the outdoor market.

"You're a small wonder," Nafta grinned. "Not a picture of the restrained Saudi woman."

"I'm not?" Sasha asked innocently. Nafta giggled.

They stayed for forty-five minutes, sampling spices, pausing to negotiate with vendors selling jewelry and clothing, frequently abandoning the sport even before discovering how low they could badger the salesman down. "I agree. Ibrahim's very bright, but not very motivated," Nafta said, looking disinterestedly at a table full of shoes.

He's heading for a major collision with his father's image of him, Sasha thought.

Nafta continued. "And he has a temper, if you haven't seen it already, so you'll have to be careful. We wouldn't want anything to happen to you"—she paused for emphasis—"like shipping you out."

They walked in silence for a few minutes. "At least it's not a hard life, only monotonous at times," Sasha said. "And claustrophobic."

"It gets better, believe me. He takes one of the other girls skiing. I've never gone. Can't get my legs to turn that way." She smirked lewdly. "Ask him to take you again. Where did you go?"

Sasha felt warmed as she recalled her week with Ibrahim in December. "Aspen. It was wonderful. But I haven't seen him open up to me like that since." Sasha sensed surprise in the way Nafta glanced sideways at her. Jealousy? Concern?

They left the market and headed back toward the palace.

"You have to admit the work's not hard," Nafta said later after a long silence.

"No, but there's certainly a lot of it."

"He still treats you well, I assume?"

"Yes. Now he even turns the air-conditioning down for me. I froze to death the first few months."

Sasha reflected on Ibrahim's little kindnesses, sensed her longing to be close to him in a way she wasn't. Was it possible? She could get glimpses of it when he was in his more serious moments. When he revealed his intelligence and perspective as he opened up to her, for example, about Yassar's work. Yassar had said sometimes concubines became wives. *You're forcing it, now.* She laughed at herself for her adolescent fantasy gone wild. Yet it brought to her the longings she felt for a lover. She deserved it. After all, she was a woman now, fully experienced—except in matters of the heart. Sasha took Nafta's arm and pulled her close. Nafta wouldn't laugh at her dreams. They walked on that way, clutching each other like sisters.

"Lonely?" Nafta asked after a while.

"Empty. I miss people. And I can't help but ask myself, 'Is this all you're going to do with your life?' I used to believe in love as something everyone would find. Now I'm not so sure, and it's left me a bit lost." They continued on, their arms still hooked. "I'd like something to believe in again."

"The secret is to keep busy. Jammed full. So you don't think about it. Then it's fine."

"I'm used to that." Sasha looked down at the ground. "I guess I've been doing that for a long time."

Nafta brightened. "The season on the French Riviera starts soon," she said. "Things will pick up. Ibrahim gets a break from his schooling and Yassar keeps him on a longer leash."

"Yes," Sasha said, feeling her emotions flowing again. "Ibrahim's taking me to Paris in a few weeks."

"Be careful, sister," Nafta said. "Remember, I've been at this longer than you. Don't let your imagination—or your heart—get carried away into believing you've found something just because you're yearning for it. Don't hurt yourself."

Sasha squeezed her arm, thanking her without words. It was good advice.

March, Twenty-Two Years Ago. Paris, France. Sasha always felt like a princess when she descended the stairway of one of the royal family's Lear jets wearing anything other than a black abaya. Today she wore an ankle-length, midnight-blue cashmere coat, sable hat, and maroon gloves against the late-winter cold in Paris. What she liked most wasn't so much allowing herself that indulgent moment of vanity, but that Ibrahim played into it. "Lovely," he said, dark eyes fixed on her, his hand out to take hers as she alighted from the last step, himself dressed in tan cashmere highlighted by a bold blue-and-gold silk scarf Sasha had given him for the trip. For a moment the two of them stood there looking at each other in a different way than before. Like honeymooners.

When they got into the limo, Sasha wondered how long it would take for Ibrahim to start groveling in his silver case for his coke, which had been absent the entire ten hours from Saudi Arabia. *Relax,* she told herself. *Enjoy the trip.* She had Ibrahim to herself for a week, and she'd explore those possibilities she saw for them. *A week.* And in Paris, no less.

She slid her arm through his and held him close until she could smell the scent of his coat and his cologne. He said, "How about a cruise through town before we go to the hotel?"

"Great," she said. At 9:00 p.m. the lights of Paris would set the mood. Was he feeling romantic, too?

Ibrahim spoke to the driver. They entered Paris through Montparnasse, drove up past the Eiffel Tower, then crossed the Seine. Cruising past des Invalides, Sasha turned to Ibrahim. "Thank you for bringing me," she said. She kissed him. "I needed some time. Quiet time, away."

"Yes. It's nice to get away," he said.

She felt a sag of disappointment. Was she hoping for too much or reading too much into what he said? Or didn't say? *Stop being a schoolgirl.* "How much time will you be spending on your business?"

"I have meetings with the bankers on the agricultural loan program all day tomorrow, then Tuesday, then depending how it goes maybe another day. Probably a dinner or two."

"Sounds like I'll need to amuse myself part of the time," Sasha said. She allowed disappointment to show in her tone. Ibrahim stared at her as if perplexed, then looked out the window with a haughty indifference. It made her feel lonely.

Sasha thought about what she could do on her own in Paris. All the people she knew. The last time she was here was eight months earlier, only weeks before Yassar had come to the Countess' in Switzerland with his proposal. In that moment she played a few of the reunion conversations in her head. So you're well. And Christina? Smoking up her million-dollar fee. And so what have *you* been up to? Oh, just laying on my back around the Saudi Royal Palace. And what's it like? Better than a slap in the face with a cold fish.

No, not an option. What did it matter? She'd never been ashamed of herself in her life. Why start now? If the people she knew couldn't deal with it, that was their problem. *Move on and see what comes next.* Besides, what she was doing was no more mercenary than many of the marriages and less holy liaisons she'd witnessed growing up in Christina's revolving circle of barons, socialites, pretenders and snobs. Trophy wife. Concubine. What's the difference?

Sasha admired the familiar polished marble and brass in the lobby of Le Bristol Hotel as Ibrahim checked in. It would be a good trip, she thought. She felt somehow home again. Not so much at Le Bristol, although she'd been staying there on and off as long as she could remember, but Paris. She saw Renee, one of the frosty concierges who'd been melting into smiles ever since she was a preteen running up to him, pestering him about what she'd had for breakfast or where did the room service carts go at night? Now she wished she could run up to him and hug him like that again, and the thought made her feel distant from the world she'd left behind.

In the suite, Sasha unpacked her bag, humming an Indian melody. She realized how tired she was. Yet as she unpacked her negligee she felt a surge of energy, sensing her desire for Ibrahim. So far he'd been the companion she'd hoped for. Sober, dignified and authoritative, even if hard to figure. A bit of mystery was okay. Sexy. She heard him on the phone in the living room of the suite, speaking in French. He gave someone their room number and hung up.

"Ordering room service?" she asked.

"No. A little business."

Sasha's stomach wrenched. What was this all about? The way he said it implied he didn't want any discussion. She stopped unpacking and turned to him, wondering how to raise a question without him exploding, seeing him hurry past her again toward the living room. "Anything I can help with?" she asked jauntily, botching it, realizing trying to sound cheery and off-hand wasn't her forte.

"No. I'm fine," he crooned back, showing her how to do it, but adding a bit too heavy a dollop of patronizing dressing for Sasha's taste. Now her antennae were up.

Is he buying drugs?

She heard a knock on the door and walked to the doorway of the bedroom to see two men enter the suite. She observed them sourly. The one who looked like a hollow-cheeked dealer looked away from her guiltily. She felt a swell of outrage, realizing she'd never seen one of Ibrahim's transactions. Never wondered how he got the stuff.

Most of the exchange occurred out of her view in front of Ibrahim, who rounded his shoulders, as if he felt Sasha's eyes singeing his back. She saw a wad of bills come out of his pocket and it was over.

Then it wasn't over, something odd happening, the other man, taller and burly, pulling something shiny—handcuffs!—out of his pocket and slapping them onto Ibrahim's wrists, declaring in guttural Parisian French: "I pronounce you under arrest," with melodramatic aplomb.

"What are you doing?" Sasha demanded, knowing precisely what they were doing, arresting Ibrahim, but trying to defuse the drama. "Don't you know that man is a member of the Saudi royal family? He has diplomatic immunity!"

She saw Ibrahim turn to her with calm in his eyes, as if what she said made perfect sense.

"Stand your distance. Or we take you too," the smaller man said, reaching for the door handle. The burly one started ushering Ibrahim toward the door.

Sasha felt anxiety wash over her. She grabbed her purse as they had Ibrahim halfway out the door. "I'm coming with him!" she said. Why in God's name was Ibrahim so calm, she wondered. Who could she call if they actually hauled him in?

"Not unless you want to get arrested too!" the little man shouted from out of sight. Sasha raced down the three flights of stairs, watching the three men ride down in the glass-walled elevator to the lobby, wondering where they were taking Ibrahim. It was an obvious setup. She felt her heart slapping against her rib cage and wondered what they did to drug offenders—God it sounded like something from American television—in France, then *Oh my God,* what about Saudi Arabia where taking drugs was against their religion as well as the law. She arrived in the lobby just after them and followed them out the door, avoiding the stares of the hotel staff. She regretted leaving her coat behind as she entered the cold night air, leapt into a cab and actually said the words, "Follow that car," as the police cruiser pulled away from the curb.

The police car took Ibrahim into an alley behind a police station in the second Arrondisement. Sasha was obliged to enter the front door after a gendarme blocked the taxi from the alley.

The inside of the police station was stark, fluorescent lights, glossy yellowish paint over bare-walled concrete. Gray-painted concrete floor. She endured the next hours in purgatory, twisting in her mind what Yassar would think, what he would do, and how she would tell him. And what was Ibrahim involved in? Was it simply a setup bust over drugs or had Ibrahim been targeted in some way to embarrass the Saudis? She couldn't imagine how she was going to get him out of here, let alone deal with whatever the consequences would be.

She asked to see Ibrahim. No. Again. Not yet. What to do? She forced herself to think clearly. She knew a judge, a friend of Christina's, but what was his name? Then Yassar's face came to her, his mournful eyes chastising her, then enraged. How would she explain to him?

Three hours now. She asked to see Ibrahim again. Later. Now she was seized by concern for Ibrahim, how he must be feeling. She felt her strength draining out of her through a vacuum in her stomach, next the consuming need to hold him. She wanted to tell him how much she cared for him, how much she...what? Was she in love with him? What a time, what a place to wrestle with that one. Leave it until later, when she could focus, and her head didn't hurt so. Her mind kept going anyhow. And how did Ibrahim really feel about her? He'd never said it to her, that he loved her. Wanted her yes, but...?

"Mademoiselle Del Mira," the paunchy sergeant finally barked from behind his desk. Sasha approached. He motioned with his head toward the door where a young officer stood. "Ten minutes only." Sasha walked to the doorway, her mouth dry.

"You will need to be searched," the officer said, eyeing her handbag, then her body.

She just looked at him. "That will hardly be necessary," she said. The man nodded and led her down the hall to a room before stepping aside so she could enter. Three chairs and a desk. A glass wall, the classic two-way mirror. A rumpled newspaper on the floor in the corner. And Ibrahim standing, looking at her calmly, his calm making her more upset, because she felt her pulse oddly thumping in her heels. "What do we do?" she said. "We can't let them arrest you."

Ibrahim smiled. "It would seem they already have."

"How can they? Don't you have diplomatic immunity?"

He laughed. "Now you seem to think there's some question about it. Back in the hotel you were very convincing. Barking at them like my lawyer."

Sasha was pacing now, imagining the hollow-cheeked, wormy little man who had entrapped Ibrahim now watching behind the two-way mirror. She knew they were recording their conversation, certainly listening at least. Ibrahim seemed to be turning something over in his mind. She positioned herself in front of him so they couldn't see her whisper into his face, hoping they couldn't hear either. "What about it? Diplomatic immunity?" She felt her chest rising and falling unevenly.

"It's drugs. I don't know," he said. She looked into his eyes and now saw that his placid expression was only a front. There was strain at the corner of his eyes, and his mouth was tense.

She felt her heart soften toward him. They'd get through this together.

"I'll call your father."

He shook his head. "That's a last resort. I think I'll try the Saudi Arabian consul first."

"You know him?" She looked at her watch. "It's two a.m."

"No. But he'll respond. He works for us. It's his job." Sasha sensed a muffled wail from someplace within her, perhaps the sound of a belief being shattered. She continued to look into his eyes. The concern in his face, the stress at the corners of his eyes, were gone, replaced by an arrogant look of entitlement. Sasha felt a tremor of despair.

Ten minutes later in the bright entrance hallway of the police station, Sasha stood erect, muscles tensed as if preparing to defend herself from a physical threat. She felt the same melancholy she'd sensed in the interrogation room with Ibrahim. Her mind replayed his words, "He works for us. It's his job," then she remembered Nafta's words: don't let your heart convince you it's found something just because you're yearning for it. Now she was feeling like she was trapped in a stalled elevator. *No. Worse.* Inside someone else's body, another life.

Her hopes for her and Ibrahim were ridiculous, she knew. He'd just told her by implication she was only an employee. But maybe he did love her and the drugs were just in the way. She could give it more time and see. She owed herself that much now that she'd brought the question out in the open for herself.

Oh, come off it. You heard him in there. He didn't love her. She was being a fool; she was his concubine, so this pubescent pining…for what?

Deal with this: Yassar. What's he going to do? Ship her back? To where? To what? *Remember your pact with yourself. Make enough money and get out.* She didn't have enough yet, just getting started. She'd go make peace with Yassar. But it wouldn't be easy. Tears came to her eyes. Disaster. The one person she didn't want to disappoint. She now realized the depth of her bond to Yassar. Was that why she tried with Ibrahim: for Yassar? Maybe. With nobody, nothing in her life, she could at least please Yassar. Now look where things stood.

Think later. Feel later. Now, concubine, get this fixed.

March, Twenty-Two Years Ago. Riyadh, Saudi Arabia. Sasha hurried across the courtyard to the stolid granite columns and facade of the Finance Ministry, trailing a long-legged Royal Guard behind her as if he were a Chihuahua on a leash scampering to keep up. She was uncomfortable in the noon sun in her black abaya, headscarf and hijav veil, jet-lagged from her flight, but thankful that her discomfort and exhaustion kept her from obsessing more than she already had on her impending conversation—confrontation?—with Yassar. She had left three urgent phone messages since leaving Paris. No response. She hoped it was only because his aide wouldn't give priority to some girl, probably knew she was a concubine at that, who struggled with broken Arabic. *Or worse,* she feared, *Yassar knows about Ibrahim in Paris and he's furious at me, too.* Even worse, he blamed her. "Be his gyroscope," she kept hearing Yassar's words in her mind. She quickened her pace.

Once in the waiting room, she glanced nervously at the Royal Guard who positioned himself by the doorway. She wasn't as uncomfortable as he was, and probably not as much as Yassar would be with her visiting him here at the Finance Ministry. No, wrong. Neither of them would experience the sensation she now felt of a vice clamping her head. This couldn't wait, but how on earth was she going to tell him? *Some gyroscope.*

A moment later Yassar came through the door, wearing his formal Saudi robe and headdress. The Royal Guard came to attention. "Yes, Sasha, what is it?" He carried the gravity of his business in his frown. She could see he didn't need this interruption, was annoyed at it. No matter. In 30 seconds she'd have more of his attention than she ever cared to experience. She forced herself through her fear, feeling adrenaline buzzing through her system.

"It's Ibrahim," she said. She glanced at the Royal Guard, as if to say she wasn't sure she could speak in front of him.

Yassar nodded at the guard and the man disappeared. Sasha felt a palpable increase in the tension in the room.

"What about him?"

No way to position it. Do it fast. "We've just come back from Paris."

"I know. And?"

She swallowed hard. "He was arrested. Then released, on diplomatic immunity." She looked away. "Possession of cocaine."

Yassar's back went stiff, then he slowly, deliberately sat down. "Is he all right?"

"Yes."

"When?"

"Yesterday. We just got back." *I'm sorry!* she wanted to shout.

"Did the newspapers find out?"

"No. But I'm not sure for how long."

"How did it happen?"

"We were in the hotel in Paris. He bought some cocaine. They set him up, the police. I...I'm sorry. They just took him away. We were at the police station for six hours. Ibrahim finally called the Saudi Arabian Consul. Got him out of bed. He came down and sorted it out."

"I'd better call the consul," Yassar said distractedly. She could see it was an automatic reaction.

"Yes, he was quite exercised." Her breathing was shallow. She wanted Yassar to get on with it. Explode. Whatever he was going to do.

"Anything else?" Yassar looked at her again. Sasha saw the concern replaced by disappointment. It rattled in her soul. She'd let him down, too. She felt as if something was oozing out of her heart.

"Only that he's not been in a good way in general lately." She saw the questions in his eyes. "I'm afraid he's not listening to me at this point."

Yassar simply nodded. "I'll take care of it," he said.

Oh, God, Yassar, I'm so sorry.

Ten minutes later Yassar rounded the last turn toward the entrance of Ibrahim's suite. He should have anticipated such things, should have taken drastic steps at the outset of Ibrahim's slide into this self-destructive lifestyle. First off, the arrest must be kept quiet. That consul's instincts were good. And he understood the looming penalty if he leaked the story. But the police might be another matter. A tabloid headline, *Wastrel Playboy*

Prince, formed in his head. His worst fear or his self-torment for his soft hand on the tiller? Either way he wasn't leaving here without a resolution.

The Royal Guard positioned outside Ibrahim's door moved to the side. Yassar turned the knob and went in without knocking. Ibrahim wasn't in the suite. He entered the bedroom, where he opened each bureau drawer, fishing underneath Ibrahim's underwear. He found the silver case, opened it, then dumped the contents onto the top of the bureau, walked back into the living room and sat down on the sofa. He checked his watch, opening and closing a meaty fist around the silver case. This would be dealt with. Today.

An hour later, Ibrahim arrived. Yassar didn't get up.

"Father," Ibrahim said. His gaze went to his father's hand, in which he still clutched the silver case. Stoic exterior intact, Yassar saw the recognition in Ibrahim's eyes. Ibrahim bowed his head, then looked around sheepishly as if to find support from one of the pieces of furniture. Seeing none, he sat seemingly against his will in the chair across from his father.

"I understand you are making quite a name for yourself. Most recently in Paris."

The air came out of Ibrahim's lungs in a whoosh.

"Did you think I wouldn't find out?"

"No. I'm only surprised it took this long."

"Do you have any idea what this could do to our kingdom?"

Ibrahim looked up at him. "Is that all you can think about!" He leaned forward in his chair. "What it will do to the kingdom?"

"That is always the first thing on my mind!"

"Why isn't that a surprise to me?"

"What in Allah's name is that supposed to mean?"

"Only that if you took more of an interest in matters other than your precious business perhaps we wouldn't be having this conversation!"

"Don't give me some trite nonsense about the neglected son. For a young man born with every advantage you seem to be convinced you're underprivileged. Most people born to your wealth and station would be out doing something constructive instead of siphoning their lives away through some ridiculous tube!" Yassar was yelling at him now, unconcerned about giving his rage free rein. He threw the silver case on the coffee table. "You've shamed us! You've shamed the entire kingdom, your family, your religion!" Ibrahim lowered his head and averted his eyes. "What have you got to say for yourself!" Yassar stood, shouting directly down at Ibrahim. "I said, what have you got to say for yourself!"

Sasha opened the door from her room to Ibrahim's suite. Her heart felt as if it would fly out of her throat. Oh God, Yassar's unleashing on him! She had to see if she could intervene, at least slow Yassar down. And Ibrahim, with his temper! She lowered her head and ran into his bedroom.

"Sasha, your presence is inappropriate. Leave us," Yassar said.

"Please, Yassar, I'm as much a part of this as anyone." She saw him hesitate, and she sat down next to Ibrahim, clasped his hands in hers, as if to say she was here now, she would help, do what it took to sort this out.

"She stays," Ibrahim said, emboldened by her presence. "What do you want from me?"

Don't overdo it, Sasha thought.

"You're going to straighten out."

Ibrahim opened his mouth to speak.

"No discussion," Yassar said. Sasha had never seen him look like this.

No one spoke for a half minute. Sasha saw the glazed look in Ibrahim's eyes. He was still high. She wanted to slap him.

"Perhaps we can go someplace," Sasha said to Ibrahim. "A few weeks, a few months, whatever it takes. One of those clinics." The prince didn't reply. He hung his head as if he were waiting for his father to leave so he could crawl out of his shame, then finally straightened himself in the chair. "I'll only go if Sasha comes with me."

Sasha looked at Yassar. "I'll take him."

Yassar walked to the doorway and paused with his hand on the doorknob. He looked back. "Our Secret Police will make the arrangements. The events of the last two days will never be repeated, or spoken about." He opened the door and walked out.

<hr/>

March, Twenty-Two Years Ago. Ford Clinic, California. No bars. Not even latticework. He could walk out of here any time he wants, Sasha thought, looking out the windows in Ibrahim's simple room. She heard him stir in the bed and turned to see him observing her, wide awake, lucid and eyes clear. "Feeling better?" she asked.

He nodded. "Physically." They sat in silence for a few minutes. "Has father called?"

"Yes. I told him you had a few rough days, but that now you're doing splendidly.

"And?"

"I think he's prepared to forgive you."

"Thank you for joining me here." A breakthrough. Particularly after he'd insisted he wouldn't come without her to attend to him. And God only knew what Yassar had to do to get them to bend the rules to allow her to stay with Ibrahim. "You don't know what it's like, to have a famous father to live up to," Ibrahim said. "Everyone admires him. Everyone. The leftists, the rightists. Foreign governments. Even the fundamentalists admit he's the only one inside the royal family they think they could deal with. He's a giant. How do you live up to that?"

His words tugged at her heart. They stirred her own feelings for Yassar, at the same time giving birth to new feelings for Ibrahim. Tenderness toward him welled in her, and even as she tried to savor it, she realized it was more sympathy than affection. With all his talents, all he was born to, he amounted to a spoiled adolescent afraid to live fully because he couldn't measure up to his father.

She stroked his head, as she would a child's, and he nodded off to sleep again.

CHAPTER 16

JUNE, TWENTY-ONE YEARS AGO. RIYADH, Saudi Arabia. It's okay, you can admit it to yourself. You like it here. Sasha hurried through the perimeter corridor in the Royal Palace toward Prince Yassar's study for her lesson in Islam, wearing her abaya and headscarf. The lesson was at a later hour than usual, after the second evening prayers, because Yassar wanted her to have prayed twice to purify herself before this session, which he said would be a ceremonial one. She didn't want to be late. Not just because she knew it was to be a special evening, but out of respect for Yassar.

She'd long ago noted that Yassar was rigorous in his adherence to the five-times-a-day prayers, that he made his annual pilgrimage to Mecca, and that he insisted that those who worked with him in his ministry do the same. He had shown her from the outset that the Muslim religion formed a part of the daily routine, the daily temperament and interactions with others, as distinct from other religions she had observed. Indeed, it was akin to her experience at Swami Kripananda's ashram in India.

Her role in Ibrahim's life wasn't inconsistent with either teachings, she reflected. While Swami Kripananda neither espoused nor condemned them, the Tantric Yoga studies she'd brought with her from India taught that shared sexual experience was a natural celebration of one of the gifts of life. *Not so different from the Islamic teachings: sex as the gift of Allah, the bliss of Paradise in advance; celibacy as ingratitude toward Allah.* She was no longer troubled about enjoying her role as a concubine.

Yes, I've settled in all right. She'd seen how, when she'd arrive for her Islamic studies, Yassar's eyes glowed with parental pleasure at seeing a favorite child. She knew that his feelings grew for her well beyond simple fondness, and that he came to care for her as a daughter-in-law, even though she was not a Believer. And these days Yassar did not do all the talking. Many times while Sasha sat at his knee as she had with her Guru's swamis, she told him stories from the Indian myths she had learned as a child, about Ganesha, her Remover of Obstacles. Ganesha, the elephant-headed boy, whose statue—now that as the "favorite" she had a single room—she secretly said Sanskrit prayers to on a makeshift puja she set up on an end table.

Yassar opened the door, the Koran in his hand. "Come in, Sasha, you're right on time."

They sat together, Yassar in his chair, Sasha on a low stool in front of him. She held her gaze at the floor, not wishing to be perceived as too aggressive or disrespectful, but she knew of the kindness in his black eyes and the sereneness of his demeanor.

He's tired, she thought. His role as Finance and Economy Minister was beginning to weigh on him. That and the growing rift between the royals and the Saudi people that Ibrahim told her he and Yassar dealt with daily, now that Ibrahim was back for the summer from his first year at Harvard and involved in helping his father with the jobs programs.

"The entire Koran was revealed over twenty-three years by the angel Gabriel to the Prophet Mohammed, who had to recite every word back to Gabriel shortly before Mohammed died, so that the entire text could be checked," Yassar said. "Many say this process was done twice."

Perhaps that's what killed him, Sasha couldn't help thinking.

"As one who has indicated she can respect the teachings and who has the intellect and the integrity to understand them, I present to you this copy of the Koran." Yassar held the book out to Sasha, who took it with a flush of guilt for her thought. She held it in her lap and momentarily hung her head as if in prayer, feeling a warmth flow into her at the gift, then simple peace, a grace. He handed her an embroidered cloth like the one he wrapped his own Koran in, and she placed the Koran he'd just presented to her in it and held it to her breast.

"Thank you," she murmured. She knew the feelings the senior prince stirred in her were precious. She wondered if other young women who had grown up with fathers to guide them, scold them, teach them, and protect them felt as she did now.

She stood, still clutching the book in both hands and leaned forward. *Dear, dear Prince. Constant, gentle Prince. You are my anchor, my rock.* She kissed him softly on the forehead. "Thank you," she said again.

———◆———

July, Twenty-One Years Ago. Nice, France. People really do live like this, Sasha thought. *But sometimes I feel like my heart's going to dry up and blow away.* She walked with Nafta into the Sea Wall Cafe and Lounge at the Baron David de Duval Hotel at the quiet, east end of Nice. Ibrahim always stayed at the Baron David because it was more subdued than the hotels in the center of the city. Sasha loved Nice. She had visited nearly every season with the Countess at the Negresco, in the center of town facing the sea. But Sasha now preferred to be both figuratively and literally above it all on the outskirts of town, high on the hill where the elite Baron David was located.

Prince Ibrahim was already seated at a table with two Arab men a few years his senior when Sasha and Nafta entered for lunch. They kissed their benefactor in turn.

"Abdul and Waleed," Ibrahim said, "you have met Sasha and Nafta?" The two men barely acknowledged them.

"I question the validity of a government that isn't truly committed to Islam," Waleed said.

"If the Saudi regime can't uphold shari'a, how can it act as steward of the Muslim world's holiest sites?" Abdul added.

"I understand what you're saying," Ibrahim said, "but you must also understand the extent of the influence I can have on our government policies."

Oh my goodness, Ibrahim, listen to yourself! This was really getting to be too much. First he's going to the ministry every day—in part due to her urgings—and the next thing he's carrying on about how much he can influence Saudi government policies. Trying to impress these toads with his importance. She wondered if she didn't prefer him stoned on cocaine. At least he made less of a fool of himself that way. She felt that curious emotion again, now like dread, then as an ache.

Maybe it's time to get out. She mentally tallied the twenty-four monthly envelopes of $75,000 in cash she received—1.8 million dollars, U.S., as she had stipulated—and the roughly 2.6 million dollars in jewels she'd accumulated. *Maybe, maybe not.* Her restlessness of the past few days now seemed as if it had gone on longer than that. A few months? Ibrahim had become opaque, distant, perhaps because he'd become so absorbed in his father's work. But more than the distance from him, she'd come to realize she didn't love him, couldn't imagine ever wondering if she did. So what was to keep her from moving on?

One thing was clear. Sasha didn't like these strange young men tagging around Ibrahim here. They preached to him, seemed to be all over him. And she too had been accosted by political as well as religious zealots. She remembered with particular discomfort the questions of an elitist young Englishman with whom they had shared a table at a dinner earlier that season—probing into Ibrahim's perspective on the bombings of the American military bases in Saudi Arabia—and the conspiratorial conversations he had exchanged with a scruffy American on the yacht *Christina*, on which they had dined last week.

"They must return to the ways of shari'a themselves if they are to be respected and to lead their people," Waleed continued.

"They've become too close to the Americans."

"I'm not in a position to deal with that just yet," Ibrahim said, "but we can use the Americans to our advantage. Don't underestimate the value of that."

Use the Americans! Who did he think he was fooling? He actually seemed as if he *believed* the nonsense he was spouting. Sasha was seized by a desire to return to her room, pack a few things, and disappear. *Forget about the politics. That isn't the half of it.* She looked at Ibrahim. *Your need to make a name for yourself is getting the better of you.* Then she saw Yassar in him. The thought calmed her. She stroked Ibrahim's head, and he turned, startled, then kissed her hand peremptorily and leaned further into his conversation.

There it was again, that sensation, which she now realized was so indistinct because she was fighting it. Ibrahim was engrossed in his conversation. She felt the distance from him again, then gave in to her emotion. It *was* an ache. Then overwhelming sorrow, like mourning. She knew what it told her, what she needed. She wanted to be loved. She stood up and walked from the table, knowing she wouldn't find it here.

At 3:00 a.m. the Beautiful People were just switching from their drugs of choice to their drinks. Sasha sat on the afterdeck of the *Staid Matron*, drinking Dom Pérignon with Nigel Benthurst, their host. Only half listening to him, she was merely conscious he spoke in the affected, stuttering manner she'd frequently identified with those who attend the best English schools, and exuded an attitude reminiscent of the glory days of the House of Lords. Even Sasha found his impassioned superiority difficult to counteract, at least in conversation.

"I gather your Ibrahim is enjoying his new friends, Abdul and Waleed. Are you?" Nigel said in his clipped speech.

Eton? The little creep was beginning to annoy her. She glanced back into the cabin of the yacht where most of the party was going on, but couldn't see Ibrahim.

"Sorry. Off base. Bad form," Nigel said. "I'll start again. I'd like to talk to you, Sasha. Rather feel it's in, in, your best, uhm, interest."

"How?" Sasha glanced back into the cabin. Her eyes met those of a midthirtiesish guest seated ten feet away, luxuriating in his cigar. *The scruffy American.* The man Nigel had talked politics to all night on the *Christina* a week earlier.

"I rather think Ibrahim's getting in on the wrong side of things," Nigel said. "It's a little uhm, uhm, scary, actually. These fellows Abdul and Waleed are extremists. Linked to terrorists. They're trying to recruit Ibrahim."

Sasha played with her string of pearls, as if to dismiss everything Nigel had just said. *Leave me in peace.* She was full up with
this kind of talk. Bloody politics. And what *were* these men up to
with Ibrahim? What was Nigel up to? She looked at the scruffy
American again. Was he in this in some way, too? "Are you talking to me?" she asked Nigel.

"Well, actually, yes."

"And?"

"I said I think those fellows are extremists."

"What do you want, Nigel?"

"Well, actually, uhm, your help. Our people want your
Ibrahim to resist, or at least, to, to render them harmless. We're
looking after him."

"You mean you're watching Ibrahim?" *What's going on here?*

"No, them."

Sasha leaned forward to address him eye to eye. "Why are
you telling me this?"

"I, uhm, checked you out. You're smart. And you know
better. Sense of values and all that. You've seen how the average Saudi lives. Double standard. Royalty. Poverty. Right next
to each other. The country's getting ready to slide into the bog.
Oil, social unrest, more oil, ninety-five percent of the population
making less per year than the interest on ten minutes of oil revenues. The royal family's still rather above it all and doing quite
well, thank you very much. *Particularly* well on the commission
it charges for anything coming into the country. Military hardware. Industrial equipment. Agricultural supplies. You name it."

"The family's committed to doing better for the country.
They're building a future," Sasha said. She thought of Yassar,
knowing how enraged he'd be to hear Nigel's words.

"Wake up. There's trouble brewing in their jolly old kingdom. You'd know that if you were paying attention."

Sasha looked for Ibrahim, but couldn't see him. She wanted to escape. The only problem was, what Nigel said made sense. And as quickly as she thought this, she realized someone had rehearsed him. This wasn't some random conversation on some rich Englishman's yacht in the midst of a party. In fact it was oddly reminiscent of what the scruffy American had said on the *Christina*.

"Are you having me followed?" Sasha asked.

"Not unless you want us to."

"Of course not. What do you want from me?"

"Let us watch. You watch. Tell us what's going on, come see me, us. That's all."

She thought about telling him to go to hell, but instead said, "All right, you've got my attention. Now who are you?"

He looked at her for a long moment, seemingly measuring her. "A concerned friend."

"I see. Some fellow who hangs out on yachts and warns off girls from their boyfriend's new cronies." He didn't respond. "Do social work on the side?" She decided to ease off, see if she could find out more before her attitude put him off. But she was angry. Angry at Nigel for staying after her. Angry at Ibrahim. Angry at the scruffy American sitting a few yards off in his disheveled khakis, rumpled cotton shirt, smoking his stupid cigar. Angry at everybody tonight.

"Ibrahim's new friends are going to get him in trouble. He'll wish he never got interested in anything but sex, drugs and rock and roll. That little vacation to California a year or so ago may have done him more harm than good."

She felt a flash of—fear. How the hell did Nigel know about the Betty Ford Clinic? Who was this Nigel? And he and his people, whoever they were, *were* watching Ibrahim. And her. "What's that supposed to mean?"

"Only what I said earlier. We've been watching him. And, uhm, very closely since he picked up those two stray dogs. Help us. Help yourself."

She needed to think, regroup, so she got up and strode off toward the cabin to look for Ibrahim. The scruffy American smoking the cigar nodded to her and smiled. She strode past him, pearls flying, shoulders erect, all on instinct, because her mind was elsewhere, churning with what she wanted to talk to Ibrahim about once she got him cornered.

Prince Ibrahim and Sasha busied themselves dressing for the evening in their duplex suite at the Baron David, he upstairs in the bedroom, she downstairs in the living room. She enjoyed dressing downstairs, feeling the evening breeze through the screen doors, seeing the glittering curve of lights, feeling the grounding cool of the marble floor under her feet. She wished the view could pull her thoughts away from what was troubling her. She tried on another of the dresses scattered across the sofas, ready to call up to Ibrahim for his opinion.

She'd been trying to segue into a discussion of Abdul and Waleed and their politics all evening. So far she was frustrated by his ability to dodge her. *Well, I'll just have to blurt it out.* "Ibrahim, this Abdul and Waleed. What is it they want from you?"

He looked down at her from the balcony and shrugged. "Nothing." She looked at him, unsatisfied, and he saw it and turned away from her. She figured he must have felt her eyes on his back because he turned back and added, "We simply share similar views."

She thought it was a limp response. *You're getting me all the more concerned by your nonchalance.* "More like they're forcing their views onto you."

She saw him frown and turn away. It annoyed her, made her want to be more persistent. "Such as you may think," he added, and walked away from the railing and out of view into the bedroom.

I'm not finished with you yet. Sasha selected another dress. "How about this one?" she asked, holding a flowered print.

He walked back to the railing. "Too English countryside."

"You know, they really are taking positions that run contrary to anything I've ever heard you identify with." There. Enough to provoke him? She wasn't about to let him off that easily and she figured he expected it of her anyway.

"Hardly."

You still refuse to engage. I'll not be sloughed off. "Hardly? You family's not fit to be the steward of Islam's holiest sites? They won't recognize the Saudi government as valid?"

"They never said that."

"They stopped just short of it. What's got into you? Why listen to them?"

Ibrahim sighed. "I'm going to be one of the leaders of Saudi Arabia one day," he said. "Exposure to the ideas of our constituents is healthy. There's nothing wrong with challenging the conventions of our own thinking." He leaned down at her now, Sasha thinking she couldn't imagine a more arrogant posture.

I hate it when you adopt that long-suffering paternalistic tone with me. She thought of mimicking his pose, showing him how ridiculous he looked, but realized he either wouldn't understand or would become completely inflamed. "Nothing is wrong with a dialog. But I'm afraid they're using you as a shill to co-opt others to their views. Making you into some kind of trophy so they can say 'see, look who is with us' to the people who follow them."

"You don't know what you're talking about."

"Don't I? What would your father say if he knew you were agreeing with a bunch of tripe challenging your own family's convictions, their religion, their—"

"Who are you to talk about my religion?" he cut her off.

Good. That got your attention, finally. Before she'd wanted to grab him by his hair and force him to listen. But now she knew she had him. She'd drive it in a little more. "I dare say I know almost as much about it as you do. I've certainly spent more time on the teachings than you have over the last year and a half."

"Oh, I forgot you were a Koranic scholar." His sarcasm rolled off the balcony. "And you know as much as I about Saudi politics, and my family, I suppose?"

Well at least he's engaged now, even if he's being a bloody, ignorant boor. She lowered her eyes to show him she was contrite, that she wouldn't challenge him completely. *You're really not that hard to figure out, Ibrahim.* "I'm only asking you what's going on," she said.

"What's going on is I am becoming ready for my role in the future of Saudi Arabia."

Her own anger rose. "How can you say that if you're agreeing with people who are questioning the very validity of your family's rule? These people are poison. They're threatening your family, your religious values, and you don't even see it."

"What on earth are you prattling on about, woman?"

Prattling! Woman! She felt her face beginning to flush. "Your need for recognition, to make a name for yourself, has gotten the better of you! These people are fundamentalist extremists, and you're letting them drag you around like their trained monkey! You seem to forget you're one of the royals!" She saw his face and regretted it. *Uh oh, there he goes.*

He grasped the handrail. "I've never forgotten who I am! It's you who seem to forget who you are, concubine! Now shut your mouth or consider the consequences! You can be shipped off to wherever you came from just as easily as my father brought you here in the first place!"

Sasha felt the words strike her as if he'd spat on her. Her mind tried to catch up with the whirl of emotions that stirred in her, sort through the thoughts that now came rushing, almost two years of them, reality pushing through the notion she had created—had she created it?—that she was part of this family, a member of the Saudi elite. Now she had it thrown at her that he could discard her like his used laundry. A man who didn't even understand what the concept of laundry was, who didn't know what happened to his clothing after he left it crumpled on the floor. Her brain caught up with her. She stepped forward, slowly, deliberately. *Oh, Ibrahim. How can you? After I picked you up and straightened you out.* "I don't deserve to be spoken to that way," she said. "I've done nothing to deserve your disrespect."

He looked down at her, and she saw the anger flow from his face. He seemed to be reading her thoughts. He showed gentleness, then—was it possible?—shame? He descended the stairs and walked over to her in silence, picking up a dress. She tried it on, saw he didn't like it, and removed it.

He put his hands on her shoulders, caressed her and kissed her neck. "Sometimes you're not capable of understanding what you are asking me about," he said softly. Then: "I like that one." He pointed at a dress on the sofa. "But I think it would look better on you without this." He unhooked her bra, removed it and turned her around to face him. "And you won't need this," he said, sliding her garter belt down to the floor. He held it while she stepped out of it. Then he helped her step into the dress, slid the straps onto her shoulders, turned her around, and zipped it up.

She guessed Ibrahim figured the argument had ended, he doing his princely best to appeal to her and she accepting that his words were just so much detritus from a momentary spat. *Just like him.* But he'd soiled their intimacy and there was now no way to deceive herself into putting it back. *Time to get out.* Then she thought of Yassar, and knew she couldn't leave without making sure he was aware, probably before Ibrahim was consciously knowledgeable of it himself, that the son was choosing sides against his father. She remembered Nigel Benthurst's words about Ibrahim's new friends: they're dangerous. Concern for Yassar now replaced the disgust she felt for the man standing in front of her. Yes, Yassar must learn of this. From her.

BOOK 3

CHAPTER 17

AUGUST, THIS YEAR. NEW YORK City. The stale remnants of the sandwich Daniel ate for dinner and the soggy fries he left untouched lent an aroma to his office akin to the conference room for the last week. *Yassar's demanding and sharp as hell. I need to be on point.* The words he'd used to spur himself all week blended together as a mantra in his brain. *That and twenty-five percent of the fees.* He hunched over a draft presentation of six refining and marketing acquisition targets he and his team were preparing for his meeting with Prince Yassar in Vienna. His neck was crimped from being in the same position. *Or is it from tension?* He noted the time on his watch. *10:30.* With relief he reflected on the fact that Lydia hadn't intruded on his train of thought for hours.

His three colleagues perched on the edges of their seats across his desk from him, their own faces buried in the presentation. Walter Purcell—the Vice President—and Steven Pace—the Associate—both showed signs of the extended push to finish the project—ties and shirt collars open at the neck, tousled hair and rolled up sleeves. Daniel was still crisply starched although he knew his eyes must be betraying reddish signs of fatigue. And his movements were jerky with stress.

Eyes downcast, rigid and unsmiling, Daniel continued perusing his copy of the presentation. The two subordinates exchanged sideways glances as Daniel neared the last page. They'd been this close before over the last few days, only to be thrust back into another draft.

Daniel exhaled and sat back in his chair, cracking his neck from side to side. "I'd say we're looking good, fellows. Nice job." Purcell smiled and relaxed his shoulders. Pace shifted in his seat and stretched his arms over his head. "How long will it take you to turn these new comments?"

"One, maybe two hours." Purcell said.

Daniel nodded. The two stood and left.

Daniel looked out the window. *Three days. No call, no sign of her since Friday.* Then his mind burned and his stomach twisted inside out for the thousandth time since Lydia disappeared. He clenched and unclenched his fist. *Damn you.* She'd walked out and hadn't even given him the satisfaction of throwing her out now that he'd made that decision. He started to spew the speech he'd conceived and involuntarily rehearsed on autopilot six times every few hours since the previous Friday night. He slapped his fist on the desk, wondering how long it would be before he'd be able to deliver it, then refocused on the presentation in front of him. In the next half hour he drafted the first few bullet points of the summary of the strategic rationale for the Saudis to acquire additional refining and marketing operations.

Then his mind curled back upon itself. *Never even tried to come up with a logical explanation for what she was doing with my computer. Or the passports or the money.* He slumped back in his chair, threw his pencil down, and exhaled heavily. *Or the files. And the whole stash disappeared with her.* He wondered again where Lydia came from, who she really was. He felt his guts turning over again as his mind worked through what the passports and money meant—a scam? Or was she just nuts? Again his heart moaned with a sense of betrayal.

Who cares, he tried to tell himself.

Daniel stood up, circled his neck to crack it again, stretched. He walked from behind his desk and looked out the window at the glitter of lights in Midtown, his features jagged and coarse in his reflection in the window. *Does she love me?* It was a question he'd repeatedly asked himself the last three days. He felt a painful lump of air muscling its way to his throat, then spun from the window, glaring at the wall as a surrogate for Lydia to satisfy his anger.

I don't need this now. Not during his first presentation to Yassar, the first step in creating the liberating windfall the Saudis could bring him, his first opportunity to put the excitement back into his business life. *Even if the bubble's burst again in my private life.*

"I actually believed in you," he said aloud, fighting back the swelling in his throat and the sting in his eyes.

He walked to the window again. His heart cried out to her. *Who am I kidding?* And then he was off someplace else in his mind. Now seeing her, close enough to reach out but unable to move, touch, sense her, as if his nerves had ceased functioning. Unable to satisfy his hunger. It was then he admitted he was in love with her.

August, This Year. New York City. Kovarik reached down and rubbed his shin. Man, his leg hurt today. *Must be the humidity.* He sat at his desk, waiting for Kareem Kapur, or whatever the hell his real name was. Two copies of his 26-page list sat on his desk, one for Kapur, one for him. No title, just a list of 14 oil and gas investment bankers, their 56 clients who provided operating software to the industry and 4,128 oil and gas industry customers of the software vendors. It was in rank order by banker with the most clients, with Daniel Youngblood at the top of the list.

That made him smile, even as he rubbed his leg. Maybe through all of this he'd somehow fix Daniel's ass for smashing up his leg, for one thing. Sonofabitch put his Aston into the wall on the S-turn at Watkins Glen that Memorial Day; Kovarik had watched that crash in his mind five thousand times, and he still couldn't understand how Daniel had the balls to hold his line while Kovarik tried to take him on the inside. *Enough.*

He shook his head and glanced at his LCD screen to check the markets. His assistant buzzed him. "Mr. Kapur is here."

Kovarik pointed to the sofa in his office when Kapur arrived. He walked out from behind his desk with the two copies of his list and sat down next to Kapur. The guy was wearing the same brown suit—looked like he got it at Kmart, hung on him like a sack, sleeves too long. And that rumpled polyester shirt and $10 tie.

"Welcome," Kovarik said, shaking Kapur's hand.

"That the list?" Kapur looked intense, and not at all friendly.

"Yeah." Kovarik handed him a copy. "You'll be pleased."

Kapur leafed through it for a minute or so. "I see you're pretty far down the list."

"I didn't want to be too conspicuous. I can change it to add the rest of my clients if you want, but it won't make much difference."

"I'm surprised you put your name on it at all."

"If it finds its way into the wrong hands, I didn't want to be conspicuous with my absence, either."

"Only way it finds itself in the wrong hands would be through you," Kapur said, still looking at the list. "It does and I know who to look for." He looked up, glaring.

Kovarik's neck tensed.

Kapur flipped back to the first page. "This Youngblood. Looks like he's got half the business if you count the end customers."

"Yeah, he's a player." The words tasted bad in Kovarik's mouth.

"You know him?"

"We go way back."

"Any issues if he gets tangled up in this?"

Kovarik felt his pulse quicken. "Nothing I'd like to see better. He's a self-righteous, holier-than-thou asshole."

"Sounds personal."

"Yeah, so see if you can make something bad happen to him." Kovarik smiled. He thought about Angie, then rubbed his shin.

Habib hung around the lobby of the Waldorf Astoria until 8:00 p.m., waiting long enough that he figured the investment banker from Credit Suisse, Philip Adair, would be home from the office. He got out of a cab two blocks from Adair's co-op building at 90th and Park and walked the rest of the way. He felt comfortable in the FedEx uniform. When he got to the concierge's desk in the lobby of Adair's building, he said, "Package for Philip Adair, twelve-G." He kept his sunglasses on.

"Leave it here, I'll sign for it."

"I gotta have *his* signature."

The concierge looked at Habib with disdain, then picked up the phone and called upstairs.

In the elevator, Habib felt the familiar race of adrenaline, the heightened senses—he could smell the lemon oil on the elevator's woodwork, see the prickly little hairs on the back of the elevator operator's neck—he always experienced before an engagement. Better to handle this himself. Now that he had the list from Kovarik, he didn't need Adair. And Adair wanted more money than Kovarik, and he was dragging the process out, sounding whiny and scared in their last conversation. The last thing Habib needed was Adair chickening out and going to the Feds. Habib knew doing Adair himself was best. Besides, if he turned it over to the Sheik's people, they'd probably either botch it or call too much attention to themselves. And risk the Sheik thinking Habib couldn't handle his own problems.

Habib got off the elevator and walked slowly enough that he could hear its door close before he approached Adair's apartment door. He stopped in front of it and looked to each side, checking, then pulled the silenced Sig Sauer automatic from his bag. He knocked. His pulse thundered in his ears.

The door opened.

"Mr. Adair?"

"Yes."

Habib raised the Sig Sauer and put a single shot in Adair's forehead. He pulled the door shut and walked toward the stairs.

CHAPTER 18

AUGUST, THIS YEAR. VIENNA, AUSTRIA. The Hotel Sacher stands across the square to the State Opera in their marriage to the traditions of the Hapsburg monarchy that established the culture of old Vienna. Yassar had slept peacefully in the Madame Butterfly Suite, the Sacher's most opulent, because his flight had arrived in sufficient time for him to have a pleasant dinner and retire by 9:00 p.m. After his prayers he showered, dressed, ate a modest breakfast in his suite, then took the Sacher's Rolls Royce to Obere Donaustrasse to the OPEC offices for the general session of members where he joined his cousin, Prince Naser, the Saudi Oil Minister.

Yassar's mind drifted during OPEC's routine update reports—production vs. quota, pricing grids, and on and on—oblivious to the 1960s décor of the 40-by-60-foot central meeting room in OPEC's building. His sad eyes were deceptively lifeless, his overall presentation one of outward calm despite his inner animation. From his seat next to Prince Naser he glanced deliberately around the room at his colleagues, the Oil Ministers of all the other 11 OPEC members, including all seven representatives of the United Arab Emirates. His eyes involuntarily found Hectar Vincenzio, the Venezuelan Oil Minister, and his lip curled. *Pork-eating bastard.* He again affected nonchalance, but steeled for his opportunity to speak, in which he would formally sponsor and propose a vote on the project to put the cartel in the 21st century. Four hours of discussion later and after the vote was tallied, Naser clasped his hands and winked at Yassar in a Western gesture of victory. Yassar arose from his seat to leave, his formal Saudi robe and headdress swishing behind him. *Today,* he thought, *we take the first step to join the diversified Western conglomerates—BP, Exxon/Mobil, Royal Dutch/ Shell—who rule the oil business, and the world.*

Two hours later Yassar sat in his suite amidst the scattered remnants of his dinner on the room service cart. He took no pains to mask his fatigue from Assad al-Anoud, the head of his Secret Police, who sat across from him.

"That's the last of the surveillance reports on our financial and legal advisors, Minister," Assad said. "Do you have any further questions?"

Yassar shook his head no, distractedly fingering an eyebrow. *I'm almost afraid to ask what's going on at home.*

"As you wish. And we'll have a team stationed to observe Mr. Youngblood's comings and goings while he's in town for your meeting tomorrow."

Yassar understood and agreed. Assad placed the folders he held in his lap to his side on the end table. "There's something else I need you to be aware of, Minister Yassar."

Yassar heard the change in his tone. *What now?*

"We had another demonstration at the Ministry of Labor yesterday. This time five thousand students."

Unrelenting, these problems. And they will become unbearable if we do not act quickly. Yassar sought a reserve of strength within him and found little.

"And our Intelligence reports indicate the student organizations at the main two universities in Riyadh are organizing a march with the Shiite Muslim groups."

Bin Abdur. We haven't much time. He felt a soul-wrenching desire to take the man—Sheik bin Abdur—once and for all eternity in his hands, squeeze his throat until his eyes popped, then throw his body to the worms that ate the refuse in the desert night. Seeing Assad watching him with concern in his eyes, he felt his face burning with shame. Yassar knew Assad's next topic, dreaded it. He waited a few moments before asking, "And what news on bin Abdur's other plans?"

"Our agents now confirm that he is actively soliciting computer hackers for some kind of sabotage of the oil and gas industry."

"And?" Yassar rubbed his forehead, staring at the wall.

"We have agents posing as hackers to try to find out more." He paused, seeming reluctant. "And we may have had one bit of luck. A hacker he has hired appears to have brought in one of our own agents, called Alica, who may be able to ascertain his specific plans."

"That's fortunate," Yassar said. "Good work." Only now he looked up again at Assad, who was pushing out his chest, probably from the compliment. "But don't get carried away; stay vigilant and see where it might lead us. You had best get home to Riyadh immediately."

Assad seemed to deflate. "Yes, Minister."

CHAPTER 19

AUGUST, THIS YEAR. VIENNA, AUSTRIA. Yassar saw the note slipped beneath the door of his suite at the Sacher. He hoped it was from her. He was expecting news. He opened it to see a neatly typed message transcribed by the hotel's Business Centre:

WE ARE INSIDE. OUR MAN HAS NOW AGREED ON PRICE TO HIRE ALI FOR STAGE ONE. HE'S PAYING TOP DOLLAR FOR THE BEST. SEVENTY-FIVE THOUSAND ADVANCE AGAINST THREE HUNDRED THOUSAND SUCCESS TO HACK INTO SAUDI ARAMCO'S COMPUTER NETWORK. I WILL KEEP YOU POSTED.

ALICA

"Good," Yassar said aloud. Now he'd see how bin Abdur would make his move. He began pacing, thumbing his eyebrow. One more meeting tomorrow morning and he could fly back to Riyadh. He crossed the room to phone Assad. He would need to put Saudi Aramco on alert.

CHAPTER 20

AUGUST, THIS YEAR. VIENNA, AUSTRIA. Delta Flight Number 2770 left Kennedy Airport at 6:30 p.m., with passenger J. Daniel Christian Youngblood III the last to board after receiving the handoff of six copies of a critically important client presentation from a breathless, wild-eyed James Cassidy outside the security checkpoint at 6:14. Daniel landed in Vienna at 9:20 a.m. By the time he walked across the Philharmoniker Strasse to the Sacher, its international flags hanging limp in the still summer morning, its bold, red awnings gleaming in patches of sun, he felt the tear in his arm sockets from the weight of his bags and the taste of the cognac he'd drunk in order to grab at least a few hours sleep on the flight.

This presentation better do the trick, because it's my best shot. The Sacher didn't let Daniel down; the staff pressed his suit to store-mannequin perfection while he showered, and delivered a steaming breakfast with a punctuality that would have made a Swiss hotelier cry. The shower put some glow back into his cheeks, despite his darkened eyes. At 11:00 he knocked on the doors to Prince Yassar's "Madame Butterfly Suite" chuckling to himself at the butterflies in his own stomach. His briefcase didn't seem so heavy now. Six copies of his presentation and his wits about him were the only other things he needed at this point. He felt his adrenaline rise.

Yassar opened the door. Daniel tried not to show his surprise at seeing him in his Saudi robe and headdress. *Of course. He must still be in the middle of their OPEC meetings.*

"Daniel, come in, come in, you're right on time." He waved his hand in an arc.

Gracious and polished as ever, but seems distracted. And his face looks as bad as I feel.

"Did you have a pleasant flight?" Yassar asked as they headed toward a conference table at the far end of the suite.

"Fine. Uneventful."

"I took the liberty of ordering some tea, coffee, juice and breakfast things for you," Yassar said.

"Thank you," Daniel said and fixed himself a cup of tea, though he didn't want one. When he turned around, Yassar had sat down at the head of the conference table, contemplating its polished surface. *This guy's mind is someplace else. I hope I can get his attention. Maybe I can loosen him up.*

"I've had a few changes in my schedule, including some urgent matters that have come up at home," Yassar said without looking up. "I recognize you've come a long way for this meeting, but would it be too much to ask if we commence immediately so that I can get on with the remainder of my day?" Yassar's look was friendly but Daniel saw the creases in his forehead and the anxiety at the corners of his eyes.

"Absolutely," Daniel said. He felt a nerve someplace inside him twang. He sat down, took a sip of his tea, and pulled out the presentation from his briefcase. He felt one more ripple of doubt, then slid a copy of "Presentation to the Kingdom of Saudi Arabia on Selected Refining and Marketing Acquisition Opportunities" across the expanse of now-forbidding mahogany. *Breathe. Pace yourself.* "As you'll see from the table of contents, we have a general overview of the strategic rationale for your expansion of refining and marketing activities, followed by a succinct review of six specific acquisition targets. They range in size from five hundred million dollars up to forty billion dollars in value." Yassar flipped open his copy and started skimming through it.

Okay, roll with it. Stay with him. He's in no mood to go page by page. "Ah," Daniel said, adapting, "I see you've focused in on ConocoPhillips' refining and marketing already. As you'll see, I believe the strategic rationale for them specifically…"

"Too concentrated in one geographic region," Yassar said without looking up.

A little abrupt, Yassar. Okay. Let's try to get something more of a reaction, even if only to help me know what you don't want in order to zero in more closely on what you do.

Yassar turned to the next acquisition target. He seemed uninterested.

Damn, Daniel thought. His eyes darted back and forth from Yassar's presentation to his own. "Dorchester Refining. An interesting play for you. I know the situation intimately, having helped the LBO fund to acquire it out of bankruptcy earlier this summer. They've barely owned it for a month, but they've been known to flip things in the past, so…"

"Tired old facilities, limited brands." Yassar looked up. "There's no long-term franchise here for us to buy." He turned the next three pages, looking down again at the book.

Daniel made himself sit straight. Forget the butterflies in his stomach. Now a knot was forming. He saw Yassar looking at the first summary page for the refining and marketing operations of Forrester. "This next one would be the smallest deal in the group. As I noted earlier, we estimate it to be a half billion dollars." Yassar took in the page for the next thirty seconds. *A spark of interest?*

Yassar flipped past the next three pages.

Damn.

At one point Yassar ran his finger down a page and flipped back a few pages—cross-checking what?—then stopped and pondered the page he had turned to.

Daniel adapted again, following Yassar. "I'm a little reluctant to give you a full commentary, since you seem to be in quite a hurry, but if I may make just a few points on these last few?" He studied Yassar's face, telling himself to relax, that the situation was salvageable. *No catastrophe, I'll come back at him with another group of targets.*

Yassar smiled, first with his eyes, then the corners of his mouth. "Nice job. These last three make an interesting opportunity in combination. Simco has refineries and a network of service stations under different brand names throughout Scandinavia, while Petro and Dontol have similar assets across Southern Europe and the East Coast of the United States."

Daniel forced himself to appear nonchalant, then decided he might as well be candid. "True, but Dontol has weak market share in its region and there might be a better play if you want to build some gas station operations in the United States."

"I'm not concerned."

Daniel felt some of the tension go out of his shoulders. *Fine with me if you know what you're letting yourself in for.*

"Only thing is," Yassar said, "you have to deliver all three, or it's not worth doing."

Daniel felt it like a slug in his stomach. "That's tricky," he managed. He made eye contact to get his point across. "As you know, deals are unpredictable, and we could invest months…" *That is, I could invest months.* "…and come up empty-handed because we couldn't put the pieces of the puzzle together at the same time."

Yassar returned his gaze without blinking. "I know that. But that's what we're paying you for, isn't it?"

"Absolutely." *Okay. Message received. Figure it out later. Take the assignment and run.*

Yassar flipped perfunctorily through the remaining pages of the presentation, then stood to indicate the meeting was over. "Thank you for coming, Daniel. I apologize for rushing you off, for not being a better host." He smiled. "But now you have a lot of work to do. And I have other obligations. I'll show you to the door." He stopped, then said, "Oh, and I almost forgot this," and handed Daniel an envelope. "Your engagement letter, signed, and a check for your first retainer."

Daniel extended his hand. "Thank you, Prince Yassar. I won't let you down." A smile was frozen on his face. *Why is it I feel like 'Be careful what you wish for, you might get it' just bit me in the ass?*

Daniel's stomach was gnawing at him when he got to his room on the second floor of the Sacher. He looked at the executed original of the engagement letter Yassar had handed him. *A signed engagement letter. And a check for two-fifty. And a million bucks payable from the firm upon signing Yassar up. And Dieudonne can't wriggle out of this one*, he thought, remembering the deal he'd struck—in writing—with the senior partner in his year-end bonus negotiation. But it rang hollow.

He thought about the deals Yassar just told him to go ahead with. *Looks like total transaction value of five to six billion. Probably twenty-five to thirty million in fees.* He didn't need a calculator to figure out what his 25% of that was. *Still, all or nothing, and because of it, I could burn through a good six months trying to get all three, and then if one falls apart, I've got zilch.*

"It certainly puts the pressure on," he said aloud to the empty room. Something else was still bothering him. He'd seen clients make decisions on half-baked information before, and plenty of great ideas dismissed virtually out of hand, but Yassar had just authorized him to spend five to six billion dollars in less than fifteen minutes.

Yassar sure was in a hurry. *If I'd served him up cat food he would have eaten it.*

CHAPTER 21

AUGUST, THIS YEAR. VIENNA, AUSTRIA. After Daniel left his suite, Yassar felt the jitters, anxious to get back to Riyadh. *One more thing to do first,* he thought again for the fifth time. He glanced at the phone, then his watch, and drummed his fingers on the end table, turning his mind back to the business at hand. The phone rang. He checked his watch. *11:59:32.* "Hello, my dear, you are twenty-eight seconds early," he said without asking who it was.

"You know how risky this is?" Alica said at the other end of the phone.

"I know, but I thought it critical we talk directly. You sound like you're a middle-aged man stuck in a wind tunnel."

"I'm using a voice scrambler. Can we make this quick? This line could very possibly be traced—or tapped."

"As you wish, but please dispense with the scrambler. I need to hear your voice, to know that it is really you. Things are heating up and I am not sure who I can trust without confirmation." Yassar settled into his chair, listening.

"Okay." She switched off the device. Her voice sounded strained, but he was almost certain it was her.

"What have you got for me?"

She began speaking hurriedly. "It's like this...God, this is crazy over the phone...Sheik bin Abdur has hired us to hack into Saudi Aramco's main refinery as a test run, and we now know he wants us to plant logic bombs." Her voice slowed down, as if caught up in the romance of the technicalities she was describing. "Logic bombs, in case you don't know, are specifically tailored programs designed to attack software that controls systems. In this case, mechanical processes—automated oil pipelines, refineries, drilling rigs and so on. And at the coordinated time, they all go 'boom,' or such as it is."

No question. It was her. "What other targets?"

The staccato nature of Yassar's question seemed to remind Alica of her urgency over being overheard. She paused. "I'll call you back from a different phone."

"Extraordinary," Yassar said, looking at the receiver. Two minutes later the phone rang again.

"This is making me really uncomfortable," Alica said.

"What other targets?" Yassar repeated.

She readopted her blitzkreig. "I don't fully know yet. That comes after we get into Saudi Aramco. It's complicated, that much I know. Bin Abdur wants us to hack into the computer programs of the oil and gas industry's dominant computer service providers. I don't know who they all are yet, but the biggest is called Intelligent Recovery Systems. The company's programs do everything you can imagine in the oil service sector, ranging from refinery control, drilling rig control, secondary and tertiary recovery, everything. The company does routine online updates of its software programs every two weeks. We plant our logic bombs in the company's software as it's being sent out online to its customers' computers with the routine updates."

"When is the 'boom'?"

"I don't know."

Yassar heard the tension in her voice again. "Anything else for me, my dear?"

"Isn't that enough?" Yassar heard a rasp of static on the line, then it cut off.

He felt a burst of adrenaline. "Are you there, my dear?" Nothing. He wondered if their call had been intercepted, or worse, if someone had grabbed her. He hadn't counted on anything like that.

CHAPTER 22

AUGUST, THIS YEAR. NEW YORK City. Daniel still hadn't shaken the kinks out of his legs when he arrived at his apartment at 6:00 p.m. the day following his meeting with Yassar. He'd had an opportunity to stretch them during his brief layover in Heathrow, but the next eight hours on the final segment into JFK always wreaked havoc on him. His nostrils still curled with the cocktail of garbage, street grit and exhaust fumes from his cross-town ride that only a sweltering August day in New York could concoct. *The glamorous life of business travel.* He stepped out of the elevator to the private landing to his apartment, bedraggled but at least comforted by the familiar sheen of the ivory-painted woodwork, the walnut door, and the secure feeling of parquet under his feet. He turned the doorknob, the nagging sense of something wrong supported by the continued churning of his stomach.

The sight of Lydia's suitcases in the entrance foyer dwarfed the ill-defined sensation of discomfort. *Finally I get to end it. Closure.* He exhaled heavily and felt his stomach turn over. He dropped his mail. A dozen rehearsed lines flooded into his consciousness. He became aware of his pulse thumping in his ears. Then his mind went stiff, a practiced monologue stuck there, like concrete setting before it was properly smoothed over. He sensed Lydia's presence, smelled her perfume. His eyes darted around the foyer.

Then he heard Lydia talking on the phone in the living room, and froze. It was unquestionably Lydia's voice, but he'd never heard her speaking…what was it?…Arabic. Her back was to him in the living room when he entered. She was gesturing, waving her arms and pouring words intensely into the phone. She shot an arm toward the ceiling emphasizing a point and spun, her jaw slackening and eyes like saucers as she saw Daniel. She turned back toward the wall, said another few sentences in measured tones and hurriedly hung up.

Daniel's pulse was racing. *What the hell was that?* "I didn't know you spoke Arabic." He felt a rumble in his chest. "This gets more and more weird."

Lydia stood in the center of the living room, wearing a modest cotton blouse and jeans. The curve of her waist, the lithe strength of her legs crashed over him in a wave. *God, so beautiful.* He felt the sensation of holding her in his arms as an ache in his chest. The soft moisture of her eyes warmed him. A lump coursed up his throat. *How'd I get myself in so deep so fast?* He struggled against the emotion and conjured a firm tone in his voice, full of the resolve that wasn't really there.

Lydia walked toward him, a smile changed instantly into openmouthed alarm. Looking at her now and asking her to lie to him, talk him out of it. Feeling that swimmy feeling, like falling, in his stomach.

He got his nerve back. "I trusted you, believed in you, let you into my life. Opened my home to you."

"I know, I know, I'm sorry."

His gaze was locked on her eyes. They drew him into their vulnerability. "I was completely open. And you were running some kind of ruse…"

"I can explain…" she interrupted.

"...whatever it was, I don't even care at this point." He knew that was nonsense. Of course he cared, even if he was going to break it off, he was itching with curiosity. No, the airy hope she'd explain it all away.

He saw her eyes grow large, the color drain from her face.

Daniel's heart softened. *This isn't going to be easy.*

Her eyes now implored him. "I know you feel betrayed. I know you're angry..."

His anger flared. "You're damn right I'm angry."

"...I know that stunt I pulled in the dining room was childish..."

"Stunt? Childish? Christ, you tried to burn my goddamn house down."

"Daniel, please." Lydia moved toward him, her lower lip trembling.

Don't start anything with me now.

"Don't be absurd," she said. "If I'd wanted to burn the house down don't you think I'd have managed?" She paused, took a deep breath. When she spoke again it was softly. "Please. Won't you let me at least try to explain?"

Daniel glared at her. "Okay." *But this better be good.* In the same moment he felt the resurgent hope her explanation would satisfy him.

"Won't you come sit?" She walked back into the living room, choosing a seat at one end of the sofa, leaving room for him to join her.

Daniel didn't move. The brief flurry of his anger had spent any desire to harangue her. Now, for his as well as her sake, he wanted it over with. Nothing to be served by sitting and talking it through. His trust was violated. She'd misrepresented who she was—whoever that was—and whatever she was up to, and he wanted out and needed them both to face it.

Daniel reluctantly chose a Queen Anne chair facing the couch. Lydia's hands were clasped contritely in her lap, her knees together. "Let me start by explaining that I reacted emotionally. I felt my privacy had been violated. You entered my room in the Milford house without my permission. You upset me, then angered me, and it just escalated."

"That doesn't justify your behavior," Daniel said, feeling sadly distant from her.

"I'm not making excuses. I'm only trying to explain. And I know my reaction was harsh, but you did, after all, say that room was mine. My private space."

Daniel moved in his seat, wondering what difference it made. And yet he responded. "And what about all that cash? And the passports?" He heard the resignation in his voice. He was going to follow through with it, insist she leave. Wondering if he was supposed to feel good about winning the internal struggle to stick to his objective. But now he saw how much it was going to hurt him. And he found himself worrying about Lydia.

"It's not as bad as it might seem." She appealed to him with her eyes, leaning toward him. "All right, I'm not a photographer. I'm an exporter. The passports and cash are part of how I operate to get around government restrictions." She probed his face for a reaction. He offered her no encouragement. "Sometimes I do work for foreign governments. Nothing illegal, not like arms or anything of that sort, but I export machinery and equipment, computers. Sensitive things."

"So why the lies? What was such a major issue you couldn't talk to me about it?" He watched her closely now. *Come on. Get this over with.*

"Sometimes I'm being watched. I was afraid if I told you everything I'd scare you off. It's that simple. I would have told you eventually."

"This isn't making sense." Why would she concoct such a story? The explanations he'd coursed through in his mind in the last few days—none of them good—turned back on him again. Drugs. Some scam, even espionage. The thought made his insides cringe at ever sleeping next to her. He sat up straight, as if shaking off the bad dreams twisting in his mind. Then: "I love you." He paused, not believing he'd chosen that moment to say it, even to say it at all. "But you lied to me. I don't trust you. I don't even know who you are." He looked at her detachedly, feeling the bittersweet ache of the ended affair. Lydia's eyes were brimming with tears.

"There isn't much I can say except to tell you how much you mean to me, how sorry I am, to try and explain."

Daniel wanted her to stop. Why was she still going on? Insisting on explaining?

"Sometimes the truth sounds a little strange," she said, leaning further forward.

Strange isn't the word.

Lydia inhaled deeply. "If I told you all the times I had to skirt around that IRA nonsense—for example." She looked up at him. "Have you ever tried to get into Northern Ireland with a British passport—or get into and out of an Arab country with visas to Israel stamped on your papers?" She sighed. "It simply isn't worth dealing with those kinds of complications if you have a way around it. Believe me, that's all it is." She looked up at him again, her eyes showing pain.

"Why are you going on like this?" Daniel finally said. She opened her mouth to reply but he continued. "Can't you see I don't believe you?"

She stopped, leaned back in her chair, as if never considering that was a possibility. After a pause she lowered her head and looked him in the eye, uncompromisingly. "I'm going on like this because I know I screwed up and I don't want to lose you. And I'm staying here until you believe in me again. Or throw me out."

Daniel saw her leaning forward there, the little dancer, the force, and wondered if he could say no to her. But that made it into an almost philosophical discourse. Something to prove? He leaned forward toward her, as if to stress a winning point in a negotiation. "Uh huh. And what about my computer?"

Lydia froze. He saw her look into his eyes, her cheeks hollow. She seemed to be turning the question over in her mind.

Daniel eyed her with detachment again. He wondered what she was thinking, why she was taking so long to answer.

Still she hesitated. She drew in a breath and he knew it was a moment in his life coming, held in her answer. "I'm sorry I violated your trust," she said. "But it was nothing, really." Daniel heard the words as an afterthought. He'd already concluded he wasn't going to believe her response. *That look and the long pause mean something.* And immediately after that he'd decided there was an explanation that made sense, because his gut told him she was trying to tell him but for some reason wouldn't let herself, all calculated and rejected in her pause. And he wasn't going to ask her to leave until he figured it out because his feelings for her were real. He remembered the old adage, that if you had to ask, you weren't really in love. He wasn't asking, because that wasn't the question. The question was what was she up to, and what was the explanation that would let him make sense of it and not lose her.

His stomach was now turning over.

Daniel opened his mouth to speak, but the words escaped him before he could seize them, like marbles scattering on a tilted table. "Maybe you should just go," he said. He saw her look of suppressed horror. He was glad for it: at least she was reacting, instead of displaying the dead eyes of a liar.

Lydia put her hands up as if to stop him. Tears hovered in her eyes. "You just told me you loved me. Do you think I'm going to walk off after hearing that?"

Why is it I feel like she's playing me again? First alarm, then on the verge of tears. Daniel's eyes narrowed. *But she's damned good at it.* "What am I, some dupe in a scam?"

"Daniel, please. I need to talk this out with you."

Daniel heard the nervousness, no, panic, in her voice and stopped. "What's wrong?"

"What would you say if I told you I'm being watched? That you're being watched." Her face showed fear. "I did some wild, stupid things when I was young." She leaned back into the sofa. "The things I told you about my background. When I met you, and even just now. They're not true. Well, some of it was, but the facts weren't all there; basically I was abandoned by Sophie, let's still call the woman who raised me. Her name doesn't matter. I got into a difficult situation I'd rather not tell you about." Her gaze was exploring his eyes, his face. He could see her urgency. "I got involved in a political situation. And then everything exploded. That's not the half of it. Oh, God," she continued in an emotion-clogged voice, "people are chasing me, have been ever since. For years. Religious zealots, they're fanatics. I've been living by my wits. Odd jobs. And as I'm sure you've feared, espionage."

Daniel again felt the sense of falling, deeper and deeper into that pit he'd entered upon returning home, unsure where the bottom was. "This is all so vague." Daniel wondered who "they" were, wondered what "everything exploded" meant.

"Please, don't ask me more. You wouldn't want to know me if I told you everything. At least leave me my dignity."

"Stop this. Now."

"I have to go. I'll pack my bags and get out of here."

"No. I'm not letting you. Particularly not if you're in danger. You're staying right here. We'll figure this out together." Daniel heard the command in his voice. Now he wondered what she'd done that made her say he wouldn't want to know her. Wondered what he could do about her situation. Trying to reason it out. At least get the right questions framed. One, just one mental step at a time.

"You can't figure it out!" She moved her face to within inches from his, and he could see the hopelessness in her eyes. "You just run from it. Constantly. These people are crazy."

"I said we'll figure it out." Daniel felt a shock of urgency. "But the first step is, you need to tell me the whole truth. Who are you and what's going on?"

She threw her arms around him. "Oh God, just hold me."

BOOK 4

CHAPTER 23

AUGUST, TWENTY-ONE YEARS AGO. NICE, France. Tom Goddard had invented himself, years earlier, Jay Gatsby style, on a Greyhound bus from Troy, Michigan, to New York City. Thinking that made Tom smile. He supposed that made him the ultimate spook: even his own past was made up. He went back further into his bio, killing time, thinking he was good at it, because that's what he did. Lots of time to kill. Cops on stakeout ate donuts; Tom thought about things. Smoked cigars. Thought about politics, like why the al-Mujari kooks he was working in Nice did what they did. He'd tracked Abdul and Waleed here, and now watched their involvement with Ibrahim, but still didn't have much more than what he knew when he arrived two months earlier: Muslim fundamentalist group with terrorist ties fomenting Saudi dissent, all stewed in the pressure-cooker of the increasing gap between the royals and the average Saudi shlub. He thought about things like that and smoked cigars, and watched.

He was watching for his mark, the black-haired girl. He figured she'd see him if she came out, realize he was looking for her. He knew from his conversations with Nigel, and those he'd overheard the other night, she wasn't stupid. And she was pretty well primed. All he needed to do was see if he could get her to open up. He sat on the patio of the Sea Wall Cafe and Lounge at the Baron David de Duval Hotel. It was a typically gorgeous day in Nice. The air smelled of sweet flowers, the pungent Mediterranean dirt and dried vegetation. A cool breeze on the hill where the Baron David sat offset the sweltering midsummer Mediterranean heat. A few guests populated some of the tables. He could hear the clinking of glasses and the rattle of silverware as the waiters prepared the tables for lunch.

He saw a midfiftiesh man wearing a silk Hawaiian shirt, tan slacks that drooped in the ass, and cheesy-looking perforated shoes walk out to a table with a leggy brunette on his arm. He thought for a half second it was the black-haired girl. Girl was maybe twenty-five, with pushed-up breasts and a great ass but it wasn't her. She also wasn't this guy's daughter. Guy kind of slithering into the tan canvas seat like he had a herniated disk. Probably Miss Boobs-in-Your-Face worked him over. You knew the only reason she was with an old fart like that—ugly, too—had to do with his solid gold Rolex.

He'd need to kill more time, so he went back further in his bio to where he was born Terrance Godchaux, in Flint, Michigan, the son of a plumber and a cocktail waitress. His own undistinguished high school career, playing second-string tight end in football, no chance of a scholarship to college. His mother constantly having "friends" over, then him realizing it's for money, his father not doing anything about it and—Jesus, *enough* already, I'm out of here—and off to the Greyhound station with one bag and only a copy of *Gatsby*, of all things, and by the time he's to New York, Tom Goddard had been created. Tom summoned a waiter and had a plate of the Baron David's Famous Nicoise Salad with Seductive Anchovy-Vinaigrette Dressing. That killed another forty-five minutes.

After getting to New York, Tom Goddard wanders around for a while, waits on tables, manages two years at SUNY, then a degree in Political Science at NYU. He gets recruited by the CIA directly out of undergraduate school. That he'd lied on his application was a plus. The recruiting head for New York thought it showed an enterprising nature, and pursued Tom aggressively. After four years as a junior intelligence operative in home base in Langley, he moved around. Costa Rica. England. Israel. Saudi Arabia.

A bony kid, maybe twenty-five, strutted out toward a table behind the maître d', a tall dark-haired girl following him, print sundress, yellow with green flowers, thin legs with a nice tan. Nope, not her either. This one's wearing mirrored sunglasses, must be pissed at the kid because she's staring straight ahead after they sit down, not moving her head or saying anything while the kid has the sinews in his neck standing out, talking at her while he looks at his menu, talks at her now while the fat busboy pours water, *still* talks at her as she gets up and walks back into the hotel.

Sasha looked toward the dining area at a tall girl in a print dress and mirrored sunglasses, her jaw set as if in anger, walking briskly toward her. She focused over the girl's shoulder and felt her pulse pick up. It was the scruffy American. He was seated at a table, lounging with his cigar. He wore a rumpled cotton shirt with a few buttons to just above his chest hairs, and characteristically wrinkled Bermuda-type shorts and sandals. Only his farm-boy blond hair was trimly in place like he'd just walked off a movie set. What was he doing here? She doubted if it was a coincidence. Yes, she wanted to talk to him. She lowered her eyes, stepped forward and, yes, he saw her. She walked toward a table under an umbrella near the wall. Directly in his line of sight in case he needed encouragement. She settled herself in the chair, behind her sunglasses, watching, as he flicked the ash off his cigar. Yes, she'd wait before going to Yassar, until she knew more. She'd watch Ibrahim, see what Nigel, and perhaps this scruffy American knew, then go to Yassar.

*Now, at thirty-five, Tom Goddard was a Station Chief based in Riyadh running fifteen agents in Saudi Arabia...*he was going on in his head, then: *Ah, there she is.* He flicked his ash off his cigar and stood up. The black-haired girl walked in and sat down underneath an umbrella, looking out from behind big round sunglasses. Tanned skin, sandals, blue bikini showing through a white cotton beach cover-up barely down to her ass—a fine ass at that.

Good, Sasha thought, seeing the scruffy American stand. He sauntered without even trying to appear nonchalant, heading toward her with a smile of recognition as if he were going to say something silly like "We meet again." He reached her table. He wasn't bad looking if one got past the wrinkled pants and shirt. The sandy hair was something out of a Midwestern high school yearbook and he had blue, blue eyes that almost looked like they weren't real. She guessed he was about six feet tall, and he had athletic, broad shoulders that even the baggy shirt couldn't hide. He appeared to be in his midthirties.

"Hi," he said. "I'm Tom Goddard. We've met before. Once or twice at parties."

Meeting implies being introduced. You observed me. Or listened in, rather I should say. "Yes, I recognize you. I remember you and Nigel were intensely engaged on the *Christina* a few weeks back." She took her glasses off, wanting to seem approachable, to make sure he sat down. Yes, of course she was going to invite him to lunch with her.

"Are you alone?" he asked.

"Not if you'll join me." He pulled the chair back and sat down. "I'm Sasha," she said, extending her hand. They shook. She was observing his eyes carefully. They were more than blue, impossibly blue, and she imagined that if she hadn't seen so many, hadn't lived the life she had, they could induce her to tell him things. "One of the idle rich of Nice, or just visiting?" Sasha asked. Not too casually, she wanted to make sure he knew she had an agenda, so this wouldn't be a waste of time. Besides, he'd come over to her table anyhow. He probably had his own agenda, and she doubted it involved trying to pick her up. After all, he'd seen her with Ibrahim, knew their connection.

He chuckled like it wasn't something he was used to doing. "Neither. Just here on business." She imagined most women found him quite fetching.

"I'm surprised. Seems you fit right in, at the parties I mean. I met your friend Nigel on the *Staid Matron* a few nights ago. I saw you there too. What is it you two are up to?"

He heard it without blinking. "I don't know what you mean. I just met Nigel myself this year."

Oh, come on now. This man could get annoying. She looked at him skeptically, but he either didn't pick up on it or wasn't acknowledging it. "Really? I've seen the two of you locked in such conspiratorial conversations all summer."

"Oh, that. We share certain political views."

Politics. Exactly. "Judging by my conversation with Nigel I guess they have to do with what's happening in Saudi Arabia."

"You might say that. It's part of my beat anyhow."

"Oh?" Yes, he was beginning to get annoying, coming over here and only wanting to pitter-patter with roundaboutness. What did he want?

"State Department. U.S. Embassy in Riyadh."

Sasha allowed herself to smirk and made sure he saw it. *Right. Got you pegged. Just happened to be here. A couple of spies, you and Nigel, I'll bet.* "I didn't know U.S. State Department employees could afford vacations on private yachts in Nice."

He repeated that infrequently used chuckle. "I'm on special assignment for some State Department business."

"Oh?" *I'll bet. And just what are you snooping around about now?*

"Agriculture. How to grow grapes in Saudi Arabia."

She looked at him even more skeptically. Now certain he was seeing it and reacting to it, a bit defensive.

"Agriculture's the second-fastest-growing industry in Saudi Arabia, believe it or not," he explained. "It's a big priority for the government."

She was now bored with the chitchat. "Funny. I've never heard Yassar mention it." *That ought to get a rise out of you.*

Tom remained serene. "Oh, you know him? He's greatly admired. Very impressive."

You aren't going to ask me how I know him? He'd seen her with Ibrahim, but just being Ibrahim's consort wouldn't necessarily give her access to Yassar. Not the kind of woman one normally bothers to introduce to Father. No, this Goddard was intentionally sitting back. "Well, I'm ordering," she said, with an edge in her voice. She motioned to a waiter. "I'd be grateful if you'd put out the cigar, now." *He's definitely up to something. Holding out on me. So why the approach from Nigel, and the stonewall today? Who are these people?*

Tom put his cigar in the ashtray and handed it to the waiter at the moment he walked up.

Sasha said, "I don't need a menu, I'll have the Nicoise salad, dressing on the side, and an iced tea." She looked at Tom. "Will you be joining me for lunch?" she said, now with more than an edge, a curtness in her voice. "I'd recommend the Nicoise salad. It's famous."

"So I've heard." He nodded to the waiter. "And a beer."

She stared off over his shoulder now, telling herself to calm down. No sense in taking out her frustrations on some State Department functionary, since maybe that's all he was anyhow. *Have lunch with the unfortunate sot and be done with it.*

Goddard leaned forward in his chair, the way she'd seen him do in those hushed conversations with Nigel. "I'm not intruding or anything, am I?"

Sasha felt her face flush with embarrassment for her impatience with him.

"You sure you wouldn't like to be alone?" he said.

"To the contrary." Now she was feeling guilty about her curtness. Maybe he was just trying to be friendly. Maybe he wasn't up to anything, even if Nigel was. She sighed and felt the tightness in her shoulders. "I'm just a little tense today."

She realized he was observing her. He was definitely thinking about something, poised on the edge of saying it. No, this chap was no dolt. He leaned back in his chair now, as if he were still luxuriating in his cigar, hand poised aloft as if cradling it. "That's what Nigel said about the other night," he said. There was an insinuation in his voice that told her that her initial instincts were correct.

She met his gaze, letting him know she wasn't uncomfortable. "Go on," she said. "What else did he say?"

He was silent, giving it more thought. Then he relaxed. He smiled now, with his entire face, accentuating the wrinkles at the corners of his mouth and eyes that gave him that rugged look. The real smile and not the stifled grin that had accompanied his earlier chuckles. "Just that you were tense," he said. She knew he was holding back on her again, but sensed the recognition that passed between them, aware he knew he'd made contact, sent his message, however veiled, and that it had been received. She knew then he'd been testing her, whether it was to see if he could trust her, whatever, she didn't know. But she knew she'd passed and she'd be hearing more from this Tom Goddard.

CHAPTER 24

AUGUST, TWENTY-ONE YEARS AGO. CAP Ferat, France. Tom sat in the dining room on the *Staid Matron*, anchored off Cap Ferat, killing time as usual, waiting for Nigel, his counterpart from British intelligence. Three generations of boredom had overcome Nigel and he'd joined the British Secret Service. Nigel was one of the few Brits Tom could rely on, and he'd done so throughout his career. And now he needed all the help he could get.

Waiting for Nigel to get back after seeing "where the hell his bloody waiter was." He felt the boat sway incongruously in the blue-green water he'd noticed was almost perfectly calm as he'd motored out to the yacht. The scent of some fowl—sweet aromas accompanying, maybe citrus—being roasted in the galley intermingled with the pungent salt air. He looked at the hand-rubbed mahogany walls, heard the ice pop in his gin and tonic, then watched beads of sweat roll down the sides of a crystal highball glass. He picked it up, wiped the mahogany table with his hand and put the glass on the coaster.

Nigel came back. "You were saying?" he said.

"I think she may be ready to listen to us."

Nigel nodded. "Got that sense in our latest chat." He wore a yellow woven silk tie against a white cotton broadcloth shirt. His blue blazer, brass buttons with little anchors on them, was laid over the chair. Tom was listening and at the same time thinking that Nigel was probably the only guy in Nice on a boat this big wearing a tie. And today it had two dimples, right below the knot where he always had one, perfectly in the middle. Must've gotten dressed in a hurry.

Tom said, "She's pretty twisted up inside."

Nigel said, "Uhm, agreed. Senses she's in a jam."

Tom wondered if he should tell Nigel about the double dimple. But was that like telling a Brit he had bad breath? "Yeah, she mentioned Yassar. Wanted me to know she knows him."

"And?"

"That may be our hook. All our checks say she's almost like family with him." Nigel nodded. Tom thought again about his conversation with John Franklin, his Section Head back in Langley. "Use her if you can but be careful," Franklin had said. "Assume she likes things the way they are." Tom didn't think so, but he'd see.

"Ditto from Whitehall. Ari's people in Tel Aviv as well." A fiftyish waiter with sandy hair brought in a silver tray. Two gold-edged bone china plates of Duck l'Orange. Hardly a roll-up-the-sleeves working lunch. Tom was thinking he'd be happier with a turkey sandwich when Nigel asked him, "Like some wine?"

"No thanks." He held up his gin and tonic, saw Nigel glance down at the coaster, then the moist spot on the table. "Where is Ari?" Tom asked.

"Back in Saudi Arabia playing his role of Mosin Mahavandi, oil broker."

Tom felt his juices start to flow. He thought about those bastards Abdul and Waleed, that nut who sent them, Sheik bin Abdur, Mr. Happy Face the Clown, the holy son of a bitch who at the drop of a turban became an epithet-spewing lunatic.

"Okay, so where are we? You got anything new?"

"Nothing particularly new, just uhm, uhm, more confirmation of what we've had, some more clear links to the Sudan terrorist training camps. Although we do know the Sheik's brother, rich bastard based in London, has been funding them. But he's been bloody clever; no clear ties, at least no paper trails." Nigel squinted as he talked, showed a mental toughness beneath that frail exterior, the tenacity Tom liked so much.

"We've got nobody inside," Tom said. "Our guys were the ones who turned up Abdul and Waleed with Ibrahim at Harvard. Based on your guys linking them to him back in Saudi Arabia last year." Tom felt impatience welling up inside him, and forced it back down. These al-Mujari bastards were getting to him, making him feel the old urgency he'd learned to restrain as a junior operative. "But still no luck in turning up any of the U.S. splinter terrorist cells they're linked to."

"Ari thinks he's found three splinter organizations linked to them out his way, and we've got to have some in the UK if the Sheik's brother's there, but no luck uncovering them."

Tom sighed. "So, add all that to the Sheik and his fundamentalist cronies sticking pins into the Saudi faithful to get them agitated about jobs, and what do we have? And now these guys trying to turn Ibrahim, not even being subtle enough to whisper, about returning the country to fundamentalist Muslim values. Sounds to me like the same deal we had in Iran after the Shah. A bunch of fundamentalist bastards drag the country back into the Stone Age, for who knows how long? So how much time we got in Saudi Arabia?" Tom felt his heart pump faster.

"Hard to say. I can tell you what we're afraid of, old boy," Nigel said. "They topple the Saudis and we've got precious little but the bloody Russians to look to for our oil."

"That and you've got a bunch of terrorist nuts running all over the globe, funded by the richest oil nation in the world." Tom squeezed his palms together under the table.

"Wouldn't be the last Muslim nation to go. Turkey would be next, I'm sure. Perhaps even Pakistan."

"Not to mention what Ari's afraid of," Tom said. He remembered seeing Ari's face the first time he met him, at the '72 Olympics as one of the follow-up team after the Arabs murdered seven Israeli Olympic team members. He turned to look at Nigel. "You sure Sasha and Ibrahim are coming tonight?"

"Absolutely. Ibrahim wouldn't miss this big a party. I'm becoming quite the rage this season, old boy," Nigel said. He raised an eyebrow. "I'm sure she'll be here."

"Good. Then I can set up a chance to make our pitch."

Tom was thinking about another cigar, but decided against it, his mouth stale after four Havanas in one day. He was sitting on a deck chair at 2:00 a.m., watching the party still throbbing around him. Last time he spied Nigel he was still wearing the tie with the offending double dimple. Now watching Sasha, her not acknowledging him after they'd set up lunch for tomorrow. It had been easy after her fight with Ibrahim, them going on at each other in Arabic with nobody paying much attention. Her sitting stiffly by herself. *She's ready.*

His work was done for tonight, but he was still watching, now just for sport. Sasha had earlier glided from group to group, all the sudden tonight letting herself look available—she must be really pissed about what Ibrahim said to her—then seemed to tire of dodging guys who didn't know better to lay off her, didn't know what they were messing with. Still, Ibrahim had acted like the loudmouthed jerk he could be with too much scotch in him. Now she was rubbing it in again, sitting with some pasty-faced Italian in black leather pants and a white silk shirt open to his chest hairs. *Careful, girl. Don't get yourself thrown out of here. Then I'm back to square one.* Sasha looked strained in her smile, like she'd bite her lip if she were inclined to show her feelings that much. He started to feel sorry for her. Then she made it worse by meeting eyes with him with that "help me" look, buried beneath the I'd-be-bored-with-it-all-if-only-I-weren't-having-so-goddamn-much-fun glaze of sophistication, the facade he recognized well.

Yeah, she's ready.

Tom continued watching Sasha, saw her body move inside that silk dress, all that youth and energy. He had a grungy feeling. Usually the people he recruited were shady sleazeballs, out for their own profit. The ones like this girl, just a kid, the ones who did it out of commitment, those were tough. And this was as shitty as it got. He tried to feel better about it, telling himself she was a whore, and probably rich from it. But watching her now he felt soulless.

It made him revisit their other possibilities. Try Yassar again through government channels? Not much hope. And that wouldn't get them inside the al-Mujari. If Ibrahim was inside, Sasha could get them enough to slow down, even cripple the entire organization.

But what about using some of the other girls they thought of? This Nafta? He immediately rejected that, as they had earlier. Nafta wasn't as close to Ibrahim. And this kid Sasha had nerve. Brains. They needed her. They'd have to get her to do it. And then he remembered her file. *Some life. Screwed over by the Drug*

Queen and the Prince himself. How the hell was she still so close to Yassar?

Yeah, they needed her and he'd go through with it. But he'd handle her himself, not pass her off to one of the other guys who ran agents for him. He'd do that much for her.

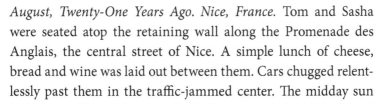

August, Twenty-One Years Ago. Nice, France. Tom and Sasha were seated atop the retaining wall along the Promenade des Anglais, the central street of Nice. A simple lunch of cheese, bread and wine was laid out between them. Cars chugged relentlessly past them in the traffic-jammed center. The midday sun had warmed the stone on which they sat and already softened the cheese to produce oily stains on the paper wrappings. They sipped burgundy from paper cups.

"I see you and Ibrahim had another fight last night."

"Yes, it's getting to be *de rigueur.*" Sasha was feeling like raw nerves today. A little afraid to be so open around Tom, unsure where this conversation was going, but knowing he was finally going to surface his agenda. But then he was open now, too. He had a warmth today that made her start to trust him. And a gentleness beneath the rugged exterior.

"You okay?" he asked. She liked the quiet way he said it.

"Yes, thanks."

He looked at the cheese like it was some new species. She couldn't tell if he was delighted or astonished.

"Explorateur."

"Oh. Amazing," he said. She smiled. She decided she liked him. The aw shucks facade that wasn't always a facade.

"So, not that I wouldn't be flattered, but you obviously didn't invite me out to try to seduce me."

She saw him look at her like he was trying to think of a snappy response, then a smile, then his face turned serious. "No. As Nigel said, we've been watching these guys hanging around Ibrahim for some time."

Sasha was silent. She felt her heart rise, hoping he would plunge right into it. But now he was hesitating, just looking at her, seemingly thinking. "Go on," she urged.

"They're dangerous. And we think you can help us."

"How?"

"Like Nigel said. Watch and listen. Tell us what happens. We'll do the rest."

"Who are you?"

"CIA. Nigel's British Secret Service. There's another one of us you haven't met yet, Ari Verchik. He's Israeli Mossad."

"I thought so." She felt a surge of blood to her face, a sense of minor triumph at having her suspicions confirmed, then a tingle of fear. "Who are these people Abdul and Waleed?"

"They're part of an organization called the al-Mujari, a Muslim fundamentalist group based in Saudi Arabia. Led by a cleric named Sheik bin Abdur. They're talking about overthrowing the Saudi government and returning it to the Saudi people. Of course, led by themselves."

"And Ibrahim? How does he figure into it?" She felt she was hearing too much too quickly, but was still greedily compelled to absorb more.

"I guess they figure if they can turn him, they'll use him as an example for others. Plus I guess it gives them someone on the inside in the family so they know what's going on."

"They've already turned him." She felt like someone was pushing on her stomach and saw Tom looking at her, watching, not blinking his eyes.

"How so?" Now she was seized by concern. How did she know who Tom was? Or Nigel? Tom must have seen her face change because he asked: "What's wrong?"

"I now realize I have only your word as to who you are."

"Unfortunately, we don't exactly carry IDs." He reached into his pocket and handed her a State Department business card with the words: *Thomas A. Goddard—Deputy Assistant Ambassador.* "Here. Call the embassy in Riyadh. Better yet, call information and get the number yourself so you know it's not a phony card. Give them your name. They'll be expecting your call. Then the embassy will patch you into CIA headquarters at Langley. Will that do it?"

Sasha nodded. It struck her that she was getting herself involved in something much more serious than she'd imagined.

"What? What's wrong? Talk to me."

She liked that. Concerned about her. And that gentleness again. Yes, she liked him. He was contemplative, thoughtful, like Yassar. She imagined Yassar would like him too. "Nothing." She looked back up at him. "Just that one doesn't start a life of—spying every day." She laughed nervously. "So, back to business, I guess. So what's going on?"

"I told you. Their plans are to take over. Throw out the royal family, and they're recruiting Ibrahim."

"Like you're recruiting me."

"Yeah."

"Sticky business."

"Yeah." He was again watching her without blinking.

"I'm wondering why I don't just run away from the whole thing. Leave."

"And?"

"I think you know. I'll bet you know a lot about me. You're careful, thoughtful. I'm sure you know how close to Yassar I am."

"Yeah." He looked down at the ground for a moment, then back up at her. Was he ashamed?

"So you know…" Her voice trailed off. She realized he probably knew everything about her. Christina. Her relationship with Yassar. Her life with Ibrahim, her role as a concubine. She remembered thinking that before, anticipating encountering someone from her prior life, and had just as quickly decided she'd never been ashamed of herself before and wasn't going to start now. Not then, not now. *So what?* "So you know I'd be worried about Yassar."

"So are we," he said gravely.

She looked up at him, her mind spinning. "You said these people want to…you used the word *overthrow.*"

Tom was silent, giving his answer some thought. Observing her. Now Sasha's brain flashed with panic. She'd never allowed herself to think it through. But now it made sense. It meant that Yassar might actually be in *danger.*

"We're trying to stop them. Will you help us?"

"What's your intention? Why not just go directly to the Saudi government? To Yassar?"

"We've already tried. They insist it's a domestic issue. Private." He leaned forward toward her, the way he had at her table at the Baron David, as she'd seen him lean forward to speak with Nigel. "Will you help us?" he asked again.

"I'll think about it," she said. Sasha felt the sense her decision would change her life in ways she couldn't possibly imagine, then wondered if it hadn't already irrevocably changed. Her relationship with Ibrahim would never be the same. She recalled how she'd had to steel herself to respond to Ibrahim's advances the previous afternoon and yet realized she could get through it. And she thought of Yassar, felt her heart ache, and wondered if she had any choice. How could she leave if he was in danger?

CHAPTER 25

AUGUST, TWENTY-ONE YEARS AGO. CAP Ferat, France. Sasha imagined they must look like a casual group, seated on the rear deck of the *Staid Matron,* four friends having a drink under a brilliant blue afternoon sky. But what was going on in Sasha's mind told a different story. And she knew her body language—arms resting on the chair, both feet on the floor, as if poised to jump—gave off something of the vibrations generated by the turmoil in her mind. Tom, Nigel, and the new one, Ari something or other, the Israeli Mossad agent, sitting around her, positioned as if to set up a crossfire. The gentle rocking of the yacht added to her sense of uncertain footing.

"What did Ibrahim say?" Tom asked Sasha.

"He didn't say anything. Are you satisfied?" She saw Tom watching her, knowing he sensed she was angry. And why shouldn't she be? Invited out for a drink by Tom, knowing he'd be interested in following up on their chat, but ambushed by the three of them. She anticipated perhaps Nigel, but this Ari? She fired her gaze back at Tom to punctuate her last comment.

"That doesn't prove anything," Tom said. "We wouldn't expect him to step forward with any information to you."

"He still talks to me. He still listens to me."

"Sasha, it's, uhm, not obvious to us that you're ready for this. We don't, uhm, uhm, think you want to hear it and all that."

Nigel waved his hands in the air. "But I'll say it anyhow. Abdul and Waleed are in regular contact with the al-Mujari. We know they were trained in a terrorist camp in Sudan. And we know that they and their, uhm, Shiite extremist friends are serious about overthrowing the Saudi government. The Saudi royal family corrupted by its exposure to Western infidels. You know the story." He paused.

What's going on here? She looked at Tom. Yes, they were setting her up for a high-pressure sell.

"It's worse than that, actually," Ari said. "We've heard about assassination plots. Death squads." He was watching her face for a reaction. "You're close with Prince Yassar, too, aren't you?"

Damn you if you're playing with me! "Yes," Sasha said guardedly. "I'm close with him."

"The al-Mujari have been working on this for years," Tom said. His tone was almost apologetic. "I've been telling you, you're in danger."

"What are you talking about?"

"We're convinced they're trying to get inside the royal family," Nigel said, "they've been working on Prince Ibrahim since he started college, trying to turn him to their cause."

She looked at Tom as if to say they'd been through this before. But then they hadn't, at least not all of it. It was news this Abdul and Waleed and whoever they were with had been working on Ibrahim for that long. "I already told you Ibrahim's spouting their views," she said to Tom. "But that's hardly what I'd call getting inside. What do you mean?"

"We know that they've targeted the king and the crown prince for assassination," Tom said. "But we thought you should know that Prince Yassar is also on their list."

Sasha involuntarily threw her head back, as if she'd been slapped in the face. Her eyes showed anger, fear and outrage at the same time. *How dare you manipulate me this way!* She leaned forward in her chair. "Listen, gentlemen," she said. "I don't appreciate the hard sell!" She looked at Tom, into those blue eyes, and couldn't conceal her feelings of betrayal. "Cheap tricks, shock tactics—whatever you people in your business call it." She inhaled, trying to get her composure back. "First you take turns trying to get me off balance. So what comes next?"

Nigel and Ari looked at Tom as if to say "you've got a handful here." Tom motioned to the others with his head. "Let me talk to her," he said. Nigel and Ari got up and left, Nigel making an awkward sort of bow. Tom sighed. "I'm sorry. We weren't intending to gang up on you. We were trying to make sure you understood that Yassar's in jeopardy. So if you call that a hard sell, maybe it was. It was my idea, so don't blame them. We can stop this if you like."

Sasha watched him with her hands clamped on the arms of the chair, guard still up, still angry. They knew she wasn't likely to walk away from her concern for Yassar. "How do you know all this? About targeting Yassar?"

Tom had a look that exposed his vulnerability. "We can prove it," he said softly. He was silent for a moment, giving it more thought. "What do you want to do?"

Sasha didn't answer because she'd already been wondering that before he asked it. She still didn't have anything to go to Yassar with but more unsubstantiated bits and pieces. And if she asked Tom to give her what he had, he might or might not. But probably not. Maybe she should play along with them for a while. Maybe she could trust Tom, at least, as long as he didn't try to pressure her like this again.

"We do need your help," Tom said. "I've thought this through carefully, thought of the other ways we could try. They won't work. You're our best shot." He was speaking slowly, as if he were choosing his words carefully. He leaned forward in the chair again, which she now recognized was his way of under-scoring an important comment. "If you agree to help, I'll be your contact. Nobody else. All we're asking is that you stay inside and report to us. Information, that's all."

Sasha felt herself nod, not wanting to commit herself, but wanting to find a way to work through this.

"You mind if I ask you something personal?" Tom asked.

"Okay." She suddenly felt worn out, de-energized.

"Why are you so close to Yassar? I mean, after—everything?"

Sasha felt pain in her throat. "We always had a bond." She looked off into the distance, over Tom's shoulder. "I forgave him. And he showed me that he was sorry even before he apologized. It's complex. Let's leave it there." She looked back at Tom. "I'll consider your proposal. I'll discuss it with Yassar, fly back spe-cifically for that if I have to."

Tom's head rose, his eyes charged with fervor. "You can't. Yassar can't know. I told you we tried that."

"I can't lie to him!" Sasha felt a slam of panic, only now beginning to understand what they were asking of her.

"Imagine how it looks—a gaggle of foreign secret services recruit you to watch his own son. Even if you say it's to protect him. He just won't buy it. There isn't enough proof. That's what we need you for."

Sasha had the sense she was losing her balance, that the rocking of the boat was unbearable. A sense of nothingness, a complete absence of any emotion or concept of reality enveloped her, as if the only foundation she'd possessed had been removed from her. How could she do this without telling Yassar?

Sasha entered the duplex apartment she shared with Ibrahim, maintaining the same oddly vacant, emotionless state she'd experienced on the *Staid Matron*. She took in the apartment through trancelike eyes. Standing in the center of the room, she removed her shoes so she could feel the cool marble under her feet and offset the sense of groundlessness. Thank God Ibrahim wasn't there. She wondered what her reaction to him would be in her zombie state.

Was it possible he knew these people were planning to kill his own father? Why not talk to Ibrahim? No. Absurd. There was no going back with him. No emotion, no trust.

And go to Yassar? She'd heard Tom. They'd already tried. No luck. And they must have more concrete information than she did. Yet, they were outsiders. She wasn't. She could get Yassar to listen to the facts. But they weren't about to divulge secret intelligence to some twenty-year-old concubine to the royal family. Certainly not Tom; he was too careful. These men were professionals. Could she agree to help them and then tell Yassar? Not until she had some hard information. And there was still the fundamental question: how could she possibly do it their way without telling Yassar?

Now she felt a surge of the anguish that must have been stored in her when she realized what they were asking her to do. She sensed that her deathlike state was a result of her inevitable estrangement from Yassar, the barrier she would erect by concealing her activities from him. She threw herself into a chair and her face collapsed into her hands. She might lose Yassar. Wherever it led, he might, probably would, find out eventually. This wasn't all just going to go away. Not if what Tom and the others said was true.

She raised her head slowly. The only way out was to do it. And she realized why: she didn't just have a bond with Yassar, she loved him. Like a father. She'd do it for him, because she loved him, and her belief in that would sustain her through it, even if it meant she might lose him.

CHAPTER 26

FEBRUARY, TWENTY YEARS AGO. RIYADH, Saudi Arabia. Sasha lay on the bed in Ibrahim's suite, pretending to sleep, certain she was carrying it off, as she'd been doing for the last six months. Now listening to Ibrahim, Abdul and Waleed talking in the living room before Ibrahim's nightly party, Ibrahim filling his belly full of scotch, Abdul and Waleed filling his head with fundamentalist rhetoric. She tried to overhear all of it, but was afraid to move to the door. *This is impossible.*

Since she'd agreed to work with Tom Goddard she'd been frustrated. Ibrahim had been unwilling to fully open up to her since their arguments in Nice. And he was smart enough to speak in hushed tones, or not at all while she was nearby, particularly when Abdul and Waleed visited him.

She was only catching every third word in the other room, and finally decided to move to the door despite her concerns about being detected. If someone came toward the bedroom she'd pretend she was just waking up, staggering around half asleep. *Pretty lame.* But it would have to do. She slid out of the sheets and removed her panties so at least she could hope for the element of shock, then tiptoed toward the door.

"U.S. military…Air Force…army…training…like the oil companies…" she heard, leaning toward the crack she had left open. She thought it was Abdul's voice.

"...bombing, they'll see..." She picked up another snippet, Waleed.

Definitely Ibrahim: "Destabilize...but careful." She leaned in toward the crack, peered out through it. *Ibrahim!* Walking straight toward the bedroom door. She felt a blast of adrenaline and ran back toward the bed, threw herself under the sheets. She pretended to sleep, feeling her pulse thumping, wondering if he'd heard her.

Ibrahim walked in, paused as if to allow his eyes to adjust to the light. She noted he didn't turn it on. He walked over toward the bed, sat down on the edge and stroked her hair. His touch was gentle, and under other circumstances, a year ago, she would have thought he was being sweet. Perhaps he thought he was. He bent over and kissed her. She pretended to awaken.

"Oh," she said. "Is it time for the party?"

"Yes. We're leaving soon. Time for you to get dressed."

She turned herself over, reached up and hugged him. It made her feel unclean, but she thought of Yassar, then tried to relax her body so Ibrahim wouldn't sense something was wrong. She was getting good at it, particularly when she was having sex with him. It was like going to her job every day, dreaming all the while of somebody who didn't exist to get her through it. Not as difficult as she thought it might be.

"I'll get up now," she said. "I'll be ready shortly."

But she was thinking this wasn't any good. It wasn't working. Picking up a few words here and there just wouldn't help. She needed to get something of substance. And now, during Ibrahim's spring break from Harvard, while Abdul and Waleed were here, she was certain what they were saying was what she needed. The time was right to convince Tom that they needed a different plan, make a change so she could get the evidence.

She'd helped Yassar work Ibrahim out of one bad habit; maybe she could do it again, perhaps not so easily, but with enough evidence perhaps she could put Yassar out of jeopardy and get out of here and on with her life. Wherever that led.

Sasha heard the clatter of the typewriters and the teletypes in the communications room of the American Embassy in Riyadh. College-aged clerks, most of them blonde-haired blue-eyed girls, cruised back and forth with papers in their hands and airs of self-importance. She took in the back rooms, the bustling center of activity belied by the facade: the opulent, old-world majesty of the main entry rooms and public spaces, accessible by other diplomats and the occasional American citizen looking for relief from trouble with the Mutawwa'iin.

"What excuse did you use to get here?" Tom asked. He looked at her disapprovingly, as though she were a high school student late with a term paper.

"Nafta and I went out shopping. I'm going to the United States with Ibrahim next week. Spring break is almost over. I need a visa, so that's why we're here. We're with a Royal Guard, and Nafta and he are both in the outside room. I don't have much time." She gave him a look that said she didn't need his paternalistic disapproval.

"I think I can slow the process down so you'll have to come back in order to get it. More time for us to talk if we need it." He paused, then nodded at her. "So what's so important?"

"I need the tape recorder," she said.

"I told you that was too risky." He observed her calmly, as if trying to say that the conversation was over.

"I don't care. It's not working like this. They're here now. But I'm only getting bits and pieces."

"What if you get caught?" Tom said, showing her that studied pace of his, trying to slow the conversation down. "I appreciate your zealousness, but shoot-first tactics won't cut it. This is a methodical, careful business." He paused. "You push this too fast and you'll get yourself killed."

His words were unexpected, hit her like an insult. Her instinct was to retort back. "Then you and your secret-agent friends will have to start all over again, right?"

"Not only telling me how to do my job, but telling me what I think, too?" Tom said.

She regretted her sharpness, aware now of how stressed she was, and frustrated by Tom's resistance. "I'm sorry."

He listened without blinking. "And maybe I'm being over-dramatic. But what if you're caught?"

"My only exposure is on the way in."

"What about bringing the tapes out?"

"I won't bring them out. I'll just listen to them. And report back to you by phone."

"We've never done it that way. They might tap the phones."

Wasn't he being overly conservative? Wasn't he supposed to push her to take the chances? If she got caught, he'd be able to wash his hands of her. Why was he being so obstinate? "Then we'll do it the usual way. Letters to my 'friends.'"

He looked at her, seemed to weigh it in his mind, then finally nodded. "Okay."

"And if I find out anything that's absolutely electric, I can decide if it's worth the risk to bring the tape out."

"Don't piss me off."

She wondered if there was something he wasn't telling her. Or maybe he was paranoid. Or maybe that's just the way they worked. *He's careful*, she reminded herself.

Placing the tape recorder was a problem. Where was the appropriate place? The question plagued her while Ibrahim and she had sex. The subject had distracted her from her customary spirited performance. And that wasn't the half of it. The timing, when to place it, was a conundrum as well. There was the cleaning staff constantly turning Ibrahim's suite upside down. Nobody around for a few minutes, then one of the bellgirls coming, or even Nafta.

She felt the urgency of other things, too. Such as staying the favorite, so she could keep her access to Ibrahim, her ability to observe him. There were new, younger girls around, not a serious challenge, but it made her think. A reminder, just as it made her shudder seeing Ibrahim "loan" two of the girls to Abdul and Waleed the other night. She sighed, now giving in to the release after her climax; the release from the pressure and her mental agitation as well. It made it easier for her to focus. She watched Ibrahim.

He was stroking her thigh. Didn't he suspect anything? Were men so dense? Or was Ibrahim just so arrogant? As long as he was getting what he needed, would he even question anything?

"I thought I lost you in a fog there for a while."

"Really?" Had it shown? Maybe he wasn't so obtuse after all.

"Thinking about whether or not that new dress shows off your thighs?"

She cringed at his condescension. "No, just anguishing over a broken fingernail."

He laughed.

"I got over it," she said.

"You sure did." He leaned over and kissed her. Did he have to be so pleasant? She felt a rise of self-reproach.

He patted her on the behind. *Good.* His signal he was ready to get up. He rolled off the bed.

"Time for a quick shower. Then off to the ministry."

Sasha waited until she heard the water running, gauging time in her mind. It might take a few minutes to locate the appropriate place for the tape recorder, figure five minutes in all. She got up, still naked, and walked into the anteroom. She eyed the sofa, remembering the radius of the tape recorder—sixty feet. She looked at an end table with a latticed door, never used to store anything. That was it, she'd do it now. She walked into her room adjoining Ibrahim's anteroom.

A woman stood in the center of the bedroom. Sasha felt the blood surge to her face, the jar of a shock. "Nafta!"

"You're underdressed, sister."

Sasha laughed. She kissed her friend on the cheek. She'd get her robe, then go back into Ibrahim's anteroom and hide the recorder. But what if Nafta followed her in? And what *was* she doing here? "What are you up to?"

"I didn't want to be available," she said. Sasha could see now that she was upset. "For entertaining Abdul and Waleed." She looked away. Sasha thought she must be ashamed to even be worried about it, knowing Nafta had once been the favorite herself. Nafta turned back to her. "I hope you don't mind. I figured they wouldn't look for me here."

"Not at all." She hugged Nafta, then put on her robe, with the tape recorder securely in its pocket. "I'll come back once Ibrahim goes to the ministry. We'll have a snack."

Sasha returned to Ibrahim's anteroom, feeling pain for her friend. Everything quiet, and Ibrahim still in the shower. Good. She opened the two doors of the end table, fingers steady, mind working but her breathing shallow. She placed the recorder inside and hit the switch to the slow speed, remembering Tom said that would allow for four hours of recording. As she closed the doors she heard Ibrahim's shower turn off, and headed toward the bedroom. Then a lurch. She hadn't wiped off her prints! No time now, she'd have to do it later. Then she thought, maybe if they found the recorder they might suspect one of the other girls. She thought of Nafta in her bedroom; she'd leave her prints on the machine. If it was discovered, she wasn't having anyone else arrested in her place.

She removed her robe and slid back under the sheets, but a troubling thought filtered through her mind, destroying the momentary sense of relief that her job was finished: she'd be taking just as much risk retrieving the tapes as planting the recorder. And listening to them. And making the copies and stashing them so she'd have backups for Yassar. She felt an ominous rumble of dread.

Sasha realized she must look as if she meant business, because the self-important U.S. Embassy girl paused to let her pass and enter the conference room where Tom was seated.

"I'm stunned. You won't believe it," Sasha said. She had the tape in her hand, remembering her argument with Tom on the phone about bringing it out—about even calling him at all—but it was urgent.

"I'll believe it."

"Listen," she said, as Tom put the tape into the machine and turned it on.

It was Abdul's voice. "So it's decided. We bomb the military targets once we have access to the plans."

Then Ibrahim: "I'll get them. It may take some time. But I'll get them. I'll be back from school in late June."

Waleed was next: "That's too long!" Sasha pushed the fast-forward, saw Tom raise his hand.

"Wait," he said.

"You can listen to the rest of it later." She stopped the tape, found the next reference.

Now Waleed: "I'm authorized to speak for Sheik bin Abdur. You will be installed as the new head of the Saudi government, afterward. He sees you as a righteous Muslim. He knows both the Shiites and Sunnis will accept you. You've been well trained, as well as well schooled in our Islam."

Next Ibrahim: "What about my father?"

A long pause, some fumbling, then Abdul: "He'll be retired. A consultancy if he wants it. You can't fight the will of the people. Of Allah."

Waleed: "There is no god but Allah!"

Voices—were there more than the three of them?: "La ilaha ilallah!"

Sasha hit the fast-forward again. Next it was a voice she didn't recognize, somebody on a speakerphone: (faintly) "Ibrahim, you are a righteous Muslim amongst a sea of infidels...We choose you to be the successor to power."

"Appalling," Sasha said. She felt her blood racing, now repulsed at the thought of the things she did, her body, her hands...with Ibrahim...Tom had a look on his face she'd never seen before. Much calmer, much more reserved. "Whose voice was that?" she asked.

Tom looked at her, words on his lips. She could see he was thinking, trying to decide.

What does that mean?

"It's him," Tom finally said. "Sheik bin Abdur."

CHAPTER 27

JULY, TWENTY YEARS AGO. PARIS, France. Tom always thought the American Embassy in Paris was more designed for the French than the Americans—those silly narrow doorways a broad-shouldered man could barely get through, the ceiling-height windows that had an effeminate quality about them, and the skinny columns that never carried off the sense of stolidity of good old American thick-stoned bulk, something like the Washington Monument. Nigel fit in there, he thought, looking at him across the table, always the dandy.

Ari, swarthy, hairy and earthy as ever, came up to give him a good-natured hug. Within minutes they were hunched over a polished oak conference table, all business.

"Ibrahim's out of control, even Sasha's convinced of that. We need to move our agenda up, way up," Tom said. "These bastards are better organized than we thought. They're planning bombings on the American bases at Dhahran and Riyadh. Then hits on the royal family. Disrupt the relationship with their allies, then topple the government. Crazier plans have worked."

"How soon?" Nigel asked.

"Next week," Tom said. Ari and Nigel exchanged a sideways glance. "How soon you think we can be ready to move?"

"We can get close enough to do three of them, we think," Ari said. "And we have a chance to make it look like it was power struggles within the splinter groups and local al-Mujari cells that would implicate other members. Maybe we get lucky and start some infighting within the al-Mujari."

Nigel was looking at Ari with admiration. "Brilliantly conceived," he said. "We could get to one ourselves. High up in the, uhm, organization. We think he's the cell leader."

"And you're thinking?" Ari asked Tom.

"They're planning to install Ibrahim as their new leader. Only one thing we can do."

"And that is?"

"We light up Ibrahim." Tom knew better than the others what he was saying. He was already thinking about Sasha, knowing she could handle it, at least once she knew everything. "Ibrahim is the only one on the inside of the royals. Take him out and it stops there for now."

"How're we going to do it?" Ari asked.

Tom felt his stomach curling into a ball. He said, "Sasha. She'll have to do it. She's the only one who can get close enough. Leave it to me," he said. "I'll talk to her. She's my agent, it's my job."

"Unpleasant. The chap she sleeps with," Nigel said. "Does she love him?"

Ari answered for Tom: "No way."

"Still, lads, not going to be easy for her."

"She'll understand once we tell her everything," Tom said. "Sleeping with him or not, she's got the grit to do it."

July, Twenty Years Ago. Riyadh, Saudi Arabia. Sasha stepped out of a limousine in front of the French Embassy in Riyadh. She walked with her head erect, arms folded across her chest beneath her black abaya. A Royal Guard escorted her through the gate and into the building. She'd received Tom's urgent message and had come to meet him there under the guise of obtaining a visa for her trip to Nice. Her nerves were frayed. Feeling an ache in her legs. As if the strain of maintaining this shadow life weren't difficult enough, it was compounded by the constraints of being a woman in Saudi Arabia. Not free to come and go as she pleased without one of these bloody beefeaters trailing along behind her. It had gotten wearying. But she was hostage to her desire to protect Yassar.

She knew Tom wanted something more from her; and she'd already made up her mind she wasn't about to agree to it. She was worn out. Literally months had passed since she'd given him the tapes she felt would be the evidence to go to Yassar. *He said things move slowly in this world.* But now she was beginning to think things didn't happen at all. Maybe she'd bring what she knew and her duplicate tapes to Yassar without waiting to learn anything else of what Tom and the others knew.

A French girl wearing a suit led her to a small conference room while the Royal Guard seated himself in the lobby.

Tom was sitting alone behind the conference room table, looking grave. "Hello, Sasha."

"Hello," she said. She made certain her tone revealed her annoyance with him. "You said it was urgent."

"Yes. How much time do we have?"

"As long as it takes to get a visa." She glanced around the room. "Technically, we're in France. So, forever?" She laughed, but it didn't make her feel any better. Tom smiled, but there was no warmth in it.

"This whole thing has taken an abrupt turn," he said. She saw him fingering the edge of the desk, a little nervous oddity she'd never noticed before. "It's become more serious and needs some immediate steps from our side."

"Our side?"

"The U.S., the Brits and Israelis are taking the lead. NATO is involved, or we wouldn't be here in the French Embassy." Sasha raised her chin expectantly. Tom went on. "We're coordinating some measures against the al-Mujari…"

"Measures?" she cut in. She heard the edge in her voice.

"I'm not sure you want to know all this, but you probably need to, and certainly deserve to." Sasha felt her breath quicken. "Some people are going to disappear, or at least stop being a nuisance." He looked at her with a hard glint in his eyes. "The world will be better off, believe me."

So they were talking about killing people, she realized. She felt a numbness in her fingers. Then a flare of anger. "And you'll be asking me to do something, no doubt. What?"

She saw him frown at the aggressiveness of her question. "We aren't enemies here. You and I are on the same side, remember? There's no need for tension between us."

Sasha realized he might be right. Still: "But you didn't call me urgently to tell me this. You want my help, right?"

"Yes." His eyes were now softer, connecting with her as usual. But she knew he was asking her help in killing someone. Why not just ask her for information, use it to do it and not even tell her? Despite herself, she asked, "Who?"

The answer was immediate. "Ibrahim."

The shock was a blow inside her brain. "Oh my God, you can't be serious!" His face didn't move. "Are you out of your mind? I thought somebody, some faceless…somebody I didn't know. He's Yassar's *son!* For God's sake, I sleep with him. Yes, he's an unwitting, egotistical fool who's being taken advantage of. But kill him?"

"It needs doing."

"Don't tell me that!"

"Maybe I should let him tell you himself." Tom put a tape recorder on the desk, hit the play button. "We recorded this yesterday in Waleed's hotel room."

"We do not need to tell you the solution," Abdul was saying in near frenzy.

"Shari'a does not permit the killing of an Arab brother, but it does permit driving out the infidels!" Waleed said, incensed. Obviously at the end of a long, passionate exchange. Sasha heard a low grunt of acknowledgment, unmistakably Prince Ibrahim's. She tensed her shoulders. "There is no sin, no violation of shari'a in driving the infidel Saudi regime from the holy Saudi peninsula. There is no violation of shari'a if they must be killed in order to wipe out the stain of the infidels from our holy land, the home of the two holiest sites in all of Islam!"

"Then, our holy friend, you must choose between the life of your own father or the preservation of the purity of the Islamic state! Either your father and his brethren in the Saudi government must die or the infidels will eventually pollute our holy land and destroy the nation of Islam!" Sasha was unsure whether she heard the murmur of Prince Ibrahim's acknowledgment. Her breathing had accelerated to the point she had to make a conscious effort to slow it down.

"Do you accept this grave challenge, this test that Allah has chosen for you? Do you choose the preservation of the nation of Islam? Do you choose the return of the holy Islamic sites to the

Muslim people? Do you choose the expulsion of the infidels? Do you choose death for the Saudi royal family?"

"Yes!" came Prince Ibrahim's unmistakable reply. Sasha felt a slam of anger, and simultaneously tears flushed to her eyes. "Damn you!" she yelled at Tom. "Damn you!"

"Would you rather we do nothing and let them kill Yassar?"

Sasha slumped back into her chair, hearing her pulse slamming in her ears. "And killing Ibrahim is the alternative? So I help you kill his son—God, I've already helped you!" Tom sat still, his expression betraying nothing. "And have Yassar hate me for the rest of my life?"

"There's no other way."

"Take Yassar the tape!"

"They'll kill him anyhow!"

"If you won't, I will!" She reached for the tape recorder. Tom yanked it back and started the machine again.

"Will you do it?" Abdul asked.

Waleed jumped in, still at a fever pitch: "You are the only one who can! Nobody else can get close enough!"

Sasha thought her lungs would burst. "Yes! Yes, I'll kill him!" Ibrahim cried.

Sasha's slammed her fists down on the table. "All right! Enough!" Tom turned the machine off. "What do you want me to do?" she asked. Tom reached into his jacket pocket and Sasha saw the blue-gray steel of a Beretta in his hand when it emerged, a silencer in the other.

"Oh my God! You're not suggesting...I...?"

———◇———

Five minutes later Sasha's breathing was still coming in deep gusts; she couldn't get enough air, and fought the urge to vomit. Her throat was jagged with pain.

Tom motioned to the glass of water he had brought her. She sipped. "And you're convinced if we go to Yassar he won't believe us?" Her voice was faint, and she heard the tremor in it. Yet her mind was clearing.

"Even if he did, if he hesitated, or he went to Ibrahim, it might be all over before we could intervene," Tom said. She saw now the fatigue in his face, the lines around his eyes. She thought they were sympathetic now. "Besides, it's not just about Ibrahim at this point. There are others. And as I told you, it's a coordinated program. If you go to Yassar, they'll find out about it and go underground, and if we don't take as many of them as we can out now, they'll get to Yassar eventually. Even without Ibrahim."

How could she not tell Yassar? She sat, staring at the gun on the table until Tom put it back inside his coat.

Sasha's gaze went to Tom's eyes. "Okay. When?"

"Three days. At night. You'll call into the hotel every day, to your 'friend' Maria who's visiting from Italy, visit her if necessary. We'll do what we need to do to communicate. And three days is enough time to teach you to shoot."

Sasha felt her anger subsiding, then thought of Yassar and felt clarity, purpose. "Not necessary. I've been shooting since I was ten, shotguns, rifles—and pistols. Besides, I'll be at close range." The tremor was gone from her voice.

Sasha allowed herself to take in everything in Yassar's study, knowing it would be the last time she would visit with him. *Two days left.* Yassar got up from the floor following their lesson and sat in one of the stuffed chairs. Sasha lingered for a moment, kneeling in front of him, wrapping her Koran in its special cloth. So far she'd gotten her wish: a quiet evening, studying the teachings with Yassar. She'd asked for a special lesson because she wanted to say good-bye, and to leave him with enough facts for him to fill in the gaps afterward so that hopefully he might at least understand.

She got up and sat in the chair adjacent to him. "Thank you," she said. She observed Yassar, the drooping eyelids, the prominent nose and the serious, contemplative forehead. He still had gentle eyes.

"You're welcome. Still an enthusiastic student." There was pride in his voice.

She poured tea. "Yassar," she began. "I was thinking the other day, we've now known each other over ten years." She saw him nod. She felt content. "And I remember the first time you mentioned Ibrahim, when you used to come visit Christina's after the oil meetings in Vienna."

He sipped his tea. "Yes."

"I remember the high hopes you had for him…" She trailed off to see if he'd pick up on it. Was he disappointed in him? She knew he was helping him at the ministry now that he'd returned from Harvard, but was Yassar aware of any change in Ibrahim's views?

"I still have high hopes for him. He straightened out wonderfully. Thanks in part to you, my dear. I hope you can continue to keep him company, even while he's away at school."

Sasha didn't respond, didn't know how. *God, this isn't easy.* "Do you believe he's helping you at the ministry?"

"Absolutely. He's been critical to the jobs program, even in the short time since he's returned from school."

"And is he still keeping up with his religious studies?"

"You are modest, my dear. I'm certain it's your influence. He even quotes the Koran now."

She wished it were her influence. She knew it was the tip of the al-Mujari iceberg. Or ice pick? "I've been finding him a little overbearing at times since he's gone to school," she said. "At least in his political views. They're not exactly always in line with the family's."

Yassar waved his hand. "Ibrahim is open-minded. Harvard has had an influence on him. He respects other's views."

She grabbed at the hope she could get him to listen to her tapes, intervene, go to Tom…"What if he was to get involved with some people with wildly different views? Not the Saudi royal family way?"

"Don't trouble yourself. If that happened, I'd get involved." He winked. "Besides, he'd need to take you on first, and I know how persuasive you can be." She felt a lump in her throat. He went on, making it worse. "And he and I have never been closer, particularly since he's been back from school. I've never been more dependent on him at the ministry, never more hopeful for him." Her anger rose now. *Diabolical.*

"I confess I've never felt more confident he'll succeed me," Yassar went on. "He's become—righteous."

Why was he so blind? But how could he help being taken in by his own son? She was having trouble suppressing her rage. "You might find yourself with a totally new perspective after you have a chance to reflect on things from a distance—perhaps when he goes back to school in the fall."

Yassar almost cut her off. "Not true. This year it will be much more difficult to see him go back." He paused. "As one gets older, one lives more through one's children. Hopes, dreams are for them. And Ibrahim is my oldest son. There's no pride in the world like that."

Sasha didn't know which focused her more—her anger at Ibrahim or her love for Yassar. What she did know was that she needed another answer, realized she couldn't stop Ibrahim the way she'd planned. Forget about what she'd told Tom. How could Yassar lose Ibrahim, and not at least have her around to take care of him? And how could she stand leaving Yassar? Tom wasn't going to like it, but the plan needed to change. And immediately, because there wasn't much time.

CHAPTER 28

July, Twenty Years Ago. Riyadh, Saudi Arabia. Tom Goddard was getting his ass chewed over the phone by John Franklin, his Section Head at Langley. His mind raced. Two hours earlier Sasha had dropped in his lap the fact that she wasn't going through with taking out Ibrahim, part of six coordinated hits mostly under his direction. She'd smuggled in the Beretta Cheetah with the custom-made silencer like a pro, an iceberg, then a day later plopped down on the stool in the bathroom in their cover suite at Le Meridian Hotel Riyadh for the final debrief, her black abaya draped over her down to the floor, and said, "We need a change of plans."

"Everything's set," he'd said, trying to sound reassuring. But he'd seen something was wrong. His next thought had been to just get her through this. *Take her in. See how she's doing.*

She looked like a little boxer there on her stool, waiting to go at it. "I know," she said, looking at him as casually as if she were telling him what she had for breakfast.

He chalked it up to fear, then sensed she wasn't afraid at all, and at once he realized that he had no idea what was going on.

"Everything's been coordinated. We can't change things. Just tell me what's going on. I know you can do this."

"It's no use, Tom." Her eyes softened as she said his name. "I'm not afraid. I'm just not going to do it the way we planned."

She sat back a little on the stool, slumped to the side with her elbow on her knee, like she'd finished whupping him and was just waiting for the judge's decision.

"What are you talking about?" He felt sudden anxiety.

"I'm not leaving Yassar. Come up with some other way to do it. I've tried dreaming up other solutions, but I'm out of ideas." She lowered her head and looked at him just so, almost coy. "*You're* the spy. You think of something."

Tom wondered for a moment if it was a bluff. She wanted Ibrahim taken out as much as they did. Was she pushing for something? He'd never seen her have any ulterior motive. No hidden agendas. Still, he had to ask: "What do you want?"

She tossed her head back. "Nothing. Except a change in plans so I can stay. I'm not leaving Yassar. He needs me, and especially will afterward. And I don't want to leave him. He's all I've got."

Tom was snapped back into the moment by Franklin's voice bellowing over the phone. "…and now after all this she's chickening out."

"She's not chickening out," Tom said.

"I can hear her clucking from all the way across the Atlantic."

"She'll do what we need. I think she wants to get rid of the guy more than we do."

Then Franklin was off on his griping about the timing again, still hadn't vented it all. "Christ, we've done the planning work in days that'd normally take weeks. Six hits within forty-eight hours. Timing is critical, and everything's been coordinated. How many times you gonna change things?"

"She doesn't want to leave Yassar," Tom repeated as evenly as he could.

"Jesus Christ, she think he's gonna hug her and forgive her afterward? I mean, what kind of bimbo—?"

"She's no bimbo."

That stopped him. "What's your proposal?" Franklin asked.

"Put a team on Ibrahim."

"We tried to make that work before."

"We dropped the idea when Sasha agreed to do Ibrahim herself. Plus it was tricky to get the team in. Now Sasha will let them in."

"You'd rely on her? After this?"

"She'll do it. Believe me."

"She better do it. But where the hell you gonna get a team at this stage?"

"Only way to work it is to pull a team from one of the other targets. We're using all mercenaries."

"Oh, great."

Enough, already. Give it a rest. "I can work this out. It'll take a dozen. The squad goes in undetected. One shooter. Everybody using silencers. Hopefully a clean exit."

"Crazy," he heard Franklin's low murmur. Then: "Can you get these guys to do it?"

"They'll do it. We'll have to up their fees, but yeah."

"And these guys are untraceable."

"Yeah. This can work." Tom said it as much to convince himself as Franklin.

"If not, it's your ass."

If not, it's Sasha's ass. "It'll work," was all he said. He had a grungy feeling.

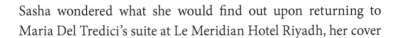

Sasha wondered what she would find out upon returning to Maria Del Tredici's suite at Le Meridian Hotel Riyadh, her cover meeting place with Tom. After firmly planting the responsibility on Tom to come up with something new that would preserve her life here with Yassar, she was now afraid she'd thrown events into motion that she couldn't control, and that she might not like the outcome. What would he expect her to do?

She felt her soul screaming in pain; in less than 36 hours she was going to help these people kill someone. And not just anyone: a man she had lived with for almost three years. And regardless of her feelings for Yassar, it was still hard to believe she was going to do it. She would offer her prayers to Ganesha tonight, her Remover of Obstacles. Would that he could remove her guilt as well.

"Hi. Ready?" Tom asked when she arrived at Maria's room. He was serious. She saw him observing her, checking.

Never mind. I'm okay. She nodded.

"Good." He pulled out a diagram. She recognized it as the plans for Ibrahim's suite and the surrounding corridors. She now had an odd sense, an absence of emotion toward Ibrahim. Was it her guilt that caused it, out of self-defense? No, she still found him repugnant. But there was an anger, too. Something that needed to be there, yet controlled in a determined, equally diabolical response to Ibrahim's deception. She kept reminding herself of his words on the tape: "Yes, I'll kill him." She saw Tom's eyes watching her again, still checking.

"I'm okay. Go on."

"All right. We'll be using a dozen men. The team comes over the perimeter wall here." He pointed to a spot on the diagram. "Once inside they pack it with charges—C-4 explosive—in case something goes wrong and they need to blow the wall for their escape."

Sasha listened and observed, but felt curiously detached, as if she were watching this on a movie screen.

"The team will be using silencers, so if there are guards in the courtyard, they may still be able to take them out without being observed and continue the plan. The team leader will make the judgment at that time. Your part of the plan is next." He pulled out latex gloves and slid them on. "You'll deactivate a microswitch that triggers the alarm on the window they'll come in through." He pulled out a plastic strip from his bag, holding it up and peeling a cellophanelike substance off the front of it. She smelled the acrid odor of the adhesive. "Cyanoacrylate, extremely fast drying and activated by exposure to the air," he explained. He moved it up toward the metal window frame. "You'll slide it between the window and the frame like this, and then use this electromagnet"—he pulled a clump of metal the size of a tennis ball out of his sack—"to clamp the steel window molding against the frame." He unraveled the cord from the contraption. "It's very powerful." He plugged it in and positioned the device against the window frame, flipped a switch, and she heard the clunk of the magnet pulling the window molding against its frame. He moved his hands and left it securing itself in place. "You getting this?"

"Yes, go on," Sasha said. She was feeling the unnatural calmness she experienced before a riding competition. She knew her rising excitement would be next. Even a thrill. She was impatient for Tom to continue.

"This is a different type of window, it slides down while the ones in the palace push open."

"I know," she said, thinking about how Ibrahim had opened the window for her to warm the room until she had adjusted to the air-conditioned palace. A sharp sensation. Remorse?

"The cyanoacrylate will dry in less than 30 seconds, after which you crack the window open so the team can enter. The glue will hold the microswitch for the alarm in place, but the plastic backing to the glue strip will keep the window from sticking to the frame." He reached up, switched off the electromagnet and placed it on the floor, then slid the window down, showing her that the plastic strip had been bound to only one side of the window frame. "The microswitch is pressure sensitive, so it should hold indefinitely." He sat back down. "That's it for your part. Leave the gloves in the bag next to the electromagnet. After that you go back to the room and wait. The lead man on the team is the shooter. A Beretta with a silencer. He goes to Ibrahim's room, does it quietly and cleanly. My advice is you pretend you're asleep after they do it. Then wake up comfortably after the team is gone—the entire job won't take more than three to five minutes—and then react as you normally would waking up to find..." His voice trailed off.

"A dead man in bed next to me."

"Exactly."

Sasha now saw the coldness in Tom's recitation. This was a job for him, something he needed to do. It would be over soon, and for all she knew, she might never see him again.

"The team leaves," Tom continued, "going out the same way. That's it."

"And what if it doesn't work?"

Tom inhaled. "Depends on when it goes awry. If they're even partway through, the plan is to blow the wall and get out. There'll be three escape cars stationed outside. Black BMW 535s. You'll have to make your own decisions. Your cover—this is what you wanted—is you were an innocent bystander to an assassination team coming in. Unless you're detected as you're disengaging the alarm, there's no reason for you to run."

The word "run" hit her like an electrical charge. She hadn't thought of that: if it went sour and she had to run, too. Then it might all be for nothing, because she'd be forced to leave and Ibrahim might still be alive, free to…She stopped herself thinking about it.

"If for some reason you need to get out, get down the ropes and through the wall with the team. Run into one of the escape cars. They'll leave you at a drop point and I'll pick you up and get you out."

"And then what?" she asked. Not to Tom, but off over his shoulder. Tom must have seen the nature of the question because he didn't answer. She focused back on his face. "Who are these men? Yours?"

"They're professionals. Untraceable. Trust me, they know what they're doing. And if any of them are caught, they can't be linked to us. Or to you. We've even taken steps to make it look like it was planned from factions within the al-Mujari."

They sat not speaking for a few moments. Sasha's mind was whirling now, asking what happened next. Where would she go, what would she do if she had to run? And if it didn't work, and Ibrahim survived? Again she forced herself not to think about it. "What's the backup plan?" she asked.

He looked her in the eye. "That's up to you."

She knew what he meant. "I figured that's why you didn't ask me for the Beretta back."

"It's up to you," he repeated. "Whether the plan works or not, unquestionably they'll find it. It will be impossible to explain. You can still get rid of it if you want to."

Sasha shook her head. "No. I already decided. I'll work it out myself—afterward. Remember what you said when we first discussed this?"

"What?"

"This needs doing." She heard the firmness in her voice, knew it was from the purity of her motive. Her previous uncertainty was gone, replaced by the words she'd just spoken.

Sasha stayed at Ibrahim's side at the party that night, *the* night. It was where she had been all day, except when Ibrahim was at the ministry, and when he had an afternoon date with Rachel Prinea, the new concubine. That was all right with Sasha. It was Friday, and after all she was his for the evening. And he was hers.

Sasha wore her hair up, showing off her neck in an ivory silk Chloe gown. Her solitaire diamond drew the eyes to her breasts. She'd reflected as she put it on that it wasn't her style, but she figured it would appeal to his lust, and she was taking no chances on keeping Ibrahim's attention tonight. She wanted him in bed, shown a good time and passed out as soon as she could manage it, by midnight if possible.

He's not drinking enough. She found a bellgirl and pointed at Ibrahim's scotch.

"Let's go soon," she said later. "It's almost bedtime, and I don't want to be too tired."

He smiled. "I'm not concerned. You've never disappointed me." The bellgirl handed him another scotch. "The band's just getting ready to start up again. A few songs, then we'll go." He held his hand out to one of the girls, and they began to dance.

Sasha realized she was staring at him, looked away, made certain she kept her poise. She turned the plan over in her head. The bag was in the closet. Put on her abaya in case she was detected in the hallway, or needed to run. Don't forget the latex gloves.

To the window, unroll the electromagnet, plug it in, peel off the backing from the adhesive, slide it into the window frame, then put the electromagnet in place and switch it on. Count to thirty, switch it off, place it on the floor, turn the lever and push the window open. Just a crack. Ditch the gloves. Then back to the bedroom.

Now she felt a flutter of nerves, impatient as she saw Ibrahim continue dancing with the girl. She'd had enough, and walked directly over.

"Mind if I cut in?" The girl looked at her with malevolent eyes. Sasha saw the mild amusement on Ibrahim's face as she gave the girl a glare as if to say "I'm still the favorite." Ibrahim swung Sasha in a circle away from the girl, leaving her behind like discarded lingerie.

"Ever Sasha." He was looking at her through gloating eyes. "Why don't we go away again?"

She felt a jolt of emotion, unable even to identify it.

"I'm busier now," he said, "but I could get away for a few weeks. How about Venice?"

"Okay," she managed. Her soul, she realized, was fighting to be heard. Moaning at what she must do. She forced herself to remember: Yassar. Ibrahim's words on the tape. Tom's simple statement: *This needs doing.* She rested her head on his shoulder again, unable now to look him in the eye.

Sasha lay awake in bed, staring out at the blackness across the room, the green light of the display of the digital clock the only illumination. Ibrahim lay next to her, sleeping. She'd treated Ibrahim to some particularly extended pleasures. She glanced at the clock: 1:02 a.m. That was the part she hadn't needed to figure out: how she would awaken at the appointed hour. She couldn't, wouldn't sleep. And now her mind continued to work on how her life would change. No matter which way it turned out, if it succeeded or failed, or the team didn't arrive at all. And if it worked, would she be able to stay? Could she actually live on here, in essence as Yassar's daughter—and his son's killer? She now saw that as absurd, felt her emotions crumbling.

She checked the clock again. Waiting.

Footsteps in the hall: the Royal Guard on his rounds. She felt a renewed sense of the commitment that spurred her to what she would do. *It's time*, she told herself, and she slid, inches at a time, from the sheets to the cool marble floor.

Yassar will never forgive me. She breathed deeply, then felt exhilaration at the cool detachment her purpose gave her. She stood, naked, shoulders erect and head back, observing Prince Ibrahim, the man she had served as concubine for three years. *But you don't deserve to see it coming.*

She inched toward the closet...

CHAPTER 29

July, Twenty Years Ago. Riyadh, Saudi Arabia. Sasha was pressed facedown on the floor of the escape car, her ears still ringing from the sharp bursts of the machine guns and that C-4 blast. Her head was throbbing and she had to force her stomach muscles tight to keep each bounce of the road from causing over 200 pounds of mercenary from knocking the wind out of her. She was sickened by what she'd done: stood and fired a round into Ibrahim's chest from not five feet away, then put another one in the back of his lifeless skull for good measure. She could hardly believe it. She knew it was only her belief in her love for Yassar, and his for her, that gave her the courage to do it. Then she felt a crushing wave of anguish. She'd lose Yassar. She'd never see him again; there was no chance that she could return to him with her improvisation after the plan had gone wrong. She shut her eyes against tears. And now rage welled up in her, first at Tom for getting her involved, then at Ibrahim for being so weak, and finally at herself for not going directly to Yassar with what she knew.

Her face was contorted and her breathing was shallow. She could feel something moist on her face, was able to reach up and wipe it off. It must be Ibrahim's blood that had splattered up on her. She wanted to vomit. She felt every bounce in the road, smelled the cordite from the explosives and garlic on the hot breath of the man jammed in on top of her in the BMW.

Now what? Where would she run? Would Tom be able to get her out of Saudi Arabia? She'd have to rely on Tom. Tom and his flawless plan. No, that wasn't fair. He'd advised her of the risk. Ibrahim was dead, Yassar was alive; that much had been accomplished. She felt an explosion of guilt: but the squad leader and at least two more of the men had been killed, and she was responsible for that. *Oh my God.* She'd shot two innocent men, the guards, and the other guards that were killed were on her head too. If she hadn't insisted on the change of plans, none of that would have happened. Her heart wailed, desperate, damned. And now she'd never see Yassar again anyway.

Impossible. She'd have to figure out a way to come back later. But how could she go to Yassar? She couldn't bear the thought of him knowing she'd been involved—or had done it. And they'd find her gun. There was no way she could go back. They'd probably kill her. Desperation clogged her thoughts.

The tape! She'd get it from Tom. He owed her that much. Owed? Did that matter in this business? Yes, she'd get the tape of Ibrahim swearing to kill his father, then go to Yassar. But would Tom do it?

She'd figure it out. Convince Tom. She had to. Otherwise she'd be on the run, estranged from Yassar forever. Or dead. Now the car slowed almost to a stop, then revved its engine and ran up a ramp. The engine cut. She felt the coarse fabric of her abaya chafing her thighs, the man on top of her press down on her to raise himself. She heard the car doors fly open, the jangle of equipment as the men climbed out. Her breath was coming in gasps. She felt despair and panic at the same time.

She climbed out of the car to see they were inside a dimly lit tractor trailer, the rear doors already closed, and then felt the lurch of the trailer moving. She fell to the floor as it accelerated. Four men in uniforms were collapsed around her, dusty and sweaty, one kneeling and rubbing his thigh, attended by another. One of the men helped her up.

"We carried you out of the crater," he said.

She averted her eyes. "Thank you."

"How many men down?"

"I saw three," Sasha said. "Including the team leader."

"Damn," the man who'd been nursing his leg whispered.

"He never got to him, to the target," another said.

"I did," Sasha said.

Four pairs of eyes were locked on her. "You sure?" the man with the sore leg asked.

"I'm sure." Sasha leveled her eyes at him. "Point-blank. Two shots. The team leader's Beretta Cheetah. Just like mine." She saw their gaze on her. She didn't know if it was horror or admiration, or simply surprise. She wasn't sure of her own reaction yet either, the absence of emotion, as if stunned to be saying it. *Out in the open now, a murderess.* They rode in silence for another ten minutes.

The tractor trailer stopped, then the back doors opened to the inside of a warehouse. Sasha saw Tom Goddard walk toward the trailer, his face tense, like a mask. A surge of horror at what she had done came over her again. Two other men she didn't recognize walked behind Tom. The death squad team clomped in their boots out of the trailer.

Sasha walked toward the edge, feeling her bare feet against the coarse steel and grit on the floor inside the trailer. One of the men helped her down while the others stood and talked with Tom and the two men. Tom walked over to Sasha. She felt torment searing at her, as if she needed to confess to Tom what she'd done. Her breathing was labored.

"We need to get you out of here," he said, his eyes scrutinizing her face. "Are you all right?"

"I…" She needed to tell him, wanted the cool efficiency with which he told the men in the trailer to come back to her, but now was stunned and disbelieving that she'd done it at all. "Ibrahim…I…"

"I heard." He took her by the arm and walked her toward a door into an office. Papers were strewn on a dilapidated desk and scattered around it on the floor. All the windows were painted black on the inside. He sat her down at a wooden chair by a dusty table, took a seat in front of her. He looked at his watch.

"We don't have much time. First we get you to the embassy, then some clothes, cut and dye your hair. We've got your documents and a U.S. passport to get you out as the wife of an oil broker from Houston. The sooner we leave the better."

Sasha felt her strength returning. "I'm not leaving."

Tom looked at her as though she'd lost her mind. "What?"

"I'm going back to Yassar."

"No you're not."

"I have to."

"Are you crazy? They'll have you killed."

"No," she said, looking up at him with as much steel in her eyes as she could muster. "You're going to help me."

"How?"

"Make sure he understands, believes me."

Tom just looked at her, speechless.

"I get proof. Then I go back." Now she wasn't just putting on a good front, keeping her poise. She had her mind in the right place again, knew what she was about.

"What kind of proof?"

"The tape."

"Absolutely not. They'll link it to us."

"You owe me."

"Why?" She saw the flicker of doubt in his eyes. He was good at this, but she saw that he felt he did owe her something.

"You made me a pawn."

"You went into this with your eyes open." His eyes were hard again. She stared back at him, wondering if hers were as hard as his. Did he always have somebody else do his killing? She'd just done his. Her eyes must be harder.

There was a long pause. "What do you want?" he finally asked.

"I already told you. The tape. To prove to Yassar why I did it."

"And I already told you that will never happen."

"You can do it, make a copy."

Tom looked at his watch, then ran his fingers through his hair. "I can get you out. Safe. On the run, but safe. We can even bury you. A fake death and a new ID."

He sounded cold. She said, "No. I'm going back to Yassar." She saw him sigh, then lean forward toward her, the way he always did.

"Okay," he said, his eyes tender. He reached up and stroked her forehead, something he'd never done before. "Okay."

Sasha felt emotion welling in her throat, all of the exhaustion, shock and agony of the last days flowing upward. She mouthed the words, "Thank you."

"We'll need to figure out how to get you back inside." He checked his watch again. "We already have a cover story—part of our contingency planning in case the whole plan got blown." He was talking as much to himself as to her. "I was a loosening cannon, then finally came unhooked and led a renegade group within the agency, piggy-backing on the joint U.S./British/Israeli operation to take out the other al-Mujari heads, and I decided to take out Ibrahim as well." He was looking off in the distance now, as if he were thinking through where he would go from here. "They'll send me back to Langley. Probably would have gone back soon anyhow, become a Section Head running this whole region. But now, after this, who knows, after it plays out this way..." He stopped himself and turned back to her. "But there's something we can't help you with."

"What's that?"

"Even if he believes you, you still killed his son."

Sasha swallowed hard. *Yassar will never forgive me.*

Yassar felt as soft and formless as the fat upholstered chair in which he sat in the living room of his suite. He'd wondered earlier if he were in shock, but knew the pain in his chest and the effort it took to hold his head erect meant the reality of Ibrahim's murder was with him. He glanced over at Nibmar, still a crumpled form in the corner of the sofa, balled-up Kleenex surrounding her, hair disheveled, wearing a bathrobe over her nightdress. With some effort he lifted himself from the seat, sat down next to her, put his arm around her tiny form, and pulled her close. Always such energy and internal strength. Now look at her. She sagged against him, looking at him through reddened and swollen eyes. Now he felt his own sorrow overwhelm him, pushed the tears back from his own eyes, but Nibmar saw it and collapsed, face in hands, sobbing again.

Yassar reached into himself for his wrath. There it was. His newborn hatred. He remembered his vow of last night, his vow to avenge Ibrahim. And now he thought of Sasha, felt a tide of pain. How could she do such a thing? How could she hurt him like this?

Someone knocked on the door. "Enter," Yassar said.

Assad al-Anoud, the head of the Saudi Secret Police, came in and stood stiffly. "Still nothing," he said. "We found one car—a BMW."

"And the dead men?"

"We can't identify them. Probably mercenaries. We're checking now, but we don't expect it to lead us anyplace soon."

Yes, it would probably be a long hunt, but he would chase them down. He almost preferred it that way. A long hunt, let them fester with worry, always looking over their shoulders. Make it miserable for them until they're caught. And Sasha, too. The ultimate betrayal.

"Keep checking."

Sasha emerged from the safe house dressed in a black abaya and headscarf, an Arab man in full Saudi robe and headdress accompanying her. They walked toward the Royal Palace, through a mile of winding, dusty back streets lined with shopkeepers hawking their wares. She felt relief rather than tension. She'd be at the palace within minutes, and then whatever happened, so be it. She probed for the tape recorder inside the purse strapped around her waist, then for the key to the locker with the duplicates of all her tapes. She would play Tom's tape for Yassar, and then...

The front entrance to the Royal Palace was now in sight. Guard stations were set up with makeshift barriers to keep pedestrians at least one hundred fifty feet away. She realized she'd encounter the Royal Guards well outside the perimeter walls. Despair flared in her breast, and she pushed it away, her commitment surging in her. She passed her escort, found a spot in the barricade between two guard stations, ducked under and was inside.

She walked across the courtyard, Royal Guards calling to her in Arabic, dust swirling in her face. She reached the perimeter wall and stopped in front of a Royal Guard. "I must see Yassar," she said into the man's astonished face. "I am Sasha."

Yassar stood and paced. The low murmurs and occasional wails of his three other wives attending to Nibmar made him edgy. He gestured to a servant for more tea. His other children were here, sitting in formal mourning—all eleven of them—and at least they gave him some relief from his misery, especially little Assan, now three, his youngest, from his fourth wife, Liva.

He heard a sharp knock on the door, turned weary, hooded eyes and said, "Come." Assad entered again. Yassar crossed the room. Assad said only one word: "Sasha."

He shuddered at the wail Nibmar emitted at overhearing Sasha's name, then palpably felt it as it rumbled into a growl and then a howl, a sound almost inhuman. He saw Nibmar standing, fists clenched and face contorted into a scowl of hatred, a face he couldn't deny. He felt a tremor in his being, as if he now fully understood the new purpose of his life.

Sasha sat in a hard metal chair at a table in a hot interrogation room in the bowels of the Royal Palace. The concrete walls hadn't seen paint in decades. No windows. Only a heavy wooden door, looking as if it had been constructed centuries ago. A room from another era, one less enlightened than that of the current Saudi Arabia. Or was it? She would soon find out. She wondered if Yassar would come to her. She'd been sitting here for fifteen minutes. They'd stripped-searched her, taken the shirt and slacks she'd worn underneath her abaya and left her to wait. No interrogation.

Sri Ganesha, she prayed to her Remover of Obstacles. She finished her prayers, heard sounds in the hallway, and tried to recapture the cool sense of determined composure with which she'd approached the palace, but couldn't. She felt tension in her legs and knots in her neck. She wondered if she could face Yassar with her guilt.

Now her mind was working again, a semblance of the confidence she'd felt earlier filtering back. She knew it could work. They'd taken the tape and the recorder from her, as expected, but they'd undoubtedly play it, and that was her proof. Then a start. What if the guards played it and decided to destroy it? She'd murdered a number of their own. They'd want to see her killed as revenge. And what if someone else was on the inside, assisting the al-Mujari in their plans? Tom wasn't available to her now; she had no backup.

She recognized the sounds from outside as footsteps in the hall, then the sound of metal against wood as the bolt of the door slid back. Yassar and two guards stepped in. He glared at Sasha, who raised her head to look at him and she felt the blood drain from her face. "Leave us," Yassar said to the men. They closed the door behind them.

Sasha felt a blast of emotion, and then struggled for sanity. She saw the pain in Yassar's face beneath the hatred. She needed to get through it to his heart, his mind. This was it. "Yassar. I came in voluntarily. I needed to see you."

"The fact that you ran establishes your guilt. No doubt we will find your prints on the weapon. We found another gun in your bureau." He stood by the door, his body rigid.

Now her heart was wailing. *Forgive me!*

"No doubt," she said.

"Is that a confession?"

"Only to wanting to save you."

"Preposterous! What are you talking about?"

"There was a plot to kill you."

"That is ridiculous. Our secret police are well informed."

"I can prove it."

"How?"

"Hear me out."

"The only thing I'm interested in hearing is the answer to one question: Why?"

She felt as if she were shrinking, and he became a giant looming over her. How could she say it now? That she loved him, what she'd done for him. It wasn't happening as it should, but how could she have expected anything else? She forced herself to raise her head. She was going to tell him. And she knew he wouldn't accept it. She saw it, heard it in his voice. And then, almost as if her words came from someone else, she heard herself say, "Ibrahim. Ibrahim and these people. They were planning to kill you."

"What?" He took two quick steps toward her, leaning over her across the table. "Do you expect me to believe that my own son…!" he bellowed. The bolt slammed and the door flew open, two guards rushing in. Yassar turned. "Leave us!"

He turned back toward her, pausing as if he were forming his words. She leaned back in her chair, away from him. She could see the fatigue and stress in his face more clearly, the lines at the edges of the eyelids, and could smell the pungent scent of his body, as if he'd awakened from sleep and thrown on his clothes. Now she wanted to let him rage. Vent. Better to let him get past it so she could speak to the rational, contemplative Yassar once he was through. Then there'd be an opportunity to reason with him. She knew it, had confidence in him, and ultimately, how he felt about her. She needed to get to that. She felt her heart beginning to ache as she thought those words—the contemplative Yassar.

"What was your involvement in this?"

"I passed information."

"To whom?"

"The Americans, the British, the Israelis. At least that's who they said they were. They were tracking the al-Mujari."

"How do you know this?"

She saw it register on his face. The al-Mujari. She remembered Tom said they'd contacted the Saudi government. Maybe, just maybe he'd connect it, believe her. Her heart soared. The first hopeful sign! She felt her hands trembling. "First they told me. Then I heard it for myself. Abdul, Waleed and Ibrahim. Talking, planning." She saw anguish on his face, his great graying head sagging.

Yassar raised his chin. "I don't believe you."

She felt as if he'd slapped her with the back of his hand. "I know this is hard to believe. But Yassar, think of how much I care for you, do you honestly believe I'd do anything to hurt you?"

He snapped his head back as if at an affront. "Tell me why I shouldn't have you killed on the spot," he barked through clenched teeth.

It sucked the strength from her body again, her brain filled with a sense of doom. *Focus! Get control of yourself!* "Because I can prove it, if you'll let me."

"Let me understand this," he said. "You helped a team to assassinate my son, which you're going to justify on the basis he was involved in a plot to kill me, his own father?" His face was awful; it tore at her heart to see him look at her that way.

Sasha plunged on. "Yes. He was involved—seduced—by these al-Mujari extremists, murderers, and sucked into their plans to overthrow the government, return the country to fundamentalist rule. And install *Ibrahim* as head of a puppet government." She felt herself starting to break, and she leaned forward in the chair. "Yassar, you're like my father. I came back for you. I could have run." She heard the desperation in her voice but was unable to stop herself.

"Proof!" he said. His eyes were cold, distant now.

"The key in my purse. Did they tell you about it?"

"They did."

"And the tape recorder and the tape?"

She got her voice back, "The key is to a locker at the bus station. All of my tapes, everything, duplicate copies are there. I saved them just in case. And the tape and the recorder I brought. That is the ultimate proof."

Yassar walked back to the door, pounded on it. "The tape recorder," he said, and it was immediately handed to him. Yassar waved them to close the door, crossed the room, and placed the recorder on the table.

He switched it on and Abdul's voice filled the room. "Then, our holy friend, you must choose between the life of your own father or the preservation of the purity of the Islamic state! Either your father and his brethren in the Saudi government must die or the infidels will eventually pollute our holy land and destroy the nation of Islam!" Sasha watched Yassar's face, her heart going out to him as belief crept across it.

Abdul went on: "Do you accept this grave challenge, this test that Allah has chosen for you? Do you choose the preservation of the nation of Islam? Do you choose the return of the holy Islamic sites to the Muslim people? Do you choose the expulsion of the infidels? Do you choose death for the Saudi royal family?"

"Yes!" Ibrahim's voice rang out, seeming to knock the wind from Yassar. He slumped where he stood. She wanted to go to him, but restrained herself. He must hear the rest.

Abdul again: "Will you do it?"

Waleed now, urgently: "You are the only one who can! Nobody else can get close enough!"

Now unmistakably Ibrahim's voice, his betrayal: "Yes! Yes, I'll kill him!"

Yassar seemed as if he would topple to the floor like a giant tree. He moved forward, pulled one of the metal chairs out and slumped down into it.

Would his heart open to her now? She saw his eyes soften, then felt her hopes rise. Yes, they would get through this. Then his face went blank. "Why did you not come to me?"

"I tried," she said, reaching for his hands across the table.

He pulled back. "You tried? My door was always open to you."

"Yassar, please believe me. Think. I questioned the views of his friends, their influence on Ibrahim." She saw him look away, as if considering. She went on. "Listen to the other tapes—their plans, Ibrahim's involvement, it's all there."

"Maybe," he said. "But you still betrayed me."

"I did my best. I tried, but there wasn't time to convince you. I had to save you."

"And now what do you expect?" There was a hardness in his voice.

"I don't have any expectations." She was calm now, resigned. "I wanted to come back to you. Help you to get through this if you will allow me. Ask you to forgive me."

"For your betrayal?"

She forced herself to find the same commitment that had gotten her through the horror of last night. "Was it any worse than your betrayal of me? Your tearing me from whatever life I had to bring me here the way you did? At least I had a reason to do what I did. What was yours? You wanted a good fuck for your wayward son?"

Yassar stood up.

"Yassar!" Sasha leaped up from her chair, sending it toppling to the floor. She arched her neck toward him in a fury. "I'm not letting you go!" She ran around the table and clutched his robe, pulled her face up to his. "All your teachings, all your prayers! For what? So that you can throw them aside and be consumed by hatred for the rest of your life?"

"You helped them kill my son!" he shouted.

"I *killed* your son! I did it to save you!" She saw his eyes go wide and he tried to force her away. "And if you want to hurt me back, do what you will! But I stand by what I did, because I love you! That's what kept me coming back to you! Even after you betrayed me! And now you're all I've got! So if you're going to reject me, then just kill me and get it over with!"

Yassar stopped struggling against her, then pressed her to his breast. She felt his body convulsing, buried her head in his chest, and knew he was sobbing.

"I'll help you find these people. We'll do it together. Please—Father, let me stay, say you'll forgive me." She felt his hold grow tighter; it was her answer. She held him back, drew him against her soul, felt a fulfillment that made everything that had gone before in her life seem just.

BOOK 5

CHAPTER 30

AUGUST, THIS YEAR. NEW YORK City. Daniel paced from one end of the living room in his apartment to the other. His insides felt like they were gnawing on themselves. He looked at the bathroom door, behind which Lydia was freshening up, seemingly emotionally exhausted after her confession to him. And yet, she still hadn't given him more than a sketchy overview. How many layers existed in peeling away the skin of this onion? And now to add to his tension and mental disorientation, he was worried about her.

It was surreal: he was involved with a woman who said she lived a life that was something out of the thrillers he read on vacation. A life of running from shadowy figures, using multiple passports, doing odd jobs—for whom? She hadn't said. He wondered if she'd ever killed. Then he pushed the thought out of his mind.

Sasha looked at herself in the bathroom mirror. She was weepy, teary-eyed. Daniel's words had moved her, not just because they were unexpected. *He loves me. And he said we'll figure it out together.* How could she not be touched by hearing that from Daniel? Her head was erect; she felt proud.

And now she knew how she felt: she loved him. She knew now that was the real reason she'd come back after her blazing exit from his weekend house, after her cover had almost been blown. Not because of her mission, but because she was in love with him. How could she not have known that before? It was what she'd always wanted. Somebody who loved her and whom she loved back, something the two of them could believe in.

She took a deep breath, leaned back and felt the cool brass towel bar behind her, held onto it to ground her. *I love him.* After all these years she had what she wanted sitting in front of her, if only she could figure out how to make it happen. Funny how life knocks the legs out from under you when you least expect it. And oh, what a change it makes. *Now everything's different.*

She called to mind the first day in Riyadh with Nafta, her fellow concubine, an unimaginable life just dawning. Childhood desires to experience "tempests in her heart" or "rivers of passion"—squelched. Now she prepared to go to the lover she'd chosen, and felt her love for him glowing. This *was* what she wanted, sending it hiding that day with Nafta, but waiting ever since. The sum total of her emotional life.

She knew what she had to do. Tell him everything, then let him decide. That and show him how she felt; be honest.

She opened the door, stood looking at Daniel for a moment, then started across the room to him.

Daniel was still pacing, slowly, like a boxer staying loose between rounds, when Lydia emerged from the bathroom. He turned at the sound of the door opening, thinking he'd cut right to it, when her countenance set him back on his heels with a thud.

She stood in the doorway beaming at him, as if she'd just awakened after their first night of lovemaking. Her eyes possessed a dreamy softness, and yet showed the steadiness of clarity and intent. She stood with her head characteristically aloft, shoulders back. More than poised, in a state of grace.

"Thanks for letting me regroup, darling," she said. "I'm better now." Daniel took her in as she crossed the room toward him, her body language, the tone of her voice, her demeanor, everything, Svengali-like, telling him it was okay now. Soothing him. Her eyes now with the expressiveness of the night they met. No, Svengali-like was wrong; no sleight of hand, just Lydia. "I'm sorry for all the stress this has put you through." He felt the warmth and firmness of her body as she embraced him, as if he were taking her in his arms for the first time. She kissed him, then led him by the hand to the sofa. Daniel complied, somehow quieted by her mixture of tranquility and purpose.

Sasha seated Daniel on the sofa, positioned herself in a chair diagonally from him, her knees touching his.

"You're right," she whispered, feeling herself beginning to tremble. *This is the moment.* "I have to tell you everything."

She prepared to plunge on, ready to describe a mosaic of events in her life—kneeling for prayers to Ganesha at Swami Kripananda's ashram, Islamic studies with Yassar, life with Ibrahim, Tom Goddard and the CIA...It was all coming down to this. Her trembling increased. "I've lived a lie with you from the start. First, Sophie wasn't Sophie. It might not matter, but she was Christina, Countess Del Mira. My name is Sasha—"

"What?" he interjected.

She shook him off. "Sasha Del Mira. Christina raised me as her ward—never legally adopted me. She started taking drugs, then became desperate, actually. Addicted." She swallowed hard. "She 'sold' me to Yassar." Her heart was crying. "Sold me as a concubine to his son, Ibrahim."

She saw Daniel's head snap back, watched emotion flood into his cheeks.

Pain washed over her, but she went on. "Ibrahim became involved with these Islamic fundamentalist fanatics who I'm sure you've heard of—the al-Mujari."

She saw him nod stiffly, eyes glazed over.

"I was recruited by the CIA as an undercover agent to report back on Ibrahim's and the al-Mujari's activities. When they influenced Ibrahim to help them kill his father—Yassar—and install Ibrahim as their puppet ruler of Saudi Arabia, I helped the CIA kill Ibrahim." *No. Not enough.* Her omission burned in her soul. "I—I killed him myself."

Daniel leaned forward now. It was a few moments before he realized he was staring off at the wall—at nothing, his mind working. *Jesus.* He was aware his mouth had started moving well before any sound came from him, then heard a gulping noise from his throat. He swallowed hard and looked at Lydia. "Go on," he said in a hollow voice.

"You haven't heard the worst."

Now he felt his breathing ragged. He motioned with his head for her to continue.

Sasha saw that the pupils of Daniel's eyes had shrunk, watching her as if wondering how much more there was, Sasha herself afraid because she couldn't read his reaction. Would he get through it? She went on. "I went back, pleaded, explained to Yassar. He was like my father—he's still the only father I've ever known—and he took me back. I lived on in the Royal Palace, started doing what I'd been trained for—covert intelligence. The multiple identities, the passports, the money. You were right to question it all."

Sasha spoke slowly, felt each word was like giving birth. "I did it for years, to thwart these terrorists, living on and off undercover. I even helped Yassar with you, Daniel." She heard a roar like jet engines in her ears. "When Yassar learned the al-Mujari might be planning some form of computer-based terrorism on the oil and gas industry, he sent me here to spy on you. I couldn't tell you because we didn't know if we could trust you. I was sent to meet and get involved with you, pass on information and, most importantly, wait to see if any of the rumored al-Mujari terrorism surfaced."

She pushed on, talking faster, wanting to get through it now, all the while watching his face. It was frozen, a death mask.

"It has: the terrorists plan to bring down the Saudi royal family, install a Shiite fundamentalist government, and cripple the world's oil capacity. Their plot leads directly to you and your clients. They'll hack into and sabotage the industry's software programs that run all its operations. And it appears their main window into the industry is through your links to your clients. But there must be others, probably through other advisors to the industry. I'm even using an alias as a computer hacker, Alica, to learn of their activities. That's why I hacked into your computer." She continued searching his face, her heart wailing. "Will you trust me again? Will you help us? Daniel, I fell in love with you, too, and I don't want to lose you." Her voice was thin. "I'm sorry, darling, so sorry…"

She felt her nerves sandpapered raw, and yet she was clear. They could do this, the two of them. Get through it and live it. Just a little longer. She clutched Daniel's hands in hers. Don't let him fade, not now, not after all this. "Daniel, don't doubt that I love you." She threw herself beside him on the sofa.

"Stop it, stop talking," he said.

She felt his arms around her, his chest heaving. She wanted to tell him that she'd never leave him, but kept silent. Now words didn't matter, because she felt the command in his embrace and was infused with a soaring sense of completion. It was as if she'd arrived abruptly at a destination—as if "Oh, here so soon" had taken the wind out of her, blanked her thoughts, and left her unable to describe the impression. All at once something was singing inside; she knew it not from any sound, but from feeling it, a wonderful tickling vibration, like humming in her soul. What a way to know his love! A lyricism from within. She realized there would be no more searching.

Daniel was still experiencing the release of pushing through to the other side of his fears, having heard her words as so much flotsam from a past that didn't exist anymore. She loved him back. Now it was all about their future. He leaned back and took in Lydia. She looked urgent, intense. Then seeing her discern his acceptance, her face grew joyous, and she was again the little dancer he'd met across the room at Gary and Jonathan's. Daniel now experienced her anew, saw her smiling, the mixture of languor and energy. He was almost unbelieving, nearly unable to stand the intensity of simply embracing her here this way. Then in the next moment it all seemed so effortless. He sighed and felt perfection. No, not perfection, realizing that didn't happen, wasn't for him, but that she was for him, for as long as he could earn that of her.

Lydia was watching him, her expression peaceful. She spoke again. "When I realized I loved you, it was as if my spirit stirred with recognition, as if it was always there and I just needed to understand it. Not preordained I'd find you, but since our souls had once touched, you were there to help us both nurture our love with belief, teach ourselves what we already knew."

Daniel didn't respond, had no voice to speak even if he'd be able to formulate the thoughts. Then, slowly, words came, and with them a sense of gravity.

"If all this is true, there's a lot more at stake than the Saudi royal family. If this sabotage means what I think it does, thousands, maybe even hundreds of thousands could die. And it could cripple more than the oil and gas industry. Energy, transportation, industrial production—everything grinds to a halt. Economies will topple like dominoes. We can't waste time. We need to move—now."

CHAPTER 31

AUGUST, THIS YEAR. NEW YORK City. Sasha kissed Daniel on the forehead as he slept on the sofa, where he'd crashed from exhaustion within fifteen minutes after they'd finished talking.

He stirred. "What time is it?"

"Almost midnight."

"Jesus, why didn't you wake me?"

"Darling, you're exhausted. You did a one-day out-and-back to Europe, then had the last twenty-five years of my life dumped on your head."

He smiled. "I'm looking forward to the next twenty-five."

"If it's not longer than that I'm going to feel awfully cheated. I waited a long time to find you."

He kissed her. "Agreed." Then his eyes narrowed. "Hey, we should get going. We have a lot of work to do."

"First thing tomorrow. Right now I'm putting you to bed."

"Just me?"

She felt her own face change, her lips pull taut and her brow furrow. "I have something to do before tomorrow."

After she put Daniel to bed, Sasha went to Daniel's study and pulled out her notebook computer. She typed an email:

ANYTHING NEW? I AWAIT NEXT INSTRUCTIONS FROM BIN
ABDUR.

ALICA

She encrypted it and hit "send." A few minutes later her computer beeped. She deencrypted and opened the email response.

NOTHING. QUIET. WILL LET YOU KNOW.
ALI

She felt her arm muscles tense. *Stonewalled again.*

August, This Year. Online. After responding to Alica's email, Ali gazed at his computer screen. His eyes blinked in rhythm with the cursor that pulsed on the green background.

He decided it was time he hacked into Saudi Aramco's system himself. The username and password Alicia gave him worked, but now he couldn't be certain he could trust her. Always asking questions, probing for next steps. What if the username she gave him was a plant, and therefore traceable? Perhaps her questions and probing were only that she was greedy and wanted more involvement for more of the fees. But even if she were trustworthy, now that he had seen the scale of the Sheik's ambitions and the commensurate size of the fees, he wasn't sure he wanted to share them with Alicia if he could do it himself. Besides, he had a half-dozen other hackers, all of whom he'd known and trusted for years, he'd need to pay in order to get all the Sheik's work done in time.

So he'd start by hacking into Saudi Aramco and getting his own username and password on their system.

He started to hack his way in but ran into the company's firewall. After an hour of trying, he guessed the firewall was the formidable Raptor Eagle and finally gave up.

He sat down to what he now knew would be a long siege. He checked the personal profiles he had created on three of the Saudi Aramco system managers. He didn't have to go further than the first.

Let's see, Mr. Bopal. You are thirty-one years old, you attended private high school in Bombay, were shipped off to MIT to under-graduate school and for a Master's in computer sciences. You worked for IBM in Armonk, New York, as a systems programmer for two years, then moved directly to Saudi Aramco, after which you made your way up through the ranks to system manager. Oh, infidel, you like to visit the sex.fun.com website, you're an avid follower of cricket, you enjoy Shakespeare plays, you're a religious Hindu.

Bopal had visited the cricketnews.com website 52 times over the preceding month. *That's it.* He got right to work. He logged onto one of the half-dozen websites he'd commandeered over the past two months for use as an anonymous remailer, a program that cloaked the identity and location of the sender of email messages anywhere on the Internet. From there he logged onto the cricketnews.com website, then logged off. He reviewed the files on his hard drive and found the cookie files the cricketnews.com website had created in his directory. The cookies stored details about users' activities on the website, and allowed the website to customize responses to individual users based on their activities in prior website visits.

Ali opened the cookie file and appended a file of his own, a trojan horse. Then he logged back onto the cricketnews.com website; by doing so he deposited the trojan horse he had appended when the site grabbed the cookie from his hard drive. He logged off to wait.

The trojan horse program waited, too, in this case for the cricketnews.com website client with the username Bopal to show up. The program's first line read:

If user = Bopal, then attach

At 7:56 p.m. local time in Dhahran, Saudi Arabia, Marij Bopal sat at his computer at Saudi Aramco and logged into the cricketnews.com website to check on the day's worldwide cricket scores. A few minutes later he logged off the cricketnews.com website, and Ali's trojan horse stole into the Saudi Aramco system. As the system manager, Bopal enjoyed the highest level of authority available within the Saudi Aramco refinery's system. It was 8:32 p.m. when Bopal logged off his account, or thought he did. It was Ali's trojan horse that mimicked the log-off sequence and kept it open. A beep on Ali's computer told him it was time.

Ali stepped into Bopal's shoes, then scrolled around the account. He worked rapidly, not out of fear he would be caught, but with the thrill of having cracked a difficult system. As a superuser—with power to manipulate the computer system at the system-manager level, he scrolled around the system. Everything seemed to be routine. A few engineers were running diagnostic routines and some research calculations. The refinery programs slowly chugged through their monitoring and control functions. A few users dabbled with the Internet.

Four accounts hadn't been used in over three months. *Good.* As a superuser all he needed to do was delete the passwords for those four accounts, then later log back on the system as each of those users, inputting a new password, which only he would know.

Ten minutes later Ali logged off as Bopal and then dialed back into Saudi Aramco through his anonymous remailer program and logged back on as user name "Portnoy," one of the four accounts he had stolen. He entered the new password, "Stolen," that he'd replaced Portnoy's password with.

"Now the fun begins," Ali said aloud. He looked on his directory for the logic bomb program he'd written and loaded it onto the Saudi Aramco refinery routines.

———◆———

August, This Year. New York City. The next morning Sasha was up by 5:00 a.m. She was in the kitchen making tea when she decided she couldn't wait any longer. Still hearing Daniel in the shower, she dialed Nafta at the clinic in Paris, feeling apprehension as they connected her to Nafta's room.

"Hello?"

"It's me," Sasha said.

"Sister, how are you?" Sasha heard a lift in Nafta's voice.

"How are *you*?"

There was a pause. "As feared."

Sasha gripped the phone tighter. "What does it mean?"

"Caught it too late. Cervical cancer, and it's metastasized into…" Her voice trailed off, then came back. "…everything."

Sasha felt as though a meteor had fallen out of the sky on her. "I'm coming."

"I have time, sister, don't drop everything. I want to hear how things are going with your man."

Sasha barely heard her, now thinking. *How long does she have? Weeks? Months?* "I'm coming."

"Sister…"

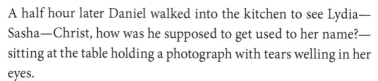

A half hour later Daniel walked into the kitchen to see Lydia—Sasha—Christ, how was he supposed to get used to her name?—sitting at the table holding a photograph with tears welling in her eyes.

"What's wrong?"

"Someone's sick."

"Who?"

"Her name is Nafta. She's my oldest friend." She showed him her photo.

"You could pass for sisters."

"It's as if we are—we love each other like sisters."

"Is it serious?"

"Cancer. And she doesn't have much time."

Now Daniel saw her head sag. "I'm sorry," he said, taking her hand.

She squeezed his hand. "I want to go see her, but with all this going on…how can I?"

"For God's sake, lover, if she's your oldest friend, why wouldn't you go to her right away? Most of our work tracking down my clients is stuff only I can do anyhow. I can make do without you for a day or two."

She looked into his eyes. "I'm not sure there's time."

Daniel's stomach tightened.

"Sheik bin Abdur's lead hacker has most likely started his terrorism. He's gone silent on me, and it doesn't feel right."

Daniel felt a tremor in his chest.

In a taxi on the way to the office, Lydia sitting at his side, Daniel turned the prior day's events over in his mind. It *was* surreal. The woman he loved was a spy, with a past you couldn't make up if you were a pulp novelist. It was so crazy it was believable. But this elaborate computer terrorism plan, the scale of it, a strike at the heart of the engine that drove the world—oil—it just seemed so fiendish it was hard to accept. Maybe he needed to give it more time to sink in.

He clutched Lydia's hand in his, felt her internal tension in the firmness of her grip. He sighed and tried to stop thinking about himself, consider how Lydia must be feeling. She was clearly shaken by the prospect of losing a friend, not being able to go to her and maybe never seeing her alive again. He'd comforted her as well as he could. But that was a pain she might not be prepared for. And then he felt a twist of the emotions he'd felt after Angie passed away, that unique, unfathomable agony. Then he conjured the unthinkable: Lydia herself could be taken from him as swiftly as her friend Nafta would from her, as Angie was from him.

That put the whole terrorism scheme in context, personalized it. Even as frightening as the big picture was—thousands dead, industries and economies melting down—the possibility of losing Lydia made it more horrible still. He felt a wallop of realization that if Lydia were gone, and given the space she occupied in his life, so overwhelming, so surprisingly large, that it was impossible for him to grasp that level of absence. He didn't need time for the transforming force of that epiphany to sink in.

CHAPTER 32

AUGUST, THIS YEAR. NEW YORK City. Shortly after arriving at his office, Daniel sat behind his desk briefing his best team: Walter Purcell, Steven Pace and James Cassidy, who sat facing him. Lydia—she'd admonished him to keep calling her that in public, as if he needed to be reminded—sat off to the side in one of his lounge chairs. Purcell kept looking out of the corner of his eye at her as if wondering what she was doing there. Maybe he'd understand later. They were almost finished reviewing their approach to ferreting out which of Daniel's software vendor clients were potential targets for infiltration, and then in turn, which of their customers might be sabotaged.

"How deep a dive you want?" Purcell said.

Daniel said, "For starters I want the eighty-twenty rule. Find eighty percent of the customers in twenty percent of the time it will take to find them all."

Purcell squinted and tightened his jaw.

"What's wrong?"

"You need all three of us for that?"

"You mean do I need *you*, too? Yes, I'm interested in speed." Daniel stared at him a moment, then looked at his other two colleagues. "Understand?"

They both nodded.

He looked back at Purcell. "Walter, you split up the software vendor clients with these guys any way you want, but I want you on IR Systems."

Purcell nodded.

"Okay guys, thanks, get going. I need a status update in two hours."

Daniel followed them to the door and closed it after they left. He turned to Lydia, who sat with her hands in her lap, dressed down in a simple blue skirt, silk blouse and blue pumps. Her face showed she was deep in thought. He now took in her hair, which hung over her shoulders and curved with the shape of her breasts. He smelled the scent of her shampoo, or was it a subtle perfume she wore for business? They hadn't made love last night, even after the climax of that emotional roller coaster. She smiled at him. He felt a rise of desire.

Focus. Not now.

"That would've been a lot easier if we could've told them what's really happening," Daniel said.

"Not yet. Let's wait until we have facts to confirm it."

"What more do we need?"

"Evidence of sabotage. You know how alarming it would be to your team? And how fast it would get out, maybe even to the media? Without hard proof we'd have no credibility."

"Yes, but we don't want it on our consciences if things start blowing up."

Lydia paused, looked away for a moment, then back up at Daniel, thinking. "That's not my call, darling. It's Yassar's."

"Why don't we just call him?"

Lydia tightened her lips. "Can we finish this first? How long will it take?"

Daniel started turning it over in his mind, then talked it out, thinking aloud. "These guys are good, and I gave them all of my software vendor clients off the top of my head, and a few dozen of their biggest customers…it's the customers that we're after… I'd say six to eight hours to get all of what I asked for."

Lydia winced. "Still, let's wait, then decide."

Daniel nodded. *Yeah, plus this is still pretty hard to believe. Better to wait.*

At 7:00 p.m., Daniel thanked his team and sent them home. As he walked them to the door to close it behind them, he saw Purcell and Pace exchange sideways glances, probably now not only wondering about why Lydia was there, but what Daniel was up to. The office smelled like steaks, broccoli and onion rings— Daniel had ordered in from the Palm for the entire team. He turned from the door. Lydia's dinner still sat untouched on the end table. She'd been too anxious to eat while they awaited the team's results, and now she was already poring over the 22-page Excel spreadsheet his team had prepared.

"It's hard to believe," she said without looking up. "So many. Thousands. I had no idea."

"I've never tried to figure it out myself," Daniel said as he sat down next to her, his own copy of the spreadsheet in hand. "I've always only looked at it from the standpoint of my twelve clients who sell operating software to the industry, and, I guess, the bigger customers they provide services to."

"Yes, but this goes down to another level. How many primary, secondary, tertiary wells. How many drilling rigs. How many refineries…it's almost impossible to absorb." She looked up into Daniel's eyes. He detected a note of alarm. It made his stomach rumble. He felt an airy feeling in his chest as he inhaled. *Is she starting to lose it?*

He smiled and stroked her hand, trying to calm her. "It's a little overwhelming if you take it in all at once, but if we break it down, take it one step at a time, maybe we can sort it out." She nodded and smiled, but her face was brittle. "Why don't you eat something, let me absorb it, then we can attack it systematically together."

"Okay," she said almost timidly, then tore into her steak like it was her first meal in a week.

Ten minutes later they were sitting side by side on the sofa, their spreadsheets in their laps. Daniel was leading Lydia through the data. "The first four pages are the master list." He flipped forward to the fifth page. "From here on it's sorted by type of customer end use." He started flipping pages, calling them out. "Exploration well drilling, production well drilling, refineries, pipelines, primary, secondary and tertiary well recovery, etc… you see how it's organized?"

Lydia nodded.

"It's too much to chase them all without some organized approach. So I asked my guys to set up the list so we could sort it. We just need to figure out what's the most logical approach."

"Triage," Lydia said. "Like battlefield medics—work on the most critical cases first."

"Great. So, who would they hit first? Production wells? Pipelines? Refiners? Exploration companies?"

Lydia looked up at him with eyes displaying urgency. "You know the business. Use your judgment. If you wanted to cripple the industry, how could you do the most damage in the shortest time, and how would it be the most enduring?"

"Refiners," Daniel said without hesitating. "That would bottleneck the industry. Nobody could process raw oil into end products." He paused for a moment, looking up at the golf print on his wall, thinking.

Lydia grabbed his forearm. "Don't stop, just let it flow."

"And refineries would take years to rebuild, and would cost the most." He looked down into Lydia's eyes. "That's where I'd look first."

Lydia started flipping pages.

"Don't bother. Intelligent Recovery Systems is the biggest player in the industry, and their systems run by far the most refineries. If I wanted to screw up the oil and gas industry, I'd start there."

A half hour later Daniel put his phone back in the cradle. "I couldn't get either of them, not even on their cell phones."

Lydia stood up from the sofa, shook her hair out, walked over and seated herself in one of the chairs in front of Daniel's desk. She slid it forward so she could sit with her copy of the spreadsheet on his desk. Now her eyes were flashing with energy. She bent over the spreadsheet, her hair hanging down. "Intelligent Recovery Systems has five hundred fifty-seven customers, seventy-three of which are refiners, with two hundred twenty refineries. Dresner Technologies has two hundred fifty-six customers, twenty-six refiners with seventy-eight refineries." She looked up at Daniel. "How much of the industry is that?"

He'd already done the math. The two clients totaled 99 refiners with almost 300 refineries. "Worldwide? About forty percent of the refineries."

Her eyes went wide. "My God, and that's with only two of your clients."

Daniel felt a surge of adrenaline, then a flare of tension in his chest. *No question about it, this could get really ugly.* He reached across his desk and took her hand, looked into her eyes. "We're on the right track, I think. Not bad for a day's work, lover. And if these two guys don't get back to me tonight, I'll be all over them tomorrow morning."

She squeezed his hand and smiled. "I love you, Daniel."

"I love you." He leaned back in his chair. "And in a few minutes I'm going to take you home and do something about it." Lydia smiled again. "But first I need to make one more phone call. I thought of something when I was looking at the list of my clients. There's this guy I used to work with, Bob Kovarik, who also has a few sizable clients who supply software to a few dozen refiners." Daniel picked up his office phone and punched the keys. *Voicemail, damn.* "Bob, it's Daniel Youngblood. I've got something I need to talk to you about. I know this is going to sound crazy, but somebody's trying to infiltrate some of my clients' software systems, with the intention of creating real havoc in the industry. You have a few clients, particularly Resource Systems, who may be infiltrated as well. I know we've had our differences in the past, but this is something we should discuss, urgently. Please call me. Use my cell number."

Lydia was sitting up straight in her chair, her jaw taut when Daniel hung up the phone. "That should get a reaction."

"Yes, if for no other reason than he'd look like a hero to his clients if he helps them avert all this. And because even *he'd* want to do the right thing."

He hoped he was right.

CHAPTER 33

SEPTEMBER, THIS YEAR. NEW YORK City. The next morning Daniel was sitting finishing his tea, admiring Lydia's profile as she glided around the kitchen, reliving in his mind her lovemaking the previous night, when his cell phone rang.

"Daniel," Dick Jantzen, Chairman and CEO of Intelligent Recovery Systems, said. "I got your message. Sounded like it was important. What's up, tiger." Daniel could tell Dick was on his cell phone, probably driving.

"Thanks for calling me back, Dick."

"No problem. My main man calls, I'm there."

Daniel's stomach gurgled. This early in the morning and he's laying it on this thick? *Give it a rest.* "Thanks. Since this may be a little shocking, I'll just blurt it out." He squeezed the phone tighter, felt his arms tense. *Here we go.* "I have good information that someone may be infiltrating the computer systems of the oil and gas industry's software vendors. I also believe they may be doing it to target refiners. Since you're the biggest player, I have to assume your systems have either already been compromised or will be shortly."

"You gotta be kidding me."

"Would I say something like this if I weren't serious?"

"You have any idea of the consequences of what you're saying?"

"That's why I'm calling you."

"You tell this to anybody else?"

"You're my first call."

"Good, because if this gets out, I'm gonna spend the rest of my life doing nothing but babysitting my customers. What the hell is the source of your information?"

Daniel swallowed; his throat felt like it was full of sawdust. He closed his eyes and took a deep breath, exhaled slowly. "I'm close to someone with the Saudis, who are one of my clients, whose covert intelligence has uncovered this."

Jantzen said, "Covert intelligence? You mean spies and shit? Are you crazy?" He paused. "You say you're close to someone. What the hell does that mean?"

"A woman…"

"Oh, here we go, some babe you met…"

"It's not like that."

"Oh, it's not? So it's serious, she's your girlfriend, then?"

Daniel felt the energy draining from his legs. This wasn't going at all like he'd planned. "That's not important."

Jantzen laughed into the phone. "Okay, my man, so what's the master plan with all this?"

Daniel clenched his teeth, now starting to get angry. He wanted this conversation over with. Either Jantzen would buy into it and do something about it or not. "According to Saudi intelligence, a Saudi Islamic terrorist group, the al-Mujari, has plans to infiltrate computer service providers to the oil and gas industry and sabotage the industry's operations."

"So you're telling me your girlfriend's some kind of spy and she knows some Saudi Islamic terrorist nuts are gonna infiltrate my company and screw up the whole industry?"

Daniel chose not to answer. He was already thinking a few steps ahead; what would Jantzen do with this information:

probably nothing. How would Daniel play his next conversation with Stan McDonald at Dresner Technologies: do it face to face.

"Daniel, I think you're hanging around with the wrong broads. You should stop thinking with your Johnson and ditch that bimbo. If I send my systems guys to my customers with a harebrained story like this, they'll drop me like a hot potato."

"Dick, I realize this is hard to believe. But I think it would be irresponsible of you to just ignore it."

Jantzen didn't say anything for a few moments. Daniel heard the static on the line, knew he was still connected. "Okay, I'll tell you what I'll do. I'll have my head guy do some checking to see if anybody's busted into our system. I'll let you know if he finds anything. But don't ever call me back on this subject unless you've got either the CIA or the Saudi King on the line." Jantzen laughed, then the line cut off.

Daniel put his cell phone down on the kitchen table, looked up and saw Lydia standing with her back to the counter, both hands clasped to the edge of it, her arms tense. Her lips were drawn into a thin line. "That went well," she said.

Daniel shrugged. "I guess I should have expected it."

"What are we going to do?"

"Learn from it. When I talk to Stan McDonald at Dresner Technologies, I think I'll suggest I fly down to Houston to visit him. This might be better done in person."

"And without your bimbo spy."

Daniel laughed, a welcome release of tension. "You heard that?"

"How could I not, the man speaks at about ninety decibels."

"Yes, and you could say he's difficult."

Lydia cocked her head to the side. "Darling, the man's what you Americans refer to as an asshole."

September, This Year. Houston, Texas. Daniel flew to Houston the next morning. Sitting in the conference room at Dresner Technologies, waiting for Stan McDonald to show up, Daniel played back the end-less loop of thoughts he'd been assaulted by on the airplane. Dick Jantzen did have a point. Why not just go to the CIA or the FBI? Was it because Daniel wasn't convinced it was all real, afraid to make a fool of himself? Was he so much in love with Lydia—Sasha—that he was willingly living in the bubble of her own delusion? Why not just call Yassar and put an end to his doubts? Because he was afraid that would prove he didn't really believe in Lydia?

Daniel was staring out the window at the glass-and-steel office towers rising in all directions from the sun-baked prai-rie, still turning things over in his mind when Stan McDonald showed up. Daniel gave him a firm handshake, made eye contact and handled the meeting like any client presentation. Low key. Working his thought process from the client's side, addressing likely questions and skepticism. Selling it.

A half hour later Daniel was sitting elbow-to-elbow with Jim Fredrickson, Dresner's Senior Vice President, Systems Security. Fredrickson pointed at the monitor on his desk. "I can't show you how the firewall works. I can only show you the printout of security checks, a list of attempted assaults, and the catalogue of viruses, network worms and spyware detected." Frederickson looked over at Daniel to see if he understood.

Daniel nodded.

"And as you'll see, nothing here looks suspicious. So unless what somebody's doing is very subtle and extremely sophisti-cated, our firewall is intact."

Daniel said, "What about my email access?"

"Let's check," Fredrickson said, typing at his keyboard. Daniel saw his name come up on the screen, then the printout of an email inbox showing his communications with Dresner personnel. "Nothing unusual on the surface."

"Would my email account on your system make it any easier for someone to hack his way in?"

"Possibly, but unlikely, since our internal intranet security picks up the same kind of viruses, worms, etc. as our external firewall. But still, it's possible."

Daniel thought for a moment. It was a major coup for him to be accepted onto Dresner's intranet system as if he were an employee, as the firm's trusted advisor and a confidant of Stan McDonald. It gave him access to all internal employee memoranda and strategic white papers, and in general kept him in the inner circle of decision makers at the company. Something any investment banker would kill for. That's why he felt a flutter of butterflies when he said, "If that's the case, maybe you should eliminate my account. I can live with communicating with you guys the way the rest of the world does for a while. Then if this turns out to be nothing, you could reestablish my account in the future."

"Okay," Fredrickson said. He typed a few more keys that led him to another screen and hit "delete." Daniel felt a brief gasp of despair.

Fredrickson promised to keep an eye open for any hacking attempts. Daniel left him then swung by Stan McDonald's office to shake hands, and headed for the airport. He hoped his mind wouldn't get stuck on that same infinite loop on the way home.

September, This Year. New York City. Kovarik was itchy; mad. He hated it, getting mad. It was the downside of letting a son of a bitch like Youngblood get to him. It made him sweat, made him pit out his shirts, wrinkle his suits. That was the worst part, his suits. He had to dry-clean them instead of just having them brushed and pressed—wore them out prematurely, all that caustic chemical shit attacking his English superfine worsted wools. Sweating was okay for the masses, dopes who rode the subway and wore cheap-shit JoS. A. Banks suits, but not for him. He sat scratching, rubbing his shin, because now it was starting to hurt. Goddamn son of a bitch Youngblood.

He sat with his feet up on his desk, shoes and jacket off, tie loosened, blasting the air-conditioning so he could try to keep cool. Poor Tracy in reception was freezing her little buns off, nipples standing up like soldiers at attention. He'd been waiting for Kapur since two o'clock. That was another thing that made him mad; the guy was 45 minutes late. Finally his assistant buzzed him: "Mr. Kapur is here."

Kovarik swung his feet off the desk and into his loafers, hitched up his tie and stood up just as Kapur walked in.

"What's so urgent," Kapur said without even saying hello. Wearing that same Kmart suit, same rumpled shirt. He walked over and sat down on Kovarik's sofa, looking mad himself: brow furrowed, jaw set. Kovarik remembered this wasn't a guy he wanted to mess with and so he eased the door closed instead of slamming it like he wanted to.

"I got a phone call from Youngblood."

Kapur looked at him like he was saying, "So?" and shrugged.

"You know, Mr. Top-of-the-List Youngblood."

"And?"

Kovarik walked over to his desk and turned his phone around facing Kapur. "I'll play it for you." He hit the speakerphone and fast-forwarded his voicemail to Youngblood's message. He watched Kapur's body language as the message went on. He played it cool, but when it was over he sat up on the edge of the sofa and leaned forward with his elbows on his thighs. He put his head down and sighed.

"This man is just an investment banker, no?" Kapur said, looking up at Kovarik.

Just an investment banker. The hell's that supposed to mean? Kovarik said, "As opposed to what?"

Kapur just looked at him, then said, "As opposed to somebody whose business it is to figure things like this out."

"Yeah, in that case he's just a banker." Kovarik realized he was still sweaty. He wanted to scratch his thighs because of the wool on his sweaty skin, but resisted.

At that moment Kapur stood up. "Anything else?" he said.

"Yeah, I was thinking, how about setting it up to frame Youngblood. Make it look like he's the one who gave you all the information."

Kapur was scowling, shaking his head.

"What? You couldn't make that work?"

Kapur took a few steps toward the door, then turned back to face him. He said, "If this guy, Youngblood, screws this up on me, I don't get my success fee. Frame him, my ass. I have other ways to deal with this." Kapur glared at him. Kovarik felt fresh perspiration break out on his forehead and upper lip. "And if you have any contact with him, or screw around to pursue any personal agenda, I'll deal with you the same way." He turned and left, closing the door behind him.

Kovarik felt a spasm of panic flare in his chest. His next breaths came in short gasps. He reached down and scratched his thighs.

CHAPTER 34

SEPTEMBER, THIS YEAR. ONLINE. ALI stared at the flat-screen monitor on his desk: his world. His computer beeped. *Another email from her.* He de-encrypted it:

WHAT NEWS? WAITING FOR NEXT STEPS.
ALICA

He typed, encrypted and sent:

NOTHING.
ALI

He hoped the woman would get the message and quit trying. He turned back to the business at hand. He was inside this Daniel Youngblood's account at Ladoix Sayre, ready to penetrate Intelligent Recovery System's computer network through the email account IR Systems had created for Youngblood as a user on their system.

It was the same approach he'd taken with three other of Youngblood's clients, planting trojan horses in the software code that would be sent out to the company's customers in routine updates to their programs. Trojan horses with prearranged timing to drop their embedded cargo—logic bombs—once the program updates containing them had been installed.

He checked the IR Systems' brag sheet on its Internet website: seventy-three refinery customers running over 220 refineries in all. *This is the big one*, he thought.

He worked smoothly now, familiar with the process. He'd create a "buffer overflow" in a security flaw in an appointment calendar program that was shipped with the server that IR Systems' system ran on. He'd make an entry in the calendar program in Youngblood's account, but his entry was a carefully designed clump of information too large to fit the storage space that the program allotted for it. The resultant overflow spilling out into the computer's main memory allowed the code he had appended to the email to run a short routine that granted him root access. Able to do anything he wanted.

He loaded his code containing his software routine into an email file on Youngblood's computer. Then he emailed it into his account on IR Systems. *There.* The buffer overflow. He sat back from the screen, watched and waited for him to get root access. Seconds later he was in. He logged back into Youngblood's email account, downloaded his trojan horse program, its logic bomb appended, and scrolled into the refinery update code. His trojan horse and logic bomb now sat waiting to be beamed out over the Internet to the IR Systems' customers as a routine software update at 6:00 a.m. Moments later he logged off the system and closed out his circuitous link to Youngblood's computer.

Well, Sheik bin Abdur, I think you'll be surprised and impressed at what happens over the next few days.

September, This Year. Langley, Virginia. Tom Goddard, CIA Mid-East Section Head, was ready for the videoconference to start, his last chance for input from his fellow Mid-East experts prior to his flight to Saudi Arabia. He fixed his eyes on the 20-inch Sanyo flat-screen computer monitor on his desk, killing time, seeing a blank background in the right half, a smaller-than-life Nigel Benthurst in 1,700 pixels per inch shrug in his confident, superior way in the left. Tom was waiting for Ira Land, Ari Verchik's replacement in the Mossad, killing time. He noted Nigel's decadent look and manner, carefully cultivated over the years, was now starting to show dissipation.

The right side of the screen flashed on, Ira video-streaming at him through secure OC-3 fiber-optic lines at 1.5 gigabytes per second. Real time, not like the old big-screen TV satellite hook-ups where everybody moved in that herky-jerky 56k world.

Nigel had been speaking, Tom realized. "...I tell you they're a bunch of tent dwellers from centuries ago. And, uhm, that's all they'll, uhm, likely ever be...oh, hullo, Ira...only difference between now and two thousand years ago is that they've got five thousand bloody princes running the place instead of fifty."

"All right, fellas, let's get started," Tom said, a stale, dry taste in his throat. Ira's chin was just barely above the bottom of the screen. Shorter than five-foot-five-inch life. "We've got a situation in Saudi Arabia. Intelligence and military alert status; potential use of force required."

"When are you going over?"

"Today at noon. The red-eye into Riyadh. Our meeting starts at noon tomorrow. I'm bringing a team of computer jocks with me. Our own CIA and some Joint Terrorism Task Force guys." He dreaded the meeting.

"We'll provide resources on request," Ira said. "Full government clearance." His dark beard looked like a five-o'clock shadow, accentuated by the video monitor.

"Appreciated."

"Same from my colleagues in London," Nigel said. "*Actually, we wish we'd been invited to your meeting ourselves.*"

Tom sighed. "It's a bitch of a trip. And it brings back old memories. Bad ones." He thought of the hit on Ibrahim, Yassar's kid, then of Sasha. Now he had that feeling. Grungy. Was it remorse? *Just leave it.* Sasha had gone into it all with full knowledge of the consequences, and the risks. And she'd at least helped Yassar avoid getting lit up by his own kid.

"We all should have expected this," Ira said. "Sheik bin Abdur's been rebuilding for years. We should have assumed he'd make a move sooner or later."

"Yeah, but it's not just that. I'll be seeing Yassar himself." *First time since we killed his kid.*

"I still think it would make everything a lot easier if the Saudis would just blow Sheik bin Abdur away," Ira said. "They had their chance—we all did—years ago. You'd think they'd have learned their lesson now that he appears to be going critical again."

"No, not this time either," Nigel put in. "You know. The undesirability of making him the martyr and all that…"

"It's really the whole Muslim thing that's stopping them," Tom said. "Brother against brother and all that shit." He'd spent most of his career covering the Mid-East. Was he now worn out with it?

"Didn't seem to trouble them too much during the first Gulf War," Nigel said.

"Yeah, but we were the ones dropping the bombs. And they kept at arm's length from the '03 Iraq invasion."

"Maybe they should let us neutralize him, then."

Tom grunted in the affirmative.

"Let's not get ahead of ourselves," Ira said, "let's make sure this isn't just some false alarm. Maybe it's not the al-Mujari after all."

"Possible," Nigel said. "We're not hearing any unusual chatter in our monitoring of their cells."

"Don't count on it," Tom said. "My bet is in a week we'll be looking for somebody to get inside, get close enough to light up bin Abdur."

"Not an easy type to find," Nigel sighed.

"Whatever happened to this girl, Sasha?"

"I don't know," Tom had thought about it before Ira asked. He was the last one to have any contact with her. Maybe she was still alive. "As far as I know she's fallen off the face of the earth. Or dead." Now he remembered a few possible sightings over the years, usually when a bomb was going off someplace, but never sure it was her. "But we haven't been the only ones looking for her, that's for sure."

September, This Year. New York City. By 7:42 the morning Daniel left for Houston, Lydia was in a taxi and on her way to JFK, having chartered a Gulfstream V from Falcon Aviation. She could be to the Cayman Islands and back by early afternoon. Once on the airplane, Lydia felt a sagging sensation, as if a weight was on her chest. Heartsick. Thinking about Daniel, hoping he wasn't in danger. Then putting it out of her head. *Deal with business.* She called her banker from on board.

"It's your black-haired friend. Account number one two four six seven nine three." There was no emotion in her voice, but her mind was racing. "I'll need three hundred fifty thousand in U.S. currency in two and a half hours. Hundreds will do. I have a suitable bag with me."

"I'll take care of it right away," her banker said.

With a sense of detachment, she phoned Herr Schinkelhaus in Switzerland. "Wilhelm, it's Sasha. I'll need your services again. It's a rush job. Swiss passport."

At 11:35 the Gulfstream V landed at George Town, Grand Cayman. She went first to the Federal Express office and over-nighted Daniel's passport photo to Schinkelhaus, then to the Royal Cayman Trust Company, where she withdrew the $350,000 from her numbered account. "Thank you, Austin," she said to her banker. Errands accomplished, she went back to the airport and boarded the Gulfstream. Counting the rivets around the window, she remembered other flights on which she'd used that diversion from mental maelstroms. By 2:45 she was at Kennedy Airport. Customs didn't search her bag, the one with the false bottom for the cash, with the clothes and lingerie on top of it. She rented a car and was in Kent, Connecticut, by 5:00 p.m.

She drove into the light-industrial section of town, past an equipment rental shop, some dusty, tan manufacturing build-ings, a hardware store, and then parked the rental car in front of a white-painted brick building with four garage bays. Normally these operations were buried in gritty auto body shops with smashed cars scattered helter-skelter out front. This building was landscaped with grass and shrubs, with a crisp sign read-ing "Farrington Auto." Two of the four bays were open, showing a spotless gray-painted concrete floor. Mechanics in matching blue overalls worked beneath cars on lifts.

Sasha walked in the office door, found nobody and went through the back office door into the garage. She found a tall man with gray sideburns who looked like Sean Connery, a "Frank" name patch stitched to his blue uniform. "Hi, Frank. I called earlier. Sandra," she said, extending her hand.

He took her in with probing, intense eyes. After a moment he shook her hand. "Not what I expected." He inclined his head to the side. "It's out here."

In the back lot, two dozen cars were parked in neat rows surrounded by a cyclone fence. Frank pointed at a maroon coupe.

"That's it. Mercedes SLS AMG. Two years old, thirteen thousand miles."

"Never driven over a hundred forty, right?" Sasha smiled.

Frank looked sideways at her as if annoyed at the interruption, then back at the car and continued, "They come stock with a hand-built six-point-three-liter V-eight, five hundred eighty-three horsepower, zero to sixty in three point eight seconds. A barely street-legal racing car."

"Sounds like what I need."

"This car's an animal. Sure you can control it?"

"I hear they handle like sixties-vintage Aston Martins tricked out for the track."

Frank looked over at her again, eyebrows raised as if impressed. "You race Astons?"

"No, but the man who'll be driving this did. He raced the Northeast Aston circuit for three years."

Frank nodded. "You want it?"

"I'll need clean papers and New York plates."

"Part of the deal. Two hundred thousand all-in."

Sasha felt a tingle of irritation. "Roger told me you dealt straight." She looked him squarely in the eye, held it when he tried to back her down with a glare.

"Lady, whatever your real name is, I only deal straight. These puppies list for over one-eighty new. I got expenses for papers and plates, plus my time to make sure it's top-notch mechanically—I got a reputation to keep—plus my margin. Plus a premium for the time factor. Roger said you needed it today."

Sasha didn't flinch, but nodded. "I'll need three keys."

She drove the SLS AMG back to New York. Any other time she'd have been smiling like a jackal, pushing it to the limit around curves, opening it up on straightaways. Today was all business. She pulled into the basement garage of Daniel's building and parked.

Daniel smiled and felt a rush of warmth in his chest when he returned from Houston to his apartment. "Wow." Lydia was wearing a thigh-length emerald kimono embroidered with birds, an emerald necklace at her throat. Her eyes were seductive. "We going out?" he asked.

"No, I've ordered in Chinese," she said. She kissed him and held him. "Darling, I've made some plans in case we need to run. I'll explain later but first I need to show you something that's part of them."

"What are you up to?" Daniel said, smirking.

"This is serious."

She took him out the front door of the apartment to the elevator, rode it down. The elevator door opened at the garage level and she led him out by the hand.

She pointed to the Mercedes coupe in the first space where she'd paid Lloyd, the garage manager, $100 to put it. "It's not registered to either of us, but the papers and license plates are clean. If things get too hot, we can outrun almost anything in it. One key for you, one for me and a spare that's duct-taped behind the left front tire. If we get separated, first one to the car takes it. We meet in Milford."

He blew all the air out through his cheeks. "An SLS AMG. Puts my old Aston to shame. I've never driven one, but that's one angry-looking car."

"Let's hope we don't need it." Then she looked at him with urgency in her eyes. "But darling, if we do, and if we're separated, we need to anticipate each other. The situation will be fluid. Be intuitive."

CHAPTER 35

SEPTEMBER, THIS YEAR. NEW YORK City. Daniel and Lydia sat at his kitchen table strewn with open boxes of Chinese food, packages of sauce, dishes of mustard and chopsticks. The lights, at the brightest end of the dimmer, gave the room a stark quality; the smell of hot and sour soup and Chinese hot spices lent an exotic air. *How incongruous*, Daniel thought, admiring Lydia's beauty in her elegant dress—hair up, emerald jewelry jiggling with the movements of her head—eating with chopsticks directly from the box. She saw him observing, licked her lips, smiled and blew him a kiss. It was equally as incongruous as this everyday scene of two lovers eating a casual meal, juxtaposed against the overhanging weight of a plot that threatened to crash down a major portion of their world.

"Quit hogging the moo goo gai pan," Daniel said, wondering how much the terrorists had advanced their plans in the 48 hours since he'd learned of them.

"You've been clutching the orange chicken like it's a long-lost child," Lydia said. "I'll swap you."

Daniel passed her the box, took hers. *Screw it, I can't do this.* He put the box down and pushed his chair back. "I can't concentrate. My mind's moving in two directions at once."

"Isn't trying *not* to concentrate what we're doing?" She reached over and took his hand, looked at him with soulful eyes.

"Darling, I don't know what else to do except behave as if everything's normal. If we let this twist in our minds we'll drive ourselves crazy."

Daniel squeezed her hand, then stood up and started pacing. "It's been forty-eight hours since we talked about this and we haven't made anything happen."

"You said it yourself yesterday—not bad for a day's work."

Daniel stopped pacing and turned to her. "That was yesterday, but what have we got to show for ourselves today? One of my clients thinks I'm nuts, another's convinced his systems are still uncompromised."

"Maybe they are. But both your clients have been alerted and will be sleeping with one eye open. Believe me, even your charming Mr. Jantzen."

Maybe she was right, but it wasn't good enough. He gripped the back of a kitchen chair. "You know, Jantzen has a point. Why don't we go to the FBI or CIA? How do we prove this—?"

"We're trying."

"Too slowly—"

"You just said it, we've only been at this forty-eight hours."

"I don't think there's any 'only.' Were acting as if we're being chased by a glacier while an express bus is speeding to run us over from the opposite direction."

Daniel saw her jaw sink against her chest, her jaw muscles protrude as she tightened them. He saw her hands ball into fists and then looked down to see that his own knuckles were white from clenching the back of the chair.

Daniel said, "What we're doing isn't a waste of time, but we need to call in somebody to kick this onto a bigger stage."

Lydia waved her hand as if she'd heard enough. "You're right," she said and stood up. "I'll call Yassar first. I have a satellite phone in my luggage. It's not perfect, but it's harder to trace than a landline and harder to triangulate to than a cell phone."

Two minutes later Daniel watched Lydia dial a 3 by 10 inch contraption that looked like an early 1980s cell phone.

"It must be about two a.m. there," Daniel said.

"Three. He'll be up in an hour and a half for prayers anyhow—it's ringing."

Daniel heard a click followed by mumbled words in Arabic. Lydia spoke back in Arabic, restrained at first, probably apologizing, because she bowed her head as if in submission. As the conversation went on she grew more animated, waving her arms, standing up from the bed and walking, arching her head back, punching the air with a fist. Then her voice grew quiet, her demeanor softened, and she sat back down on the bed. She uttered a few gentle words, paused, and then whispered with affection. She hung up and looked at Daniel, her eyes wide with surprise, but a smile on her face.

"Well?" he said.

"Yassar's already called the CIA. They found a logic bomb in the Saudi Aramco refinery control program. Bin Abdur's lead hacker must have planted it after I gave him access—I'll explain that later. The American team will have CIA and Joint Terrorism Task Force computer experts with them."

Daniel felt as if his entire body was exhaling with relief.

"And there's more," Lydia said. "A CIA team will be here tomorrow morning with a satellite hookup for us to participate by videoconference."

"Progress. But let's hope it's not too late."

Teske arrived late to the top of the tower of St. Patrick's Cathedral. First the cleaning staff kept him away from the doorway accessing the stairs, then one of the priests was doing some mumbo-jumbo near the candles for 20 minutes.

He took his time removing his .338 Lapua Custom from its case, attached the 24X enhanced magnification Zeiss scope and screwed the tripod onto the bottom of the Lapua. He took his time, because he needed to catch his breath from the climb so he'd be steady for his shot. Three hundred yards to 30 Rockefeller Plaza wasn't that far, but even a slight tremor of his hand could send a round a foot off target. And it was complicated enough with a shot through the 30 Rock's half-inch-thick tempered glass. He was using armor piercing rounds, but even they couldn't assure a perfect trajectory on the other side of the glass, and Habib had insisted on a head shot.

When he finished setting up, Teske sat down on the cool granite to fully collect himself. After five minutes he stood up, positioned the Lapua and looked through the scope. He counted one window down and four across from the left. The light was on in that office and the target was working at the computer on his desk. He lined up the Zeiss' crosshairs, exhaled. He pulled the trigger, saw the target disappear, dropped the Lapua and started back down the tower stairs.

CHAPTER 36

September, This Year. Riyadh, Saudi Arabia. "You're right, it's a logic bomb," CIA Mideast Section Head Tom Goddard said, his hand clamped around an English bone china coffee cup. He looked around the conference room in the Saudi Royal Palace. Everything was marble. The walls, the floor, the ceiling. Even the windows might as well have been marble, given that you couldn't see much out of them. He'd been told they were inch-thick bullet-proof glass that would withstand a Scud missile. That had been a design change after scores of windows had been shattered from the explosion that blew a 40-foot-wide hole in the perimeter wall the night Prince Ibrahim was murdered. Tom was uncomfortable, not just in the suit, shirt and tie, which he was unaccustomed to wearing, but because Yassar was observing him through cool, blinking eyes. It was the first time he'd sat face to face with him since they'd killed Ibrahim.

He and Yassar sat across from each other at one end of the conference table. On the credenza about 10 feet from them stood a satellite video hookup from New York with some guy and woman that Yassar had insisted participate. The guys at Langley had done an overnight security clearance on them while Tom flew in on the redeye. The two CIA computer systems analysts and two Joint Terrorism Task Force computer experts Tom brought with him sat all the way at the other end of the table. So did four Saudi Council of Ministers members, along with a cadre of fifteen of their own experts. Tom had been at the game long enough to know that's how it was done in Saudi Arabia. *It's no democracy.* Yassar here, the other guys in the cheap seats.

One of the JTTF computer jocks was talking, booming it out from the bleachers, "The logic bomb is a computer program carried inside another program called a trojan horse. The subject sneaks it in undetected, it lies around for as long as the subject wants, then drops its bomb from the inside. It's a program that's timed to go into a destructive subroutine at a specific moment. In this case, tomorrow." If the logic bomb the Saudis had found was anything like the one the Brits had discovered in the Stockton refinery near the North Sea, there wasn't much time to be lost. Tom knew he had to convince the Saudis to let them place the sniffer program to help chase it back to whoever planted it. Tom added, "And when it does, your main refinery complex at Dhahran is ashes," he said.

"Go on," Yassar said. Back in Langley they'd told Tom it was Yassar who'd called to ask for help, seemed to understand the problem, how destructive the logic bomb could be. And they'd said he'd asked for Tom Goddard to lead the team. "The youthful boy genius of Saudi Arabia. And of Nice," he'd said.

Tom took in Yassar. *Pretty cool, but sort of an enigma. Doesn't show much.* Tom thought the man looked peaceable enough, even gentle, but barrel-chested, big, and capable of coming across the conference room table at him. His nerves were on overload. He felt the butterflies he'd experienced as a schoolboy before a fight. "As my colleagues explain it to me," Tom said, nodding to his computer jock, "at twelve hundred hours tomorrow this program would invoke an infinite loop in the refinery's catalytic reformer heating cycle, gradually raising the tempera-ture, then spiking it upward to cause an explosion."

"Go on," Prince Yassar said.

"That part is fairly simple. We know what the logic bomb is intended to do. We don't know who put it there, whether it was from the outside or the inside, and whether it was designed to be a prank or a terrorist attack." *Stupid*, he thought. They both knew this was no prank. For a second he wanted to tell him about the logic bomb they'd found in BP's North Sea refinery. But he wanted the JTTF techs and his own CIA experts to get a better look at this one first, confirm that the one the Saudis found had the identical design. "It's a simple piece of software, really. At a certain time, the program has the built-in logic to be triggered to go into its routine. In this case, it's a loop that won't allow any of the other software to shut down the heating cycle." His voice grew stronger. "Do you have any idea who would want to do this? Have you made any traces to see if you can figure out who planted it?" Tom was almost certain he knew the answers, but wanted to hear what the Saudis thought.

"We both know with whom we're dealing," Yassar said.

"Right. It's gotta be bin Abdur and his al-Mujari."

Yassar nodded. "What do you recommend?" Yassar asked.

This was his opening. Would Yassar go along with it? "We put in a sniffer." Tom knew the Saudis had to trust him com-pletely, and that he was probably the wrong guy to pitch the idea. At least to Yassar. He felt worse than grungy. Still, he had to take a chance.

"We have no such programs, although we have heard of them," Yassar said. "Tell me about these sniffers."

Man goes right at it. "It latches onto anybody who comes in and accesses this program, and lets us to trace him back to where he came from." He was aware he was hurrying his words, felt the tension pressing in on him.

"And you can give us one?"

"Well, it's proprietary. We put it into your system, monitor it, and remove it once the situation is secure. That is, if anybody ever comes back to check on this program."

"You're a clever man, Mr. Goddard," Yassar said. "I don't need to tell you how sensitive that would be for us. To allow you access into some of our most important computer systems."

"We're aware that might be an issue. At the same time, we can't give out this code."

"A matter of national security," Yassar said, "just as it is for us."

"We'll just have to trust each other."

Yassar smiled. "No. I understand the situation. It's we who will have to trust you."

"Right. But why wouldn't you?" Tom regretted the words even as they left his lips. Yeah. Why wouldn't this guy trust somebody who'd orchestrated the assassination of his son. And turned some woman who was almost like his daughter into a trojan horse so she could help them do the job.

"Because we have history," Yassar said. His voice was calm, which made it all the more menacing.

"Yes," was all Tom could manage. He had the crazy notion to apologize to Yassar. *Screw it.* The only way to do this was to go right at it. "What happened to Sasha?"

Yassar didn't answer, just looked puzzled, then glanced at the video screen.

"It was me who arranged for her to get back in. She said she needed to come back to you."

Yassar remained silent.

"We were the ones who got the tape," Tom said. "I gave it to her." He looked into Yassar's eyes. "Those were bad times."

"Yes," Yassar said. "Yes, they were." He sipped his tea, then looked at the video screen again.

What's with the damn video screen?

Yassar said, "So. What's our plan of action? You put in the sniffer, then what?"

Tom felt relief flood through him. Yassar was letting them do it. "As I said, the sniffer latches onto anybody who comes back in to access the logic bomb. That means we have to re-inject the logic bomb, obviously defusing it first. Then we hope someone comes back to check on it, maybe to see why it didn't go off." He took another sip of his coffee. Inky, bitter stuff but he needed it. "Not much hope of anybody coming back in before that, though. As I said earlier, the thing's set to go off tomorrow."

"But let's assume someone does go back in. Then what?"

"If we're lucky, we find out where they are. Maybe through a domain name on the Internet. Then if it's not too late, we take tactical action. We'll take the lead."

Yassar's eyes narrowed; he didn't look gentle now. Tom felt an ominous sense of blackness. And just as quickly he felt guilt wrenching his guts. He looked into Yassar's now cold eyes and wondered why he'd ever helped Sasha go back to him.

September, This Year. New York City. It had taken Daniel a few minutes to sort out what he was seeing and hearing on the satellite screen. Figuring out the players wasn't easy—he'd never attended a business meeting where people didn't at least introduce each other in the beginning. And then the discussion seemed to be dancing around the real issue. He motioned with his head to Lydia to step out of his study. He didn't know how to put the satellite hookup on mute, and, besides, he didn't feel like talking in front of the CIA technician. Lydia wrinkled her brow, confused or annoyed, but got up and followed him into the bedroom. He closed the door.

"What the hell's going on in there?" Daniel said.

"What do you mean?"

"What do I mean? Are you intentionally playing dumb?" Lydia looked wounded. He softened his tone. "Lover, in the first place, the head CIA guy, Tom, doesn't seem to know you're here, or maybe even alive. In the second place, they're only talking about a single logic bomb at Saudi Aramco. Nobody's even mentioned the real issue of an effort to sabotage the whole world's oil and gas operations. Why's Yassar holding out?"

Lydia listened with her mouth ajar and hands clasped to her chest. *Off balance. What's going on?*

Lydia said, "They won't believe it without some proof."

"The Saudi Aramco logic bomb proves it."

"It's the wrong time to bring it up."

Daniel couldn't believe this. "Then when's the right time? One of my guys got murdered last night, undoubtedly intended for me. We've got a half-dozen CIA guys in that room. What more do you need?"

Lydia didn't answer. She just stood there, looking stunned, maybe thinking.

Daniel said, "I'm going back in there." He strode back into the study, head lowered. He sat down again at his desk in front of the video screen, pulse starting to thump, confidence flowing. Lydia sat next to him and rested her hand on his arm. He turned and saw her nod to him to go ahead.

"Excuse me, gentlemen," Daniel said. He saw Yassar and Tom turn toward the screen. He waited a moment. *Take yourself down a peg. Treat it like a group negotiating session.* "I think it's important I interject some new facts that will bring us down a new line of discussion." He saw Yassar lean forward to speak to Tom, thought he heard his name murmured. Then he saw Tom do a double take at the screen as if he'd just seen a ghost. He had. *I guess now he knows it's Sasha.*

Daniel cleared his throat. *Let them have it.* "My name is Daniel Youngblood. I'm an oil and gas investment banker based in New York. Everyone in that room may or may not know that this logic bomb is not an isolated situation. Lydia—Sasha"—he looked to his right—"has told me she is aware of a suspected al-Mujari plot to sabotage the oil and gas industry by placing logic bombs in its operating software. In the last forty-eight hours she and I have developed a list of my clients who provide operating software to the industry who we believe may be part of the means through which the al-Mujari will accomplish that. I believe analyzing this logic bomb will tell you what to look for in the al-Mujari's other terrorist attacks, and help you figure out how to defuse their entire operation."

Daniel had seen somebody suck the air out of a conference room many times in his career, but never witnessed the near-perfect vacuum he'd just created. A full 30 seconds passed with Tom and Yassar looking at each other without anyone speaking a word in the room. Then Tom got up and walked toward the video screen, put his hand down near it and the screen went blank.

Daniel looked over at Lydia, who now slid her arm through his. "Tom's the man who recruited you, had you kill Ibrahim?"

Lydia nodded.

"Lover, I think it's time I started calling you Sasha."

She clutched Daniel's arm tighter. He felt her breast press against him, saw her eyes get teary.

"You okay?" he asked.

"I'm a little emotional. I'm very proud of you right now. I don't know what I was thinking earlier. I've been keeping things secret so long, and I've been so caught up in the Saudi royals versus the al-Mujari, that maybe I've lost perspective. Of course we need to do everything we can to stop these people. Maybe I was stunned silent by the shock of seeing Tom and Yassar together, then hearing Tom bring up…Ibrahim."

"I saw Yassar looking at you at that point."

"Yes, I'm sure he was making certain I was alright."

Daniel unhooked his arm from hers and pulled her close to him. "We'll have a lot to talk about when we get out of this thing." Daniel turned to the CIA tech. "What now?"

"I guess we wait. Nobody tells me."

Daniel stood up, then led Sasha by the hand into the kitchen. He made them both tea. A half hour later the CIA tech walked in and said, "We're back online."

Daniel and Sasha walked in to see Tom's face on the screen, Yassar at the far end of the table in the background talking to the other Saudis. Tom said, "Daniel, I'm gonna need a full dump on everything you and Sasha have come up with—your client list, contact information for all of them, everything. I know I don't need to tell you how critical your help will be to this. We need to get out in front of this thing and stop it. Is Intelligent Recovery Systems one of your clients?"

Daniel felt a rush of adrenaline. "Yes."

"We understand they're the largest provider of operating software to the industry."

"That's right."

"BP is a customer of theirs. We found another one of these logic bombs in their North Sea refinery."

Another refinery. "We figure they're targeting refineries first. Maximum impact to the industry, hardest to repair."

He saw Tom nod. "We're scrambling a CIA and JTTF team of computer analysts out of New York. I need you two on a plane to Houston within an hour."

"Absolutely."

"Good. You got all your contact information in your Blackberry or something or other?"

"Yes, and I have all the analysis we've done on my software clients and their customers in my laptop."

"Our computer techs can offload it onto their system on the plane. Get IR Systems on the phone, tell them you're coming in with our guys. I'll be flying back into New York shortly. I'll coordinate however many teams we can get on this from the air." He looked at Sasha for the first time. "Sasha, sounds like we have some catching up to do." Tom looked back at Daniel. "Okay, get going. Good luck."

<hr/>

Daniel called Dick Jantzen on his cell phone from the car on the way to JFK airport.

"Can this wait?" Jantzen said. "I'm on the golf course."

"No, it can't. Remember what you said before about not calling you back unless I had the CIA?" Daniel didn't get a response. "Well, I'm flying into Houston with a CIA and Joint Terrorism Task Force team of computer analysts. They want your systems guys in the office by five p.m. You too. And you'll get to meet my bimbo spy girlfriend in person." Daniel hung up.

CHAPTER 37

SEPTEMBER, THIS YEAR. BURAIDA, SAUDI Arabia. Sheik bin Abdur knelt in prayer in the simple dirt-floored room in the building next to his mosque in Buraida. It was the place from which he conducted the business of his dual roles—religious cleric and head of the al-Mujari, both part of his holy calling.

Eventually the Sheik closed the Koran, wrapped it in cloth, kissed it, replaced it on its shelf, then summoned three Saudis who had been waiting for him in the outer room.

"You all know what day this is, do you not?" Sheik bin Abdur asked. "There is no God but Allah!"

"La ilaha ilallah!" they called in unison.

"These are historic times. Today our jihad begins. Abdul, have the wire transfer arrangements been made?"

One of the Saudis spoke. "Yes, ten million U.S. dollars in four separate two-and-a-half-million-dollar transfers to accounts in Switzerland and the Cayman Islands designated by the man who calls himself Habib. Four million dollars in two separate wire transfers of two million dollars each to bank accounts in the Cayman Islands and the Netherlands Antilles on the instructions of Ali. A check for four million dollars from an account at Bank of America on the instructions of the man in New York, Kovarik."

"Good. I wish to have the reputation for promptly honoring our commitments." The men sat in silence for a minute, then began to speak among themselves in low whispers. "What is it?" Sheik bin Abdur asked.

"We are concerned for your safety, Sheik bin Abdur," Abdul said. "What if the infidel nations or even our Saudi brethren who have been polluted by the infidels strike out against you?"

"My brothers, I am a religious leader who must interpret the way for our Islamic brothers in these times." The Sheik trained his eyes on them in turn so they could see the fire of his commitment. "I must be available to counsel the Believers on the one true path." He paused. They reluctantly bowed in agreement. "There is no God but Allah!"

September, This Year. On the PeakOil Challenger, two hundred seventy miles southwest of New Orleans, Louisiana. A consortium of three oil companies had been formed to tap the estimated 15 billion barrels of high quality crude oil in the Jack field, one of the largest oil discoveries in the Gulf of Mexico. The project had an estimated 50-year lifespan.

Robert Nesbitt, one of 126 crew members on the PeakOil Challenger oil platform anchored to the ocean floor 270 miles southwest of New Orleans, was nearing the end of his two-week evaluation. Nesbitt had been the lead engineer on the design and construction of the 1.2-million-ton structure. Now he rolled his chair back from his computer-controlled monitoring station. He was a proud parent and the PeakOil Challenger was his baby. Nesbitt had even assisted in the alterations to the software adapted from Intelligent Recovery Systems' most sophisticated exploration program. He'd allowed himself to imagine the accolades he would receive for this first-of-a-kind drilling platform, designed to drill 30,000 feet down into the lower tertiary rock below 7,000 feet of Gulf waters.

What the hell? There was something odd on the sensors. Nesbitt punched keys on his computer and got another reading, then another. He dialed Frank Jamison at the drill controlling station. "What you got on sensors twenty-seven and thirty-nine?"

"Jesus," came Jamison's reply. "Hundred ninety degrees at twenty-seven and hundred eighty-seven degrees at thirty-nine. That what you got?"

"Yup. What do you think? Is it over-revving?"

"No question about it," Jamison said. "And it shouldn't be. The software's set up to rev it as fast as it can take it, but only if the temperature is within operating parameters." Jamison typed at his own computer keyboard. "Shit, I got 3,150 rpms. That's not too fast, that's *way* too fast."

Nesbitt had a curse on his lips but felt a quake of despair deep inside. When he spoke he tried to sound calm. "Something's definitely wrong. The drill head is down about ten thousand feet. That's solid bedrock, not some north Texas sand and shale substrate." Nesbitt cradled the phone in his neck and began playing with the computer keys. "Through rock that hard this puppy shouldn't be cranking any faster than 2,100 rpms without risk of a burnout. Slow it down, Frank. Override the software and reset it to 2,100 rpms."

"Righto." Nesbitt watched on his screen while Jamison typed in the commands to access the manual loop in the software. Now it would be hours before the system could run normally. Something must obviously be out of kilter with the software. *Maybe bad sensors? Nope. Can't be, there are multiple sensors. The good ones would override a bad one.* He watched on his screen as Jamison accessed the drill functions software routine.

```
Welcome to drill functions parameters
Command: reset drill speed
Current speed 3162
Enter new speed: 2100
Resetting..........
Current speed 3166
Command:
```

"What the hell?" Jamison said into the phone. "You see that?"

"Yup. Should've started slowing down right away." Nesbitt typed. "I got three other sensors showing the same thing. Now over 3,170 rpms. Temperature on twenty-nine and thirty-nine up to one ninety-six and one ninety-two degrees."

"I'm trying it again," Jamison said. "We've got a problem with the software."

"I'm afraid so," Nesbitt agreed. His stomach dropped. He imagined the conversation with the head of operations in Dallas, played it out in his mind in three or four different ways. He didn't like any of them.

"Bob? You still there?" Jamison asked.

"Yup. I'm phoning this in to Dallas. I'll call you back."

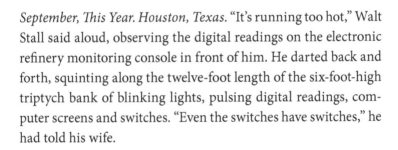

September, This Year. Houston, Texas. "It's running too hot," Walt Stall said aloud, observing the digital readings on the electronic refinery monitoring console in front of him. He darted back and forth, squinting along the twelve-foot length of the six-foot-high triptych bank of blinking lights, pulsing digital readings, computer screens and switches. "Even the switches have switches," he had told his wife.

"Damn these digital sensors. Just give me my good old pressure gauges I can kick to make sure they're working properly." He squinted at the panel. "Too hot."

Walt liked being known as the Wizard around the refinery. He knew Rouge North down to the wiring diagrams, and could sense what was wrong just from listening, smelling, feeling its rumblings. He hadn't liked it at all when new management at Dorchester Refining replaced the manual controls with new computer hardware and software systems. Walt's phone rang. "Walt Stall," he answered.

"What the hell's going on down there? I can see you jumping around like some jackrabbit." It was Carey Struthers, talking from his plant manager's perch at the far end of the refinery.

"She's running too hot."

"Which section?"

"The catalytic reformer."

"Shit. You think we picked up one of those bugs that Youngblood and Feds called about?"

"Could be. Sorry to be so abrupt, Carey, but I don't have a lot of time to be screwing around with you on the phone." Walt hung up and looked at the temperature monitors for the Number Six through Number Ten catalytic reforming reactors, then typed:

Reactor function: catalytic reformer
Function desired: reactor temperature
Reactor(s) desired: Number 6...10
Temperature desired: 850
Resetting.........
Current temperature:
Reactor Number 6: 1002
Reactor Number 7: 1003

Reactor Number 8: 1006
Reactor Number 9: 1002
Reactor Number 10: 1007
Command:

"Swell, just swell." Walt stood. He picked up his cell phone and dialed. "Daniel? Walt Stall." Daniel had phoned to warn Walt from the army transport plane on the way to Houston two hours earlier. "You're not gonna believe this, but my catalytic reformer controls have gone haywire. I think those bastards may have stuck one of those things in it."

Daniel said, "I'm in a car about ten minutes away. I'll bring the computer team with me." Walt spent the next ten minutes pacing in front of the monitoring console, checking the readings. The ten minutes felt like an hour.

When Daniel arrived he could see something was wrong. Walt Stall, whom he knew from the Dorchester deal he'd just closed, was walking back and forth in front of the control panel. Three other refinery employees stood around him, observing. Other groups of employees were huddled together, nobody manning their stations. Daniel and four computer techs hurried up to Walt.

"What's the status?" Daniel said.

Walt turned to see him, then back to the screens. "All the reactors are over a thousand degrees."

"What's that mean?" one of the computer techs asked.

Daniel said, "Another couple hundred degrees and the plant could blow."

"Not if I can help it," Walt said. He typed at the screen:

Command: emergency shutdown
System command not recognized
Command: emergency shutdown
System command not recognized
Command:

"That's it!" Walt yelled. He stomped to the end of the console and slammed his left fist onto the three-inch red emergency shutdown button.

Nothing happened. No alarms, no lights, no change in the sound and rumblings from Rouge North. Daniel stepped to the console and looked at the digital temperature readouts. They were all over 1,150 degrees Fahrenheit. Walt grabbed the phone and punched some digits.

"Yeah! Talk to me! I can't believe this!" somebody yelled through the phone.

"Pull the plug! Sound the fire alarm and get everybody the hell out of the plant!" Walt bellowed.

The room filled with sound.

A lot of good that's going to do, Daniel thought. *Unless these guys can run a lot faster than me they've got about two minutes to get about a half a mile away.* He knew that at another 50 or 60 degrees the entire catalytic reforming section of the plant would erupt. He thought of Sasha, waiting in the car outside with the other techs, felt a blast of panic.

"Where's the computer room?" he yelled.

Walt pointed and started running across the plant, limping, his fat legs pumping. Daniel saw the door all the way on the other side of the plant and passed Walt after a few yards, sprinting as fast as he could.

C'mon, c'mon! he told himself. He had only another fifty yards to cross to get to the door, and he closed his eyes against the pain in his lungs and pushed his legs to carry him faster. Then he was at the door, and he crashed it open without turning the handle, burst through the outer electrical room and through an inner door that someone had left open, into the computer room. He froze. In that 1.67 seconds of immobility he felt as if the world was moving in slow motion, but in an instant he charged across the room and reached down behind the main bank of computer servers and one, two, three, four in turn he pulled out the plugs. He gasped for breath and braced for the shock of the explosion. But then he heard the whine diminish, and he felt through the wall and the floor the slackening rumble of old Rouge North.

Walt burst into the room a moment later. Tears were in his eyes. He hunched over, panting, then sat on the floor. "Saved you, old girl," he said and slapped the floor. He looked at Daniel, then at the backs of the four servers in front of him. "Gotcha, you dumb sons of bitches."

September, This Year. On the PeakOil Challenger, two hundred seventy miles southwest of New Orleans, Louisiana. "I can't shut it down!" Nesbitt yelled into the phone to Jamison. He was standing in front of his computer screen, having just been told by the Vice President of Operations back in Dallas to cut all power.

"What the hell is going on?" Jamison yelled back. "I just hit the manual shutdown button and nothing happened!"

"So did I up here!" Nesbitt was worried about his job, the repercussions in Dallas. The mud was overheating. Soon the drill hole would seize. The "mud," a mixture of clay, oils and chemicals, was pumped down into the drill pipe to the bottom of the shaft and out of the drill bit. It was designed to flow up the outside of the pipe back to the surface of the rig, cool the bit shaft, and bring up ground rock before being filtered, cooled, and recycled back down into the pipe again. If the temperature rose only a few more degrees, the mud would seize and harden into rock around the bit and drill pipe, and the entire ten thousand feet might have to be abandoned. A new hole would have to be started. That would cost millions.

"Ah, Jesus Christ, Frank, there goes my pension," Nesbitt moaned into the phone. "Look at the temperature for Christsakes. I've got sensors twenty-nine and thirty-nine at two hundred ten degrees! We're gonna have boiling mud in a couple of minutes."

"There's a first time for everything," Jamison said. His voice had the calmness of resignation in it. "I've never seen one of these things seize before."

Nesbitt felt the words like a smack in the face. He thought about what he was going to say to his wife about losing his job, about how the VP of Operations in Dallas would carve him a new asshole.

A software subroutine ordered the spray injectors in the mud pump to switch the chemical mixture to 100% naphtha, the volatile solution used for cleaning during shutdowns. At that level of concentration, once the drill shaft reached a temperature of 222 degrees it was only a question of moments before the entire ten-thousand-foot length would constitute one of the most effective and largest pipe bombs ever manufactured.

Nesbitt was still thinking about how he was going to explain to his wife when the mud near the top of the shaft exploded. The blast shattered the steel superstructure of the PeakOil Challenger, blew the drilling rig itself off the platform, and split the huge platform's concrete base in half. The entire crew was incinerated in the initial thrust. The PeakOil Challenger sank within fifteen minutes, its massive concrete base sucking it to the bottom of the Gulf of Mexico 7,000 feet below.

CHAPTER 38

SEPTEMBER, THIS YEAR. RIYADH, SAUDI *Arabia*. Tom Goddard heard the news about the PeakOil Challenger in his hotel room on CNN. Up and pacing, now not killing time, killing brain cells, wondering why he hadn't prevented it, why he was a step behind.

Tom picked up the phone but did not dial, still riveted to the television. *I should have made a move after we found the North Sea refinery logic bomb. Might have prevented this.*

"The crew reported computer malfunctions shortly before the drilling platform exploded and sank. Authorities believe all one hundred twenty-six crew members were killed and…" Tom dialed the Washington incoming CIA satellite line.

"Where are you?" Jim Rattison, Tom's divisional head, asked.

"In my hotel room in Riyadh watching CNN. Jesus."

"It's worse than you think," Rattison said. "We heard from our computer techs that a refinery explosion in Houston was narrowly averted. Their computer systems went off the reservation. I was hoping you'd have some answers by now."

"I'm heading out now. It's gotta be the al-Mujari."

"And I don't see how we hadn't picked it up. How the hell could anybody catch us so completely flatfooted?" Rattison's anger rang in Tom's ears.

Not completely, Tom wanted to say.

"I thought you had the computer jocks on it."

"I do. Our guys, JTTF, the NSA, and now some top-level FBI guys from the Bureau's Com-Tech group. I've got them chasing down the clients of some investment banker from New York who we think are how they're targeting the oil and gas industry."

"Enough talk, get going," Rattison said. "I've got a C-5 Army transport warmed up down in Riyadh. I want you and the computer guys on it pronto. We can hook them back up to our systems via wireless into satellites when you're in the air. By that time, we'll have figured out how to patch in all the people we need from the Bureau's Com-Tech jocks, their anti-terrorist team and anybody else you think you'll need."

"Get me Nigel Benthurst from British Intelligence and Ira Land from the Israeli Mossad," Tom said.

"You got it. Call me on the way to the airport."

"Right." Tom headed for the door, his breathing short, the image on CNN of the fireball as the drilling rig exploded, filmed from 20 miles away, etched in his mind.

September, This Year. Buraida, Saudi Arabia. Sheik bin Abdur was seated cross-legged on the dirt floor of the back room in the ramshackle building next to his mosque. Six of his devotees, many of his closest, including Abdul and Waleed, were seated across from him. He couldn't contain his exultation. "The manifestation of our power is beginning! It is clearly the work of Allah to reunite the Muslim world!" As he spoke, he began to comprehend his own words. "There is no god but Allah!"

"La ilaha ilallah!" the others said in unison.

But now he was overcome by the presence of Allah. He felt he was imbued with Allah's power, knowing the new purpose, the certainty of his faith, the justification of his actions. Surely, only the work of Allah could have effected it, an undeniable sign, the justification of the jihad, the reunifying war that would create an Islamic state and return control of Saudi Arabia, with its holiest of the holy Islamic sites, back to the Believers. He felt his very being burning with the knowledge that he was the earthly manifestation of Allah's will.

"My friends, this is the manifestation of the spirit of Allah, with which I am infused. Abdul," he said, looking at the fine Islamic young man. "Publish my words in our Muslim newspapers in London and Pakistan. I will take full responsibility for this, our jihad. We will proclaim that it will unfold and unite our brothers in a new holy Islamic state."

He paused, then motioned for Abdul to approach. He whispered to him, "I will need you to contact the man who calls himself Habib. I require an additional service from him."

He waved Abdul away and turned his vision inward, his eyes closed, the eyes of his soul, searching skyward. Yes, it was Allah, in him. Nothing could stop them.

September, This Year. New York City. Kovarik's eyes were stuck to the TV screen in his office like he was a kid watching his first pornography. The PeakOil Challenger explosion was all over the news. He could hardly believe it. Things like this only happened in the movies, not real life. At least not in *his* life.

What a rush. At first he was embarrassed to even think it, then as the idea sank in he let himself feel a thrill like never before in his life. He wasn't just a player, he was a grand-scale, major-league titan. The exhilaration of being a part of—hell, he was the guy who made it all possible—a game-changing series of events that would rock the world was intoxicating. It made him tingle all the way down to his balls. He couldn't wait to see what happened next.

If only he could tell somebody about it. That gave him the chills, made him think of somebody finding out. These nuts had paid him well, but if anybody traced anything back to him, he was cooked. He thought about Daniel's phone message again. Maybe there was an angle there. He thought it through. A well-timed phone call to the FBI offering his help as an oil and gas expert with insight, like strategic information on whose client supplied the computer software that ran the PeakOil Challenger.

He smiled. *Not a bad idea.* He picked up the phone, then put it back in its cradle. He rubbed his shin. *No, script it out first.*

Habib wasn't crazy about dealing with one of the Sheik's terrorist cells in New York, but the little job the Sheik wanted him to do paid well: $100,000 for just locating the investment banker, Youngblood, and the girl, Sasha. It was a mystery how the Sheik found out where the girl was this time, or that she was with Youngblood. But it was always a mystery. The crazy old man seemed to have antennae for the girl. But that wasn't his business. All he had to do was find them. Then let the Sheik's men take care of them so the Sheik could regard that he'd cleansed them from the world himself. That is if the Sheik's men could get out of their own way. It didn't matter to him. If they botched it, he'd probably get paid to do it right. Thinking that made him wince. Teske blowing away that kid who worked for Youngblood was a rookie mistake, one he wouldn't let happen again.

CHAPTER 39

SEPTEMBER, THIS YEAR. RIYADH, SAUDI Arabia. Prince Yassar reacted with outward calm. Assad al-Anoud, the head of the Saudi Secret Police, stood before him, his message brief, a summary of the day's events.

We are dealing with monsters, he thought. *This bin Abdur. These al-Mujari fanatics.* And the old emotions, those he had not felt since Ibrahim's murder, assaulted him. Venom rose from a place deep within him.

Arab brother against brother it shall be.

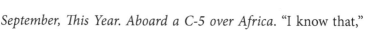

September, This Year. Aboard a C-5 over Africa. "I know that," Tom Goddard said. "But the PeakOil drilling rig proves they're not just going after refineries. That multiplies the problem."

"Exponentially," Nigel Benthurst said.

Tom sensed he was the conductor of an orchestra with no score; 30 or so professionals—computer jocks and intelligence wonks—on a conference call. They were working on the fly, improvising. He hoped the collective experience and brains on the line would allow them to muddle toward some answers.

"There are about a thousand refineries worldwide," Terry Jenkins, Tom's lead CIA systems analyst, said into the conference call from across the aisle on the plane. "If you add drilling rigs, that's gotta be another twenty or thirty thousand. How the hell do we chase all of them down?"

"There's no way they could hack into that many individual systems," an FBI Com-Tech analyst in New York interrupted. She had a deep, Lauren Bacall voice.

Tom said, "Sasha said their plan was to plant the logic bombs in the software vendors' programs and feed them into the individual customer locations with routine updates."

"That makes perfect sense," the throaty voice came on again. "And so far we've only got one vendor, Intelligent Recovery Systems. They sold the software for all the sabotaged locations— the BP North Sea refinery, the Saudi Aramco refinery, the River Rouge refinery, and the PeakOil Challenger."

"Youngblood gave us their customer list," Tom said.

"It doesn't matter," somebody said. "If the logic bombs are being placed with software updates, we can defuse them at the source; we don't need to chase them down at all the customers. We've analyzed the three logic bombs from the refineries and they're all the same. And they were only in computer systems on hardware platforms running Unix, or on IBM AS400s running on IBM's proprietary TSO operating system."

"Who said that?" Tom demanded.

"Stone. FBI based in New York." It was the throaty FBI voice he'd been hearing.

"Good. Youngblood's got eleven other software vendor clients," Tom said, happy to have something to grab onto. "Stone, can you chase them down? See if anybody else's software runs on those platforms? That might be the key. Maybe peel off with a few analysts and chase that lead?"

"I'll take one of my techs here in New York," Stone said. Two voices, one from Homeland Security in Maryland and one from CIA in Langley, volunteered.

Tom said, "We can keep looking for other leads while we're checking on that one." *One small victory.* He exhaled and cracked his neck. "Okay, what else do we know?"

Stone spoke up again, "Before I go, somebody should start working on a patch."

"A what?" Tom said.

"A patch," Terry Jenkins said. "Some software code to defuse the logic bombs we've already found. I already have the guys in Langley working on it. I'll get an ETA from them."

"That you, Terry?" Stone asked.

"Yeah," he said. "Stay close. If you find logic bombs in any more of Youngblood's clients' software, I'll ship you the patch—when we finish it."

"What do we do with it?" Tom said.

"Send it out to defuse the logic bombs the same way they were deposited in the first place," Stone said. "Zap out a software update."

"How long?" Tom said, feeling a tickle of anticipation.

"Hours," Terry said, "maybe a day."

Jesus, Tom thought. "What's the good news?"

"That is the good news," Stone said. "The bad news is the patch will only work for the logic bombs we've seen—for refineries. We don't know what the one that went active on the PeakOil Challenger looked like, or what subroutine in the program it attacked."

Tom remembered the number of drilling rigs that someone mentioned early in the call—20 to 30 thousand. He felt his throat constrict.

⊰◇⊱

September, This Year. Houston, Texas. Sasha was sandwiched between Daniel and two CIA computer analysts in the lead Chevy Suburban in a three-SUV convoy. They hurtled through the streets of Houston toward Intelligent Recovery Systems' offices, escorted by police, sirens blaring, lights flashing. Two computer techs sat in the third seat behind them, two more in the front. The techs to her right were like Jack Spratt and his wife: a bone-thin man and an overweight woman whose skin was sticky from perspiration against Sasha's arm. She felt as if she was on a bus in Bombay, where the Indians jammed together in the seats out of habit, even when the bus was half-empty.

A cell phone rang. *The skinny one.* The man passed it over to Sasha. "For Daniel. Tom Goddard."

"Hello," Daniel said. Sasha watched him, awed by his command, proud to be his. Daniel had shown his mettle today, most recently in the crisis at Rouge North. She'd watched from the doorway of the refinery—unable to sit in the bloody SUV anymore while he was at risk—as he dashed across the floor to save the plant.

"I know, I know," she heard him say. "Yes, I'd say twenty to thirty thousand is a good estimate. But if it comes to production wells—man, there are forty thousand in California alone. I'd say eight hundred thousand worldwide."

She could hear Tom barking, agitated, on the other end of the phone but couldn't make out his words.

Daniel said, "Well that's good news on the refinery fix. You should get it to…"

She heard Tom again, almost yelling.

"That's what I was trying to say. You have my client list. I've called them all. Your guys I'm with have sent teams to all of them. Dresner Technologies would be my second priority. They're across town." She heard the authority in his voice, saw it in how he emphasized his words with his free hand.

Then more from Tom, quieter now, calmer.

"Right." Daniel hung up and held the phone out to Jack Spratt. "They have a fix for the refinery logic bombs," Daniel said. Sasha saw the relief in his eyes. "And they're sending it out to their techs at all my other clients."

"A software patch?" she asked.

He nodded. He turned to look into her eyes. She clutched his hand. "And so far no other incidents."

"Maybe we're not too late," Sasha said.

"Maybe. But the PeakOil Challenger brings up a different problem Tom wants us to jump all over once we get to IR systems. Find the logic bomb that targeted the drilling rig and come up with a fix for that, too." He looked to the front, his eyes focusing off on the distance, at nothing. "And even if we solve that, it could get worse, still. So we need to hurry."

Sasha felt a flash of alarm at the new concern she saw in Daniel's eyes.

CHAPTER 40

SEPTEMBER, THIS YEAR. HOUSTON, TEXAS. It was after 5:00 p.m. when they arrived at the offices of Intelligent Recovery Systems. Sasha was amazed as she saw the bodies pile out of the SUVs. It looked like almost two dozen of the technicians from the various CIA and other federal agencies were there, more than she saw on the plane from New York. The conference room they entered was dimly lit, as if for an evening ball. She assumed Dick Jantzen was the man seated at the center of the head table that was arranged perpendicular to the other conference table like the top of a "T". He wore a ridiculous outfit—pink pants, green golf shirt and crocodile loafers with no socks. Her eyes found Daniel's, who motioned at the man with his head, then nodded. Yes, it was he. A gray-haired man in his 60s sat to Jantzen's right. They were both flanked by four others on each side.

Daniel strode to the head of the perpendicular conference table, as close as possible to Jantzen and his group. Without looking at Sasha he said, "You feel comfortable starting off?"

She said into her handbag, "Ever known me to be bashful?"

She heard him chuckle. "I think your background on the computer terrorism is essential here. You heard Jantzen on the phone with me. Go heavy on the Saudi intelligence, the al-Mujari. Lay it on thick, lover. That guy to his right is Stanley Walters, senior partner of his law firm."

Sasha waited until the others had filed into the room, then stood up before anyone else had a chance to speak. *Okay, wing it.* "Ladies and gentlemen, perhaps I can give some brief background perspective. I am an agent of Saudi Arabian intelligence, working jointly with U.S. intelligence on this crisis. What we're dealing with is a now-confirmed terrorist plot, we're certain by the al-Mujari, to cripple the oil and gas industry, and in the process topple the Saudi government and destabilize the Mid-East region."

She was speaking directly to Jantzen. She saw his eyes get large. He whispered something into his lawyer's ear.

"Their method is to infiltrate oil and gas software vendor programs and plant trojan horse code that will jettison logic bombs to sabotage key processes in oil and gas operations. You've seen the results in the PeakOil Challenger drilling platform explosion today. Three other logic bombs were found in refinery programs."

She saw Walters nod back at Jantzen and lower his gaze at her as if to be intimidating.

"One was arranged as a decoy that I helped create by posing as an accomplice computer hacker and allowing the terrorists access to Saudi Aramco's Dhahran refinery. Our efforts were successful. We found a logic bomb they planted, then called in the CIA. That has led to creation of a patch for the refinery logic bombs. Through my undercover efforts I became aware that Intelligent Recovery Systems was one of the prime vehicles to target clients via routine software updates."

Walters stood and opened his mouth to speak. Sasha held up her hand to stop him.

She went on, "All four logic bombs to date were planted in IR Systems software code, resident in its customers' systems."

Walters said, "That presumes a number of things, including that the PeakOil Challenger explosion was not an accident…"

"Yes, a fairly good hypothesis given that the crew reported out-of-control software prior to the explosion…"

"My client has not acknowledged or been accused…"

Sasha heard the rustle of a chair behind her and turned to see one of the team stand up. He said, "Just a minute. I'm FBI, with full authority to intervene. I don't like how this is going."

"Sir, stand down, please," Walters said. "My client is anxious to cooperate in stopping this terrorism, but simply waltzing in here with a lot of accusations and two dozen people to begin poking around his software…"

"Who said anything about poking around?" the FBI agent said.

"I think that's fairly obvious…" Walters said.

"That's exactly what these people are here to do," Daniel said. "First, they need to install the patch for the refinery code, then find the logic bomb for the drilling rigs."

At that point Sasha saw six technicians stand up. One said, "Who's your head systems analyst?" Sasha saw potential chaos dissolving into action.

A member of Jantzen's group stood. "Frank Desoto," he said. The techs started at him like pit bulls after a rabbit.

Jantzen now stood up. "Just a minute," he said. He looked tentative, but pushed out his chest as if to project bravado. *A short man. That explains a lot.* Sasha looked over at Daniel. He didn't show any emotion, but she hoped he was at least enjoying this moment. Jantzen continued. "Stanley's right. You can't go poking around our code. It's proprietary. Plus that means screwing around with our clients. It exposes us to liability." He looked at his lawyer for support.

"I'll tell you what I'm gonna do," the FBI agent said, approaching. Sasha watched the man walk behind the table, pull something out of his pocket—handcuffs—and cuff Jantzen.

"You can't do that!" Walters shouted.

"Yeah? Obstructing a federal investigation of a matter of national security." He pulled out another pair, spun Walters around and cuffed him. He motioned to one of his men, started walking Jantzen and Walters out. "We don't have time to screw around with shit like this." Partway across the room he turned back to look at Jantzen's team. "Anybody else?"

The man who identified himself as the head systems analyst said, "Who has the refinery patch?" One of the CIA techs who'd approached him earlier raised his hand. The man pointed to two of his colleagues. "These two will work with you on installing it and feeding it out to our customers." He turned and pointed to two more of his people. "And these two will get you set up on the drilling rig code. We've already started on it."

Daniel turned to see Sasha nod as if handing it off to him. She sat down. "Frank?" Daniel said to the Director of Systems Analysis. "Can I get you a second?" Frank walked around the table toward Daniel. Daniel turned to the techs. "Who's next?" Four of them walked up. He turned back to Frank. "Tom—the CIA head of this operation—talked about other targets they might be going after. Sasha and I did what we were calling triage. We figured refiners would be the top priority to inflict the most damage, but now that approach is off the table after the PeakOil Challenger. I figure it could be ten, maybe fifteen different types of attacks, each with separate code for the different types of operations—production wells, pipelines…"

Frank was shaking his head.

"What?" Daniel said.

Frank said, "We've only got four types of program platforms, subject to modifications to adapt them to different applications in the field. Refineries, drilling rigs, wells and pipelines. Any other operations work off those basic designs."

One of the techs behind Daniel said, "Okay, so we need two more teams for wells and pipelines. Where do we start?"

Frank said, "Come on," and motioned with his head toward the side door the other techs had exited through. "I'll get some more of my guys," and started walking.

One of the CIA agents came up to Daniel. "Tom just called. He wants you and Sasha back in New York ASAP. We got it under control here anyhow. Our guys will get you to the airport."

Daniel was nervous about leaving, but figured he and Sasha couldn't do much more good down here anyhow. Besides, something was bothering him that he needed to check out back in New York.

CHAPTER 41

Early a.m. September, This Year. New York City. The C-5 rumbled and shook, buffeted by a sharp side wind.

"Hang on, this won't be pretty," the captain said over the intercom. Tom looked out the window as the plane landed with a bounce. The pilot threw the thrusters into reverse, trying to get off the runway as quickly as he could to get the team off the aircraft.

Tom was back on his cell phone to Stone at the FBI regional office in Midtown Manhattan as he hurried off the plane to the waiting helicopter, "Where are we?" Tom had to strain to hear her over the chopper's rotors. He wished he had his hands on bin Abdur's throat.

"Multiple teams working, a large one on the Intelligent Recovery Systems' programs. Others at Youngblood's other clients. Another is chasing down your Saudi sniffer trail. The guys from JTTF are working with Sabre, the computer reservations system in Dallas, on it."

"The sniffer picked something up in Riyadh?" Tom felt his blood pumping now.

Stone went on. "About one a.m. our time, the Saudis contacted CIA in Langley. Your sniffer went active. Seems that one of the Saudi Aramco systems manager's accounts had been tampered with and the hacker used it to go into the subroutine in the refinery software to see why the logic bomb hadn't gone off. Your sniffer traced him out and into the Sabre airline reservations system. The Sabre guys helped us trace it back out to Switzerland then back via satellite to right here in New York. He's still online, believe it or not."

"Where is he?" Tom had his first real taste of success. And some heat in what until now had been only cold fury.

"A PC in an office in an investment bank called Ladoix Sayre right here in Midtown. Thirty Rockefeller Plaza."

"That's Daniel Youngblood's. Sasha said they might be using it for access." Tom wondered for a moment, but Daniel was on the way back from Houston. "Anybody checked it out yet?"

"No, we're scrambling tactical agents right now."

"I'm coming along."

"Shouldn't we leave it up to the muscle guys?"

"No," Tom said. "I want to be there when we catch the son of a bitch, whoever it is." Tom paused to savor the thought. "What else you got?" he asked.

"Good news from IR Systems, too. They've installed and sent out the refinery patch. And we think they've traced back the entry port into IR Systems' network through an email entry from, you guessed it, a PC at Ladoix Sayre. The email address is youngblood@ladoix.com."

Tom's anger rose again.

"The guys at IR Systems think we're dealing with four different types of logic bombs, all placed in subroutines in different types of IR Systems' software," Stone said.

"Do you think somebody at the company was helping him out in order to plant stuff in four different types of programs?"

"No. It's really very simple," Stone said. "Somebody writes a different subroutine for each of four different types of programs—some function in a refinery, one in a drilling program, one for a production well, and one in a natural gas pipeline program. Then he hacks into IR Systems and plants it in four master IR Systems versions. Those master versions automatically go out over the Internet to update every one of IR Systems' programs, like Microsoft sends out Windows updates."

Tom still didn't think it was simple.

"So then on four different days, an auto-update mechanism at IR Systems logs into each of its babies, gives them a shot of new and improved tweaks online, and plants the logic bombs at the same time. Really very easy. The only hard part was hacking into IR Systems' network. And apparently whoever's on Youngblood's computer right now found a hole someplace to plant the logic bombs."

Tom got the gist of it. Pretty slick. But if Stone was right it could have been one or two guys, or a small group. The chopper landed. Tom ran across the pavement to a waiting car.

He spoke from the back seat. "Stone, I'm on the ground at Thirty-fourth Street on the West Side. My guys are coming to your office. I'm heading straight for Rock Center. Stay on the line and let me know what the Sabre boys and the Saudis are saying about our hacker."

Tom wondered what kind of person would help out these bastards. Freshly scrubbed computer kid? Yeah, he wanted to be with the team that caught up with him.

The lobby at 30 Rockefeller Plaza was deserted. Four FBI agents, escorted by a half-dozen New York cops, convinced the security guards to let them go upstairs. Eleven men piled into one elevator.

"All right, now listen up. This is an FBI operation, tactical on-site, subject to CIA command via Mr. Goddard here," Johnson, the FBI tactical commander, said. "We'll take the lead," he said to the cops. "We don't know which office he's in, but we know the phone number's extension 6193. Two FBI agents will take the lead to the left and the other two to the right. You guard the rear, with one man at the elevator."

The cops nodded. "Thanks fellas." Johnson now addressed his men. "Simms, you come with me to the left. Walters and Vixen, you go right. I want weapon hands free, coats unbuttoned, and holster thongs unsnapped. Unidentified subject may be on premises, no description. We want the unsub alive. No green light on weapons unless threat-risk detected. I'm primary through each door." The doors opened and they crossed the lobby to the locked entrance of Ladoix's offices. Agent Vixen picked the lock in fifteen seconds.

The two teams fanned off. Johnson saw the layout, made a signal, and all of them drew their weapons. Tom wished he was carrying one now, if only to club the son of a bitch.

Johnson and Simms worked efficiently and coolly. They stalked up to each office door and wherever they saw a computer screen illuminated, looked inside to check. Johnson checked the phone numbers, slowing down after he realized the extensions were in descending order.

6195...two to go, Tom thought. Johnson and Simms passed one more office and Tom saw light dancing in the next doorway. Johnson made a hand motion to Simms, who sneaked behind the secretary's station and went down past the office. He circled back along the outside wall, approaching the office in the opposite direction from Johnson. They both inched their way to the door, automatics raised to eye level. The door was open. No sounds emanated from the office, but the green light continued to dance. Tom held his breath.

Both men leapt into the doorway. They froze for a second, then lowered their weapons.

Tom ran in behind them. "What?"

"Damned if I know," Johnson replied, "Looks like somebody's online. Look at the thing." Johnson pointed his gun at the computer screen. Typed commands ran across it, scrolling upward with each new line entered.

Tom flipped open his cell phone and called Stone.

"Nobody's here," he said. "The damn computer's running commands by itself."

"Our hacker must be logged into his computer, using it as a remote terminal from someplace else," Stone said.

Damn. All this for nothing. Or was it nothing? Could this guy, Kovarik, who called the FBI about Daniel, be on the level? Could Daniel be dirty and only helping out the CIA to throw them off the scent?

Tom's cell phone rang.

"It's Daniel. We just landed. Where do you want us?"

"FBI headquarters. The driver will know. We need to talk."

"Yes. I have some ideas I need to discuss with you, too."

I'll bet you do.

CHAPTER 42

SEPTEMBER, THIS YEAR. NEW YORK *City*. Daniel and Sasha got off the elevator at One American Plaza, FBI Headquarters in the city. Daniel could see Sasha was tentative, walking slowly, head down. *She's not herself.* Just before they reached the receptionist's desk, Daniel turned to Sasha. "You okay?"

"No. I'm uneasy. Seeing Tom face-to-face brings up that awful night of Ibrahim's assassination all those years ago."

Daniel squeezed her hand. He'd keep an eye on her.

Tom met them at the receptionist's desk. Daniel watched his eyes meet Sasha's. He looked different than Daniel expected, younger than he had on the satellite screen, perhaps early 50s, with healthy color and full hair. Penetrating blue eyes. Daniel saw Tom glance at him, then look away as if guilty. *Of course.* Tom knew he and Sasha were lovers, knew Daniel must have had heard Sasha and Tom's history from her, how he used her in Ibrahim's murder. He looked at Sasha, saw her emotions rise as she looked at Tom. There was pain in her eyes, but also something more. He wondered. Were *they* ever lovers?

Tom ushered them in. The lighting was fluorescent, stark, the furnishings functional and cheap. Tom showed them into a conference room, the blinds drawn. "Have a seat," he said, taking one himself.

They sat for an awkward few moments, Daniel glancing on and off at Tom, seeing Tom observing him as if sizing him up. He didn't like it. Then a 40-ish woman, tough-looking, burst through the door like she owned the place.

"FBI Special Agent Stone?" Tom said.

"Who else?" she said. She looked at Daniel. "Youngblood?"

"Yes."

Stone nodded. She said, "So, I've got good news. We now have patches for all four of IR Systems' program platforms. Bad news, the logic bombs were timed to go off starting tomorrow at noon, and we don't know where else the buggers hid them."

Nobody said anything.

Tom looked at his watch; Daniel checked his own: 2:05 a.m.

Stone said, "Daniel, I've been meaning to ask you how you saved the River Rouge refinery."

"I pulled the plug, literally."

Stone looked at him in stunned silence for a few moments.

"How come nobody thought of that for the rest?" Tom said.

"It's no good," Daniel said. "Rouge is an antiquated plant by today's standards. I'm sure you know modern plants have redundant computer backup, hardwired into the power grid."

"Yeah," Stone said, "If the computer system went renegade, it wouldn't let you shut it down."

"You'd have to shut down the entire plant. For a failsafe fix of this thing, that means you'd have to shut down the whole oil and gas industry." Daniel looked over at Tom.

Tom appeared to be thinking. He said, "You'd need the President to shut down the United States, then talk to all foreign heads of state."

Daniel said, "By the time you did that we'd either have debugged this thing or they'd have all blown up."

Tom thought for a moment, appeared to be turning it over in his mind, then said to Daniel, "You said you had some ideas."

Sasha watched, amazed, as Daniel stood up from the conference room table and started pacing, rattled off 15 other oil and gas investment bankers on Wall Street he competed with, then dozens of their clients who supplied computer software systems to the oil and gas industry. How did he retain it all?

"That should give you a good percentage of all the worldwide systems the terrorists would infiltrate," Daniel said. He was looking at Tom, clearly seeking a reaction.

Tom seemed to be thinking about something himself. After a pause, he said "I'll get some more of our guys in here and get on it." He looked at Stone, then spoke into his cell phone.

Stone said, "I'm gonna need to rouse a lot of people from bed, get access to their offices and computers, and trace a ton of trails to find out if we've got other tainted software."

"There's something that's been bothering me," Daniel said. "The terrorists had to have had expert help. Nobody but an industry insider would have the insight to target these operations so effectively. If we can find out who, we might be able to get a roadmap, find a solution. Otherwise it will take too long."

Sasha saw Tom's gaze darting back and forth between Daniel and Stone. She had an odd feeling about it, shifted in her seat. *Something's bothering him.* Then Tom said, "Interesting you bring that up. We got a call from a guy named Kovarik, who suggested it was you, Daniel, helping them out. He phoned in his lead to the FBI yesterday and now we can't find him."

Sasha saw Daniel do a double take, then sit back down in his chair as if now everything made sense. "Kovarik. Bob Kovarik," he said. "We were best friends, came up together at Goldman. He dated Angie, my wife, before I met her. She dumped him, and I don't think he ever forgot about her. In fact, he hit on her right up until the day we got married. Then he stabbed me in the back for partner of oil and gas at Goldman."

Sasha was watching Daniel closely, seeing his eyes tracing off into the distance, feeling the pain he was experiencing as he spoke. She wanted to embrace him, support him in some way.

Daniel said to Tom, "The light bulb just went off. It's Kovarik. He's a slimeball and he hates me enough to sick the FBI onto me. Something's not right, and under the circumstances, that means a lot. We need to track this guy down."

Tom said, "I worried about you for a minute or two, including when we found the hacker online on your computer. But it didn't add up. So I'd like to talk to this guy, Kovarik."

"Me too," Daniel said.

"His call means something," Tom said.

"Maybe everything," Daniel said.

When the team didn't find Kovarik at his townhouse, they went to his office. The security guard at 299 Park was dozing when they arrived, but sat bolt upright at seeing four men and women dressed in business attire surrounded by six hulks wearing body armor with FBI logos on their backs, automatic weapons in hand. A half-dozen New York cops rounded out the ensemble.

Upstairs, Daniel was hoping they'd use a battering ram on the office front door, but one of the agents picked the lock in less than a minute.

"Where's his office?" Johnson, the lead FBI agent, asked.

"I've never been here," Daniel said. "But if I know Kovarik, it's big. Look for the one with the throne in it."

Daniel saw Sasha turn on a lamp on an end table, observe the paintings on the wall, the furniture. *What's she doing?*

They went in the first office past reception. Daniel saw Kovarik's face in framed photographs on shelves and the credenza. Framed merger deal announcements hung on the walls and Lucite deal mementos sat on the credenza. Kovarik's deals. "This is it," he said. Two of Johnson's agents stood guard at the door, Daniel thought, absurdly, as if anyone would be showing up at close to 3:00 a.m. Daniel walked behind Kovarik's desk, wondering what he was supposed to do. *Open drawers? No, the computer.* It was still turned on.

Johnson and two other agents fanned out around the room, opening credenza drawers, lifting the few piles of paper that lay exposed. Daniel stared at the computer screen, pondering. He felt anxious, powerless. *All dressed up and no place to go.* He saw Sasha looking at each photograph in turn, studying it, then moving onto the next. *Now what's she doing?*

Daniel sat down and clicked the mouse on Kovarik's computer, saw the screen saver vanish and Kovarik's desktop appear. Neat rows of icons were stacked along the desktop, maybe 40 or 50 in all. *Jesus.* He clicked on the control panel to find Kovarik's documents folder. It held another 50 or 60 folders.

He glanced up to see Sasha staring at a photograph on Kovarik's shelf. She said, "He's standing next to an Aston Martin." She turned to look at Daniel. "Is this the one he raced with you?"

"Yes." He felt a flash of excitement. Was she onto something?

"Is he a man who names his cars?"

"Yes." Daniel leaned to the side to get a better look at the photo. "That's 'Destroyer.'"

"Is this the one you forced into the wall at Watkins Glen?"

Daniel's pulse quickened. He knew where she was going. "No," he said, looking back at Kovarik's computer screen, "that was 'Eliminator.'"

"Try that," she said, but before she'd finished saying it, he'd already found the 'Eliminator' icon on Kovarik's desktop. He clicked on it and an Excel file opened up. He felt a blast of adrenaline. "That's it." The file showed a list of investment bankers, Daniel's name at the top, followed by lists of software vendor clients and their customers. Daniel scrolled down, guessed the list was 20 to 30 pages if printed.

When he looked back up, the entire team surrounded him, Sasha's face beaming at him over the top of the computer screen. She mouthed the words, "I love you." It warmed him.

"You sure?" Johnson said.

"Absolutely."

Johnson punched a fist in the air. His teammates slapped each other on the back. Daniel felt a surge of triumph. They still had time.

"I'll get Stone," Daniel said, flipping open his cell phone. "Hey," he said to her. "We got your roadmap."

"You dog, you," Stone said. "Email it to me, then print it, scan it, make a couple copies on memory sticks and hand them out to Johnson's team. We don't want anybody getting hit by a truck carrying the only copy."

Daniel hung up, then looked back up at Sasha. She was still beaming at him.

CHAPTER 43

SEPTEMBER, THIS YEAR. NEW YORK City. Back at FBI Headquarters, Tom greeted Daniel and Sasha in the reception area. Daniel chuckled to himself at the smirk that poked through Tom's attempt to maintain a grim face. "Great work," Tom said. "The list totaled fourteen investment bankers, fifty-six of their software vendor clients. We scrambled foreign intelligence services and all our computer techs. We're on half of the list already, patches moving into place. With a little luck it looks like we'll lick this thing."

"Wonderful news," Sasha said. She let out a nervous laugh.

Daniel grabbed Tom's hand, shook it and clutched his arm as well. Tom allowed himself a smile, then said, "Let's not start celebrating yet. We've got a lot of work to do. And let's just hope these bastards didn't have a different design of logic bombs for any of the other vendors."

Daniel felt it like a body blow. He hadn't thought of that. He looked at Sasha and saw alarm in her eyes.

Tom said, "Nothing left for you two to do for the moment. Go get some sleep. I'll call you if I need you."

Sasha said, "A few hours in our own bed sounds like a smashing idea about now."

"Better not," Tom said. "We have a team watching your apartment, just in case. Looks like somebody else might be staking it out, too." Daniel felt a chill. "You got someplace quiet nobody would think of to look for you?"

"Yes," Daniel said. "I used to go a small hotel once in a while on weekends when I didn't want anybody at the office to know where I was."

Sasha stood looking out over 64th Street from Barton Manor, the hotel tucked away off Madison Avenue that Daniel had taken them to. Her focus went from the empty street below to her own reflection in the window. And from there into her thoughts: the moments she'd shared with Daniel, the realization she could be at one with him, that perhaps this would all be over soon.

She heard Daniel washing up in the bathroom; then the water stopped. He walked through the door. "I love you," he said.

He came to her. Sasha felt her need throbbing in her arms as she reached for him. She breathed his name in his ear, then, "Oh, how I love you." She felt his arms around her. He moved her toward the bed.

After they made love, Daniel watched Lydia fall asleep, her head nestled in his shoulder. After only a few minutes she awakened and propped her chin on his chest. "Darling, I can hardly believe I found you in all this craziness," she said. "You've redeemed me from a life of searching for a love I never thought I'd find. You've made me believe in love again."

Daniel felt his chest swell, his throat clog with emotion. Then he saw her brow furrow, her eyes darken. She said, "But we aren't out of this yet. I know it's only a question of time before these lunatics locate me again. They've been chasing me for decades now."

"We need to find a way to get these al-Mujari nuts off your tail for good." Just thinking about it made him queasy.

"I've tried, using assumed names, trying to vanish, but eventually they catch up with me."

"Maybe Tom can help."

Her eyes went far away. "Nafta and I discussed a radical idea. I'm not sure I could bring myself to try it." She focused on Daniel again, smiled. "Let's get through this crisis, then deal with a long-term solution later. The important thing is that we'll be together."

Neither of them could sleep, so a half hour later they got up and dressed. Daniel called Tom. "Steady progress," Daniel said when he got off the phone. He started pacing.

"You want to go back over?"

"He said he'll call if he needs us."

At that moment, someone pounded a hard object against the door. "Get out!" Daniel yelled just as the door flew open and a man hurtled through it brandishing an Uzi. Daniel grabbed him before he could get off a shot, flinging him to the floor. He saw Sasha poised with a bookend in her hand, then heard the crunch of it striking the man's skull. Daniel grabbed the Uzi and squeezed off a burst at two other men who now entered the doorway, handguns drawn. They both went down.

"Get out!" Daniel screamed again, saw Sasha disappear into the bathroom, and remembered the fire escape running from the roof to the courtyard below. He picked up the Uzi and ran to check the hall for more attackers. *Clear.* Then he ran toward the bathroom door. Out he went through the open window, and down the fire escape. He stood panting in the courtyard, looking, but Sasha was gone. Only a terrible silence.

He felt an anguished sense of injustice. They'd been so close, and now this. He looked down and saw that his shirt was splattered with blood. He'd just killed two men. And Sasha had taken care of the other. *Arabs. The terrorists.*

Someone must have heard the shots. There'd be police. He had to think, get help. And find Sasha.

Sasha knelt behind the parapet of the roof on a townhouse two buildings over from the hotel, looking at the gun she'd grabbed from the man's belt after she'd crushed his skull with the bookend. It brought a rush of the past: a blue-steel Beretta Cheetah with a custom-made silencer. Like the one she'd wrenched from another man's belt the night she'd killed Ibrahim. *Focus.* No more shots. She'd seen the first two men go down in the line of Daniel's fire as she'd grabbed her computer case and purse and darted into the bathroom, then up the fire escape, responding to her training as much as to Daniel's command to escape. Time to go back, find him. She leaped over the parapet onto the next roof, freezing as she saw a man, his back to her, crouching against the parapet on the other side of the roof.

She saw the door to the stairway to the roof swinging in the breeze, the barrel of a rifle extending beyond it. A backup. In one motion, she fired two rounds at the man behind the parapet, then another two quick shots through the wooden door. She watched the man at the parapet fall to the surface of the roof. She hurried to the door, jerked it open, stepped over the other body and pointed the Beretta down the stairway. *Clear.*

Then there was a scuff of feet on the stairs below, two, perhaps three people coming toward her. She jumped to the roof next door, hunched behind the parapet, heard voices cursing in Arabic.

She remembered she'd fired four rounds. The Cheetah in her hand was .22 caliber. Standard magazine. *Four rounds left.* The men were fifteen, maybe twenty yards away. She wasn't sure she could hit all of them, and decided not to try it. She looked behind her at the next roof, then ran from her hiding place. She heard the voices of the men behind her and the scramble of feet. She took the next parapet, onto the next roof, two feet up to the next level, then glanced back to see the men coming toward her. There were four of them! She found the doorway to the stairs below, fired a round into the lock and it fell away. Then she pulled the door open and flew down the stairs.

Daniel was safe, she told herself, willed it in her heart. She ran panting down the stairs, thinking. She'd need to get to the car if Daniel hadn't already, then to Milford. She knew he wouldn't forget their plan to rendezvous there.

CHAPTER 44

September, This Year. New York City. Tom was awakened by the alarm on his cell phone. *Oh, yeah. FBI Headquarters.* He fumbled for his watch. *6:30.* He dialed the phone.

"Stone, it's Goddard. Where are we?"

"You sound like you have a mouthful of cotton. You okay?"

"Yeah. Just a catnap. What's the status?"

"Progress on all fronts. We're getting all the help we need from the foreign intel services. Fifty-six teams of computer techs on it. Patches either in place or in process."

"Any other types of logic bombs."

"None so far. The ones we've found, forty or so, are all modeled on the four IR Systems designs."

Tom felt a flood of relief. *We just might pull this off.* "Great work." He forced himself not to relax. The real proof would come at noon. If they didn't get them all…"Go on. Any bad news?"

"Yeah. You obviously haven't heard that Youngblood and Sasha were attacked at some hotel."

The news jolted Tom fully awake. "How in the hell?"

"They're missing. But some bodies—Arab—in their room and on the roof."

The thought of it sapped his strength.

Son of a bitch bin Abdur. That did it. Even if they hadn't debugged all the logic bombs yet, he was organizing countermeasures. Countermeasures his ass, he was gonna set up hits to kill all the bastards. Bin Abdur first. Then light up every quasi-terrorist nut they'd ever put on their list.

The first things Tom received from Langley later that morning were jagged-edged photocopies of the published versions of Sheik bin Adbur's manifesto that had appeared in London's *Islamic Times* and Pakistan's *The Believers*:

A CALL TO ALL ISLAMIC BELIEVERS

Islamic Believers unite! These are historic times. Not since the first caliph, abu Bacr, the successor to the prophet Mohammed himself, have the Shiite and Sunni Muslim brothers been united in our spirituality or our way of life. We call all our Muslim brethren to unite with us under the al-Mujari banner and join us in our jihad, our holy Islamic war! We seek the overthrow of all Middle Eastern non-Muslim governments and the reestablishment of the Khilafah, our worldwide Islamic state. The infidel nations, led by the grandchildren of pigs and monkeys, who pollute our Islamic states, will be brought to their knees! There is no god but Allah!

Witness the power of Allah in the events of the last twenty-four hours, the commencement of our jihad! We will continue. We will remove the stain of the infidels upon our all Muslim brothers. Witness the current monarchy in Saudi Arabia, the al-Asad family succession, which purports to act as a protector of the Muslim principles on which our kingdom was founded, and upon the guidance of the Koran and the guidance of shari'a, our Muslim law. Until now they have had the support and approval of our religious leadership. We, the clerics, the religious leaders of the Muslim faithful, have allowed them to assume the title of Iman, the lawgiver.

But as the Koran says:

"If anyone walks with an oppressor to strengthen him, knowing that he is an oppressor, he is gone forth from Islam."

They have wedded themselves to the infidel American government, profited from the Gulf Wars they instigated, and in doing so taken up a war of Muslim brother against Muslim brother. All in direct contravention of shari'a. The Americans, and with them their fellow pigs, the al-Asad monarchy in Saudi Arabia, only understand the language of violence, and now they have seen our wrath. They run away only after there is major bloodshed. So we will give them bloodshed.

And we declare the al-Asad monarchy, this puppet government of the offspring of dogs and swine, to be infidels. As infidels, they, like the Western infidels, must be expelled and destroyed. We declare this government illegitimate. They have permitted infidels to inhabit our sacred Arabian Peninsula, site of Islam's two holiest places.

The jihad has begun! The Khilafah will be reestablished! Islamic brothers, Believers, hear our call!

Sheik Mohammed Muqtar bin Abdur

Jesus. As verbose as he is crazy. This nut had to be stopped before every lunatic in the world jumped in.

Tom's office at Langley took forever to get him a secure line to Nigel Benthurst at British Secret Service and Ira Land at the Israeli Mossad. But soon they were on the line.

"Are you fellows current?" Tom asked. He was antsy. He wanted to get on with it.

"Ira and I were just, uhm, talking about it when you rang," Nigel said.

Tom grunted, then said, "We've had just about enough of this shit. I've talked to my guys at Langley. We think the manifesto published in the London and Pakistani Islamic newspapers is genuine. The al-Mujari. We're gonna do something about this son of a bitch bin Abdur. Are you guys in?"

"Do something, uhm, like we did when we took out Ibrahim, you mean?" Nigel's voice was emotionless.

"Exactly. Light the bastards up. Only go all the way this time."

"Agreed."

"I've already got resources allocated," Ira said.

"Good. All hands meeting in New York tomorrow morning at ten a.m."

"Whitehall's on board. We'll carry our end."

Ira just grunted.

This had been a long time coming. Tom felt the urge to gloat, savor the revenge, then realized it was too soon. He checked his watch. 10:30. An hour and a half left. The last time he spoke to Stone, she'd run out of leads to chase. All 56 software vendors on Kovarik's list were debugged, 47 tainted with logic bombs, 9 clean. At noon they'd know for sure.

Then he thought about Sasha and Daniel. *Still alive?*

Daniel hung out in Times Square until noon, watching the big screen and the news ticker, hoping. At 12:15 he was starting to feel more confident. When no reports of oil and gas facilities exploding appeared by 12:30, he smiled and let out a sigh. *We did it.* That was all the celebration he permitted himself. He had to find Sasha. He started thinking through how to get the Mercedes SLS AMG out of his building's garage if it was being watched, that is if Sasha hadn't gotten to it already.

CHAPTER 45

September, This Year. Buraida, Saudi Arabia. Habib watched the throng coming up the street from a few hundred yards off; two hundred men trudged in the streets of Buraida around Sheik bin Abdur. The Sheik had finished his evening prayers and apparently couldn't resist the urgings of his senior aides to walk among the people, inspire them with his presence and encourage them that now that the jihad had begun the Believers would prevail. Habib had already received his payment in full via wire transfer, but Sheik bin Abdur's summons had been so urgent and his intermediaries' assurances so great as to how lucrative the new job would be that Habib had to accept. For the money, but also out of curiosity.

He saw the cleric disappear inside the ramshackle hut that constituted Sheik bin Abdur's headquarters. After fifteen minutes the crowd began to dissipate. By the time Habib knocked on the door, only a few dozen people were still in the street, apparently waiting for the great man's return. One of Sheik bin Abdur's aides let him in. The anteroom to the chamber where Sheik bin Abdur customarily held forth was faintly lit with two candles. The man ran in front of Habib and opened the other door without knocking. Sheik bin Abdur's chamber was also faintly lit. Habib smelled the omnipresent dust.

Here we go again. Bin Abdur wore a traditional plain head-dress, his deep-set, intense eyes alone setting him apart from his followers.

"As usual, you are prompt, man who calls himself Habib," the Sheik said. "Now we wait. Perhaps an hour. Until nightfall."

They passed almost an hour in silence. Then: "It is time," Sheik bin Abdur said and turned to Habib. "Abdul has been instructed to wire one million dollars to your Swiss bank account if you will accept our assignment. We have taken the liberty of preparing the transfer already." His eyes burned. "You have brought your vehicle, this Land Rover?"

"Yes."

"Good. All we will require for this payment is your service and your silence. And your agreement to provide additional transportation if the situation warrants. It is as you call it 'a package deal.'"

CHAPTER 46

September, This Year. Milford, Pennsylvania. Sasha returned from her morning walk around the grounds at the Black Walnut Inn bed and breakfast. Her legs were stiff, as they always were when she was stressed. Her concern for Daniel dominated her thoughts—and spurred the reverberations in her heart. Had he escaped? She'd clearly drawn off the attackers. But where was he?

She'd been acting on instinct and training. Fleeing. A rental car after she decided not to retrieve the Mercedes SLS AMG, leaving it for Daniel. A hundred thousand dollars in cash. Her own passports and another two hundred thousand in multiple currencies in her satchel, as well as Daniel's new Swiss passport her contact had sent. *Ready.*

It was that ache, the terrible consuming ache for Daniel, that scrambled her thoughts.

She stopped at the steps to the porch, willing herself under control again. The men on the roof. Arab voices, the al-Mujari. How could they have found her? It wasn't inconceivable that someone had gotten inside the royal family again.

She went to her room, opened the window, took in the rolling green of the field through the eyes of a trained observer. *Nothing unusual.* Then those last tender moments with Daniel visited her again, their embrace, then her rage at the injustice of their being torn apart.

Her skills, her training were operating now. She pulled out an electronic device from beneath the bed, plugged the phone into it and called out, listening to Daniel's voice on the answering machine at the New York apartment. She looked at the device. A red light flashed on, the voltage meter dropped halfway down, fluttered, and then plunged all the way to the bottom of the scale. Her heart went cold. *Still bugged.* It was the same at the Milford house. She reluctantly tried Daniel's cell phone—she was afraid if she got through they might triangulate to his location—and got the recording that he was either outside of the service area or the phone wasn't functioning. She was still afraid to call Tom. He and his colleagues were the only ones who knew Daniel and she went to Barton Manor. There must be a leak or an al-Mujari plant at FBI Headquarters. *Wait. Daniel will show up.*

She drove her rented Toyota Camry back through town, wearing sunglasses, her hair up under a wide-brimmed straw hat, and circled by Daniel's house. Nothing seemed out of the ordinary. She drove back to the Black Walnut Inn.

September, This Year. New York City. Tom Goddard was thinking that if they'd had this big a team twenty years ago they probably wouldn't be here today. He was looking around the suite in the New York Hilton, ready to address the room full of members of the various intelligence and military agencies cooperating on the retaliation against the terrorists. His shoulders still ached and he still had cottonmouth at 10:30 a.m.

There were forty-two people in the suite, organized in three major groups. Each group clustered in a geometric arrangement of furniture around PCs placed on makeshift platforms out of end tables. Each team had a projector that beamed light onto the walls. Computer wires from notebook PCs streamed in all directions from the outlets. Food was set up in the entranceway.

"All right, everybody," Tom called. His eyes found Ira Land with his Israeli colleagues in one of the groups around a projector, Nigel Benthurst and the NATO team in another and his own crew by the third. "You all know why we're here." The voices in the room grew silent. "We've got the group broken down into three teams. The Israelis, headed by Ira Land, an expert in the Middle Eastern region and familiar with the al-Mujari and their methods, will head up the Mid-East sector. Nigel Benthurst, my counterpart from British Secret Service, also an expert in the Mid-East, will head up the European team, joined by Nathaniel Crow, a representative from NATO," Tom looked at that grouping. French, Belgian, German and Austrian. Scads of them. Half the people in the room. "And I'm heading up the North American team, joined by my colleagues from U.S. Intelligence."

He looked out at the faces, some grim, some with chins raised expectantly, all professionals. These were the men who would select, plan and execute the hits. Most of them had been waiting for a moment like this and had fallen all over themselves to get in on it. "All right. Your team leaders will go through the targets and as much intelligence on them as we've collectively gathered. Fifty-five lieutenant-level and higher members of Sheik bin Abdur's extremist group, the al-Mujari. All targets for tactical operations, some covert, some dynamic, over the next few days, coordinated with military strikes, mostly cruise missiles and laser-guided bombs. Each team has a couple of members of each of the U.S. Navy, Air Force, British, German, and NATO air and naval commands as well. Each of you has a primary contact for mercenaries if you need them. Overall coordination by a consortium of British Secret Service, the Israeli Mossad and CIA— Ira Land, Nigel Benthurst and me, Tom Goddard." He smiled for the first time. "Hopefully you'll get to know and love us." His smile broadened. "And then forget who the hell we are and what we look like." He looked around. "Okay. We've got one shot at this. Let's not screw it up."

"We should have done this twenty years ago," Tom said to Nigel Benthurst three hours later.

"As I recall, that was the advice both you and I gave to our respective superiors at the time," Nigel said. "Take it all the uhm, uhm, way, get to as many as we can, including bin Abdur himself." A few wisps of his thin blond hair hung down in front of his face. His shirt was still freshly starched, but seemed a size too big. "Don't even think the bloody Saudis will mind us doing some of it on their soil. After the scale of this attempted terrorism, they and the entire world will thank us." He half closed his eyes. "If we'd done this last time none of this would be necessary."

Tom grunted a reply. Nigel was right, he allowed. Back then, they'd capped five al-Mujari senior operatives, as well as Prince Ibrahim. It was enough to cripple the al-Mujari for years, but not snuff it out. This time they'd do it right.

Tom surveyed the room. Styrofoam cups, sandwich wrappings and paper plates littered any horizontal surface, and a half-dozen laptop PCs were still plugged into the walls. Within the space of three hours they had reviewed all fifty-five dossiers, projecting faces and key facts on the wall from PC screens.

"I'm afraid I've lost track of the total count, old boy," Nigel said.

"One hundred forty-six," Tom said. "Including the related groups and bin Abdur."

There would be thirty-two teams. All of those in Saudi Arabia, Sudan, Iraq, and Iran would be made up of local mercenaries. On the Continent the assassination teams would be a mixture of mercenaries, CIA, Mossad and British Secret Service. Tom watched Ira Land talking animatedly with a couple of the field agents and suspected that Ira might be in on some of the hits himself. They would also use mercenaries in the U.S. for the skinhead and paramilitary groups they had linked to or strongly suspected were sympathetic to the al-Mujari. CIA operatives would hit the more sophisticated targets, the underground al-Mujari cells.

"You okay, old boy?" Nigel asked, resting his hand on Tom's arm. Tom didn't respond. He was thinking about Sasha. Remembering his reaction when he'd seen her on the video screen with Youngblood. It looked like she'd gotten on to a good thing. Maybe settled into a real life. Maybe the two of them got away, got good and lost. Maybe he didn't need to feel bad about her anymore.

"Tom, is it Sasha?" Nigel said. "I was talking to some of the lads about it. I heard she's missing. You have to stop blaming yourself about all those years ago. She did a real service to all of us. Nobody else could have done it but her."

Nigel's words stabbed at Tom like his conscience. "We used her."

"And she went into it willingly, as I've told you a hundred times. Did it for Yassar. You know that." Nigel waved his hand in a circle in the air. "Almost a year as a trojan horse, that's a lot of pressure, a lot of psychological trauma there, I agree. But she knew what she was doing. And if she hadn't done it, Ibrahim would have helped Sheik bin Abdur kill Yassar, his own father. Bloody hell!"

Nigel didn't ease Tom's guilt. "We used her, we screwed up her life, and she spent the past twenty or so years running around doing God knows what as a result." Maybe she really had found a life with Youngblood and Tom should leave her alone. "Maybe I shouldn't try to find her, just let her fade into the woodwork again."

Nigel looked at him warily. "Tom, old boy. You know perfectly well that if they came this close to her, it won't uhm, uhm, be long before they find her again. We, uhm, never dreamed they'd be organized enough to pull off coordinated global terrorism like they've just attempted. You don't want them catching up with her, do you?"

"No," Tom said. They all owed her. What would have happened if Prince Ibrahim had survived? Then where would they be? "There was a guy, mercenary called—among other things—Habib. Remember him? Used to be one of ours."

"Of course. We used to call him the invisible man. Rather, uhm, an, an enigma."

"What if we were to get somebody good, really good like this guy Habib, and put him on Sasha, kind of a bodyguard?" He looked at Nigel's face. "I figure a man like that might do a lot better job than some of our own."

"Oh," Nigel said. Tom saw his face go slack. "We understand he's already working for bin Abdur."

My God, Tom thought. What if bin Abdur had the same idea? Find somebody really good and put him on her.

CHAPTER 47

September, This Year. New York City. Daniel walked into FBI Headquarters.

"Where were you?" Tom said when he came out to meet him.

"Hiding out."

"Why the hell didn't you call me sooner?"

"At first I was afraid to. I couldn't figure out how they knew we were at the hotel. I thought you might have a leak."

Tom looked straight at Daniel with those piercing blue eyes. "I'm the only one who knew where you were."

Daniel nodded. "I also drove up to Milford. Sasha and I agreed to meet up there if we got separated."

"She's there now?"

"No. I don't know where she is. I was hoping you might. You know what happened?"

"Yeah, the aftermath at least. Two guys capped on the roof, .22 caliber bullets in both. Three more dead in the hotel room. One from a marble bookend, two from the same Uzi."

Daniel felt shock, blood rising to his face. "Two dead on the roof?" His stomach started rolling over. Tom had rattled it off like it was nothing. He felt sick. His thoughts raced back to the hotel, going to the courtyard, finding no one…Finally: "I didn't know about the two guys on the roof." He felt renewed terror in the aftermath of killing the two men in the apartment, then fear for Sasha's safety.

Tom said, "Then I guess Sasha did the guys on the roof. That means she probably got away."

Hearing it was like oxygen to Daniel.

"You talk to Yassar?" Tom said.

"I couldn't get through."

Tom looked at the floor, thinking.

"What?" Daniel asked.

"I can't get him either. They said he's on his way here."

"Maybe he's coming for her."

"Or after her."

Daniel felt an escalating fear. "What the hell are you talking about? She says he's like her father."

Tom looked grave. "She did a job for us once."

"I know about Yassar's son."

Tom's blue eyes were cold, unblinking. "Then nothing he does should surprise you."

Daniel felt a twist deep in his stomach.

Tom went on, "With all this shit going on I've never had time to ask you how you and Sasha got involved."

Daniel felt his face color. "She was sent to see if the terrorists were working through my clients. And probably to check me out for Yassar, before he hired me." He averted his eyes, his face now burning, humiliated.

"You sure about her?" Tom asked. "Sure she's told you everything?'

Daniel raised his head, certain. "Yes."

"Okay," Tom said, looking unconvinced. "We better get started trying to find her. I'll see if we have any leads. We're still covering your apartment and weekend house. Where's your cell phone?"

"Smashed in the hotel."

"We'll get you a new one, same number. May take a few hours with all I've got going on. She may try to contact you."

Daniel felt his tension and disorientation scrambling his thinking. It didn't make sense, Yassar double-crossing Sasha. He told himself that it was just Tom's job to be a professional paranoid. Unless he knew something he wasn't saying. Then he had to struggle to ignore the queasy sensation he felt.

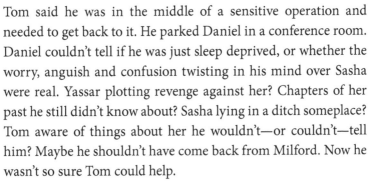

Tom said he was in the middle of a sensitive operation and needed to get back to it. He parked Daniel in a conference room. Daniel couldn't tell if he was just sleep deprived, or whether the worry, anguish and confusion twisting in his mind over Sasha were real. Yassar plotting revenge against her? Chapters of her past he still didn't know about? Sasha lying in a ditch someplace? Tom aware of things about her he wouldn't—or couldn't—tell him? Maybe he shouldn't have come back from Milford. Now he wasn't so sure Tom could help.

Daniel leaned forward in his chair and rested his forehead on the conference room table. Despair took hold. He put his hands over his head, wished he could fall asleep, just black out and wake up with his mind clear. A moment later when he tried to lift his head he felt he had no strength to do so, then thought he might simply slide to the floor and collapse, a blob of raw emotion.

He didn't know how long he sat like that, but when he focused again he was thinking about what Sasha must be doing at that moment. Probably waiting for him someplace in Milford, keeping her wits about her, planning how they'd get to safety. He thought about the Mercedes coupe. He'd parked it at the Grand Union in Milford so she would see it, know he was alive.

He sat up in the chair. *Snap out of it.* He stood up and started pacing. What still gnawed at him was how the terrorists could have guessed they'd be at that little-known hotel. If Tom hadn't told anyone, it just didn't make sense. Sasha and he had taken three different taxis, two subways, and a bus to make certain they weren't followed. The only people who knew Daniel used to stay there were colleagues from work, years ago. Then it hit him: *Kovarik.* Kovarik was one of the only people who might guess Daniel would go to Barton Manor if he wanted to get lost. When they were still friends together at Goldman, Daniel told Kovarik where he went for those "lost" weekends in case an emergency arose at the office. He had to track the bastard down; he was obviously still feeding information to the terrorists.

He burst through the door to find Tom. The woman at reception said Tom was in a meeting and couldn't be disturbed. Daniel felt like someone was peeling the skin off his flesh as he strode back into the conference room. He started pacing again. Where would *Kovarik* go if he wanted to get lost? He remembered the pictures in Kovarik's office. Kovarik proudly standing beside his Aston Martin. Kovarik's Aston peeking out of the garage on Long Island City where he and Daniel used to keep them, where Kovarik still kept his. The image tingled in his brain. *The garage.*

Daniel ran to the reception desk. "I need to get a message to Tom Goddard."

She gave him a bitchy look, "I *told* you he can't be disturbed."

Daniel wanted to throttle the woman. He grabbed a piece of paper and a pen from the desk, scrawled, "I'm going for Kovarik.

4250 12th St., Long Island city. Send backup. Daniel." He handed
it to her and said, "Get this to him now or take responsibility for
what happens if you don't."

Ten minutes later, Daniel's taxi pulled off the Queensboro
Bridge and swung onto Queens Plaza South. It cruised down 12th
Street and Daniel had the cabbie stop a few doors down from
the garage. It looked much as it did the last time Daniel was here
almost 10 years earlier. The windows were still blacked out with
paint, the cinderblock exterior sported maroon, blue and white
coats of paint peeling from it, and weeds and dried vegetation
grew up through cracks in the concrete. Litter and dust were
everywhere. Daniel walked down the side driveway to approach
the bays in the back. As he turned the corner he got a shock:
Kovarik walked straight into him, a suitcase in hand. "Ooof,"
Daniel said as their chests collided. "Shit!" Kovarik yelled as he
stepped back, then swung his suitcase into Daniel's knee. Daniel
saw stars and felt his leg go out from under him, landed on his
back in the driveway. He rolled on his side to see Kovarik sprinting down the driveway toward 12th Street, moving fast, bad leg
and all. Daniel was up in an instant, running after him full tilt,
his knee smarting with every stride.

Daniel's anger boiled in him as he ran. *No way you get away.*
He thought he was gaining on Kovarik. His knee still hurt but it
was loosening up. Yes, he was gaining on him. It would take only
another few hundred yards to chase him down. They turned
underneath the Queensboro Bridge onto Queens Plaza South.
When Kovarik rounded the corner onto 10th Street he slipped
and went down on the sidewalk. He got back up but it was all
over in another 20 yards. Daniel grabbed him by the shoulders
and slammed him against a light post. Daniel's arms were trembling with rage as he spun Kovarik around, grabbed him by the

shirt collar and pressed his back against the post. For a second he thought of hurling him in front of a car.

"You bastard," Daniel said, panting, the taste of stomach acid in his throat.

Kovarik was giving him a tough-guy sneer. He wheezed, "What are you chasing *me* for? *You're* the one who's implicated, and I've tipped off the FBI. You're gonna be disgraced and end your days in jail." Daniel clamped his hands around Kovarik's throat, started squeezing. He gritted his teeth and for a moment believed he could actually throttle him to death. Someone grabbed him from behind, pulled him off Kovarik.

"Take it easy."

Daniel turned. It was Johnson, the FBI agent who'd led the team going to Kovarik's office. Two other agents grabbed Kovarik, cuffed him and started moving him toward the street.

"We'll take it from here, cowboy," Johnson said.

Forty-five minutes later Daniel sat with Tom, Johnson and two other agents outside the interrogation room at FBI headquarters, watching Kovarik through the two-way mirror. The sound was tinny through the speakers, but Daniel could hear Kovarik whining like a schoolboy.

"He was a client. I did research on the industry for him."

"Uh-huh." The agent shook his head. "You'll need to do better'n that."

"I want to talk to my lawyer."

The agent laughed. "You watch a lotta movies." Daniel saw Kovarik's eyes widen, his head droop. "Only when I'm done with you, and I'm not done with you yet. And if you don't gimme what I want, nobody may ever even know you're in here."

Kovarik hung his head further still, staring at the table. The agent pushed a book of photographs in front of him.

"Again. Point out the guy."

After an hour of it, Daniel got up and left. Nothing on Sasha from Kovarik, and nothing from Tom's people. At least the excitement of chasing down Kovarik had taken his mind off her for a time. Now his stomach was churning with worry over her again. He was in a conference room when Tom walked in with a photograph. "Kovarik ID'd this guy. You ever seen him?" Daniel shook his head. "He goes by the name of Habib, at least most of the time. He was once one of ours. I think we might know how to get to him."

"You think it'll help us find Sasha?"

"I don't think so. Like I said earlier, I think she got away. And she's probably hiding out, waiting for you."

It didn't ease his mind. Tom had gotten him a new cell phone and she still hadn't called. But he'd been thinking about what Sasha said about anticipating each other if they needed to run. It gave him an idea.

September, This Year. Buraida, Saudi Arabia. Assad stopped his Jeep on the desert just outside Buraida. It was good to be seeing action again—so infrequent since he'd become head of the Saudi Secret Police. The green outline of buildings shone in the distance through his night-vision binoculars. *Quiet. Good.* The advance team was indicating no security force visible. That meant they could neutralize the targets without taking out the entire building with handheld rockets.

Assad motioned to Mustafa, his driver, then nodded to Ishtar, his second, in the back seat. They drove the remaining mile with their headlights off. Mustafa parked the Jeep a hundred yards outside the town's main street, and Assad and Ishtar started across the dirt. Assad could see the mosque in the distance and the shape of the building next door, but no lights through the windows.

The town was quiet, the wind picking up in the cool night air. Assad paused at the side street where it reached the center of town. As they approached, Assad could see five Arabs were seated outside the building. A half-dozen people walked the street. The advance team would be in place by now.

He pulled out his Ruger 9mm automatic, racked the slide and clunked the first shell into the chamber. Ishtar did the same.

They continued down the street, guns back beneath their parkas. Assad's eyes darted from side to side looking for anything unusual. *Still quiet. Good. Just stay that way.* He was now at fifty yards. He inhaled deeply. The cool air felt good in his lungs.

At twenty-five yards he saw the shapes of the men in the street more clearly. Four of them walked to the door of the building next to the mosque. One lifted a steel bar and slammed it against the weather-beaten wood. The door disintegrated as much as it flew open and two of the other men pitched concussion grenades inside. Blinding flashes and muffled explosions reverberated inside the anteroom to Sheik bin Abdur's chamber.

Assad saw the three men disappear inside, heard the crash of the steel against the inside door, then three more explosions. Assad entered the anteroom, smelling cordite and the dust that was sifting down from the ceiling. Three men were coughing and groaning on the floor. His two men held automatics on them. Assad nodded to his team and turned toward the anteroom door.

He heard three shots in the anteroom as he entered the Sheik's chamber, where four other men lay facedown on the floor, begging for mercy.

Three of his team stood over them. Assad told his men to turn them over, one by one. The Sheik was not among them.

"Finish it," he said. As he left the building he heard two shots, then two more. His Jeep was waiting. He climbed into the passenger seat and Ishtar jumped in the back.

Abdul and Waleed, and five others who do not really matter, Assad mused. *But no bin Abdur. No wonder it was so easy.*

CHAPTER 48

SEPTEMBER, THIS YEAR. NEW YORK City. Daniel was just leaving FBI Headquarters when his cell phone rang. It gave him a start, then a burst of joy. *Sasha.*

"Hello, Daniel."

"Yassar. Where are you?" Tom's words came back to him. Coming for her or *after* her? It still didn't seem possible.

"In New York. Is Sasha with you?"

"No. We were attacked, got split up. But I think she's safe."

"Al-Mujari. Yes, she's safe, for now."

Daniel felt a rush of relief. His breathing was short, uneven. "Thank God," he whispered.

"She's emailed me, but she's too cautious to call. I know how deep underground she can go. And she says she won't come out without you."

Daniel hesitated, then asked, "Yassar, why are you here?"

Yassar didn't respond. Then, after clearing his throat, he said, "Why Daniel, what a strange question." His tone sounded almost as if he were lecturing Daniel. He paused again. "The crisis is averted, but now Sasha is in danger and refuses to allow us to extract her. That is, without you."

Daniel paused, thinking. He remembered Sasha's words. *Be intuitive.*

"Daniel?"

"Yes. I may have an idea. Do you know how to contact her friend, Nafta?"

"Of course. I have her number at the clinic in Paris."

"She might know something. It was something Sasha said."

CHAPTER 49

SEPTEMBER, THIS YEAR. A SAFE House One Hundred Kilometers Outside Khartoum, Sudan. Habib sat cross-legged on the floor of a nondescript house in a nondescript village. About a dozen of Sheik bin Abdur's followers were seated as well, listening to the great man speak.

"An Islamic brother who murders his own Islamic brother is an infidel, who must perish!" Bin Abdur's voice was venomous.

Habib looked at the concrete walls. *Not much better accommodations than in Buraida. Now that I know where he is I figure the price of getting him out of here should be double or triple what he paid me to get him out of there. This should be a good payday, too.* Habib sat patiently for another half hour while Sheik bin Abdur finished his sermon.

"And we will continue our jihad. We will drive out the infidels! There is no God but Allah!"

"La ilaha ilallah!" the others in the room repeated.

"Now, my brothers, please you must leave me," bin Abdur said. "I must speak with our friend, the man we call Habib."

Finally, Habib thought. "You want me to move you?" he asked when they were alone.

The Sheik glared at him. "No. I want you to take care of the girl."

The girl again. Always the girl.

"This whore Sasha. She was responsible for the first acts of murder against our brethren. She, with her Western influence, seduced our young friend Ibrahim, then betrayed him. And many more over the years. Now this. Over fifty of our people murdered. I expect you to take care of it personally. Make certain *you* don't miss this time. This girl must die."

Oh, man. Trying to take someone out with all this heat? "This will be expensive. Two million dollars."

"Outrageous."

"Accept it. For once, just accept it. Every intelligence agency in the world is at full alert."

"While I would never allow my followers to learn of my disappointment at the failure of our ambitious plans for the commencement of our jihad," the Sheik said, his eyes boring into Habib, "and while I am delighted with the spectacular statement we made with the inferno of the Challenger oil rig, do you honestly believe the services the Believers received from you were fair in comparison to the compensation paid to you?"

"Just getting in and out of the U.S. with all the security now...This won't be easy. Two million."

"Mr. Farooq Abdullah who calls himself Habib, I think not. I think you will do it for us as a courtesy."

And so it was agreed.

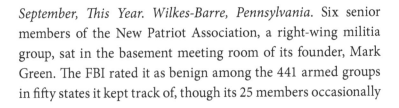

September, This Year. Wilkes-Barre, Pennsylvania. Six senior members of the New Patriot Association, a right-wing militia group, sat in the basement meeting room of its founder, Mark Green. The FBI rated it as benign among the 441 armed groups in fifty states it kept track of, though its 25 members occasionally conducted weekend war games in the woodlands around Wilkes-Barre.

Habib stood behind the semicircle of chairs. *Close to twenty thousand*, he thought, reflecting on the number of miles he'd flown in the last seventy-two hours.

He didn't mind. When the work was there he got paid. When things went cold they went stone cold. And right now things were as hot as he'd ever seen them.

The DVD was playing *The Day of the Jackal*, the scene in which the Jackal sights-in his custom-made rifle. He fires three rounds of conventional bullets, successively adjusting the cross-hairs on his scope until he's certain the sight's aim is perfect. Then he loads a custom-made mercury bullet. He fires again and a melon shatters into a million pieces with the impact of the slug, leaving no trace but a moist pool on the ground.

"I see what you mean," Green said. "How many have you got?"

Habib thought he had seen all kinds, but never anything like Mark Green. He was six feet four inches tall, skinny as a broomstick. "Live Free or Die" was tattooed across the top of his forehead. His brown eyes had the spark of a mischievous child.

"Six. They're relatively hard to come by, so don't waste them. You should only need one anyhow," Habib said. Two of the group members stood behind Green, listening. Habib judged he wouldn't trust them with much of anything important. At least Habib was sure Green could get the job done. *At a minimum this one's got good teeth*, Habib thought.

"And you say this bitch is the one who put the Feds on to the Nationalist Front in New York?" Green asked.

I'll say whatever it takes to get you to do the job. "We're certain. And two other true patriot groups in the New York area that were hit by the CIA as well. All blamed for ties to this Islamic terrorist group, led to them by this woman."

"Well I'd say that makes her a murderer, then. Six good Americans died at the hands of the Feds because of this bitch."

"Twelve, if you count the members of the other two groups," Habib said. "And if you take the others around the country she was indirectly responsible for, the total would be over fifty."

Green clenched a fist. "Well then you've come to the right men. We can do the job."

Habib dropped the six mercury bullets into Green's hand, then handed over a photograph and an envelope with $10,000. "I trust you can find Milford. The name is Lydia Fauchert. The address 521 Broad Street. Straight black hair, black eyes, about five feet four. Don't miss."

CHAPTER 50

September, This Year. New York City. Dressed in slacks and open-necked shirts, Tom and Daniel got off the elevator at One American Plaza, FBI headquarters.

Tom led him through the office until they reached a glass-walled conference room. "We call this the goldfish bowl," Tom said. The glass was a half-inch thick, so when the door closed behind them the sound of the outer office completely disappeared. Fifteen people were in the room, the men with their suit jackets off, a few women dressed in blouses and skirts. A credenza against the glass wall had two urns of coffee, scattered boxes of donuts, bagels and Danish.

Daniel still hadn't heard from Sasha. He'd checked the answering machines in his apartment and in the Milford House every few hours. Nothing. And no more calls on the new cell phone Tom had provided. Tom kept him current on the status of their efforts to find her, despite whatever else he seemed to have on his mind. But all they knew was where she wasn't.

"This is the situation room," Tom said. "And you know Special Agent Stone, our computer wizard."

"Hi, Tom—hi, Daniel," she said in her husky voice.

Tom introduced Daniel to three or four others, including Walter Baxter, the FBI Regional Director.

"I'm getting heat on somebody with good covert tactical skills continuing to light up these white supremacist and para-military groups," Baxter told Tom.

Tom shrugged. "Somebody's doing the world a favor."

"Yeah, but you need to be a little more discreet. And at some point it's not going to be open season on these guys." Baxter gave Tom a severe glance. "At least *I* answer to the Justice Department."

Christ. Daniel was itching to get on with it. He didn't need this intramural squabble.

"Hey, Goddard, you might want to hear this," an agent said. "Extension 6241. The agent's name is Stevens."

Tom hit the speakerphone. "Yes, Stevens."

"Unidentified subject matching Sasha's description has been seen driving a blue Toyota Camry around Milford, Pennsylvania."

Daniel's muscles tensed. *Is it her?*

Tom turned to him. "You think she'd wait this long to meet you up there?"

"Yes." Daniel was desperate to get moving. Why the hell were they all just sitting around?

Tom spoke back into the speakerphone. "You sure it's a woman driving?"

"Would it match Sasha's description if it was a guy? You want us to bring the subject in?"

"No, observation only, no contact and avoid detection."

"It must be Sasha," Daniel said. He wanted to scream it in Tom's face.

Tom turned to him. "Don't know. Could be a decoy. For her or for you." Tom spoke back into the speakerphone. "Give me your number, Stevens. Where are you now?"

"Parked at the Grand Union."

"We'll be there as fast as we can." Tom grabbed Baxter by the arm. "I'm gonna need a couple of your agents and a chopper. It's either Sasha or somebody's trying to set her up."

Three agents jumped up from their seats.

"Thirty-fourth Street on the West Side. We'll phone ahead for the chopper," Baxter said. He turned and went to dial the phone. Daniel felt a sense of rightness, justness. They were going to make it, Sasha and he.

September, This Year. Milford, Pennsylvania. Two days of this! Sasha felt like a jungle cat with no prey, pacing the grounds of the bed and breakfast, thinking, rethinking. Emotions twisted in her heart. Images attacked her brain. She longed for sleep, a drug, a lobotomy, anything to keep her mind from devouring itself.

Where was Daniel? His phones were both still tapped. And nobody at the Milford house after multiple drive-bys. Maybe he and Tom were working together. Tom. His Midwestern values as straight as his hair. He'd help Daniel get to her.

What would Tom do now? Nothing came to her. Maybe she should go to him. No. She needed to think for both Daniel and herself now; she couldn't allow the luxury of taking chances. She remembered the passports, including Daniel's. The money, their travel plans, the Mercedes. All they needed to do was get to Canada, then a flight to Switzerland. Then lost forever, or for as long as it took to lose these al-Mujari fanatics.

Time to move. Make sure her cover was still good. Her instinct pumped in her veins, then her longing for Daniel. Two days and he still wasn't here. When was he coming?

She paid her bill, then went up to her room, took out her laptop. She accessed the communications port, entered her account codes, then dialed out through her circuitous route of various phony accounts and international networks. She glanced at her watch, checking the online time elapsed.

An encrypted email message was waiting for her. She de-encrypted it. The words flashed on her screen:

REPEAT MESSAGE. GET OUT NOW. THEY ARE TARGETING YOU. MAKE CONTACT FOR EXTRACTION.

Not just yet. You sent me in here to think for myself and that's exactly what I'm doing. I'm not going anyplace without Daniel.

She was going back to the City. So what if she was heading right back into the middle of danger? She was convinced Daniel was there. *He's all right.* She knew it. He had to be.

A vision of Daniel's face came to her. She stood in the center of the room, her heart focused on him, swearing to herself this was the last moment she'd spend in anguish like this. She opened a window and looked to see that no one was watching, then dropped her overnight bag to the ground. Once downstairs she strode off the porch as if she were going for another walk. She picked up speed, turned the corner of the building, fetched her bag and walked behind the inn to the parking lot, breathing evenly to keep herself from hurrying too much. She drove away, looking into the rearview mirror.

The Toyota Camry seemed to turn back toward Milford by itself. As if yielding to the insistence of the car, she drove once more down Sawkill Avenue and around the curve past the Milford house on Broad Street. The driveway was empty and the house was dark. She headed back out through town, thinking of how she'd contact Daniel in the City. Or go directly to Tom?

Wait. She saw the maroon Mercedes SLS AMG parked at the Grand Union. A shot of adrenaline filled her, then a gush of joy. She drove past the Grand Union and out of town, then pulled off onto a side road. Now she allowed herself to revel in unrestrained relief. She laughed out loud, tears of happiness streaming down her cheeks. She let out one last, long cathartic sigh. Then she dried her eyes and blew her nose, steeling herself again. *All right, this is it. Get focused. You go in, get him, and the two of you get the hell out of here and get very, very lost. No more running. No more life without someone to love.*

She drove back into town, pulled into the Grand Union parking lot knowing how risky this was. She knew it would be safer to wait in the parking lot up the hill, from which she could clearly see Daniel when he got into his car.

What if he's being tailed? They'll see me follow him. Then they'll get both of us. She turned the engine off. No, her best chance was to try to get into the store without being seen and meet him inside.

She took a deep breath, murmured some words in Sanskrit, opened the door, and walked briskly into the Grand Union. She strode down the first aisle, forcing away the terror that threatened to steal her composure. Anybody could be waiting in one of these aisles.

She walked headlong into a bearded man wearing Ray-Bans and a New York Yankees cap pulled down over his forehead. *Yassar!* She inhaled a huge gulp of air in her shock.

"Hello, Sasha," he said.

"She just went into the store!" Tom yelled to Daniel over the chopper's noise, pulling his cell phone away from his ear.

"Is she okay?"

Tom shook his head, "I don't know. Two of the FBI agents just went in after her, and—"

"We're almost there!" Daniel yelled. They were about a mile out at only a few thousand feet and he could see the Delaware River, then the town of Milford looming up in front of them. *Just hang on, Sasha*, Daniel thought.

"See if you can put us down in the parking lot!" Tom yelled into the intercom. Five seconds later it seemed like they were skimming the treetops. Daniel guessed they were at about two hundred feet and he could see people in the Milford streets standing and pointing up at the chopper as it thundered over their heads.

The pilot banked hard right as they crossed Broad Street directly over the stoplight in town, and righted it in a smooth motion that squeezed Daniel into his seat.

In another five seconds he had touched it down in the Grand Union back parking lot.

Yassar felt the throbbing of the chopper's rotors at about the same moment he heard them. *Allah, don't let this go wrong.* The two men who had accompanied Yassar swooped Sasha up in their arms. He felt a crushing guilt and utter disgust at himself at the sight. They started running up the aisle toward the front of the store, holding her, past stunned neighbors who stood frozen. Yassar pushed emotion away. *It must be done.*

Sasha tried to scream. Her eyes locked for a half second on Yassar's, feeling confusion, then terror, the sense of hopelessness at the worst betrayal imaginable. The two men started running, carrying her toward the front of the store. She tried to punch the man who held her under the armpits and clamped his hand over her mouth, then scratched his hand, but he wouldn't let go. She tried to force her mouth open to bite his fingers, but his grasp was too strong. Outside, she saw a Ford Aerostar waiting with its side door open and in an instant the two men had her inside. Yassar jumped in and the door slid shut. The van sped away.

Daniel ran through the side entrance, feeling terror and anger and purpose. Where were the agents who were supposed to be in the store?

"Daniel! Out there, out there!" The townspeople, his neighbors, were pointing at the front entrance. "She's outside! They took her outside!"

Daniel ran out the front door just in time to see the van race across the parking lot. He turned back, seeing Tom ten feet behind him, and three FBI agents, semiautomatics in their hands. He felt a chill run through him, as if the cold steel of the guns had been thrust to his flesh.

"The car! Get in the car!" Daniel yelled, pointing toward the Mercedes. He took out his keychain, chirped the automatic lock and was inside. The V-8 engine roared. Tom jumped into the passenger seat and Daniel screeched the SLS AMG across the parking lot after the van. He saw the FBI agents run to another car.

Yassar! Sasha flailed and punched and scratched but the men wouldn't let go of her. *Yassar!*

Sasha felt two wheels lift off the road and then come crashing back as the van came out of a turn and accelerated off on the straightway. As it righted itself, a figure in the back spilled off the seat, her head smacking the floor a foot from Sasha's face. *Nafta!*

Their eyes met. Sasha felt her chest convulse. *Nafta.* Sasha closed her eyes and began to pray.

"He's heading for town!" Daniel rounded the curve behind the van and headed up Harford Street toward the light. He followed the van around the turn at the light, saw its brake lights, the smoke from the tires as it skidded to a stop just before his house, in front of a police car that had sped up Broad Street to block it. Then the door of the van was open and she was out of the van, her black hair streaming out behind her. A man emerged from the van and ran after her. Daniel almost collapsed as he got out of the car. Scrambling, he saw Tom a few feet in front of him running behind the man. Daniel called out Sasha's name, but she didn't turn to him as she stopped in front of the door and fumbled with her keys, and then he heard the screech of tires and the sirens behind him and realized the FBI men were there too. He heard a crack that he only identified afterward as a rifle shot someplace off to his left. And then he saw a huge red ball like a halo surrounding her head and her body falling to the floor of the porch beneath a three-foot circle of red on the white door of the house that he knew in his mind must be from blood but his heart couldn't comprehend. And the man whose face Daniel would never forget, the Arabic face with the scratches on it, the scratches of her last struggle for life, the man turned back and ran to the van and he heard the van's tires squeal and he saw it speed off. Tom turned from the sight and grabbed him and pushed him away and stopped him from looking at what Daniel couldn't bring himself to look at anyhow.

CHAPTER 51

SEPTEMBER, THIS YEAR. LANGLEY, VIRGINIA. "Hardly any traces of dental work to match. Didn't make any difference, we all saw the whole thing," Tom said to Nigel Benthurst and Ira Land, watching their pixels dance on the color split-screen. He managed a professional detachment in his voice. "I talked to Yassar. Turns out he's maybe not as much of a cold fish as I thought. Said he came back here to try to help her." *Said he loved her like a daughter.*

Nigel spoke up. "Otherwise, a successful campaign, old boy."

"Agreed," Ira said from his other side of the screen. "Our people say the al-Mujari is in shambles."

"Worse shape than the, uhm, situation we created last time."

"Yeah, but Sheik bin Abdur escaped. Again." He knew what that meant. These Al-Mujari were like jock itch—with a lot of effort, you could keep it under control, but you could never actually get rid of it.

"It'll be years before they're able to, uhm, reorganize themselves."

Ira said, "Maybe we can keep them down."

Tom didn't think he'd ever get the U.S. government to agree to another assassination plot. Not unless the situation was as extreme as the last week.

"Sorry about Sasha," Nigel said.

"Yeah," Tom said. "I guess Yassar feels worse than anybody. Trying to help her escape and it just went haywire. Still, maybe it was better for her this way. Terminal cervical cancer, metastasized throughout her system. Would've been a worse end."

"Well," Tom said after a moment, the businesslike tone back in his voice. Tom paused. He had to at least say it. "The thing that pisses me off more than anything else is that bin Abdur must have been thrilled when he heard they had...killed...Sasha." He was trying out the words. *Maybe if I say them enough, I'll get past it.*

He saw Nigel's eyes on his, watching. "We missed our, our chance at bin Abdur this time," Nigel said. "We didn't take it last time. What do they say? The third time is a charm?"

September, This Year. A Safe House One Hundred Kilometers Outside Khartoum, Sudan. Habib got out of his Jeep, shuddered against the chill of the desert night. The spring was back in his step as he walked toward the ramshackle house that hid Sheik bin Abdur. A day's rest did a mercenary a world of good.

He knocked on the door. A little man wearing a black robe opened it. Habib had been here before, knew where he was going. He strode directly toward the inner door and pushed it open. Sheik bin Abdur was sitting in the corner of the room, his eyes gleaming in the darkness as if illuminated by lights in his head. *Those damned eyes. Never seen anything like them*, Habib thought.

He surveyed the room, feeling the thrill of the dare, the challenge. He unzipped his windbreaker with his left hand, smoothly reached inside with his right and pulled out his Beretta with its four-inch silencer already attached. With a well-schooled motion, he put a single round directly between the two gleaming spots in bin Abdur's head. Before anyone could react he put four more rounds in the four others who sat cross-legged on the dirt floor, one in each chest.

Habib surveyed his work for a few seconds, then left the room, not bothering with the little man in the anteroom as he left the building.

Last time I do business with you, old man.

⋲◆⋺

September, This Year. New York City. Prince Yassar sat at the desk in his hotel room, working at his computer. He was logged in over a secure line set up a year earlier by the Saudi Secret Police and typed an email message to habib@nowhere.com.

GREETINGS. AND GOODBYE. SIX MILLION DOLLARS ACCORDING TO YOUR WIRING INSTRUCTIONS AWAITING YOU AT YOUR CARIBBEAN AND CONTINENTAL LOCATIONS. YOU PERFORMED FLAWLESSLY. YOUR WORD IS GOOD. WE WILL REMEMBER THIS.

Y

He logged off and sighed. *Know your enemies.* He smiled. *And know your friends. And know how to use your enemies and your friends for the purification of the Muslim world.* He was peaceful, even as he gloried in his revenge. Perhaps he could live long enough to atone for the stain on his soul. He looked at his watch. It was time for prayers and then bed. He had a plane to catch in the morning.

CHAPTER 52

September, This Year. New York City. Daniel felt one of those curious absences of emotion he'd experienced over the last day. He held his head erect, as if balancing an imaginary object on his nose.

He wondered if the cosmos were mocking him. He'd been sitting here like this at the beginning of the summer, just before meeting Sasha.

Eleven thirty. He told himself he'd get up soon, at least move around the office. He saw a shape. Cindy, his assistant.

"Daniel, you have a visitor in conference room two…" Her voice trailed off. She looked at him apprehensively.

He got up and walked toward the conference room.

As Daniel entered the conference room, he realized he'd been holding his breath, felt air rush back into his lungs. "Where is she?" he asked.

"Safe," Yassar said. "An airplane ride away."

"You think it worked?"

"If Tom Goddard believed it, I think the al-Mujari will."

Daniel felt a wave of guilt. "Sorry we had to put him through that, but it needed to be convincing." *She's escaped them for good.* He started to laugh and choke back tears. He collapsed into a chair. "Nafta told me she tried to convince Sasha three or four times once she knew her cancer was terminal." He felt stinging moisture in his eyes, a burning in his throat.

Yassar observed him in silence.

After a moment Daniel said, "I need to see her."

"If you choose to."

What's, he crazy? "Choose to? Where is she?"

"As I said, safe."

"What's the mystery?"

"No mystery, Daniel, I'm just protecting her. You have two choices, each with significant consequences."

Daniel waved him off as if he were talking to one of his subordinates.

Yassar continued, "Stay here, work for us as our advisor—we need a man with your talents—and you'll be well compensated."

Daniel was beginning to wonder why Yassar was being so obtuse. "Yassar—"

Yassar held up his hand. "Or go to Sasha, live on in hiding, leave your entire life here behind. Everything. Forever."

"Okay, are you finished now? When can I see her?"

"Be certain. No turning back."

"Yassar. Knock it off, will ya?" Daniel smiled from his heart. It was hers, always would be.

Daniel headed straight for his senior partner, Jean-Claude Dieudonne's office. Miss Chuckings, all ninety officious pounds of her, was sitting behind her desk outside his closed door. "Morning, Miss Chuckings, is he in there?" He walked into Dieudonne's office.

"Mr. Youngblood, you can't—"

Two guests sat at Dieudonne's coffee table. So Dieudonne was staging the Intimate Gathering today. *Closing a deal, Jean-Claude?* "Good morning. Sorry to interrupt, gentlemen. Jean-Claude, I'm resigning, effective immediately. I'm assigning my contract for the Saudis to Michael Smits, including my work in progress. Good luck with your fiscal years."

He plucked a Cohiba Esplendido from the humidor on the credenza and walked out.

CHAPTER 53

SEPTEMBER, THIS YEAR. GENEVA, SWITZERLAND. Incense and murmured prayers drifted upward in the back room of the rented chalet, which would be the first way-station in their journey. Sasha knelt in front of the makeshift puja she had created out of an end table. She recited in Sanskrit, periodically opening her eyes to gaze upon the photograph of Swami Kripananda and the statue of Ganesha. A ring of flowers encircled a photograph of Nafta in the center of the puja.

She thanked Nafta from her heart, offering prayers for her, feeling unworthy and grateful at the same time. Honoring her. When she finished she said a final farewell to Nafta and left the room, quietly closing the door, as if not to disturb her friend's sleep. Yassar turned to look at Sasha from his chair in the Great Room at the center of the chalet. She softly kissed him on the forehead before taking a seat next to him. *Dear Yassar.*

They sat in silence. "Nafta told us you were unwilling to do it," Yassar offered, "but once we had discovered the assassination plan..." Sasha's eyes were lowered, but she felt Yassar's gaze searching her face. "Daniel and I declined at first. But she said it was the only way you'd ever be free of it all. She said she didn't want you watching your back for the al-Mujari the rest of your life." He paused. "And she wanted a way for you to know some happiness now that you had finally found someone." He paused again, then murmured, "This was a true gift."

Sasha raised her eyes to Yassar's. She wondered if she could live well enough to deserve it, and as quickly absorbed that thought as one to revisit again and again, her remembrance of Nafta. They sat in silence again.

September, This Year. New York City. He had visited his parents, his brother and sister-in-law, and Sammy and Mickey. Now Daniel stood in the doorway of Michael and Brenda's apartment. "I guess this is it."

"Drop us a line or something," Michael said. "We'll be pissed if you don't."

"Bet your ass," Brenda added. Her voice was choked.

Michael bear-hugged Daniel. "Take care of yourself." Brenda stepped forward, those eyes of hers calm, accepting it, and wrapped her arms around both of them.

September, This Year. Geneva, Switzerland. The Gulfstream V must have touched down as softly as a mother kissing her newborn child on the cheek, because Daniel didn't awaken until the copilot came back to rouse him. He groaned. His contact lenses were stuck to his eyes. What a way to wake up to his new life.

"We there?"

"Yup. And a half hour early. Can we get you anything, Mr. Youngblood?"

"No, I'm fine." He looked out the window. It was just dawn, everything in an orange-and-yellow glow from the rising sun. Somebody popped the door open and he felt a flutter of anticipation, then, truly waking, a smile that seemed to emanate from someplace inside him and possess his entire being.

The copilot looked out the window. "The car should be here. I'll phone if you want."

"No problem, if the car's a few minutes late, it's a few minutes late."

He'd left it all behind. He'd wired money to the bank in Geneva and it was now just a question of selling off the apartment, the Milford house and a few miscellaneous assets. But none of that mattered. He saw the headlights of a car driving out to meet the plane.

He put on his sports jacket, checking the right breast pocket where he normally kept his Blackberry to confirm that his toothbrush, his only luggage, was there. Then he started down the steps.

The back window of the car rolled open and he could see Yassar's head, his black eyes picking up the reflected light. The other rear door opened and Sasha emerged, eyes flashing, a few wisps of hair streaming sideways in the breeze.

Daniel paused when he saw her. He didn't think there was a way to explain what he was feeling, seeing Sasha frozen there, black eyes sparkling, that one moment seeming from another time. He met her at the bottom of the steps and embraced her as though he finally knew he was home.

"What took you so long?" she said.

The End

THE GRAVY TRAIN

A WALL STREET NOVELLA BY

DAVID LENDER

ONE

Finn Keane and Kathy Fargo sat next to each other in the back of Room 12 in the McColl Building at the University of North Carolina's Keenan-Flagar Business School. Four rows separated them from the rest of the group in the Investment Banking Club meeting. At least 25 group members attended; this evening featured Jonathan Moore, the club's president, crowing about his recruitment process and offer to become an Associate in Goldman Sachs's Mergers & Acquisitions Group.

Finn leaned toward Kathy and said, "If I listen to any more of this crap I'm gonna puke. Come on, let's go get a coffee or something."

She smiled at him, nodded and they got up and left. A few heads turned as they clunked through the theater-style seats to the aisle, up the steps and out the door. Finn could feel eyes burning into his back. He was sure everybody in the club knew that Kathy and he were the only two who hadn't received investment banking offers yet.

Finn held the front door to the McColl Building for Kathy as they went outside. She wasn't a girl many guys held doors for, not much of a looker, so he knew Kathy liked it and always made sure to do it. When she'd told him she couldn't afford to fly home to Chicago for Thanksgiving, he'd brought her home to Cedar Fork. Afterward Uncle Bob said, "Wow, she's a big-boned one, huh?" Even before he brought her home, he could tell Kathy wanted something more between them. And a couple of times out drinking with classmates she made it clear to Finn it was there for him if he wanted it. He was always glad when he woke up sober the next day that he didn't do it; he'd always have felt like he was taking advantage of her. He could tell she'd now settled into the knowledge it wasn't gonna happen.

Kathy smiled and mouthed, "Thank you," as they went outside.

"Moore was a pain in the ass before he got the offer, but now he struts around like a goddamn rooster," Finn said.

"Yeah, but you have to admit, he landed the big one."

Finn just nodded.

Kathy said, "I assume no change at your end or you'd have told me something."

"No."

"We're running out of time."

"I know. I'm taking the TD Bank thing if nothing else comes through. At least that'll get me to New York."

Kathy didn't reply. He knew what she was thinking. She'd said it before: she'd worked in New York for three years before business school and told him New York wasn't all it was cracked up to be.

"How about you?" he said.

"I guess I'll take that Internet startup my friend offered me."

Finn nodded. She'd told him about it, but he couldn't remember the details. Only five or six employees, he thought.

"You did computer programming before B-school, didn't you?"

"Yeah, but they want me to be CFO. They're all a bunch of undergrad computer science jocks. Don't know anything about finance."

"Sounds like it could be fun," Finn said, knowing he didn't sound convincing as the words came out. Nothing like that for him. If nothing in investment banking came through, he'd get to New York, then see if he could leverage the TD Bank commercial banking training program into a job on Wall Street, even if it took him a few years. That's where he'd make it big. He looked at Kathy. "I forget. What's the company's name?"

"Facebook."

TWO

"I WANT BODIES," SIMON BUCHANNAN said. "Give me at least thirty. Maybe forty." He stood up and looked at his four department heads across his desk, then strode out from behind it with long Senior Managing Director strides of his six-foot-six-inch frame. Buchannan took his time crossing the oversized office, wanting to seem he was looming out at his subordinates from between the skyscrapers up Park Avenue, like some avenging angel. He sat down in the semicircle where his department heads reclined in soft chairs and a sofa around Buchannan's coffee table.

"We've already hired two hundred Associates for this year's incoming class," the head of the Mergers & Acquisitions Group said.

"Then hire two hundred thirty or two hundred forty," Buchannan shot back. Buchannan's eyes accused him of incompetence.

"It's April, Simon," the Head of Corporate Finance said.

"Fellas, what is this?" Buchannan said and stood up. He summoned his best impatient sigh. "The markets are booming. IPOs. Converts. High yield. Rates are low. The economy's chugging along and corporate earnings are still going up, up, up. The entire Street's firing on all cylinders. We need to bang this cycle until it drops." He started pacing. "Bang it. Bang it hard. And BofA Merrill Lynch is still number one. You saw the first quarter underwriting statistics. I wanna beat these guys in equity offerings this year, give us a couple more years to catch them in debt underwritings, and in another year or two we'll take on Goldman Sachs for number one in the M&A rankings." He stopped and looked at his department heads, disappointed they didn't seem to be summoning some urge to go out and win one for the Gipper. Maybe they were all immune to him by now because he intentionally acted so crazy and made himself so scary looking half the time. But Buchannan meant it. He wanted to win.

"Simon, it's April," his head of Corporate Finance, John "Stinky" Bates, reminded him again.

"So it's fucking April."

"Yes, it's fucking April and all the top kids from all the top business schools are gone. We've milked Harvard, Stanford, Kellogg, Wharton, Chicago, all of them dry."

"So get me lateral hires from other firms. Dip down to the second tier business schools, hell, go to the third tier if you have to, just get me the bodies. Or it's my ass." Buchannan thought of the new house his wife had been harping about, prayed to the unknown for a $15 million bonus again, then thought of what his mistress wanted and looked back at his department heads in renewed earnest. "I didn't get to be head of Investment Banking by screwing up, and if I start firing blanks, I'm gonna be out on my ear." Buchannan gave Bates a look that told Bates he was lazy, stupid and paunchy. "Got that, Stinky?"

Bates nodded that he did. Probably even the look. The four department heads got up to leave after Buchannan signaled the meeting was over by striding back behind his desk and punching the phone keys, holding the receiver to his ear.

He saw Bates hovering in the doorway as the other three department heads left. *Rolling their eyes.* Yeah, they were tired of Buchannan's antics. Hell, they were just tired. Business was so good they were run ragged. They knew better than anyone they needed the help. Buchannan was preaching to the converted. Buchannan saw Bates turn back to face him.

Buchannan finished his call and hung up. "Something I can do for you?" Buchannan said. He hoped Bates heard the word "Stinky" in his tone even though he didn't use it again.

"I need a minute."

"You seem to be taking it. What can I do for you?"

"It's about Shane." Bates shifted his weight onto his other foot. His big gut sloshed to the side. Buchannan looked at it with disdain. "All of the department heads are cooperating—M&A, High Yield, Corporate Finance—"

"I know what our departments are, John."

"Yeah," Bates said, shifting his weight back to his other foot. "Well, everybody's working together just fine, even across the sector specialties," he paused. "Everybody except Shane. He's still a lone wolf just like he's always been since he joined us."

Buchannan stared at Bates, impatient. "You think I give a shit? Shane is Shane. He's the only other Senior Managing Director around here but me for a reason. Because he's a money-maker. He's got big clients, he's the best new business guy I've ever seen and he's one of the crispest execution guys we've got. My attitude with Shane is to stay out of his way and let him do what he does best. Just keep feeding him bodies to help him process his deals, give him his slice of the fees and then count the money."

"But it's not setting a good example, it's not good for the rest of the teams to see they can still elbow each other out of the way."

"Let me ask you something, John. How long you been head of Corporate Finance?"

"About four years."

"Well, it seems to me you should be more worried about how much longer you can stay that way than worrying about Shane. Because four years is an eternity by Wall Street standards," and in the same instant Buchannan thought of his own six-year tenure as head of Investment Banking, "so if I were you I'd spend more time worrying about your own ass than Shane's." Buchannan punctuated the sentence with a glare that sent Bates out the door.

Jack Shane descended in the elevator to the 45th floor of 280 Park Avenue. Since he'd boarded the elevator on the Penthouse, 46th floor, his eyes had been tracking his path, assuming the role of his client's first impression. His office was up there with the other senior luminaries—Simon Buchannan, the two Vice Chairmen and the CEO of Abercrombie, Wirth & Co., or "ABC" as the investment banking firm was known on Wall Street. He took in the polished mahogany and brass of the elevator doors—one of four elevators that were dedicated to the firm's seven top floors of the building—then watched them slide open into the 45th-floor lobby. The lobby was a faux-finish limestone block, a knockoff of the real limestone in the firm's former downtown offices. The detailed observer could tell it wasn't real, but the ambiance was unmistakable. Particularly when you turned to walk into the spacious reception area. Period furniture, a mixture of tasteful reproductions and genuine antiques. Persian rugs and a drop-dead gorgeous receptionist. Today she was Little Miss Something-Or-Other, a 25-year-old voluptuous brunette with a pouting mouth and soulful eyes, sitting behind a tiger maple veneer Beidermeier four-legged desk, open at the bottom to show off her legs.

Shane nodded, not so much to acknowledge her but in deference to her beauty, and Miss Something-Or-Other responded with a brilliant smile. Shane took a left down the corridor toward the conference rooms, his feet hushed on the Persian runner that ran the entire length of the building toward Park Avenue. He continued to absorb it all through the eyes of Stanley Waldwrick, the CEO of Kristos & Company. Stanley was a small-minded Boston WASP and the son-in-law of the founder of the company. After six months of Shane's nursing, cajoling and ministering to Stanley's ego, Shane had figured out what Stanley really wanted to do was show his father-in-law he could catapult the northeastern regional department store chain into a nationwide business with a major acquisition. This would be Stanley's first visit to ABC's offices in New York and Shane wanted it to go just right. He wanted the right amount of mood, panache and bare-knuckles Wall Street pressure.

This'll do, Shane thought. The marble floor of the lobby, Miss So-And-So behind the desk, the swish of feet on the plush carpets, the elements had been perfectly designed to impress with an Old World elegance. In his four years at ABC, Shane had always believed it was a good platform for him, the seventh firm he had been with in 24 years on the Street. *I just might stay*, he had once remarked to himself.

Shane picked up the pace. He wanted to get to the conference room early. In time to have a minute with Stinky Bates, the head of Corporate Finance, and Charles Fitzgibbons, the head of the Mergers & Acquisitions Group. At 50 years old, Shane was still slim and athletic, and wore his clothes with the air of a man who had them custom made for him, because he did. He was tall, six feet four inches, and loved the look of himself reflected in the glass of the conference rooms. Gucci loafers. Sharp creases, and although you couldn't see them beneath his midnight-blue suit jacket, suspenders that matched his tie. All carried off with a practiced, devil-may-care attitude. His dark-brown hair was slicked back. His eyes were bloodshot, as they always were, like he'd stayed up too late the night before or had done too much cocaine. He smelled faintly of soap. No cologne.

He reached the door of the conference room, at the northwest corner of the building facing north on Park Avenue. Bates and Fitzgibbons were already there. He'd made sure that Buchannan made sure that they would be. "Morning," he said without emotion. Fitzgibbons, the head of M&A, was on the phone and didn't look up. Bates turned and nodded to Shane. Shane closed the door behind him and stood in the doorway, again seeing the room through his client's eyes. The bright light of the day and the grandeur of Park Avenue skyscrapers gleamed in through the windows. The room was a continuation of the seductive opulence of the rest of the place. The polished antique conference table and Chippendale chairs reeked of money. Old World, New World, definitely not nouveau riche money. But better-than-you, some-son-in-law-from-Boston, money.

Shane strode across the room and stood in front of Fitzgibbons. He waved at him until Fitzgibbons put his hand over the receiver.

"Yeah?"

"I'd like a minute with the two of you before Stanley gets here." Fitzgibbons nodded and then turned his back to Shane to finish his conversation. Shane crossed the room again to the console that was bedecked with danish, bagels and fruits, and poured himself a cup of coffee.

"How's it going, Stinky?" Shane said with his back to Bates. Shane chuckled under his breath, guessing how Bates was reacting to the hated nickname. Fitzgibbons hung up the phone.

"Morning, Jack," Fitzgibbons said. He leaned on one leg, pulling his jacket open with one hand and thrusting it into his pocket, posing like a window display in Paul Stuart. "I'm all yours," he said. "How long you figure this will take?" He looked at his watch, then up at Shane again.

"Half hour for you guys, then I'll stay with him from there." He looked at each of them in turn. "Thanks for coming," he added, half under his breath as if it hurt him to say it. "I'll make this brief." Shane sat down at the far end of the table. Fitzgibbons took a seat at the exact opposite end when he saw Shane do so.

"Stanley is the CEO of Kristos & Company, a chain of 160 regional stores in the northeast. Middle-end department stores, started in the 1950s by his father-in-law, Nikolas Christanapoulas. The old man built it up to its present size, then passed the reins about a year ago to the son-in-law, because he had turned 70, wanted to retire and didn't have any male heirs." He looked at Bates, who still stood awkwardly leaning on one leg, and then at Fitzgibbons. He saw they understood. He took a long sip of his black coffee. "So Stanley decides he wants to make a big splash, and as you know, Charles, we've got him teed up to buy Milstein Brothers Stores, the 50 store nationwide high-end department store chain. It's about a $3 billion deal, worth roughly three times as much as Kristos & Company is worth." *About $15 million in fees for that piece,* Shane thought, not permitting himself to do the exact calculation in deference to his superstition. "We do a $550 million IPO for Kristos & Company, which I presume you know all about, John," he said toward Bates rather than to him, refusing to meet eyes with him, "and then a $1.5 billion high yield deal. The use of proceeds for the financings is to acquire Milstein Brothers, except for $50 million father-in-law's taking off the table by selling some of his shares in the IPO."

Shane looked at the other two, who nodded that they understood.

"You being taken care of with staffing on the M&A side?" Fitzgibbons said.

"I could use another pair of hands, you know that."

"We're a little tight right now, like we've been telling you. But we're going to get a pack of new Associates in here pretty soon. Hang in there for a while, we'll get you covered in a month or so," Fitzgibbons said. Bates shifted his weight again.

"Okay, so that's the story, which I presume both of you guys have read in the briefing books," Shane said. He resisted the urge to scowl. He knew damn well these guys hadn't read any of the materials he'd had prepared for either the M&A deal or the IPO. They probably skimmed a one- or two-page note prepared by some poor slob Associate or Vice President on their staffs. But that was it today in investment banking. Senior guys didn't really know what was going on. They just popped into meetings to wave the flag to impress clients that the head of this or that gave a damn about their deal. Guys like Shane were a dying breed, bankers who did soup-to-nuts for their clients: conceived the deals, actually gave advice on strategy and did the execution themselves. None of this specialist bullshit where a guy stepped in and did his two little pieces and then left. Well, they'd get him through this phase, because Stanley really wanted to see the head of M&A and the head of Corporate Finance to know the "experts" were paying attention to his deals.

"So we jawbone the guy for half an hour or so, and then you guys are free to go. Any questions?" They both shook their heads. Shane nodded and turned to pour himself another cup of coffee, then looked at his watch. *Ten minutes*, he thought. Fitzgibbons stood up and went back to the telephone.

"Stanley!" Shane said in his practiced, melodious baritone when an attractive blonde showed Stanley into the conference room. The blonde lowered her eyes demurely and pulled the door closed behind Stanley.

"Jack, always great to see you," Stanley said in a Northeastern-boarding-school voice, while pumping on Shane's hand. Stanley was tall, blond and thin. He parted his hair in the middle and wore a correspondingly WASPy three-button suit. Shane smiled and extended an arm toward the center of the room. He made sure his brown eyes swam with goodwill.

"Thanks, Stanley, and you, too. And let me introduce my colleagues, John Bates, Managing Director and Head of all ABC's Corporate Finance activities, and John Fitzgibbons, Managing Director and Head of ABC's Mergers & Acquisitions Group." Shane threw a look of collegial affection at each of his colleagues as he introduced them. They walked across the room to shake hands with Stanley, Bates with his jacket buttoned and Fitzgibbons with one hand still in his pocket, bright blue suspenders showing against an English striped shirt of yellow and blue, and a matching blue Gucci tie with the label splayed outward.

Coffee and breakfast was offered. Additional pleasantries were exchanged. They sat down around one end of the table with Stanley at the head and got down to business.

"Stanley, as I told you, I thought you might like to hear from the Department heads who would oversee your transactions, and whose teams would report in to me." Shane gave Stanley another of his client smiles, then nodded to each of his colleagues. "Our objective for today is to give you the comfort that we can bring the resources to bear on your proposed deals, give you a sense of the commitment of the firm to Kristos & Company, and of course to you personally Stanley, and then we can handle some of the details on our engagement structure later, perhaps after lunch. We've got a dining room booked across the floor at 12:30. I'll be introducing you to Steven Dick, the Chairman of our firm at that time. But for now, I thought it might make sense to let you hear from John and Charles, here, about what we see for the respective deals. Sound okay?" Shane said and opened his palms toward Stanley.

"Absolutely," Stanley said and rested his folded hands on the table.

"Maybe I should speak first, since the M&A transaction on Milstein Brothers Stores is the crux of the whole thing," Fitzgibbons said. "As you know directly from your own meetings with the Milstein brothers, they are favorably disposed and we're drafting the definitive purchase agreement right now. Through Jack's good offices we know you're being well taken care of, but you should also know that one of our other colleagues has the direct relationship with the Milstein brothers and he also says they're delighted with the prospective transaction. Everything seems poised for a deal thanks to Jack, and I've got some of my best guys working with Jack and your attorneys at Winston & Sterling."

Shane's mind drifted off as Fitzgibbons went through his shtick. IPO and high-yield financing and M&A fees. Then there was the bank financing of about $1 billion. *All-in about $90 million in fees,* Shane thought. *And after these guys get done salami-ing off whatever they can get their hands on, it should still about make my year. Let's hope the markets hold up.* He looked at Stanley. Shane noted the pinkish glow under his skin, a glow of vulnerability. *And let's hope you don't get hit by a truck, dear Stanley. And that old man Nick decides not to step back in and change the game plan.*

After Fitzgibbons was through, Bates did his part. Shane was actually impressed. Bates carried it off with style, relating the history of the growth of the 1,000-strong Investment Banking Group of Abercrombie, Wirth & Co., describing its downtown roots from a 50-person boutique firm specializing in corporate advisory to its current stature as the last privately owned of the elite Wall Street firms that dominated the underwriting, mergers and acquisitions, and capital markets businesses. "We're considered the guys to watch, because we're the ones with the momentum. And we're having fun," Bates said, smiling with sincerity, conveying a warmth that again surprised Shane. "We like our business, we enjoy our clients, and we'd be happy to count you among them."

Afterward Shane walked Stanley back along the same route through which he had entered, then downstairs to the 42nd-floor trading room. The trading floor took up the entire 100,000-square-foot floor and was three stories high, extending up to the 45th floor. The effect was intoxicating, as always. Hundreds of shouting, gesturing, and athletic young bodies, barking into telephones, hollering at each other, all banked in row upon row of high-tech Bloomberg and analytical trading screens stacked two and three high, blinking in multihued colors. The noise, the phones, the energy, all rose in a multitudinous din that said, "This is where it happens. This is where it is. The money." Stanley seemed awestruck.

Over lunch he spilled his wine, which delighted Shane. *Great, keep him off balance.* Shane zeroed in on Stanley after that. By 2:00 p.m. he was in front of the building with Stanley to deposit him in a limo.

"Great day," Stanley said, pumping Shane's hand again. "We'll have to do that golf game before the deal's done."

"Absolutely," Shane said and closed the limo door. *Golf,* he thought as he headed back into the building, *now there's a dumbass game.* Thousands of hours of practice to sit in a goofy little cart with a numbskull twit like Stanley for five hours. He'd rather get his fingers smashed in a car door. If Stanley'd said tennis, maybe. At least that was a man's game. There you worked up a sweat, got a chance to pound out some aggressions, even smash the shit out of the ball down the other guy's throat. *Golf, my ass.*

Five minutes later Shane sat with his feet up on his desk, an executed original of his engagement letter propped in his lap. "All right, Stanley, away we go," he said aloud.

Excerpt from *Bull Street*

BULL STREET

A WALL STREET NOVEL BY

DAVID LENDER

CHAPTER 1

New York City. Before the global financial crisis.

"If I don't have a job by April, I'm not getting one," Richard said. "At least that's the adage at B-school."

"And this the Ides of March," Dad said.

That ominous reference hit home. Richard's guts rumbled.

Richard Blum and his dad, Hank, sat in a Greek diner in downtown Manhattan near Wall Street. It was two blocks from Walker & Company, Richard's first interview of the day, and four blocks from Dad's insurance convention. Richard played with the tag on his teabag, preoccupied; this five-day trip to New York was his last chance to salvage a job on Wall Street from an otherwise failed recruiting season. It was opportune that Dad and he could squeeze in breakfast together while Dad was in town from St. Paul at the same time for his convention. They sat at a booth across from the counter, leaning in toward each other so they could hear over the clink of china, barked orders, the clang of spatulas on the grill. Richard savored the clamor and aromas of the place. It had a casual comfort, a folksy smell of eggs and home fries Richard knew Dad must be enjoying. He eased up his cuff to check his watch.

"You getting concerned?" Dad asked.

"It's never over until you call it quits, I guess, but in finance parlance I'm a wasting asset."

"Not what I asked. You worried?"

"Sweating bullets."

He looked at Dad's clothes: cotton/polyester button-down, spot on his pin-dot tie, suit shiny from wear. He smiled; it made him comfortable, too, warmed him inside. He glanced down at his own clothes. He was wearing $3,500 in Polo Ralph Lauren. The topcoat he'd sprung for as part of this last-ditch effort to land the big one was dragging on the floor. A barometer for how it was going.

"You must be making progress, though."

"I've struck out in all my on-campus investment banking interviews—the few I've gotten."

Dad just nodded, taking it in, thinking. "Anything useful to you come of them?"

"Only that Michigan's a second-tier school for the Wall Street firms. The entire recruiting season of interviews only netted all our MBAs twelve investment banking second-round callbacks on campus, four trips to New York, one offer."

"That's at least one." Dad, trying to be positive. He smiled, then squinted and pursed his lips. "There must be others coming to campus."

"No. It's too late in the season for first rounds on campus." Richard resisted the urge to squirm in his seat. "So that's it for anything through the Placement Office."

Dad winced. He looked down at his plate, hesitated, then back in Richard's eyes. "Now this trip," he said, continuing to eye him. Richard first thought Dad's expression meant he realized this was Richard's last gasp. Now he had an inkling maybe there was more to Dad's look than that.

"Yeah, eleventh-hour effort. In New York to pound the pavement, follow up on cold letters attaching my resume. See if I can beat down some doors."

Dad leaned back. "So how's the trip going?" Richard felt him zeroing in, watching him.

"Four screening interviews, down to my last two." Richard started twirling the tag from his teabag again, beginning to get anxious, knowing today's interview was his only real chance.

"Remember *A Mathematician's Apology*?" Dad said. His gaze was now locked in on Richard, intent. Richard swallowed.

"How could I forget? It's been a big influence on me."

It was the book Richard and Dad had both read as he headed to college. Richard was turning the corner from defiant teenager, starting to get close with Dad again, this time man-to-man. When Richard landed the job after college writing ad copy at McAlister & Flinn, still living at home, he and Dad developed a working relationship. Dad helped out as proofreader and critic. Richard learned Dad actually had business wisdom to impart; insurance was at least on the same hemisphere as writing copy to convince people to buy steak sauce or annuities. Business became a common language and culture that kept them up late nights, talking about interest rates, the CPI. And eventually, over a scotch now and then, they discussed the novels of Elmore Leonard or Trollope, the music of Mozart and Beethoven. Richard thought back to *A Mathemetician's Apology*, said as if reciting, "Three kinds of people. The first, I do what I do because I have an unusual talent for it. The second, I do what I do because I do lots of things pretty well and this was as good a choice as any. And the third, I don't do anything very well and I fell into this."

"I'm a good fidelity bond underwriter, and I could've done a lot of other things probably just as well. What you're going after is a world I don't understand much about. But if you think you have it, go for it." Still searching Richard's face.

"Yeah. I can do this." Telling himself, needing it for this interview.

"So don't give up. But don't compromise who you are and where you came from. Don't let Wall Street turn your head."

"Any other advice?"

"Well, since you ask," Dad said, now giving him that half-smile he wore when he launched a zinger but still wanted to show affection. "All I've heard is excuses. This isn't like you. Get primal. Think like these Wall Street guys, like a caveman who needs to win over a woman or he can't procreate. Put some oomph into it. You're on your own; nobody can do it for you."

They sat in silence a moment, Richard looking at the half-smile still on Dad's face. Dad was right. *It's all up to me.*

Dad said, "What? You think I can't still kick your butt?"

Richard felt his throat thicken. "Thanks."

"You're very welcome."

Richard looked at his watch. Dad grabbed the check, said, "Get going. Give yourself some time to collect your thoughts."

"Why don't you let me get this?"

"When you're a mogul you can buy me dinner." They both stood. Dad stuck out his hand. They shook, then hugged.

"Love to Mom," Richard said.

"Call her. Tell her yourself."

Richard nodded. "Any final thoughts?"

"If you fall flat you know you can always come home to regroup." He smiled. "But you aren't going to let that happen. Both you and I know that, don't we?"

Richard looked at his watch: 7:45. *He's late.* He sat in Walker & Company's reception area at 55 Water Street, waiting for his interview with François LeClaire. And he'd rushed through breakfast to get here by 7:30. He caught himself clenching and unclenching his fingers into his palms, forced himself to relax them.

Great. More time to ponder the imponderable.

Richard picked up a magazine from a Sheraton end table next to the antique Chippendale chair he sat in. *Fortune.* The current issue; Harold Milner was on the cover. He'd also graced the covers of *Forbes* and *Financier* magazines over the last decade. In the cover picture for the article, "Financial Engineering on Steroids," Milner stood in a conference room at Walker & Company. It was probably the very one Richard sat outside now. The picture showed Milner framed against the backdrop of the Brooklyn Bridge, the back door entrance to Wall Street. Inside the issue Richard knew the first page of the article showed a photograph of Jack Grass and Mickey Steinberg standing on either side of Milner. He was Walker & Company's most important and prolific client. Richard knew all about these guys. He'd been Googling them before Google was a verb.

The *Fortune* article got it mostly right, although it was obvious to Richard he'd done more research on Milner than its author. Milner, then Chief Financial Officer of Coastal+Northern Corporation, had taken his entrepreneurial leap at 40 years old. He'd cashed in his C+N stock options for $1.5 million, used them for his first deal and never looked back. Now his $7 billion private empire employed 17,000 people in 22 states. The article called him brilliant, eccentric, wildly creative, and a compulsive workaholic—one of the most powerful and wealthy entrepreneurs in the U.S.

Richard looked into the open door of the conference room at the table set for breakfast. He imagined Milner, Jack and Mickey discussing a deal over breakfast and felt an airiness in his stomach.

Richard saw a young guy, probably an Associate, walking toward him. He had his jacket off, a pile of papers and some presentation books in his hands, quick pace, looking tense. *Yeah, an Associate, probably first year.* He hurried past Richard and peered into the conference room. Seeing no one there, he sat down in the chair across from Richard, apparently waiting. He was twitchy and sweaty. It made Richard feel sorry for him. The guy's papers started sliding out of his lap. Richard reached out to help him but the guy shook Richard off, reined them in himself.

Richard now saw the guy checking him out, probably guessing why Richard was here.

"Who you waiting for?" he asked.

"François LeClaire." Richard saw his face show recognition, then his forehead wrinkle with tension. The guy sighed and leaned back in his chair. At that moment his BlackBerry vibrated in his belt and he sat up with a start. Richard heard someone talk fast and loud on the other end of the call. The guy left in a hurry, papers rustling. Richard got the uncomfortable sense that this could be him in a few months, stealing a moment of relaxation as he waited for somebody to yell at him about a column of numbers that didn't add up.

The elevator door opened and Richard turned to see Harold Milner, the man himself, walking toward him. Milner carried himself with an understated manner that somehow magnified his power and importance. Richard instinctively stood, and then a surge of adrenaline froze him in place like a ten-year-old meeting Babe Ruth. He realized as Milner approached he was as big as the Babe up close, too. Six feet five or so, thick in the chest like a football lineman, massive hands. Trademark shaved head. He cruised up to Richard. "Harold Milner," he said, extending his hand. Just like that.

Richard felt himself starting to speak without knowing what would come out. He said something gushy after introducing himself, his voice faint as he said, "Mr. Milner."

"Call me Harold." Milner looked into the empty conference room, then sat where the Associate had moments earlier. He glanced down at the copy of *Fortune* Richard still clutched. "And I'm not as bad as they say," he said. "Or as smart."

Richard smiled, more relaxed now. His body had unfrozen and he sat back down, now sitting with Harold Milner like they were shooting the breeze. "I'm not sure I believe that."

"Which? Bad or smart?"

"Smart. I'd say you've done okay...Harold." "Harold" came out haltingly, Richard trying it out.

"Yeah, well, 'with money in your pocket, you are wise and you are handsome and you sing well, too.'"

"F. Scott Fitzgerald?"

"Yiddish proverb. Don't believe everyone's press clippings."

"Hard to believe you've just been lucky."

"No, but the stuff in that article is downright silly."

Richard smiled. "You've done some interesting deals."

"Yeah, but this 'steroids' nonsense is just to sell magazines. My approach is about as low tech as they come."

"I don't know. On the Brennan deal it was pretty exotic the way you set up that special-purpose subsidiary to finance the receivables on the McGuffin division."

Miller gave him a shrug and a look that said, "So?"

"So, that extra financing gave you about a 20% price advantage over the other bidders. It got you the deal."

"Maybe."

"And on Dresner Steel, the way you sold off two of the divisions and merged the rest with Tilson Manufacturing and Milburg Industries within a year. How many guys could pull that off and still keep the tax-loss carryforwards intact?"

Milner looked at Richard as if pondering something for a moment. He said, "Good insights. I'm impressed. But I'll let you in on a little secret. I don't consider I've done anything particularly imaginative or creative in my life. I stick to simple, risk-averse basics. You know who Vince Lombardi was?"

"I'm from Minnesota. Our state seal has an image of the Packers kicking the Vikings' asses."

Milner smiled. "I'm like Lombardi's Green Bay Packers. We come up to the line and crouch in position for an end sweep. The defense knows it's probably an end sweep because it's second and seven, and, besides, Lombardi's only got ten plays in his playbook anyhow. Whattaya think we do?"

"Throw an eight-yard pass to the opposite sideline."

"End sweep, perfectly done. Seven yards every time. Nothing exotic, just basic execution."

Richard wanted to ask him if this "aw shucks" routine disarmed CEOs whose companies he was trying to take over, but settled for: "Good story. Works for me."

Milner put his elbow on the end table, cupped a big hand over his mouth. Richard could see him smiling with his eyes, apparently thinking. He remained silent, then: "Are you new?"

"So new I'm not even here."

Milner scrunched his eyebrows like he was puzzled.

"I'm waiting here for an interview," Richard said. Milner smiled with his eyes, his hand over his mouth again. "I think the guy who was supposed to meet you was just called away."

"Well, then you stepped in and did the job. You got my vote." He stood up and held out his hand, a big smile on his face. Richard got up and shook hands with him again. "Welcome to the firm, Richard," Milner said.

Richard laughed. Not a nervous one because he was freaked out that he was actually bullshitting with the most famous guy in finance. He just laughed because it was funny, Milner telling him to call him Harold, putting him at ease, joking around. Not some stiff, but a regular guy.

They were still shaking hands, Richard laughing, when Jack Grass and Mickey Steinberg walked up. There he was, standing among the guys who'd done 15 major deals together over the last 20 years, not including scores of financings, refinancings, divisional divestitures and add-on acquisitions; a mini industry, the three of them.

Richard heard Jack and Mickey greet Milner, saw them shake hands, exchange a few good-natured barbs. But not clearly, not like it was real, because he was now somehow out of his body watching from a distance. He zeroed in on Milner, larger than life again. The casualness that said he didn't need to make an effort to impress was still there. Now Richard took in Mickey, Walker's genius in Mergers and Acquisitions, who droned on in a monotone, frizzy Jewish hair, sleepy eyes. Mickey was probably laying out some wisdom, because Milner gave him his complete attention, nodding as Mickey spoke. Now Richard studied Jack, the firm's Chief Executive Officer. Jack stood smoothing the peaked lapels on his European-inspired suit, looking artfully put together from his French tie and matching pocket square down to his Italian loafers. Jack's eyes moved around like a big jungle cat's. Watching Milner, taking in everything, now sizing up Richard, now back to Milner and Mickey. His athletic build showed in the close-fit suit, shirt cuffs protruding Cary Grant–like from his sleeves, hair razor-cut, Palm Beach tan standing out against his white collar and cuffs.

They walked into the conference room, Milner smiling and lifting a hand in a restrained wave good-bye to Richard. Jack Grass saw it and glanced back at Richard, seeming to make a mental note.

Richard looked into the open door of the conference room. A mahogany table was set for three, bedecked with crystal, china, formal silver and fresh linen. Its subdued sheen and worn edges showed graceful age, complemented by the oriental rug it sat on. The aroma of rosemary and eggs mixed with some other scent he couldn't identify emanated from an unseen kitchen.

Richard wished he could listen in on their meeting, be in the room with them. Hell, he wanted more than anything to *be* one of them, particularly Milner. He was a big part of why Richard was here.

Just as they sat down at the table to breakfast, a trim man in a double-breasted suit walked into the reception area with an air that he owned the place. Richard took him in: slicked-back hair, pocket square that matched his bold Hermes tie, English-striped shirt with white cuffs showing below his jacket sleeves. *A Jack Grass wannabe?* He walked erect, lips pursed, projecting arrogance. *LeClaire, no doubt.* He'd be the most important person in Richard's life for the next hour.

"François LeClaire. Sorry I am late." He smiled, but modestly, as if to overdo it would wrinkle his suit. His accent had the exaggerated edge of a cartoon character, almost too pronounced to be real. "Conference call to Europe. Unavoidable," now adopting a manner like Richard, of course, knew the import of all this. He shook Richard's hand like he wanted to leave no doubt he understood the concept of a firm American handshake. He extended his other hand in the direction of the offices with the formality of a Swiss hotelier.

Here we go. Richard resisted the urge to peek back at Milner.

Harold Milner looked down at the rosemary and goat cheese omelet on his plate, then at his hands; the meaty hands of a carpenter or mason. But for some turns in his life, that could've been him. It was something he tried hard never to forget. He couldn't help laughing at himself now: he was uneasy, and trying to hide it. He'd been at the deals business a long time. Lots of tense moments, tough deals, pressure. But he rarely felt like this.

He looked over at Jack and Mickey. They sure took Milner back. Twenty years of dreaming, manipulating, trial and error, making it work. Elbow-to-elbow, the three of them. Jack, the ideas guy, sitting there now, puffing and blowing, preening himself in that $5,000 custom suit. Mickey the planner and thinker. Jack should thank God he had Mickey. He made Jack's schemes real. And it really wasn't just Mickey's brains and technical mastery; it was Jack's crazy ideas, because without Jack's dreaming Mickey wouldn't have had anything to breathe life into.

Before he met these two he was just a scrappy guy doing pint-sized deals. Then he met Jack, and a month later, this new guy he had in tow, Steinberg—Mickey, not a nickname for Michael, just Mickey—short, plump, and unathletic. They both showed up at Milner's New York office in that dowdy building he'd started out in at 8ᵗʰ Avenue and 34ᵗʰ Street. Smelled like the Chinese restaurant downstairs. Jack grinning his golden-boy grin in a $2,000 English-cut suit, still only 31 years old and Walker's top producer, already running the firm's Corporate Finance Department. Mickey blinking slowly, shaking hands more firmly than Milner expected from someone with that weasely face and punch-drunk demeanor.

Jack pitched the Caldor idea almost before they sat down, itching to get at it. Jack talking nonsense about buying a billion dollars of debt owed the retailer Caldor by its credit card customers for 20cents on the dollar. Mickey explaining that Caldor was near-bankrupt and desperate for cash. Jack saying Caldor's credit card customers would ultimately pay their bills, Milner would make a killing. Mickey laying out how to finance the deal. Back and forth, Milner's eyes shooting from one to the other like at a tennis match. Then Jack telling Milner all he had to kick in was $10 to $12 million, maybe make 20 to 30 times his investment in a few years. Milner thinking, *that* got his attention, whoever these guys were.

It had turned out to be a recipe for an incredible home run: Milner had invested $16 million of cash, almost all he had lying around, and borrowed the rest to buy Caldor's credit card receivables. After paying off his lenders in two years, Milner had netted $455 million. Jack and Mickey had propelled Milner into the big time. Within a year he bought a Lear jet and apartments in New York, Palm Beach and Los Angeles. He moved his office to the penthouse of the Helmsley Building; the anchor of the 45ᵗʰ Street entrance to New York's power alley business district on Park Avenue. And that had only been the beginning.

But now, this was the end.

"I wanna do a deal on Southwest Homes," Milner said.

He saw Jack perk up across the table like a dog sniffing a bone. Mickey was characteristically quiet, eyes blinking. Milner sipped his water, swallowing hard without worrying about that crinkly sound he made. One of the keys to his humble roots that Mary Claire always cast him a disapproving eye about at dinner parties. He didn't have to try to impress these guys.

Mickey said, "Mind if I ask why?"

Milner saw Jack look sideways at Mickey, as if to try to shut him up.

"I don't like the business anymore. Any schmoe who can sign an 'X' on a mortgage application can buy a house he can't afford."

Jack said, "Yeah, a real bubble mentality."

Milner nodded.

Jack said, "This round of musical chairs won't last very long. Better pick your seat before the music stops. Remember when the Internet stock bubble popped?"

Milner felt himself smile beneath his hand, knew it was showing in his eyes. This was Jack at his best: always selling. Milner would miss Jack and Mickey in a way, but they'd become his chaperones on a trip to the dark side. Churning out deals together that just moved pieces around on the table; they were all making piles of money but not creating anything. He'd made a commitment to himself that he'd go back to building companies again, not this "financial engineering on steroids" crap the magazines lauded him for. Even that kid in the lobby only talked about his deals that busted up instead of built things. Milner looked over at Mickey. "Mickey, whattaya think?"

"You want to sell it to a corporate buyer, or do an initial public offering?" Mickey asked.

"Take it public—the IPO."

"The IPO market's still shooting out deals like a baseball pitching machine," Jack said. "And homebuilding stocks are red hot."

"Everything's hot. Maybe too hot," Milner said.

"Yeah, white hot. All the more reason to unload a chunk of Southwest onto the public," Jack said. Why did Jack make even the right answer sound like bullshit half the time?

Mickey said, "It's worth about $1.5 billion. How much do you want to sell?"

Milner put down his fork, rested his elbows on the table and put his hand over his mouth, taking his time. He glanced over at Jack and saw him observing. Milner said, "All of it." He saw the muscles in Jack's jaw flex. Then he saw Jack inhale, sensed the animal arise beneath that bespoke tailoring. *Okay, Jack—ready, shoot, aim.*

"We can sell 100%," Jack said. "A number of 100% IPOs have gotten done lately. And with home prices setting new records each month, and getting a mortgage as easy as eating popcorn, the public markets are bidding up homebuilders' stocks like crazy."

Milner said, "I've noticed." He looked at Mickey.

Mickey said, "In general, Jack's right. But if you sell it all in the IPO you'll take a major discount versus selling, say, half. If you sell it all, people ask: 'What's wrong with it that *he* doesn't want to keep any?'"

"I know. But I like the idea of selling it all. How big a discount would I take?" Milner felt his stomach tighten.

Milner saw Jack and Mickey take time to look at each other. Milner felt himself smiling again. He had to admit he loved watching these guys, had since the beginning. Back and forth.

Jack trying to urge Mickey with a glance and body language, Mickey considering his answer, blinking, contemplating.

Mickey said, "I'd say at least $300 million."

Jack didn't move.

Milner shrugged, then nodded. "Done."

Jack looked over at Milner with his best shit-eating grin.

Milner looked down, observed his hands again. In a way, he'd get to be a carpenter after all. And put in an honest day's work.

Excerpt from *Vaccine Nation*

VACCINE NATION

A THRILLER BY

DAVID LENDER

CHAPTER 1

DANI NORTH WALKED DOWN WEST End Avenue toward the Mercer School, her son Gabe at her side. The air was cold and fresh. Minutes earlier, crossing Broadway, she'd seen tulips on the median, and the leaves on the maple trees were ready to pop. Now, scents of spring—wet earth and hyacinths in window boxes—were apparent. She yawned, bone tired from the hectic weeks of the Tribeca Film Festival wearing her down on top of work and the daily routine of single-parenting a preteen. Tired or not, she was on a high and Gabe walked close enough that she thought to take his hand. *That is, if he'd let me.* She reminded herself it was perfectly normal for a nine-year-old not to want his mom to hold his hand anymore. *Normal.* What would those morons at Division of Youth and Family Services in New Jersey say about that? Probably still call him ADHD and drug him up. She'd love to run DYFS into the ground, along with their partners in crime, the pharmaceutical industry. Legalized drug pushers.

Leave it, she told herself. Channel the anger into something productive. That made her smile. She had, and well. It was starting to feel real that *The Drugging of Our Children,* her latest film, had won best documentary at Tribeca last night. That channeled anger was doing some good, getting the word out. Educating parents about their choices, ones she hadn't been aware of for Gabe. Who knew? If she had, she might never have lost that three-year nightmare of lawsuits with DYFS in Hackensack. It forced her to accept mandatory drugging of Gabe, because otherwise the court would have taken him from her.

She looked over at Gabe now. Chin high, proud of how he looked in his Ralph Lauren blue blazer, gray pants and white oxford button-down, school tie snugged up against his neck. Only his black Vans betrayed his age. *Yes, normal.* Thanks in part to Dr. O.

Gabe caught her looking at him. "Now that you won, you gonna get a bonus and turn the electric back on?"

"You mean 'going to' and 'electricity.'" She thought about the last two weeks of burning candles at night. She'd put off the electric bill in order to scrape up Gabe's tuition for this semester at Mercer. "Besides, we were camping, remember?"

"C'mon, Mom, that worked on me when I was like five years old. I'm not a kid anymore."

"Yes, you are."

Gabe thought for a second. "All right, but I'm not stupid."

"No, I'm not getting a bonus," Dani said, running a hand over Gabe's hair, "but I get paid today and we'll be back to normal. Lights and TV."

"Next time I'm telling Nanny. She'll pay it."

"Do that and you can forget about TV until you're eighteen."

They reached the corner diagonally across West End from the entrance to Mercer. "Leave me here," Gabe said, looking away from her.

Dani didn't respond, just grabbed his shirtsleeve between her fingers and started across the street. He pulled out of her grasp and increased his pace. Dani saw Damien Richardson on the opposite corner as they approached. He stood looking at the half dozen kids grouped around the entrance to Mercer, tentative. She knew the bigger boys picked on Damien. She felt a tug at her heart. "Morning, Damien," she called.

Damien turned to them. His face brightened and he smiled. "Hi, Mrs. North. What's up, Gabe?"

"Come on, Damien," Dani whispered when she reached him. "I'll walk you in."

Ten minutes later she crossed 79th Street toward Broadway, her mind buzzing with last night's triumph and her upcoming day. She pulled her BlackBerry out of her pocket, checked the screen. *8:10.* Enough time to get through her voicemails and emails before Dr. Maguire, the researcher from Pharma International, showed up. Now she wondered again what his agenda was, why he was so anxious and secretive about the meeting. But it was something important—at least to Maguire. She'd been calling him for weeks, coaxing him into an interview for the new documentary on autism she was just beginning. She'd been referred to Maguire by his friend, John McCloskey, the KellerDorne Pharmaceutical technician who'd served as whistleblower on KellerDorne's painkiller, Myriad, after patients who took it started dropping dead from heart attacks. Dani's interview of McCloskey published in the *Crusador* was well after McCloskey went public, but somehow it managed to electrify the issue. As a result, the contributions had flowed into Dr. Orlovski to fund the documentaries he produced, including Dani's *The Drugging of Our Children.*

Maybe Maguire needed to get something off his chest, too. Dani picked up her pace. Her BlackBerry rang and her breath caught in her throat when she saw Mom's number on the screen. How could she forget? *Dad.*

"Hi, Mom. How are you doing?"

"Okay." She paused. "You know what day it is, don't you?"

Dani's mind automatically did the math. She'd been twenty-two. Seven years. "Of course." She stopped walking and leaned over the BlackBerry as if sheltering her words from passersby. She said, "Each year I think about him constantly during this day. Sometimes it seems like. . ." her voice trailed off.

"I miss him more each year, too," Mom said. Her voice was steady, like she'd steeled herself to get through the day.

"When's his Mass?"

"One o'clock."

Dani didn't respond right away. "I can't make it this year."

"I know, sweetie. I just wanted to hear your voice. I knew you weren't coming. You had a big day yesterday. Congratulations. I'm sure lots of people want to talk to you."

"It's not that. I'm just jammed with the usual stuff. Will you light a candle for me?"

"Sure. I'll speak to you later. Gabe okay?"

"He's great. Maybe we'll get out this weekend. How's Jack?"

"The same." Dani felt her hand muscles tense around the BlackBerry.

"Anything going on?"

"The usual. He was out most of the night, couldn't get up for work."

"I'll get out there this weekend," Dani said. They signed off. She continued walking, feeling guilty. Lisa and George lived far enough away that they never made Dad's Mass. And Jack was high half the time, so it was like she was alone even if he came with her. At least Mom could count on Dani. Or so she thought. This was the second year in a row Dani would miss Dad's Mass. It hurt. Particularly knowing how devout a Catholic Mom was, how much Mom wanted Dani to experience her faith the way she did. She sighed and kept walking, thinking she'd find a way to make it up to Mom, feeling unworthy.

Dani reached the entrance to Dr. Yuri Orlovski's office at 79th and Broadway. A half dozen patients already sat in the waiting room when she stepped through the door. She paused to wave at Carla behind the reception desk, who mouthed "Congratulations." Dani nodded and smiled, then headed up the steep, 20 steps to her office. By the time she reached the top, she reflected as she usually did, *What would I do without Dr. O?* It was the best job she'd ever had, even aside from him rescuing Gabe a year ago from Child Protective Services, New York's equivalent of New Jersey's DYFS. Dr. O's homeopathic remedies and detoxification had purged Gabe's body of the mercury and other poisons that Dr. O maintained were largely caused by vaccines. And he certified as an MD that Gabe's ADHD was "cured." That got Gabe off Child Protective Services' list and off mandatory ADHD medications to attend public school. This year she'd scrounged up enough to afford to get him into Mercer.

And now she ran the nonmedical practice side of Dr. O's mini-empire, as he jokingly called it. But it was no joke. It was a flourishing Internet business of whole food-based vitamins; health-related DVDs and books; and healthy lifestyle products like juicers and water filters. And a good portion of the profits funded Dr. O's real passion: documentaries on health issues, the only thing—except, of course for Gabe—that got Dani out of bed every morning.

Her colleagues, Richard Kaminsky, Jason Waite and Seth Weinstein stood talking near the entrance to Dr. O's Vitamin Shop when Dani got to the top of the steps. Richard started applauding and the others joined in. She stood, cringing from embarrassment, yet secretly relishing the recognition. They walked over and greeted her with hugs.

"I knew you'd do it," Richard said.

"Absolutely," Ralph said.

They were joined by a half dozen others, including Kaitlin Drake, her editor. Dani was gradually overcome by an odd sensation of discomfort. She recalled how she'd wilted under the spotlight when asked to say a few words on accepting her award last night. It made her feel as if her colleagues would think she was undeserving of their praise if they'd seen her frozen with panic. She'd wanted to say something about creating a film that spoke her truth, and that of thousands of other mothers, but she was unable to utter more than "Thank you," in front of 2,000 people.

It took Dani another ten minutes to reach her desk. She booted up her computer and started going through her emails. *Eighty-four today. Oof.* The usual: mothers with no money and sick children, desperate to see Dr. O. Many she was counseling on vitamins and remedies. A few like Jennifer Knox: a mother with an autistic child who Dani had interviewed for her new documentary, who needed to vent to someone who understood, keep her from going crazy. Finally, a number of congratulatory wishes. Then her voicemails. *Thirty-six, more of the same.* One was from James, at first congratulating her, next a little pathetic and finally lecturing her about not throwing away five years. As she neared the end of her voicemails she heard his voice again, and feeling nothing at all—rather than angry or impatient— deleted the message without listening to it. That one probably hammered at James' constant theme: commitment. After she finished with her voicemails she checked her blog: 3,748 pageviews yesterday, about 50% more than usual. She wrote a quick blog post thanking her supporters and urging them to continue to spread the word on *Drugging* and it's message, looked at the time—8:58—then sat back in her chair to wait for Dr. Maguire.

Stevens waited while his partner, Turnbull, double-parked their police black-and-white in front of the doc's office.

"Don't be long, Alice," Turnbull said.

"How come I gotta listen to your shit every time I go to buy my vitamins?"

"And don't catch a wittle cold while you're there, girlie-man."

Stevens opened the door. "I need five minutes, asshole."

"Five more minutes for the crooks to prey on our harmless citizens."

Stevens stepped out of the car, looked back at Turnbull and said, "Less time than it takes you to feed greasy fries and cholesterol to your fat ass at Burger Heaven." He slammed the car door and headed toward Dr. Orlovski's. At the top of the steep stairway he turned right and got in line behind three other customers at the Dutch door, open at the top, that served as the sales window for the Vitamin Shop.

Hunter Stark sat behind the wheel of a Ford Taurus across the street from Dr. Orlovski's office, a spot he'd staked out at 6:30 a.m. to make sure he was positioned properly. He rubbed his hands, admiring his custom-made nappa lambskin gloves. They were an essential element of his professional toolkit, as important as his Ruger; form-fitting and almost like wearing nothing at all. At $500 a pair from Dominic Pierotucci's shop in Genoa, they were a bargain.

Stark's gaze scanned the street in front of Dr. Orlovski's office. He was tense. These jobs were tough enough in a low-risk environment, but this last-minute bullshit didn't allow for any planning, choice of site or operational subtlety. Still, figuring out things like this and taking the risk were why he got paid the big bucks.

The girl had entered about 8:15, and now he checked his watch again—just before 9:00—as he saw a cop car pull up. One of the uniforms got out and walked through Orlovski's front door. *Not good.* It would be a complication if Maguire showed up with the cop in there.

He felt one of those odd pains he got behind his eyes when things were about to go wrong. Less than a minute after the cop went in, he'd seen a guy that matched Maguire's description on the corner of 79th Street. Stark glanced down at the picture he held in his lap. Maguire, no question about it. Shit, they told him the man was big, but he must be 6'5", shoulders like an ox. A guy who looked like he could take right lead from Muhammad Ali and keep coming. Maguire walked with his head tilted down at the sidewalk, hands in his pockets, real purpose in his stride, moving fast.

Stark felt adrenaline surge through him. *Off your ass. Double-time. Move, move, move.* He threw open the car door and headed across the street, matching Maguire's pace, then faster. He unzipped his jacket as he passed the police cruiser, slipped his right hand inside and grabbed the handle of his knife, just underneath his Ruger in its chest holster. By the time Maguire reached the door Stark was only a few strides behind him. Stark felt the familiar thud of his pulse in his ears, dryness in his mouth, his jaw clenching involuntarily. *Here we go.*

When Stark got inside Maguire was on the third step, his feet pounding like he was Frankenstein. Stark glanced up to the top of the steps just as he reached Maguire. *Nobody there.* He swung out the knife and plunged in a clean stab all the way to the hilt in Maguire's kidney.

Maguire let out a howl like a bullmastiff and grabbed his back. Stark pulled the knife out for another stab, saw blood on the blade and felt the rush. Maguire then spun to face Stark, just as they always did, so Stark could go for the kill gore just below the solar plexus. But the guy was big and strong. Too late, Stark saw the left hook coming toward his head. The knife hit bone just as Maguire's fist caught Stark on the chin. The lights went out for what must've been only a fraction of a second because Stark found himself grabbing the banister, his back against the wall but still on his feet as Maguire thundered up the steps. Stark righted himself and started after him, shoving the knife back in its holster, grabbing the Ruger with its silencer attached and sliding it out of his jacket. By the time Maguire got to the top of the stairs and turned left Stark was only about six steps below him.

Stevens heard someone crashing up the steps like a buffalo, a yell like a wounded animal, then some scuffling and what must've been a couple of guys running up the stairs. He turned and saw one guy get to the top, duck into the first office and lean against a woman standing there, then push her aside. Then another guy came up the stairs with—holy shit!—a Dirty Harry-sized piece with a silencer on it. On instinct, Stevens flipped open his holster and grabbed his service revolver. As he did, the guy with the gun reached up and put a round square in the big guy's back, and the big guy went down like a tree right in front of the woman. Stevens now held his Smith & Wesson in both hands, crouched in firing position as the guy with the gun bent down and started reaching into the big guy's pocket.

No clear shot. The woman was in the way. "Freeze!" Stevens yelled.

The guy with the gun glanced back and pulled off a round without even seeming to move. Stevens felt his left hip explode in pain and found himself on his back, looking upside down at the guy, who now turned and pointed the piece at him. Stevens' arm was outstretched. He fired a crazy round over the guy's head and when the guy ducked Stevens rolled onto his stomach, aimed and squeezed the trigger one, two, three, four times as the guy dived down the stairway and out of sight. Stevens dropped his head to the floor and everything went black.

Stark skidded to a stop about a quarter of the way down the stairway, got up and bounded down the rest of the steps and out the door. He held the Ruger at his side as he turned down Broadway, seeing the other cop still sitting in his squad car. How the hell hadn't he heard the shots? *The guy must be deaf.* Stark slid the Ruger back into its holster and turned to look into a store window to conceal his movements. He zipped up his jacket and started toward 79th Street. He'd abandon the Taurus across the street. Leaving Maguire's picture in it was dumb, but who cared? The cops would know it was a hit anyhow. Stark's heart was still thudding against his chest when he reached 72nd Street and hailed a cab. Inside, he pulled out a handkerchief and wiped Maguire's blood off his gloves. A clean kill on Maguire, no question. But the client would be pissed he hadn't been able to check Maguire's pockets, even see if Maguire had handed anything off to the girl. And she'd gotten a good look at him. He'd have to circle back on that. The cop was unfortunate. If he lived he might be able to ID him, too. And if he didn't live, well, that would make for unnecessary heat that might send him underground and out of work for a while, at least in the States. Overall, messy. Not a good day's work.

Dani didn't think it was possible to choke on air, but that's how she felt. She gasped for breath and knew air was flowing in, but somehow it seemed to be suffocating her. She stood in front of her desk. Her knees were weak and she slumped backward, supporting herself with her hands behind her on her desk. Her ears rang from those awful shots, and she felt sick to her stomach from the smells in the room—blood mixed with gunpowder. She stared down at the man lying at her feet. He must be Dr. Maguire; he'd arrived promptly at 9:00, their scheduled time. She looked across the hall and now saw two people bent over the cop, who wasn't moving. That snapped her out of her paralysis because now she knelt down and put two fingers on Maguire's neck to check his pulse. *Nothing.* She realized she clutched a USB flash memory drive in her palm, and now remembered Maguire had thrust it there before he shoved her away. She slipped it into her blazer pocket.

Sirens, and a moment later a single uniformed cop ran up the stairs, glanced at Maguire, and then went in to tend to the other cop. By the time the paramedics arrived, Dani's stomach was beginning to settle. She wanted to go back behind her desk and sit down, but was still afraid to move. As the paramedics took the wounded cop away, two men in suits appeared at the top of the stairs. They spoke to the other cop for a few moments, then came over to Dani's office. The short one bent over and started going through Maguire's pockets. Dani recoiled. Even if it was the man's job, it was disgusting. Ten minutes ago Maguire was a man who ran to her and implored her with desperate eyes. Now he was a carcass to be sifted through for evidence.

The other man who approached Dani was taller and skinnier, with watery eyes. "I'm Agent Wilson. FBI." He flipped open a wallet-sized case and showed her a badge.

Dani felt her mouth move but no sound came out. She realized she was clutching the desk behind her as hard as she could with both hands.

"Tell us what happened," Wilson said.

Dani cleared her throat. "I was waiting in my office for my appointment with Dr. Maguire when I heard a commotion on the stairs and then he ran in. His face was white and he was bleeding. He grabbed me and then pushed me away just as—" Dani heard the tremor in her voice, realized she was spewing words and took a deep breath to slow herself down, "—another man came in with a gun and shot him in the back." The horror of it come back to her. *My God.* She'd actually seen a man murdered in front of her.

Wilson didn't show any reaction, just stood looking at her through those watery eyes.

Dani went on. "Then the man bent over and started poking around in Dr. Maguire's pockets. At that point someone yelled 'freeze' or something from across the hall, and I saw a policeman with his gun outstretched, and then the policeman went down when the man shot him and I dove under my desk and heard three or four more shots. When I looked up the man with the gun was gone and the policeman was laying face down."

Wilson seemed to be waiting for Dani to go on. When she didn't, he said, "You said Dr. Maguire. Do you know him?"

"No, but we had an appointment, and I've been talking to him on the phone for some time to set up a meeting."

"You sure it's him?"

Dani paused. Actually, she wasn't. "I assume it's him."

The man looked down at Dani's hands.

"How'd you get blood on you?" Dani looked down at her hands and noticed they were bloody. Her blazer, too. "I told you. The man grabbed me and almost fell over on me, then shoved me aside."

"You just called him 'the man,' not 'Dr. Maguire.'" Wilson said, still observing her with no expression.

"I already told you, I assume it was Dr. Maguire."

"Listen, we need you to cooperate."

Huh? Now Dani was annoyed. She felt her fingernails scraping the underside of the desk behind her. "What's that supposed to mean?"

The short man finished going through Maguire's pockets. He looked up at Wilson and shook his head. "He's got a knife wound in his back," the short man said.

Wilson nodded, then looked at Dani. "You're not giving us anything," he said.

Dani just stared at him. Now she was angry. Was this guy just dense, or was he fishing for something in particular?

Wilson said, "You expect us to believe this man, Maguire—Dr. David Maguire, a senior research biologist at Pharma International—comes in here dying with a knife wound in his back to speak to you or give you something, and you don't know him?"

"I don't expect anything. You asked me what happened, and I'm telling you."

"Why did he come here?"

"I told you. I've been calling about an interview, and he wanted to meet me first."

"That's all?"

Dani decided she didn't want to tell Wilson she believed that there might have been something more on Maguire's mind than that. She shrugged.

Wilson said, "Who set up the meeting?"

"He did."

"Who introduced you? You obviously had a reason to talk to him, and you didn't call him out of the blue."

"I was introduced through a friend of his. John McCloskey."

"That KellerDorne guy? The whistleblower?"

This was getting weird. She realized that it was strange that the FBI was probing her about Dr. Maguire even before the homicide cops showed up. And this guy, Wilson, knew who John McCloskey was with no prompting. Not exactly a household name. And how did he refer to Maguire? A research analyst at Pharma. How would he know that?

Wilson said, "What did he give you?"

She leveled her eyes at him. No way she was telling. "Nothing."

At that moment two more men in suits appeared at the top of the stairs, followed by six or eight more, some with bulky cases, some uniformed cops. Wilson turned to them. "She's all yours, fellas. We're done here." The partners left.

The two suits who just arrived looked at each other as if in confusion. They turned their backs to Dani and spoke to the uniformed cop, the one who arrived first, for a few moments.

Yes, something really odd was going on. She got the idea that these cops had no clue who the FBI guys were, or why they were here. If they really were FBI.

She put her hand into her blazer pocket and felt the USB flash memory drive. It had to be why Maguire wanted to see her. She remembered that he said something to her about "being on the right side." She eyed the men talking to each other in front of her and decided that until she figured out what was going on, she'd keep her mouth shut about it.

ABOUT THE AUTHOR

David Lender is the bestselling author of thrillers based on his over 25-year career as a Wall Street investment banker. He draws on an insider's knowledge from his career in mergers and acquisitions with Merrill Lynch, Rothschild and Bank of America for the international settings, obsessively driven personalities and real-world financial intrigues of his novels. His characters range from David Baldacci–like corporate power brokers to Elmore Leonard–esque misfits and scam artists. His plots reveal the egos and ruthlessness that motivate the players in the business world, as well as the inner workings of the most powerful of our financial institutions and corporations.

2799454R00260

Printed in Great Britain
by Amazon.co.uk, Ltd.,
Marston Gate.